The Gomorrah Principle

DUANEI
I HOPE YOU
ENJOY THE STORY.

Best Wishes
Rick DeStefanis

Rick DeStefanis

ISBN: 1-4818-9680-6
ISBN 13: 978-1-4818-9680-1

Library of Congress Control Number: 2013900321
CreateSpace Independent Publishing Platform
North Charleston, South Carolina

Disclaimer-Fiction

Other than actual historical battles and public figures, all characters and incidents portrayed herein are fictitious. Any resemblance to actual persons living or dead is purely coincidental.

Dedication

This book is dedicated to all veterans, and especially to the paratroops of the 173rd Airborne Brigade, the 82nd and 101st Airborne Divisions.

Acknowledgments

There may be some few writers who have found their way into print without the help and encouragement of friends and family. I am not one of those. Therefore, I wish to thank all those who have been there for me. First and foremost, I wish to thank my wife, Janet, who has silently endured long hours alone while I obsessed with this addiction called "writing." Second, my sincerest thanks to all my writer friends who have provided support, suggestions, encouragement, scathing critiques, and all the many things writers do for one another. These include Ellen Morris Prewitt, Jonis Agee, Brent Spencer, Chris Davis, Michelle Labedis, Christian DeStefanis, Janet Severe, and Betty Halbert.

CHAPTER ONE

The Tennessee Overhill, 1967

Cradling the rifle in his arms, Brady Nash sat high above a cornfield, his back against an ancient oak tree. The evening, windless and still, was void of sound as a somber sun sank in the distant hills. With the fall foliage now gone, there remained only the skeletal limbs of winter and a scarecrow hanging ragged and forlorn amongst the dried stalks below. Brady pulled his collar snug around his neck. It was cold in the mountains after sunset, but it was a good cold, crisp and fresh. It made a person feel life, and he'd never felt it like he did now. This was his last hunt, possibly forever, because beyond the hills, beyond the Hiwassee and the Tennessee Rivers, the world awaited him.

He was leaving despite Lacey's objections. Lacey, as stubborn as she was beautiful, hadn't spoken a word to him since he told her he was leaving. Back when Duff enlisted, she'd said, "Even if he is my brother, he's crazy, going off to Vietnam that way." And Brady had agreed with her then, but things changed. Duff was dead, and Lacey had moved off to Nashville. Now it was his turn to leave, except giving her the reason for his enlistment would only make matters worse. She should already know that leaving Melody Hill was the last thing he wanted to do.

As a dusky twilight settled over the bare cornstalks far below, the faint sound of chimes broke the silence as they drifted across the hills. They came from Melody Hill, a small settlement tucked high in a mountain valley overlooking the Hiwassee River. It was little more than a cluster of houses surrounding a gas station, restaurant, and general store, but it was home. And there was the church—the Melody Hill Methodist Church. On a rise at the far end of town, its steeple rose above the trees, a titanium spire visible from miles away to the people living in the wooded hills and along the foggy river gorges of a place they called the Tennessee Overhill.

Life in the Overhill was simple. The lucky ones worked for the L&N Railroad down at Etowah or at the cotton mill up at Englewood. Otherwise, there was the copper mine, twenty miles down the highway, or one of the logging companies. Everyone did a little farming on the side and got by. It wasn't a fat life, but people here respected one another, and everyone knew right from wrong.

Earlier in the afternoon, Brady had driven his truck up a rocky back road to this remote farm. He'd come here to escape the television with its cacophony of voices telling of the chaos and conflict gripping the world into which he was going. One more brief respite before leaving was all he wanted—to sit in the silence of the hills and watch the day fade away one last time.

He snapped from his daydream as the yips and howls of coyotes echoed from a ravine below the cornfield. Coyotes were a species new to the Overhill, and this wasn't their normal squealing welcome of nightfall, but that of a chase. The sounds drew nearer as Brady peered through the riflescope. Despite the sun having set, there was still good shooting light. A moment later, he spotted movement. A doe and fawn scrambled from the rhododendron at the far end of the field. Bounding in long, graceful leaps, the two deer came up the edge toward him. The coyotes spilled up out of the ravine behind them, streaking in hot pursuit.

Propping the rifle across his knee, he contemplated firing a round to scatter the pack, but the coyotes were three hundred yards away and too close to the deer. The howling din grew, echoing from the hills, as both deer and coyotes came up the field and disappeared into the grass at the base of the ridge below. A few moments later, the doe reappeared, bounding effortlessly up the mountainside toward him. The howls of the pack drew closer as she passed within a few yards, but the fawn was lagging behind.

Still a hundred yards down the mountain, the little deer had broken stride as it slowed to a tongue-lolling canter. Knowing they had their prey, the coyotes trotted alongside. Brady drew the crosshair down on a large yellow-eyed male, but hesitated as the exhausted fawn crossed back and forth through his line of sight. He needed to wait until they were closer, but the big male lunged for the fawn's throat.

The roar of the 30.06 rolled down the mountainside and across the cornfield below, reverberating against a distant hillside as the predator's chest exploded. A second animal skidded to a stop, and the pack milled in momentary confusion. Quickly bolting another cartridge, Brady pulled the crosshair onto the next target. The second animal's head snapped convulsively from the bullet's impact, and the pack scattered into the broom sedge. After chambering another round, he waited as the echo of the last shot faded into the distant mountains. A hundred yards below, two dying coyotes quivered, but Brady focused his attention on the high grass at the base of the ridge. This was where the rest of the pack would break from cover.

In the fading light, he detected movement as another coyote cautiously raised its head from the yellow grass. With its ears erect, it gazed back up the mountainside. At least two hundred yards away, it must have felt safe as it looked back. Brady centered the crosshair and carefully squeezed off another round. The animal rolled and disappeared into the grass as the remainder of the pack broke from the brush at the base of the ridge, sprinting toward the far end of the cornfield.

"Aren't you gonna throw another shot at 'em?"

Brady jerked his head around. It was the landowner, Hubert Brister, standing behind him.

"Wait a minute, Mr. Hubert," Brady whispered as he turned, looking back at the fleeing coyotes.

"But the rest of 'em are getting away," the old man said. "Shoot 'em."

Brady peered through the scope. By now, the coyotes were nearing the far end of the cornfield—at least four hundred yards away.

"Wait," he said. "It'd be blind luck to hit one running at this distance."

The lead coyote disappeared into the ravine at the end of the field, but one of the animals at the rear of the pack broke into a series of stiff-legged hops. It bounced sideways as it neared the edge of the field. Brady waited.

"Atta boy," he murmured, "just give me a look."

Bracing the rifle, he kept the animal in his sights.

"It's getting away," Brister said.

"No, it's not," Brady muttered as he held the rifle steady.

He held his cheek against the stock, and his eye in the scope, as the coyote bounced one last time and stopped, staring back at the mountain. The wind was dead still. With the horizontal crosshair eight inches above the animal's back, Brady squeezed the trigger. The 30.06 thundered again, and the bullet knocked the coyote flat in a cloud of dust.

"Damn, you're a crackerjack, ain't ya, boy?"

Brady remained silent as he stood and brushed the dust from the seat of his pants.

"So tell me," the old man said, "how did you know that critter was gonna stop?"

"I didn't for sure," Brady said. "But you know how the Bible tells when Lot's wife stopped and looked back at Gomorrah even when the angels told her not to? Well, I reckon animals have that same fatal curiosity 'cause they do it a lot."

Brister rubbed the stubble on his chin and nodded, but he said nothing more as they walked down the ridge to his house. The house was dark except for a single bulb burning on the front porch, and when Brady opened his truck door, a hound bellowed beneath the porch.

"Hush up, Hank," Brister yelled. He turned to Brady. "Why don't you come inside and have a cup of coffee? I sure wouldn't mind some company for a little while."

Brady hesitated as he clung to the truck door. The old man let him hunt his land when he wanted, and he was a widower, with all his kids moved off to Knoxville or Chattanooga.

"Cup of coffee sounds good," he said.

* * *

The aroma filled the kitchen as the percolator bubbled and hissed on the stove. Old Man Brister set two stained cups on the table. The cups, like his hands, were riddled with the lines of age, but everything in the room was neat and clean. Each dish towel was carefully folded, and each dish was washed, dried, and placed in the cupboard.

"Word is you enlisted in the army," Brister said.

Brady nodded.

"Well, what's done is done, but you know that ain't gonna bring Duff back."

Brady eyed the old man carefully. He didn't want to be disrespectful.

"Sounds like you've been talking to Lacey," he said.

"I went to Europe when I was seventeen years old," Brister replied. "Eighty-second Division, World War One."

The old man picked up a dish towel from beside the sink and walked over to the stove.

"A war is too big and too ugly to think you can go there to get revenge."

He was certain now that Brister had talked with Lacey.

"This isn't about revenge," Brady said. "Yeah, Duff was my best friend, and since I enlisted, Lacey and I haven't seen eye to eye on much of anything, but there's more to it than…" Brady hesitated. What could he say?

Brister used the dish towel to grasp the handle of the soot-blackened percolator, then walked over to the table. His hand trembled with the unsteadiness of age as he poured the coffee.

"Ain't got no sugar or milk," he said.

"Black's fine with me," Brady said.

"Yeah, well, she probably doesn't want you to end up like Duff or Jesse Harper."

Jesse Harper was a legend of sorts around Polk County. He had served two tours in Nam as a forward air controller, piloting small planes over the mountainous jungles along the Cambodian and Laotian borders. Now he owned a canoe and tube rental business down on the Hiwassee. He drank some, and rumor was he grew a little pot on the side as well, but his biggest claim to fame was getting drunk and landing his little Cessna on rural highways when he got lost. Everyone in the county seemed to tolerate him, and the teenagers loved him.

"What's wrong with Jesse?"

"Hell's bells—you must think it's normal to get so drunk you can't find your way home and land your airplane on a road."

"No, but—"

"No, and there ain't no 'but' to it neither. The last time Sheriff Harvey found him, Harper was slobbering and crying like a baby and saying he couldn't find his men 'cause they were lost in the jungle. You want to end up like that?"

Brady had never heard this part of Harper's antics.

"Lacey thinks I'm going to get killed, but like you said, what's done is done. I just wish she'd talk to me."

"I saw her this afternoon when I was—"

"Lacey's home?"

The old man placed the coffeepot back on the stove as he spoke. "Yeah, said she came home to see you off this weekend. Then she's heading back to Nashville."

Holding the cup in front of his face, Brady inhaled the coffee's aroma, but his mind was on Lacey. It was only two weeks ago that she said she was never speaking to him again. He'd tried to reason with her, but she was too angry, and it was all too strange—what had happened those few days after Duff's funeral.

After receiving a phone call from a stranger who said he knew Duff, Brady had driven down to Athens to meet the man at the bus stop on 411. He was a soldier wearing a uniform with the same unit crests and patches as Duff's. The man didn't introduce himself as he cast nervous glances about. When he seemed satisfied that no one was watching, he drew hard on his cigarette and stared at Brady with sunken eyes as he pulled a brown envelope from inside his coat.

"Look, I'm a friend of Duff Coleridge's, and I just got out of the army yesterday up at Fort Campbell. Before I left Nam a few weeks ago, Duff gave me this letter and asked me to carry it home to you. He said his mail is being read and his life is in danger—I mean from the crazy people he's working with. Anyway, just read it. It explains everything, but don't ever mention how you got it or that you ever saw me, OK?"

The veins in Brady's temples pulsed with the beat of his heart as he realized the man didn't know Duff was dead.

"Put that envelope in your pocket and get on your way," the man said. "You don't need to be seen with me."

"Look, mister, uh…" Brady glanced at the soldier's uniform, but his nameplate was missing from above the pocket. "There's something I need to tell you."

"Make it quick. I'm catching that bus home." The man motioned toward an approaching Greyhound as it slowed to pull off the highway.

"Duff was killed in action almost two weeks ago. We had his funeral last week."

The man's face hardened, and his voice dropped to a near whisper. "Lousy bastards." He bent over and picked up his duffel bag, pulling the strap over his shoulder as the bus hissed to a stop. "Regardless of what the army tells you, Duff probably wasn't killed the way they say. Just read that letter. You can decide if you want to do something about it."

The bus driver stepped down and opened the baggage compartment, but before he stowed the soldier's bag, Brady saw the name James R. Noble and part of the serial number 410-33-. He wrote them on the envelope as the bus pulled away.

"More coffee?"

Brister's voice jerked him back to consciousness. Brady noticed his cup was empty.

"Yeah, sure," he said.

"What's on your mind, son?"

Brady glanced up. In the future, he would need to mask his feelings. But as he looked across the table at Brister, an idea came to him. And who better was there to trust than Hubert Brister?

"I've got something to show you, but first I need your word that you won't tell anyone."

The old man smiled. "Hell, son, you've been like one of my own boys. I reckon if you want it that way, you got it."

Brady stood up. "I'll be right back."

After walking outside to his truck and retrieving the envelope from beneath the front seat, he returned to the kitchen. He pulled Duff's letter from the envelope and handed it to Brister. The old man took a pair of wire-rimmed reading glasses from his shirt pocket, while Brady peered over his shoulder, reading the letter again for what was probably the twentieth time.

Brister's lip quivered as he finished the letter and looked up at Brady with eyes wide and hard with anger. "Them bastards killed that boy. You need to take this letter to the president or, like Duff said, to a newspaper or something. Them sorry bastards."

"I know," Brady said, "but I'm afraid the army might cover it up. Besides, look at this."

He turned the envelope up and emptied the contents on the table. There were several more documents, one a handwritten note on a telex message that said, "You're getting a lot of good press from the big boys in Saigon." It was signed with only the name "Spartan." The telex message read, "Tell your new man job well done. Interrogation of his captured suspect proved valuable."

There was yet another note, one Duff mentioned in the letter. It was a list of Vietnamese names. Several were marked through, and a note was scribbled below, "The ones marked off are already terminated." It was the same handwriting as on the other telex message. Brady set it aside and picked up a yellow card splotched with what appeared to be dried blood. A strutting red-and-green bird carrying arrows and sticks of dynamite in its talons was on the front of the card, along with the words "Phung Hoang."

"What is all this stuff? What does it mean?" Brister asked. "And this French woman in the letter, the one he said was his girlfriend, how is she going to know anything?"

"I don't know for sure," Brady said. "But if Duff said I should contact her, then she must know something. That's why I'm going over there and try to find some of these people."

"Boy, how do you think you can ever do that? There ain't even a guarantee you'll get sent over there, and even if you do, that's a big country with millions of people."

"I already did my homework, Mr. Hubert. My enlistment con- tract includes MOS training and duty station. I requested airborne ranger, like Duff, and the Republic of Vietnam will be my first duty station. There are only two airborne units over there, and Duff was with one of them when they recruited him."

Brister became red-faced, and the veins bulged on his forehead as he lit a cigarette.

"Son, you're being foolish. What are you gonna do if you find them? This guy in Duff's letter, what's he call himself, Spartan? That can't be his real name. You might just end up like Duff—then what?"

"That's why I'm telling you this. If something happens to me, I want you to give this letter and the other stuff in this envelope to the army and the newspapers."

"This is the stupidest damned idea—"

"There's right and there's wrong, Mr. Hubert. I have right on my side, and I'm going to find those people, no matter what it takes. Now you gave me your word."

Brister drew hard on his cigarette, then pulled off his glasses and rubbed his eyes. After a few moments, he replaced the glasses and looked up at Brady.

"You need to think again about what's really right and what's not. Remember the Good Book says that revenge belongs to the Lord."

"All I'm going to do is get names and faces, unless they try to do me like they did Duff. Can you help me?"

Brister shook his head, then nodded.

"All right, I reckon if you say I gave you my word, then I did. I'll put this letter in a safe place, but I'm telling you again, this is a stupid thing you're doing."

"You're probably right," Brady said.

It was a long shot at best, but next to Lacey, Duff had been his closest friend on Earth. If his death involved something more than an act of war, Duff at least deserved for someone to try to find the ones responsible.

* * *

As the headlights of his pickup truck fell on the house, Brady found himself gripping the steering wheel and hesitating. It was Lacey's house, and Duff's before he was killed, but it had also been Brady's home for the last twelve years. The three of them had grown up there. Shortly after Duff and Lacey's father and Brady's own father, Lyons Nash, were killed in a mining accident, Brady's mother suffered a stroke. She lasted barely four months, leaving Brady alone in the world. Mrs. Coleridge took him in to live with her children, Duff and Lacey.

This was his family, except now, with Duff's death, an estrangement was growing among them. His foster mother, Emma Coleridge, was brokenhearted over his enlistment, saying she was about to lose a second son. Lacey said he was stubborn and uncaring about their feelings.

He pulled into the driveway. Lacey's blue Malibu was parked in the front yard. Why a girl needed a 396-cubic-inch V-8 with a four-barrel Holley carburetor was beyond him, but it fit. She was as single-minded a woman as he'd ever known.

They were five years old when he first saw her at their fathers' funerals. She and Duff clung to their mother's skirts while the congregation sang "Amazing Grace." Little had he known that Lacey would grow from this child, with whom he ran the summer hills, into this woman who ruled his every emotion. He stepped from the truck to see Emma staring at him from behind the screen door. Brady walked up the steps, and she pushed the door open.

"I heard you shootin' over yonder, son."

"Just some coyotes," Brady said. "Where's Lacey?"

"She went to her room when you pulled in. Please, don't y'all go to arguing again."

Brady bent over and kissed her cheek.

"I'm not wanting to argue."

"Come on back to the kitchen. I've got a pot of coffee going. You hungry?"

They sat across the table from one another, and when Brady saw his stepmother's eyes rise to look past him, he realized Lacey was standing behind him. A moment later, he felt her arm as she wrapped it across his shoulders.

"Hey, brother, been out hunting?"

"Brother," that was what she'd always called him—until they'd fallen in love. It was an affectionate greeting, but not the same now. He turned, raising his face toward hers, but she quickly turned aside and pulled a chair up to the table.

"Back to just 'brother,' huh?"

Lacey's lips tightened, and Mama Emma's face fell.

"I came home to see you off," Lacey said. "But…" Tears filled her eyes.

"Kids, please, why don't you talk about this tomorrow?"

Lacey pushed her chair back and left the room.

* * *

Sunday after church, they sat on the front porch, Lacey on the swing, Brady in a rocker, but she refused to make eye contact. This was his last opportunity to make peace before leaving. He was catching the Greyhound bus on 411 the next morning and heading to Atlanta and, eventually, Fort Jackson, South Carolina, for basic. Lacey stared steadfastly up the road to where the gleaming white steeple of the church rose above the trees. All day, the tension between them had been a powder keg awaiting the errant spark of a misspoken word. They talked about the weather, people, anything but the gaping chasm between them. He had to make her talk.

"I didn't get angry when you said you were going to Nashville," he said.

Lacey slowly turned her head. Her eyes, normally soft and brown, were hardened granite.

"You didn't have a reason to get angry. Singing country music in Nashville won't get me killed."

"You know I love you," Brady said.

For a moment, her eyes softened, but quickly reverted to stone.

"You wouldn't even go to Nashville with me, and now you're running off to the army. How is that showing love?"

"Look, I told you I would always be here for you, and I will. Maybe when I get back, I'll come to Nashville, and we can work things out."

She turned away.

"Can't you even look at me while we talk?"

Lacey slowly turned back toward him, but her eyes suddenly reddened and filled with tears. She was still the most beautiful woman he'd ever seen: wide brown eyes, high cheekbones, and soft brown hair that flowed down on her shoulders. Her voice was husky with emotion.

"I'm not going through this again. I can't. First, Daddy died, then Duff. Now you're leaving. You have to listen to me. Please don't do this."

"I don't have a choice," Brady said. "I've already enlisted."

"Yes, you do. We can go to Canada. I'll go with you, and we can live there together."

"Are you crazy? That's desertion. Besides, what about this country music thing you're so set on doing?"

"Dammit, Brady, you're not going to do this!"

Never had he heard her curse. Rising from the swing, she clenched her fists and walked to the edge of the porch. Brady went to her, but she pushed him back, holding him at arm's length.

"Can't you see I'm willing to give up everything for you? It breaks my heart, too, that Duff's gone, but since he died, it's like you've become a different person or something. I know you two were close, but if you love me, you'll prove it. Go to Canada with me."

Brady led her back to the swing, where they sat, and he kissed her softly on the forehead. Embracing one another, they kissed again, this time with passion, and when their lips parted, Lacey gazed breathlessly up at him.

"So you'll go?"

Brady looked into her eyes. "I love you, Lacey, more than anything on this earth, but—"

She pushed him away. "No, you don't. If you did, you'd listen."

"I don't have a choice," he said.

"You do have a choice, and you're making it. You're going to get yourself killed, and if you don't, don't expect me to wait around on you because I'm not. I can't."

Breaking into sobs, Lacey hugged her knees against her chest and dropped her head. Brady touched her shoulder, but she flinched and threw his hand away.

"Don't touch me. Just go. Get out of my life. I never want to see you again."

CHAPTER TWO

The Most Dangerous Game

L acey pushed the quilt back as she glanced at the clock
beside her bed. It was seven thirty, and the first rays of
sunlight pierced her apartment window as she prepared
for another day waiting tables. The morning sun in Nashville
wasn't the same as it was back home. It rose with a sharper glare,
and her day was something she no longer faced with eager anticipation. Brady had been gone five months now, and an unrelenting
anxiety ate at her. She had read every one of his letters, but hadn't
answered a single one. If she really didn't care, why was she even
reading them? Perhaps she was the one being too stubborn.

The apartment was quiet as she shuffled into the kitchenette
to plug in the percolator and turn on the radio. The sound helped
ward off the loneliness. The percolator hissed and bumped, emit-
ting the first hint of the coffee aroma. Unlike the old metal one

they heated on the stove back home, this percolator was shiny chrome and white plastic. It was nice, but the coffee never seemed quite as good as the stovetop brew. Nothing, it seemed, came without a price.

Nashville was that way—bigger and not as friendly as the towns where Duff had taken her to play guitars on the weekends. Yet even performing in the small towns hadn't been without risk. Had her mama learned that Duff's "community centers" were actually bars and roadhouses, she'd have raised the roof, but Brady kept their secret. They'd spent weekends driving for hours to places like Maryville, Cleveland, and even Chattanooga, where they played their guitars into the wee hours of the morning. It had been just for fun and pocket money, until a man from Nashville saw them performing one night.

Hugh Langston offered her the opportunity to sing at his club in Nashville on Friday and Saturday nights. At first, there was no considering it—the offer from this man with a snake oil tongue. It all seemed too improbable, but he refused to accept no for an answer, and after a while, it seemed possible. She went for it, and Langston, a wheeler-dealer who wore cowboy hats and smoked fat cigars, also found her a job waiting tables at a restaurant during the week. Downtown near the river, the restaurant had a view of the rocky cliffs along the Cumberland, and burgundy curtains with linen napkins, and the tips were better than she ever imagined. Langston also paid her for singing at his club.

She owed him, and she couldn't simply walk away because Brady refused to move to Nashville. Besides, this was where her dreams were. Nashville was where people came to get into the country music business. And now that Langston had made it all seem so possible, it had become her passion. It was silly, but she still toyed with the idea of someday appearing at the Grand Ole Opry—little Lacey Coleridge from Melody Hill standing up there and singing live on WSM radio at the Ryman Auditorium while all of Tennessee listened on their radios.

The aroma of the coffee brought her out of her daydream, and she gazed up at the wall clock. It was already past eight. She was on the verge of being late for work. After a quick bath, she dressed and was about to leave when she noticed Brady's last letter still lying on the living room couch. She folded it and pushed it into her purse. Hugh Langston was coming over after work to talk about getting her a music coach, and he didn't need to know she'd gotten another letter.

Langston had caught her in tears one day while she was reading one of Brady's letters, and he lectured her about how the letters were too much of a distraction. He said she needed to keep her spirits up and maintain her focus if she wanted to make it in the music business. Mr. Hugh probably meant well, and he certainly seemed to care, but she decided to ignore his tactless suggestions. She simply kept the letters out of sight and no longer mentioned them.

* * *

The army training seemed to go on forever, but by fall, Brady received the orders he sought—Republic of Vietnam, Headquarters Company, 173rd Airborne Brigade. After a thirty-day leave, he would report for military charter transport to Vietnam. His plan was actually working, and he should have felt some sense of success, except for one thing—Lacey. She hadn't answered any of his letters. As stubborn as she was, he never imagined she wouldn't reply to a single one.

He needed to talk with her one last time before leaving. Anything was better than going to Vietnam without saying good-bye. Returning home, he decided to let Lacey make the first move. Surely she wanted to see him or at least talk with him before he departed. He stayed close to home and waited, but much of his thirty-day leave had passed without a word from Lacey. It was only a few days before he was leaving for Vietnam when Brady realized it was up to him to make the call.

Perhaps after a phone call, he could go to Nashville and spend the last few days with her. Brady glanced at his watch. It was nearly five thirty—four thirty, her time. According to Mama Emma, Lacey would get home around four, her time. He dialed the number to her apartment in Nashville, and after several seconds, there came a distant ring, one that sounded as if it were a thousand miles away. The phone rang and rang. Lacey should have been home for at least thirty minutes now. Perhaps she had stopped somewhere after work. Just as Brady was about to hang up, a man answered on the other end.

"I'm sorry," Brady said. "I must have the wrong number."

"Who are you wanting?" the man asked.

"Is this Lacey Coleridge's place?" Brady asked.

"Who is this?"

"This is Brady Nash. I'm…uh…a friend of Lacey's."

"Well, she's busy right now, friend. Maybe you can call back another day."

The phone clicked and went dead. Brady white-knuckled the receiver as he thought of a man answering the phone at Lacey's apartment. His hand trembled as he stared at the telephone, scarcely able to believe what he had just heard.

Mama Emma was running water in the kitchen as he quietly placed the receiver back on the hook and walked to his bedroom. The walls were closing in on him. He had to get out, get away, and go someplace where he could think. Brady pulled his duffel bag from beneath the bed, and found the bottle of bourbon he'd bought in Atlanta. Hiding it beneath his jacket, he slipped out the front door and walked up the road to the cemetery behind the church.

Most evenings near sunset, Preacher Webb went to the church sanctuary, where he played the electric chimes. And when the breeze died and not so much as a leaf fluttered, remnants of the sun often streaked the western sky while people sat on their porch swings in the valley miles away, listening to the music drifting peacefully from the hills above. Brady usually found the chimes comforting—except on this evening. He stared at Duff's grave, cutting the dead grass like an ugly scar, and the sound of the chimes was a dirge that offered no relief.

After several swallows of whiskey, he noticed something shiny on the grass and bent over to pick it up. It was a spent piece of brass from an M14. The army had shipped Duff's body back from Vietnam. There was a flag-draped coffin, and when they buried him behind the church, seven soldiers fired their M14s three times.

The rifles cracked in unison, the shots echoing for miles across the hills, multiplying into thousands before fading into silence as the bugler blew taps. Brady found himself supporting both Lacey and his stepmother as they sobbed with grief. The sound of the bugle echoed down the mountain valley—and for Brady, the echoes had never ended.

He tipped up the bottle of whiskey, but he couldn't get enough to dull the jagged edge of his pain.

"Duffy, boy, I'm going to do this for you. I promise, I'm gonna find the bastards that did this, and I'm gonna get them."

He sat on the cold granite gravestone. Two-thirds of the liquor was gone from the bottle.

"Here's to you, buddy. Wish me good hunting."

He poured the remaining bourbon over the grave—all but a small portion, which he turned up and finished. A cold drizzle began falling. Standing, he took one last look at the grave. The icy pellets of rain stung his face as he thought of that day before Duff left. Duff had laughed about going to Vietnam. He had said it would be an adventure. Brady tossed the brass shell into the air and caught it in his fist. He had no such delusions. He put the shell in his pocket. There was going to be a reckoning, and someone had hell to pay.

* * *

The killing and dying had become a surreal nightmare. As night fell, illumination rounds drifted eerily across a smoky night sky, tracers arced across the hills, and enemy rockets and mortars thudded into the firebase. Brady watched in awe as *Puff the Magic*

Dragon, a giant C-130 gunship with infrared sensing devices, flew around the perimeter, belching a thunderous volume of fire and destruction into the adjacent hills. The old heads said it made no difference, the enemy would come anyway. A firebase south of Ben Het, in the central highlands near the Cambodian border, was Brady's new home, and after two weeks, he had decided it was probably closer to hell than Cambodia.

Enemy movements in the surrounding mountains had everyone on edge, and rumors were rampant that the firebase would be attacked in earnest any day. No one played grab-ass while on perimeter patrol, nor were the watches down in the bunkers taken lightly, but it was the rabbity nervousness of the vets that made Lacey's prediction seem all the more likely. She had said he was going to get himself killed for nothing.

When the sun rose, it wasn't so bad, unless you were outside the wire on patrol. The line company patrols—platoon and company-size units—were catching hell on every hill they approached, but Brady's ranger platoon did only long-range reconnaissance patrols. Theirs was a simple but risky mission. Hide, sit, watch, and report back. Problem was their reports were all the same—hundreds of NVA regulars everywhere. After several weeks of the same reports and the loss of an entire LRRP team, the CO was using them only sparingly, which didn't hurt Brady's feelings at all.

The NVA seemed satisfied with limiting most of their activity to the nighttime hours, usually random mortar or rocket attacks on the firebase. Brady catnapped through the day, taking advantage of an unusual lull, something the old heads said could mean nothing good. Late that afternoon, he lay atop his hooch, reading a book as the sun dropped below the horizon. It was one of those rare afternoons when the rains hadn't come, but the evening humidity still hung thick over the firebase.

He hurried to finish the story as dusk sapped the last light from the sky. A short story called "The Most Dangerous Game," its suspense absorbed him. As he strained to read in the twilight, an almost indiscernible *thoomp*, *thoomp*, *thoomp* came from the jungle outside the firebase. *"I am still a beast at bay," Rainsford said to General Zaroff.*

"Incoming!" The shouts echoed across the firebase.

Brady snapped the book shut as he scrambled from his perch. No doubt the prelude to another night of harassment, the first rounds smashed into the firebase with ground-jarring *karroomph*s. After ducking inside the hooch, he peeked back through the sandbagged doorway. The sun had disappeared, leaving an orange-and-purple glow blanketing the hills. After the first mortar rounds exploded, there was a silence—almost as if the entire firebase was holding its breath, waiting to see if there was more to come.

Several moments passed before Brady stepped into the doorway, but as he did, the sky became filled with the fiery trails of incoming rockets. From somewhere to the west echoed the distant rumble of artillery, and a few moments later, a rolling barrage of thunder inundated the firebase with smoke, dust, and whirring shrapnel.

Crouching in the doorway of the hooch, Brady watched streams of green tracers arcing into the firebase from every direction—enemy machine guns. The spent but still dangerous tracer rounds bounced and ricocheted crazily as the men down in the bunkers returned fire. This wasn't the usual harassing fire, but a coordinated combination of artillery, mortar, and machine-gun fire.

A young officer bolted down the hill toward the perimeter bunkers, but before he reached his objective, an explosion engulfed him. His body tumbled like a rag doll through the air before landing in a crumpled heap. Several soldiers scrambled from the bunker to retrieve the body. Brady shuddered and tried to maintain his composure as he turned to grab his M16, ammo pouches, and frags. He had to get to his post.

Stooping low, he ran into a maelstrom of whizzing shrapnel. The recon platoon was in charge of internal security, and he had to reach the secondary perimeter of sandbagged bunkers at the center of the firebase. These positions surrounded the mortar pits and several headquarters bunkers, including the battalion CP. Sprinting wildly toward his assigned bunker, he felt the force of yet another explosion propel him forward as he dove through the doorway.

Inside the bunker, it was suddenly quieter, and a flashlight cut the dusty darkness where a medic was working over a soldier lying against the wall. The wounded soldier held the light for the medic, who was wrapping gauze around his bloodied legs. Brady made out the silhouettes of two other men standing and peering through the gunports toward the perimeter.

"I shit you not," one of them said. "This is the real one. They're coming after our asses this time."

Brady caught their silhouettes in the fading light. It was Will Cantrell and another of his hoochmates, Shaky Watson.

"I can see a couple hundred of the little bastards just outside of Bravo Company's position," Will said.

Brady stepped over the wounded man. It was one of the men from the mortar platoon. He recognized his face, but hadn't yet learned his name. As he peered out through the sandbagged gunport, the hair rose on the back of his neck. In the gathering darkness, hundreds of enemy soldiers were surging against the wire, only meters from the first line of bunkers. With whistles blowing shrilly, they had already breached several rows of barbed wire, and the last was beginning to give way before the human wave as they showered the bunkers with rocket-propelled grenades.

Brady glanced skyward through the port. There should have been illumination rounds overhead and fire support coming from the battalion mortars. Stepping to the rear of the bunker, he stared out at several large craters where the six 120 mm mortar emplacements had been. Only one remained. The rest had been destroyed. Beyond the mortar pits stood the battalion CP bunker, sprouting a conglomeration of radio antennae from its roof. Several officers with binoculars peered through the gunports, watching the drama down on the perimeter.

Up near the LZ, a group of soldiers rolled a 90 mm recoilless rifle to a high spot, frantically cranking the barrel down to a horizontal position. Chaos enveloped the firebase as a sudden burst of gunfire jarred Brady back to reality. One of the men behind him in the bunker had fired his M16. The spent brass jingled and bounced against the wood ammo crates on the floor.

"Got that son of a bitch," Shaky shouted.

"Grenade!" Will screamed.

They ducked as an explosion of dirt, dust, and flame blew through the ports. Both men came up instantaneously firing their weapons. There was another explosion. Shaky fell to the floor, screaming with his hands over his face. Brady bent over him as the medic shone the light in Shaky's face. He was burnt and bloody.

"I can't see," he said.

"I'll take care of him," the medic yelled. "Get up there and help Will."

"There's too many of them," Will yelled. "Go cover the doorway."

Brady scrambled to the small doorway on the back side. As he peeked around the sandbagged wall, he came face-to-face with an enemy soldier. The soldier tossed a grenade, but Brady cut him down with a burst from his M16, then dove back into the bunker. The grenade explosion slammed him hard into the floor, stinging his buttocks with shrapnel. Dizzy and with his ears ringing, he stumbled back into the doorway just as a group of enemy soldiers rushed the bunker. Ignoring the bullets cracking past him, he squeezed off deliberate shots, dropping several attackers. The remainder scattered and crawled back to cover.

The enemy artillery barrage had ceased, but firefights rattled furiously all across the firebase while the medic examined Brady's buttocks with a flashlight.

"It's minor," he whispered. "Looks like maybe three or four small pieces in your ass, but your balls are fine. Hold still while I tape some gauze over the holes."

"Make it quick," Brady said.

When it was done, Brady hitched up his pants while Will and the medic whispered in the darkness.

"We might not make it till morning," Will said.

"Shit. We're completely overrun," the medic replied. "The whole damned firebase might be gone by morning."

Brady joined them, looking through the gunports as shadowy groups of men darted about. It was impossible to tell enemy from friendly.

"This is insane," Brady said. "We have blind spots on both sides."

"Just stay cool, Nash," Will said. "Don't panic."

"I'm not panicking, but we can't just hide like rats till they root us out."

Brady started toward the door of the bunker.

"Where're you going?" Will asked.

"Someplace where I can see," Brady said.

"Wait," he said, but Brady ignored him as he crept outside and climbed atop the bunker. He pulled several sandbags aside, made a shallow depression on the roof, and hunkered down. He removed his helmet, and with only his eyes peering over the edge of the sandbags, he searched the darkness.

It was an exposed position, but at least he had a full three-sixty view of the area. Red and green tracers clashed everywhere inside the perimeter, while the flashes of grenades exposed the stark silhouettes of the combatants. Brady held his fire. Without the certainty of a kill, it would be stupid to give away his position. The only good choice was to wait for the fight to come to him.

After only a few minutes, there came a sudden commotion as if someone were running somewhere behind him. Brady rolled onto his side. An enemy sapper was silhouetted against the skyline, running toward the battalion HQ with a satchel charge. The darkness prevented using the peep sight on the M16, but Brady pointed instinctively as he swung through the running figure and squeezed off a round. The enemy soldier pitched headlong into the dirt.

Immediately, another sapper ran forward, grabbing the satchel charge as he passed his fallen comrade. The officers inside the bunker fired indiscriminately into the darkness, and Brady ducked as their bullets spattered around him. When the gunfire dissipated, he raised his head again to see the shadow of an enemy soldier squatting at the base of the HQ bunker. The sapper stood upright as he attempted to push the satchel charge through a gunport, but Brady snapped a quick shot. Although the sapper was eighty meters away, his knees buckled as he slid to the ground.

The enemy seemed determined to destroy the bunker, as yet another sapper ran forward in the darkness and grabbed the satchel. Again, he attempted to shove it through the gunport. Brady squeezed off another round. The bullet slammed the enemy soldier against the sandbags as the satchel fell to the ground. An instant later, the bodies of the two men disappeared in the flaming explosion of their satchel charge.

The night went on forever, as each minute seemed like an hour and each hour like an eternity. Brady lay motionless, sweating in the darkness. Groups of enemy soldiers darted about the compound. The shouts and shrieks of combatants near and far were punctuated with flashes, gunfire, and explosions. Methodically, Brady found targets and squeezed off round after round until the bodies began cluttering the area around the bunker. So far, he'd held them at bay, but exhaustion was setting in, and he was becoming careless. The corpse of the last attacker lay only feet from the bunker.

Sometime after midnight, a sound came from the doorway below. A helmeted head rose slowly from the shadows.

"Hey, Nash."

It was a faint whisper, but he recognized the voice. It was Will Cantrell.

Brady didn't answer as Cantrell inched his way toward him.

"You're doing pretty damned good for a newbie," Will said.

"Maybe so," Brady said, "but I want to be an old head too, so why don't you take that steel pot off and crawl over in this hole."

Will took the hint, and for several hours, they lay together. Cantrell seemed to have an uncanny ability of spotting enemy soldiers, tapping Brady's shoulder several times as he pointed to figures creeping toward them in the darkness. Brady dispatched them one after another until the sky finally began glowing with the first signs of daybreak. High above, the vapor trails of jets reflected the still-invisible morning sun while the distant thumping of choppers echoed in the hills back to the east.

All night, the radios in the battalion CP had been turned down low, probably to avoid drawing enemy fire, but now they crackled and broke squelch. The nearby hills and ravines blossomed with orange and black napalm, while across the firebase, small fire teams began scrambling from bunker to bunker, rooting out the enemy. Will tapped his shoulder and pointed toward a young lieutenant standing in the doorway of the CP bunker. He held a .45 in his hand as he peered out at the carnage. Another officer, an older man, stepped from behind him and pointed in their direction as he said something to the lieutenant. The younger officer began picking his way cautiously through the bodies as he walked toward Brady and Will.

When he reached the base of their bunker, the lieutenant stopped and gazed about at the bodies—some stacked two deep. After a moment, he looked up at Will and Brady.

"The colonel wants to see you two over there at the battalion CP. Let's go."

CHAPTER THREE

The Gomorrah Principle

"What the hell is your name, son?" the colonel asked.

"Private First Class Brady Nash, sir."

"How long have you been in-country, Nash?"

"About a month, sir."

"Where did you learn to shoot like that?"

"Back home in Tennessee, sir."

The colonel gave a sparse smile as he turned his tired eyes to Will. "How about you, soldier, where are you from?"

"Macon, Georgia, sir."

The colonel nodded, then turned to his XO. "Take down their names."

He extended his hand. "I want to thank you, men. What you did last night was a damned brave thing. I'm putting you both in for Silver Stars. Had it not been for the way you exposed your-selves, they'd have taken the headquarters bunker."

Brady looked at Will and shrugged. Since when was saving your ass bravery? After the firebase was overrun, it only made sense to move to the top of the bunker. If he hadn't, the enemy would have slipped in from the bunker's blind spots and tossed a grenade or satchel charge through the gunports.

"One more thing," the colonel said, "we need to replace the sniper team we lost last week. I can send you for training when we get finished up here. How about it?"

Despite his exhaustion, Brady felt a surge of adrenaline. This was what had led Duff to the people he was working for near Da Nang.

"I reckon so—I mean, yes, sir, I would."

The colonel turned to Will. "How about you, soldier?"

Will nodded. "Yes, sir."

"I'll have your orders cut as soon as we return to LZ English," the colonel said. "Right now, I want you to get back to your post. We still have a lot of unsecured areas out there."

As Brady walked with Will away from the battalion HQ, the full light of day fell across the firebase. Choppers landed in swirl-ing clouds of dust, and exhausted medics loaded bloodied sol-diers aboard, one after another. The walking wounded, with blood-soaked gauze and bottles of plasma hanging heavily from their bodies, waited their turn near the LZ. Far and near, men moved about the base, shouting to one another as they searched through debris, bunkers, and craters, accounting for their comrades. Brady and Will crawled back atop the bunker to observe the battle's aftermath.

"I'll take first watch," Brady said. "You catch some sleep."

He turned and looked down the hill toward the perimeter where officers and NCOs scrambled from bunker to bunker, reorganizing their units. Other men worked quietly, stacking the dead in long rows near the LZ. As the sun rose and the bodies were carried or dragged up the hill, the rows grew until they stretched the entire length of the volleyball court.

Will slept for an hour before rolling over.

"Where'd you get that?" he asked.

Brady scarcely realized that he had been unconsciously rubbing the M14 shell he wore on a chain around his neck. Looking down at it, he wondered just exactly how much he should say.

"It came from the twenty-one-gun salute at a friend's funeral," he said.

Will nodded, but said nothing. He seemed satisfied for the moment, but Brady knew he would eventually have to tell the whole story.

The activity around the firebase continued as choppers brought in new supplies, and now began the grim task of ferrying the dead to a Graves Registration Unit. Brady stared out at nothing in particular as he thought of the men who would see no more tomorrows. Eleven more months like this seemed unsurvivable.

"Well, at least you've seen the worst of it your first month," Will said. His voice was heavy with drowsiness. "And we got a little vacation out of it too."

Brady gave him a sideways glance. Will's eyes squinted against the morning sun. At first glance, he appeared to be older, maybe in his late twenties, but Brady quickly realized it wasn't age, but stress. Will probably wasn't any older than he was.

"It doesn't get much worse than this," Will said.

"How long have you been over here?" Brady asked.

"Seems like years," he said, "but I have five months, twenty-one days, and a wake-up till I'm out of here."

Brady nodded. He wasn't even bothering to count the days yet.

* * *

The morning their ranger platoon boarded the choppers departing Ben Het, a cold drizzle was falling, and Will was talking more than he had in the entire month Brady had known him. Along with the sniper training, they'd also been awarded R&R, three days at Vung Tau, a beach resort down near Saigon.

"Man, this Georgia boy is gonna get drunk, get laid, and get sunburned," Will said. "Then I'm gonna spend the next two and a half days relaxing."

Brady didn't respond.

"Hey, you hear me?" Will said. "Can you believe this shit? We're luckier than a couple of shithouse rats. It's raining its ass off here, but they say the sun is shining down at Vung Tau."

Brady didn't respond until later that day as they carried their duffel bags on board a C-130. He glanced over at Will. "I'm not going to Vung Tau," he said.

"What? Are you crazy? You can't do that. Our orders are for——"

"I know, but I have a friend in Da Nang, and I'm heading up there to see if I can hook up with him."

"You got big balls for a newbie," Will said. "If the MPs catch your ass way off up there, you could get into some deep shit."

Brady glanced up at him and shrugged. Will was right. Eventually, he was bound to find trouble, but it wasn't likely to come from the MPs. His quest would take him up against people who were ruthless—Duff's killers.

"I'll be OK. Just keep quiet and cover for me, will you?"

Will tossed his duffel bag into the floor of the plane. "You know, if I hadn't seen what you did the other night, I'd tell you to kiss my country ass, but I'll do it on one condition."

"What's that?"

"I want to know the real reason you're going to Da Nang."

Brady cut his eyes over at Will. Had he somehow tipped his hand?

"What do you mean?"

"You say you're willing to risk an Article Fifteen just to visit a friend. I think you're blowing some serious smoke up my ass. Besides, I'm starting to think you aren't a cherry. Now tell me the truth."

"Look, just do this for me, will you?"

Will held his gaze. "You're not messing around with drugs or the black market, are you?"

"Hell no, absolutely not, but that's all I can tell you for now."

Finding Duff's killers seemed hopeless. After all, it had taken Will about thirty seconds to realize he was lying.

"Look, I'm asking for your help. OK?"

Will nodded. "OK. I'll cover for you this time, but you have to come clean when you get back. Deal?"

"We'll see."

Will shook his head as he lay back on the webbed row of seats inside the plane.

"Nash, I haven't known you two weeks, and I'm already starting not to like you."

Brady folded his poncho into a small pillow and lay back as well.

"Just do this for me this time, and I promise I will tell you what I can when I get back. But the less you know, the better off you'll be."

* * *

Making his way through the streets of Da Nang city that Saturday afternoon, Brady headed for the embassy house. This was the place Duff had mentioned in his letter, the place where he'd met the woman he described as his girlfriend, Lynn Dai Bouchet. Duff wasn't one to describe any woman as his girlfriend unless he was pretty damned serious about her.

Brady arrived to find a compound that was nearly vacant and a Vietnamese sentry whose only challenge was a snappy salute, which he dutifully returned as he walked past. Hearing voices, he followed the sounds until he discovered several men lounging around a table in a large room, drinking beer. They wore camouflage military fatigues, and the room was clouded with cigarette smoke. Speaking a Vietnamese Pidgin English, they laughed and slapped the table. The men glanced up as Brady knocked tentatively at the open doorway.

"What can we do for you, partner?" one asked.

Brady stepped through the door. "I'm looking for someone," he said, "a woman named Lynn Dai Bouchet."

The man laughed. "Yeah? So are all the other horny GIs in I Corps. You got a date with her?"

"No," Brady said. "But I really need to see her about something important."

He barely heard the man's reply as he noticed something peculiar about the fatigues he wore. There was no insignia or rank on them—nothing.

"Hey. Hello? You hearing me?"

Brady suddenly realized he'd been distracted. "Oh, uh, sorry. What'd you say?"

The man doing the talking propped his boots on an empty chair. Faded green canvas over scuffed raw leather, this man's jungle boots had been down a few trails. The man looked at his friends around the table as he spoke. "Look, bud, she doesn't come around, except maybe a couple times a month. I think she spends most of her time in Saigon. What do you want with her anyway?"

"I just need to talk to her—that's all."

The man slowly turned his way. "Well, partner, you're SOL. She's not here."

Brady met his stare. He had to push these guys, get their attention.

"Do any of you know someone named Spartan?"

The men slowly glanced at one another. Their reactions weren't obvious, the hint of a raised eyebrow by one. Another, in the process of tipping his beer bottle, stopped momentarily, then continued.

The one doing most of the talking looked his way, but this time he tried to affect a wide-eyed look of honesty. "Nope, never heard of him." He turned to the others. "You guys ever heard of a Spartan?"

"Not around here," one said.

The others wagged their heads.

"What's your name?" the first man asked.

"Brady Nash. I'm a ranger with the 173rd Airborne Brigade."

The man's eyes ran up and down as he checked him out. "You boys have been in some shit down there around Dak To, haven't you?"

Brady nodded. "Yeah, it's been pretty bad."

"We heard y'all tied up with the 32nd, the 66th, and the 174th NVA regiments. Is that true?"

"Yeah, but about this Spartan—"

"If we run across him, we'll tell him you're looking for him. OK?"

He had to push harder.

"Are you sure you don't know anyone by that name?"

The man with his boots propped on the chair dropped them to the floor and sat upright.

"Look, partner. Can't you see we're trying to relax here? Who is this Spartan anyway, and what do you want with him?"

Brady had his alibi ready. "Like I said, I'm an army ranger, and I heard he sometimes recruits people for special operations."

His explanation seemed to put the men at ease. "Well, like we said, if we run across him, we'll let him know you're looking for him."

He'd hit close to home, but it was obvious they weren't going to open up, and there was no sense pushing his luck.

"Thanks for the help, and tell Miss Bouchet that I was looking for her too, would you?"

The men nodded, and Brady turned to leave. As he walked down the hallway, he heard chair legs scraping the floor and felt eyes piercing his back. A slight motion caught his attention as he reached the front gate. Someone was peeking through a window. He'd definitely gained their attention.

Returning to the embassy house the next day with two bottles of black market Cutty Sark under his arm, Brady was ready to bargain. And if that didn't work, he planned another approach by asking them if there were any other SOG units looking for help. After another snappy exchange of salutes with the sentry he walked inside, but the main building seemed abandoned for the weekend.

He walked down the hallway, but every door was locked. Unable to find the men with whom he'd spoken the previous day, he was about to give up, when he found a door ajar. Inside was a room full of electronic gear and a lone marine with his feet propped on a desk. Brady stepped into the doorway as the soldier, surprised and wide-eyed, tried to maintain eye-contact while folding his Playboy and nonchalantly shoving it in the desk drawer.

"How did you get in here?" he asked.

"I walked in," Brady said.

"Dumbass Nung at the gate didn't challenge you?"

"No. I'm looking for some men who were here yesterday," Brady said. "They were in that big room up front. You know where they are?"

"Uh, no, I mean, I'm with Naval Claims. Those guys work for someone else. They just hang out here sometimes."

"Do you know any of them or where they stay?"

"No."

"You mean you don't know any of their names?"

Brady noticed the man studying his uniform.

"You a ranger?" the man asked.

"Doesn't matter. Do you know any of their names?"

"A guy named Maxon is the head man. He's an advisor for the Vietnamese special police and a PRU detachment. The others work for him. They're here on TDY assignments, but I really don't know any of them."

"Do you know a woman named Lynn Dai Bouchet?"

The young marine's face flashed with recognition. "Sure, she's our Vietnamese liaison for Naval Claims Investigation."

"Where can I find her?"

The soldier shrugged. "I'm not sure. She lives on the outskirts of Da Nang city, northwest of here. She doesn't come in but maybe three or four times a month. Look, I'm supposed to be guarding this place, and no one is supposed to be in here. What is it you want?"

"Nothing," Brady said. He turned and walked out.

The clock was ticking with his three-day pass expiring the next morning. He had to return to his unit. He'd come close, but he was stymied, and it might be months before he could return. His plan had failed, and he was out of ideas. Old Man Brister was right. It had been a foolish idea from the very beginning.

* * *

Brady began what he hoped would be another uneventful day as he and Will made their way along a trail on a ridge extending from the firebase. With company-size sweeps in the surrounding hills, enemy activity was reduced, but not eliminated. He had seven confirmed kills in the two weeks since sniper school, and he was gaining a notoriety of sorts. Men who hardly knew him were walking up and talking with him. Even the battalion CO called him by first name.

The sun hadn't yet risen above the mountains in the east as they made their hide. After spreading his poncho on the ground, Brady filled his sandbag with dirt, while Will cut brush for camouflage. When they finished, Will lay on his belly and adjusted his binoculars. He began scanning the panorama of streams, elephant grass, and trees in the mountain valley below. A well-used trail ran the length of the valley, passing several hundred meters to their front.

Their daily hunts had become the routine. While larger patrols probed the surrounding hills, Brady and Will departed the firebase each day with a small security detachment. When they neared their objective, they left the patrol and set up a hide on high ground somewhere nearby. This day went by slowly, and by late afternoon, they had seen nothing. Will continued scanning the distant trails with his binoculars while Brady lay on his back staring at the sky. It had been a quiet day, with only the faint rumble of artillery somewhere up past Ben Het. Will shifted his weight and braced his arms as he refocused the binoculars.

"You see something?" Brady whispered.

"Well, I'm not sure. I thought I did a little while ago, but whatever it was disappeared."

Brady rolled over. "Let me see those things, man."

"Check that main trail," Will said.

Taking the binoculars, Brady scanned the trail, looking behind the tree lines, into the tall grass beyond, then followed the trail to where it disappeared into a ravine. He worked methodically as he panned across the valley, back and forth, slowly working his way to the base of the hill, then across to the firebase back to the east. After several minutes, he lowered the binoculars.

"I don't see anything."

He gave the binoculars back to Will and rolled onto his back again.

"So," Will said, "you never found your buddy in Da Nang. What did you do for three days?"

"I asked a lot of questions and got a lot of blank stares."

Will continued scanning the terrain below as he talked. "You don't know what outfit he's in?"

"He's on special assignment, and I—"

Will slapped his shoulder. "There! There!"

Brady sat up and looked to where he pointed. It was at the base of the ridge back near the firebase. Two men in khakis—NVA soldiers—were squatted on one of the secondary trails coming down from the firebase.

"How the hell did they get past us?" Brady muttered.

"I don't know," Will said, "but there they are. What do you reckon they're up to?"

They watched as the men worked feverishly, first on one side of the trail, then the other.

"Hell, they're booby-trapping the trail," Brady said.

He propped his rifle on the sandbag, carefully centering the crosshair on the first man's back.

"What do you think, Willie—six hundred meters?" he whispered.

Will pulled his eyes back from the binoculars. "Yeah, uh, right at six, and there's not much wind, if any."

With the rifle zeroed for three hundred meters, the bullet would drop thirty-five inches at this distance. He checked the trees for evidence of a breeze. Will was right—no wind. Raising the crosshair two feet above the man's head, he took a deep breath, partially exhaled, and settled in as he squeezed the trigger.

The armorer down at Bien Hoa had done a marvelous job modifying the M14. The trigger broke clean, snapping crisply with minimal effort, and at over twenty-four hundred feet per second, the bullet struck the first soldier just below the shoulder blades. The second soldier, apparently hearing the loud slap of the bullet striking his partner, turned to see the corpse thump to the ground. A split second later, his head turned as the distant report of Brady's M14 echoed down the valley. The soldier wheeled and fled.

Sprinting wildly through the trees and high grass, he ran parallel to the ridge where Brady and Will lay hidden. Brady followed him through the rifle's scope as the fleeing man occasionally disappeared into the folds of the terrain. He watched, but he didn't shoot as he followed the soldier's progress.

"The echo must have fooled him," Will whispered. "He thinks the shot came from the firebase. Why don't you go ahead and fire his ass up before he gets to those trees?"

Brady nodded. "I will," he said in a low voice. "Just watch him a minute."

After a couple of minutes, the enemy soldier reached a little knoll behind which the trail disappeared into the jungle. He was several hundred meters down the trail from his dead partner as he slowed to a trot.

"He's almost to the trees. Take your shot."

"Shh."

The man topped the knoll, spun around, and dropped to one knee, looking back down the trail toward the firebase. Brady dropped the crosshair down on the man's heaving chest. Apparently thinking he'd escaped, the soldier rested as he fought to catch his breath. It was a relatively easy shot, and Brady squeezed it off. The soldier fell dead before the echo returned from the far side of the valley.

"Damn!" Will whispered. "How did you know he was going to stop?"

"Human nature," Brady answered. "I call it the Gomorrah Principle, after Lot's wife looking back at Sodom and Gomorrah. Of course, a lot of animals do the same thing. Whatever it is, you can figure eight out of ten will stop to look back, just before they go out of sight."

Will shook his head with amazement as he picked up the handset on the PRC-25 to report the kills.

"Oh-Eight to Oh-Eight-Alpha, over."

"Oh-Eight-Alpha. Go ahead, Will."

Will muffled his voice with one hand while he talked into the mic. "Scratch two more NVA, Koslosky. They're on the trail just below Bravo Company's bunkers. We'll give you cover from here while you check them out. You roger?"

"Gotcha, Lima Charlie, Oh-Eight. Oh-Eight-Alpha, out."

"Man, you sure made that look easy," Will whispered.

Brady shook the dirt from his sandbag and gazed out across the valley. "I go with the same three rules we learned in sniper school: be patient, aim center mass, take one shot. I also discovered a long time ago that it's a lot harder to shoot a living target than a paper one. I think that's why some guys can knock the center out of a bull's-eye but can't hit shit when it counts. It's a mental thing."

He pushed the folded sandbag into the cargo pocket of his jungle fatigues.

"You ever think about it much?" Will asked. "I mean afterward. You know, the ones we shoot?"

Brady wasn't quite sure if Will was serious. "You're the one who's been over here for six months. I'd think you'd know by now."

Will shook his head. "Being a sniper is a lot different from what I've been doing. I mean, it's more of a one-on-one kind of thing, you know? Don't you think about it?"

"I try not to," Brady said. "Start thinking and you get distracted. War is about killing and dying, Willie boy, and I'd rather be on the killing side of the equation. Know what I mean?"

"Yeah, I reckon."

Brady glassed the adjacent slope with the binoculars, watching as the patrol worked their way down to the bodies. Will turned and finished rolling his poncho, then stuffed it in his rucksack. Brady glanced at him, then resumed watching the patrol hacking their way down the hill. Will, always the easygoing one, was suddenly becoming contemplative.

"You know, I read a story a while back," Brady said. "It was about this crazy old Cossack who lived on a tropical island. He'd hunted every kind of big game animal in the world until he got bored and began luring ships to his island with lights. When they wrecked on the reef, he'd capture the sailors and hunt them like wild animals. Think about it. Crazy as it sounds, the only difference between us and the Cossack is the Cossack's quarry didn't have guns. These do, and they're here of their own accord, trying to kill us. Know what I mean?"

Will didn't respond, and after several seconds of silence, Brady dropped the binoculars and glanced at him. Their eyes met. Will stared at him for a moment before turning away and picking up his gear.

"I know what you're thinking," Brady said, "but it's not that way at all. I just think you either commit yourself to this shit or you don't. Go at it half-assed and you'll end up dead."

As they made their way back to the firebase that evening, Brady thought about his words and the look on Will's face. There was that self-conscious blink of his eyes that had said more than words could ever explain. Maybe Will was right. Things had gotten a little crazy lately. Had he become like the crazy old Cossack killing for the sport of it?

That was ridiculous. This was a war, and he did only what he was trained to do. But he found himself subconsciously rubbing the spent M14 shell from Duff's grave that hung around his neck. Duff had been as close to him as a blood brother. They had been "the Dangerous Duo" at quarterback and halfback, leading Polk County to the district championship. They had been the pair who roamed the hills of the Tennessee Overhill, hunting, fishing, and swimming in the creeks and rivers. They'd done everything together, but all of that was now gone.

Brady drew a deep, quivering breath. Yes, there'd been a lot of killing, but if that's what it took, he'd kill every son of a bitch who got in his way until he found the ones who killed Duff. And when he found them...there was no turning back. His, too, had become a "most dangerous game," but he was determined to see it through.

CHAPTER FOUR

Run through the Jungle

When Lacey left the restaurant that afternoon, she was foot-weary and exhausted. After driving home to her apartment, she ran a hot bath and turned on the radio. The music soothed her until the evening news began. As she shaved her legs, the voice on the radio told of places with strange names where men fought and died, the Mekong Delta, the Ia Drang Valley, and a new one, Dak To. The numbers of killed and wounded mounted, and the razor nicked her knee. She leaned over and turned off the radio, but the nagging guilt wouldn't go away. Her bathwater grew cold. She had been a stubborn fool for not seeing Brady before he departed.

After toweling off, she pinned her hair back and donned her housecoat. It was time. She sat on the couch with a pen and paper. Dating her letter December 15, 1967, she wrote, "Dearest

Brother," then paused. Brady was her brother, but it was useless to keep lying. She gazed at the photo on the coffee table. She'd taken the picture of him shortly after high school graduation when they picnicked down on the Hiwassee. Bare chested, Brady sat on a large gray rock beside the river. His chest and face were bronzed from the summer sun, but his blue eyes glinted like the rippling rapids behind him. He was even more than a brother to her. He was the one and only true love of her life.

She wadded the stationary and pulled a new sheet from the box. Beginning again, she wrote, "Dear Brady." There was so much to say, but simple words didn't work, especially since she'd made such a mess of things. She should never have left him. It was tempting to write how her job waiting tables had led nowhere and how singing in the club wasn't all she hoped for, but her troubles were insignificant compared to his.

She'd seen the television reports—the bloodied soldiers being carried from the battlefields, the wrecked helicopters, the unfocused stare of the ones who made it through the battles. Brady was fighting for his life every day. If only she could see him again, she'd tell him to just come home alive. She would tell him she would be here, no matter how long it took. She wanted to say so much, but words seemed so inadequate.

Pushing the stationary aside, she lay back and closed her eyes as she thought about that afternoon, the first time they made love beside the Hiwassee River. It happened so quickly, and it was such a surprise, or was it? They had, after all, spent the better part of their lives together in school, rambled through the summer hills, and waded the river. She watched him play football when he and

Duff were known as "the Dangerous Duo" and led Polk County past Cleveland to win the championship. But their sibling relationship grew tenuous with maturity.

First came the curiosity and the mysterious attraction to one another's bodies. A kiss and a breathless moment left them at the brink of something frightening, and she drew back, but it had been something she wanted to experience again. Only the watchful eyes of a small town, Duff, and her mother had prevented it until that warm day in May after high school graduation.

Duff was now forever gone, and the job singing at Hugh Langston's club in Nashville awaited her. Lacey was determined to see the world, but Brady was reluctant. Perhaps it was her hope that she could somehow convince him to go to Nashville that was in her mind as they lay on a blanket beside the river. Staring out at the waters tumbling across the rocks, she felt her life, like the waters, flowing past and going around the bend into the future, and she wanted Brady to go there with her.

She propped herself on an elbow and curled a lock of his hair around her finger. "Whatcha thinking about?" she asked.

He pulled her down and gently kissed her, then again, this time harder. His tongue pressed hard against hers, and there came a sudden breathlessness along with the burning warmth that her T-shirt and shorts scarcely shielded. It was the same feeling she'd retreated from so many times, but this time it was different. When Brady brushed his hand against her nipple protruding inside her T-shirt, she didn't stop him. They were alone, and they were adults.

The river rapids muffled their voices as he pulled her shorts to her ankles and kicked them free. He looked deep into her eyes as he filled her deep inside. Never could she have imagined the warmth, the closeness, and the love. And it felt so right. There was no longer any doubt. She loved Brady.

Afterward, they rested, and her mind floated in the clouds. It seemed a long time before he whispered, "So what do you think?"

She turned her head to the side, and their eyes met. Brady had the bluest eyes she'd ever seen. His hair, burnt blond on the ends, curled in short ringlets.

"What do I think?" she said.

"About getting married," he answered. "We can find a little place somewhere around here and make ends meet, maybe start a business of some kind."

His suggestion had caught her off guard.

"I don't know what to think." But she did. She was at once elated and frustrated. "Marrying you is something I want more than anything, but why settle for these old hills when we can go to Nashville?"

Brady turned and stared up at the afternoon cumulus building above the mountains.

"Because Melody Hill is our home. It's where we belong."

For a moment, things had seemed so perfect, but now, hot tears filled her eyes. Brady didn't seem to notice as he stared up at the sky. Staying here and selling quilts like her mother wasn't enough. And Brady, too, could do so much better, if he would just let go.

Later, as they drove down the mountain road in silence, she sat on her side of the truck and he on his. She loved the hills, and she loved Brady, but they would never have anything if they remained here.

* * *

Lacey glanced at the clock. It was nearly midnight, but her letter couldn't wait. It still wasn't too late to tell him she cared. She walked to the bedroom and set the alarm clock for six the next morning, then began writing. When the letter was finished, she signed it and set it aside. She would take it to the post office the next morning. Lying back, she pulled the quilt under her chin, closed her eyes, and said a prayer for Brady. And just before slipping off, she once again felt the warmth of his body that afternoon down on the Hiwassee River.

* * *

Jack Maxon sauntered down the street toward a local watering hole where the troops from the 173rd hung out when they came in from the field. Much of Bong Song, its bars and whorehouses, was off-limits to military personnel, but this one was always crowded. Here he hoped to get some information or find some people who could give him information about an army ranger named Brady Nash. With his .45 strapped in a shoulder holster outside his tiger-striped jungle fatigues, he stepped aside for no one as he made his way down the crowded sidewalk.

A soldier wearing camouflaged fatigues, jungle boots scuffed to raw leather, and a camouflage bandanna knotted behind his head approached from the opposite direction. Maxon simply nodded as he passed, but the soldier gave him a wild-eyed grin, the insane look of a true boonie rat.

Nam was full of them, career gook killers, totally whacked-out on the thrill of going into the jungle to hunt the enemy. Most had severe personality disorders, slithering into the jungle day after day to collect not Bronze or Silver Stars like other soldiers, but the ears of their enemies. In some ways, they were to be admired, except they usually ended up Section-Eighted back to a VA hospital in the States.

Maxon didn't waste his time like the boonie rats. They served their purpose, chasing after the worker bees of the so-called People's Liberation Army. These were the Vietcong, the VC they called them. Maxon, though, prided himself for going after the queen bees—the VC leaders, the spies. Catch the queen, rule the hive, that's the way it was done. He knew his business, and he'd snuffed more than a few high-level gooks.

As he reached the door to the bar, a whore in a red vinyl mini-skirt stepped into his path. "GI want date? I give you good time, numba one boom-boom. You see."

She wore a black halter top and had penciled her eyes round. Shoving her aside, Maxon pushed his way inside, no time for slant-eyed pussy today. Pausing inside the doorway, he cursed under his breath. The bar was packed, not an empty chair in the house. Soldiers, most of them no more than a year or two out of high school, gathered around the tables and along the bar. A din of off-key rock music clashed with the clinking beer bottles and loud voices, and a thick layer of cigarette smoke hung a foot or two below the ceiling.

The three-piece band was a Filipino bunch with long black hair and Nehru jackets. Two played static-riddled electric guitars, while another pounded soggy drums a half beat behind the others. They were slaughtering a CCR hit, "Betta ron tru da junga." Maxon searched the room and spotted two young soldiers seated at a table on the back wall. Neither was a paratrooper. Rear echelon clerks, he figured. The soldiers looked up and smiled as he sauntered up.

"You two dips, take a hike."

Their smiles vanished.

"Huh?" one said.

"I didn't stutter, did I?"

One rose to his feet and picked up his beer. "Come on, Smitty, let's go to the bar."

The other hesitated, staring at Maxon.

"Let's go, Smitty," the first soldier said again. "It's not worth it."

The second man stood and, after a moment, followed his friend to the bar. Maxon fixed them with a steadfast glare. Little REMFs, all you had to do was say boo, and they scattered. He kicked the extra chair aside and signaled the waitress for a beer. Glancing about, he studied the boyish faces of the soldiers. Chickenshit kids, they didn't have a clue. They thought because they'd seen a few firefights they were something special.

His was the dangerous work. They could patrol till hell froze over, but he was the one who would make a difference in this war.

It took skill to find VC leaders and take them out. It took risks, risks that meant you didn't always follow the letter of the law, and you watched your back when people came around nosing in your business. That's why he was here.

When his men said a young ranger was asking about joining his SOG group, he'd felt a twinge of paranoia, the kind a good soldier recognizes as a caution light flashing somewhere in his subconscious. And the request wasn't necessarily the problem, except for two things: One was that the soldier had mentioned Lynn Dai Bouchet, the know-it-all half-breed bitch who interfered with his every attempt to ferret out the VC. Why did he ask for her? And the second thing was that he had somehow known his company code name. "Spartan" was a name used only by his bosses for certain missions.

It had taken him a while to get the background check on Nash, and he immediately realized there was something familiar, but he couldn't put a finger on it. The report sat on his desk at the operations center for several weeks before it finally came to him. It was Nash's hometown, Melody Hill, Tennessee. He'd heard the name somewhere before. More thinking and shuffling through records finally produced the connection—Duff Coleridge.

It didn't make sense. Who was Nash, and what was he up to? Was it the arms missing from the weapons warehouse? Was Nash working for Army CID? That didn't make sense either. The connection was with Coleridge. Coleridge had somehow contacted him, but how? He'd monitored every letter he had mailed home.

As he drank his beer, Maxon listened while a young paratrooper talked loudly at a nearby table, telling a story with relish. Those around him sat nodding.

"We busted out right on top of their bunker and caught them by surprise, but my damned sixteen jammed, and this gook jumped out and threw down his AK. He had his hands up, but when he saw my gun was jammed, he went for his rifle. That's when Jelks here"—he slapped a black GI on the shoulder—"stepped around from behind me with the sixty."

"Muthafucka shouldn't draw down on my man here," Jelks said.

Maxon cleared his throat and called out to the paratroopers. "Hey, any of you guys know someone named Brady Nash?"

They all wagged their heads.

"You might ask those guys over at the bar," the storyteller said. "They just came in from Dak To this morning."

Maxon picked up his beer and sauntered over to the bar. He tapped a sandy-headed GI on the shoulder. "Any of you guys know someone named Brady Nash? He's a ranger with the Fourth Battalion of the 503rd."

"Those guys over there are from the 503rd," the paratrooper said. He pointed to two men standing together near the end of the bar.

Maxon walked down to them. "Do you guys know a ranger named Brady Nash?"

"Yeah, we know him," one said. "But he's transferring out of our unit in the next week or so."

The soldier looked like he'd been in a few scrapes, a perma-fatigue look with deep lines around his eyes. Probably had the shit scared out of him more than a few times, Maxon figured. After all, the 173rd had been in shit up to their asses for two months now.

Maxon leaned on the bar. "So you're in the same unit with him?"

"Yeah, Nash is with the ranger recon platoon attached to our battalion, Fourth Battalion, but like I said, he's supposed to be leaving. Why? You heard about him?"

"A little bit," Maxon said. "What do you think about him?"

The young soldier raised his eyebrows as if the answer was a given.

"Hell, I think he's the best sniper in the whole damned army."

"That good, huh?" Maxon said.

"Yeah, that good," the soldier said.

"The real gung ho airborne ranger type, is he?"

"Not really. Matter of fact, he's pretty laid-back, but he's a motherfucker when it comes to killing gooks. Let me tell you. We were out with Nash and Cantrell. You see, we go out with the sniper teams, and they drop off somewhere to set up their hide. Then we double back and set up an ambush maybe a half klick away. That way, if the dinks get after them—"

"Yeah, yeah, I know. So what happened?"

"Anyway, it was getting late when Nash and Cantrell showed up that afternoon, said they'd seen a big NVA patrol moving our way. So we figure it's time to *đi du mau* our asses back to the fire-base, but all of a sudden, the shit hits the fan. We didn't know, but the gooks had flanked us. They bushwhacked us less than a half klick from the firebase.

"Man, you talk about a wild-ass shootout. Seven of our guys were down inside a minute. Our shit was definitely weak, and these weren't just some of the local yokels. They were NVA regulars, and they were all over us. I mean, like, there weren't but ten of us besides Nash and Cantrell, and the gooks had us flat-footed.

"Anyway, like I was saying, Nash, he's got ice water for blood, 'cause, like, we're all pinned down and knowing we're about to get greased, but it's, like, the most awesome thing I ever saw. He crawled under this brush pile behind a stump. He's completely hidden, but he's firing this M14 sniper rifle, one shot at a time! And I ain't sure, but I think every time he shoots, a gook falls."

The soldier paused to sip his beer.

"So anyway, we all figure we're still going to die, you know? I mean, I shit you not, the gooks really had us fucked. Most of our guys are lying around, all shot to hell and moaning. The only ones left who weren't hit was Nash, Cantrell, two other guys, and me, and we're all out of ammo. Then the gooks, they decide to rush us so they can finish us off before help comes down from the firebase, but that's where they fucked up.

"You see, there were, like, maybe a dozen of them, and they're maybe a hundred meters out on this little rise when they jump up and come for us. I mean, they're coming down the hill fast, but Nash, he just lays there cool as ice. Rounds are flying everywhere, but he doesn't flinch or nothing. He just takes aim, and *pop*, a gook falls. *Pop, pop*, two more gooks fall. They're only sixty meters out, weaving in and out of the trees. *Pop*, another one falls. Now they're, like, maybe only fifty meters away, and Nash is like a statue, not moving.

"There are still, like, eight left, and real quick, he goes *pop*, *pop*, *pop*, *pop*. Not real fast, but quick and steady, and the rest of the gooks turn tail and run, but Nash, he just takes his time watching them run away. They run until I think they're plumb out of sight, but he comes up on his knees, holding his rifle. Then all of a sudden, he shoots two more times."

Maxon listened intently.

"This guy is unreal. He waited until they came out of a ravine some four or five hundred meters down the valley. They must have thought they'd gotten clean away, but when they stopped, he popped two more of them. Like I said, you'd have to see it to believe it. They say he's got something like thirty-six confirmed kills."

"You said he's leaving. Where's he going?"

"He's transferring sometime after the first of the year. Him and several other rangers, including his spotter, Cantrell, are going to the 101st."

"Why are they doing that?"

"My understanding is MACV said we had to send some experienced men up there to work with the new 101st units that just came over from the States, so the colonel asked for volunteers.

"So who's asking anyway?"

Maxon turned and walked away.

* * *

As Brady lay in his hooch that night, he couldn't remember if it was Saturday or Sunday. He and Will pulled the same sniper duty outside the firebase perimeter almost every day. And they'd become deadly efficient, so much so that even the colonel had said the enemy seemed to be avoiding their AO, but the NVA had also begun taking countermeasures. They set up ambushes.

Anytime they went out, Brady and Will planned their return route to evade the ambushes. A few weeks earlier, they'd been lucky to escape unscathed after a fierce firefight left several members of their security patrol wounded. Now the enemy was trying another tactic. They were using their own snipers, well trained and armed with first-class Soviet equipment.

Brady had eliminated two, but others continued killing or maiming sometimes several GIs a day. One sniper became so emboldened as to eat a meal using his victim's body as a table. It was a GI who'd become separated from his patrol, and afterward, the sniper had apparently rummaged through his victim's rucksack, taking a deck of cards, evidenced by the single playing card he now left near his kills. When they found the GI's body, it was dotted with grains of rice and still reeked of the fishy odor of the sniper's nuoc mam.

The ARVN scouts called this one *Rắn hổ mang*, the Cobra, and said he was challenging Brady and the men on the firebase to come get him—if they dared. It was a challenge Brady planned to meet. Hunting this sniper on his home turf would be a lethal game of cat and mouse, but the clock was ticking as the casualties mounted each day.

Brady rested on his makeshift bunk, a row of empty mortar boxes and a poncho liner. It was hard as hell, but it beat sleeping on the ground.

"If I had my way, I'd go out alone," he said. "I know I can nail that bastard."

Will had the same bedding arrangement on the other side of the hooch. His cigarette glowed in the darkness.

"I thought that marine sniper they call White Feather nailed the Cobra up near the DMZ."

"He did. I reckon this one thinks he's carrying on the tradition." Brady laughed. "Son of Cobra, ya think?"

"OK, funny guy, and you want to go after him on your own? I thought you said we were in this shit together."

"Dammit, Will, we are in this together, but I figured this one was better to do alone. Can't you see that?"

"No, I can't, but I'm not going to waste my time arguing with you. The CO won't let you go out alone anyway."

"You're right. I've already talked with him, and he didn't go for it, but he did say if we nail that bastard, he'd give us another three-day pass."

Brady heard Will shuffling about in the darkness, and a moment later, his flashlight came on. He pointed it directly into Brady's eyes.

"First you volunteer us to transfer to the 101st up in I Corps, and now this. Are you crazy? What if this guy nails us first? Then what?"

"Get that damned light out of my eyes."

"Answer my question."

Brady shaded his eyes with his hand while he talked. "If he gets us, then we don't get our three-day pass."

Will extinguished the light.

"You're crazy, Nash, totally fucking crazy. They don't call that bastard the Cobra for nothing."

"That's what I like about you, Willie boy. You don't sugarcoat things."

"Stop trying to be cute. I'm serious. If you keep taking these stupid chances, your ass is going home in a body bag."

"Maybe so, but I need that pass."

"Huh?"

"Nothing."

"Why do you need that pass so bad?"

"I just need to get away for a while."

Will's flashlight came on again. He sat upright and swung his boots onto the dirt floor.

"Why do you want that pass so bad?"

Brady looked over at him. Will was still holding the flashlight and pinching the last of his cigarette. They had grown close, and his trust was unquestionable.

"Promise me you'll tell no one. Give me your word."

"OK, you got it."

Will killed the flashlight while Brady fumbled to light a cigarette. When it was lit, he drew hard, then slowly exhaled.

"I had a brother. Actually, he was a stepbrother. His mama adopted me. His name was Duff Coleridge. He got killed over here."

"That shell you're wearing around your neck—his?" Will asked.

"Yeah, from the twenty-one-gun salute at his funeral. I wear it to remind me why I came here. You see, Duff's death wasn't an accident. He was murdered."

Brady began telling Will about the letter, continuing until he'd given him every detail, including his recent visit to the embassy house in Da Nang. When he finished, several minutes passed in silence, broken only by the distant rumble of artillery back in the mountains. Brady was beginning to think Will had fallen asleep when he heard the metallic ping of his lighter and the scratch of the striker. He was still sitting on the edge of his bunk, and the flame of the lighter cast an eerie glow across his face as he lit another cigarette. His eyes were squinted, but dark and piercing, as he looked past the flame at Brady.

"If I didn't know you better, I'd think you made all that shit up," Will said. "And I can't believe you've gotten this far. I mean, you've actually gotten yourself over here and you've actually been to that place in Da Nang to find those bastards. You must be crazy."

"Maybe I am," Brady said.

Will's voice dropped. "Hell, Nash, I'm only kidding about you being crazy. I don't blame you a bit, but why don't you just take it to the CID? What's to keep those bastards from killing you like they did with your brother?"

"I don't want a cover-up, and I don't want those bastards to get away. I want to get names. When I know who they are, I'm going to send it all to the newspapers, CID, and anyone else who'll listen."

Will fell back on his bunk. "I understand what you're trying to do," he said, "but getting a pass by killing that *Rắn hổ* son of a bitch is a long shot at best. Like I said, he might just nail us first."

"Everything I've done up to now has bucked the odds," Brady said. "We'll just have to see what happens when we head out in the morning."

"So what's your plan?"

"You're gonna be my bait," Brady said.

He heard a shuffling sound in the darkness, and Will's flashlight came on again. His cigarette hung loosely at the corner of his mouth, and he stared wide-eyed at Brady.

"I'm gonna be your what?"

"You'll need to be careful."

Will threw his cigarette onto the floor, the sparks scattering in the darkness below.

"No shit! And what makes you think I'm even gonna do it?"

"Because whether you admit it or not, you want to nail that bastard as much as I do."

CHAPTER FIVE

Rắn hổ mang

The highlands of Vietnam were steep, vine-laced ridges that sapped the strength of even the most stouthearted men, but Brady traversed these slopes with relative ease. Following the game trails, he found the natural seams in an otherwise impenetrable jungle. The tropical forests were different, but the rules of nature were the same in Nam as they were back in the Tennessee Overhill. You learned to work with them, or they ruled you.

Governed by the sounds around him, Brady listened for the alarm calls of birds and monkeys lurking high in the tiers of jungle canopy. And when there were no sounds, he was most cautious, noting every movement, every broken blade of grass, and every disturbed leaf. This would be one of those days, one that dictated stealth and caution, because everywhere, there were signs of the enemy, but it was Rắn hổ mang who presented the greatest threat. The NVA sniper had every soldier in the battalion fighting paranoia, except this fear was very real, because no man knew when he might step into the crosshairs.

It was still more than four hours till daylight as Brady and Will prepared their gear and inventoried their equipment. A slight breeze stirred the night air across Brady's bare neck as he looked out across the perimeter wire. The danger was palatable, but he would soon be in his element, free from the stifling confines of the firebase. He stood unmoving, still staring down the hill past the sandbagged bunkers and beyond the piles of concertina. The jungle outside the wire was void of sound, dark and foreboding. The tops of the hills loomed, black silhouettes against the night sky.

"Here's my plan," he said in a low voice. "We'll head west across the valley, toward the old hamlet. When we get to the base of that ridge, you'll drop off and make a hide there, but not till you cut some brush and make some false hides that will be obvious to anyone on the other ridge across the valley. Four of the seven men that have been killed got it in that area between the two ridges and the old hamlet. I think it's our boy's favorite hide, and you'll be in the most logical place he thinks we'll be, but I'm going to fool him.

"After I drop you off, I'm heading farther up the valley along the edge of the hills. I should have a good view of the ridge on the other side where it runs out from the mountain toward the firebase, and he won't expect me over there in the opposite direction, that far from the firebase."

Will tossed Brady a small OD green can of apricots. "Take those damned things. I can't stand them. You know, this plan of yours might just work, but I have one question."

Brady pushed the apricots into his rucksack and looked back at Will. "What's that?"

"Do you want me to paint a bull's-eye on my ass or just stand up and wave a red flag?"

"You're not funny. I don't want you taking any chances. He's expecting us to be where you'll be hiding, but he'll be focused on the false hides. Just stay still and watch the trails coming down the other side of the valley. That way he can't flank us. I'll do the rest."

Opening his rucksack, Brady checked his gear: poncho, liner, socks, empty sandbag, insect repellent, snakebite kit, signal mirror, gun-cleaning kit, two starburst flares, two smoke canisters—one red, one purple—extra frags, canteens, iodine tabs, C rations, heat tabs, ammo, binoculars, flashlight, map, compass, extra blood expander, battle dressing…He checked and rechecked every detail. All metal was taped for silence, all shine eliminated. He was ready. Sliding his arms through the straps, he pulled the rucksack onto his back.

"Let's go," he whispered.

Cradling his rifle in the crook of his arm, Brady led the way as they followed the dirt path to the main gate. Pausing at the gate, they locked and loaded. It was still several hours till dawn, and Brady drew a deep breath. The odor of buffalo dung from the paddies hung heavy in the night air that drifted in from the no-man's-land surrounding the perimeter. The two snipers began moving, nodding as they passed the gate guards, mere shadows with eyes crouched in a sandbagged bunker.

One of the shadows grunted a barely audible, "G'luck."

After easing through the maze of concertina strung across the gate, Brady and Will eased into the black wall of darkness, moving carefully to avoid even the slightest sound of a footfall. When they were a hundred meters beyond the gate, Brady paused. He waited and listened for the night to come alive to his senses. Ten meters behind him, Will stood in silence, doing the same, as they acclimated themselves to the shadows.

First came the crick and buzz of insects from the trees, then the snickers and croaks of the frogs. And after a while, the blackness became broken with shadows and vague outlines as their eyes adjusted to the night. Brady glanced skyward at the scattering of stars that had managed to penetrate the thin film of clouds. Somewhere far out beyond the rice paddies, past the distant tree line, a bird gave a keening call of alarm. Someone else was moving as well.

Nearly twenty minutes passed before he signaled Will, and they again began moving. A half kilometer up the road, they turned onto a trail, following the narrow path through a thick growth of banyans and along the back edge of the farthest dike, past the abandoned hamlet. When they reached the base of the ridge, Brady stopped. Will eased up behind him.

"Make the false hides here," Brady whispered. "Make them obvious. Put one at the edge of that cane thicket and the other out there by that dike. I want this guy to think he's working against a couple of yahoos. Get him cocky so he'll screw up. When you're done, move back inside those trees over there and make your hide. If you make a kill, don't move. Remember, he ain't the only monkey in this show. Just stay put. I'll pick you up at dark thirty tomorrow."

Will went to work, quietly cutting brush for his hide, while Brady continued up the valley several hundred meters. Following the trail to the place he'd chosen for his hide, he moved in silence until he reached a slight rise. It was just inside the jungle's edge, a perfect spot to observe Will's position as well as across the valley to the opposite ridge some four hundred meters away. The ridge was eight hundred meters from the westernmost perimeter of the firebase and gave anyone there a promontory view of the nearest bunkers. The sniper had been making his hide there, a position that also covered the main road leading to the old hamlet as well as the crosshatched pattern of dikes and the banyan thicket where Will was hidden.

A kilometer in the other direction was a newer hamlet occupied by a few die-hard rice farmers—probably NVA sympathizers, if it could be proven. The roosters there were crowing by the time Brady slipped into his hide. Carefully, he arranged each detail: no vegetation too close in front to tip off the muzzle blast, no telltale cut limbs nearby, nothing that could draw attention. He spread his poncho liner on the ground, placed his rucksack in front, and stuffed fresh leaves into every pouch and pocket. He'd blackened his face before leaving the firebase. Now he was ready as he hunkered down for the wait, one that, if fruitless, would take him through the next two days.

This was the time he hated most, when his mind wandered. His conscience nagged him as much as his heart ached for Lacey. The truth should have been easy to find, a clear and simple answer to the right and wrong of what he was doing. But in Nam, there was no black-and-white. The truth was hidden somewhere in the shadows, like the enemy sniper who was no doubt out there now making his hide on the far hillside.

This was war, and the killing was justified, but a new realization had found its way into his conscience. He sensed it like a dawn whose first clue is not the graying of the night sky but a gradually developing instinct that tells the cock to crow or night birds to roost long before the stars fade from the sky. And when he finally saw it clearly for the first time, it was too late. He'd become this terribly efficient killer. He'd been killing men, and it had become easy, incredibly easy, like shooting coyotes.

As dawn broke orange in an eastern cloud bank and the sun's rays shot heavenward, Brady forced himself to focus on the task at hand. He could ill afford a daydream. Bracing his binoculars, he searched the valley and the ridge as the morning sun rose and moved across the sky. He searched, and it turned to afternoon almost before he knew it, but he'd seen nothing.

His was a game of patience, but with totally focused vigilance. He never stopped peering, analyzing, searching the panoramic landscape rising before him. And today, there was something more, something Brady's instincts were telling him. He'd felt it all morning, the enemy sniper's presence. He felt it as plainly as his own heartbeat. Rắn hổ mang was up there somewhere on that ridge. King of the valley, he was waiting for Brady or Will to make a mistake. A single misstep, that's all it would take to be sent home in a body bag.

Brady continued scanning the distant hillside. With the sun now high overhead, shafts of light illuminated new areas, while shifting shadows masked others. To the naked eye, the distant slope was a collage of furrowed ravines, canopied jungle, and crater-blasted clearings. It was both light and dark with mottled hues as the shadows of clouds glided across the slope. Wind-stirred grasses swayed gently in the afternoon breeze, and it was so deceptively peaceful that one could find himself lulled into a fatal complacency.

His 10X binoculars brought objects close, making them distinct: leaves, deep green with yellow spines; a lone parrot with gleaming red-and-blue plumage winging its way across the face of the slope. With the crystalline focus of the binoculars, even the shimmering heat vapor shone in the open sun, dancing with the breeze across the distant hillside. Searching patiently, Brady visually dissected the mountain, tree by tree, limb by limb, leaf by leaf, every stump, hump, and anomaly. Rắn hổ mang was up there somewhere, but who would make the first mistake?

The hours drifted by as the heat of the day increased in the afternoon sun. Brady continued scanning the slope with the binoculars, catching a glimpse of a single fly circling in a stray shaft of sunlight, something inconsequential at first take, except another appeared. After a few moments, several flies were visible, flitting in a tight orbit, silver and black dots, visible only by their insistent attraction to something in the shadows—probably something dead, killed by one of the bombs or artillery shells that pock-marked the ridge with craters.

Refining the focus ever so slightly, he braced the binoculars on his rucksack and studied the shadows beneath the flies, some seven hundred meters away. Each shape, each leaf, each stone, each sapling, each shadow, and each shaft of light began to take form as he studied them for telltale clues, and after a few minutes, he found something—something that didn't fit, a texture, an unnatural pattern, canvas perhaps. After a while, it began to take on a familiar shape. It was a haversack, a ration bag like the NVA carried. Its contents drew the flies.

And what was it in the bag that drew the insects? Boiled rice seldom attracted them. Brady contemplated, and it came to him—nuoc mam. The only thing that drew flies faster than the rotten fish sauce was a C ration. He visually picked apart the distant perplexity of shadows until something else became suddenly visible. It had been there all along, but only now did he see the distinctly slotted forestock of a Soviet SVD sniper rifle.

The rifle's owner lay motionless, as he had the entire morning, perhaps watching the perimeter of the firebase and the road in the valley below. He waited with stoic patience for some hapless patrol to appear on the road, or unthinking grunt to step out in the open near the perimeter bunkers. There would be one shot, the bullet reaching its victim before the rifle's report was even heard, and everyone would scramble about madly, but it would be too late.

Brady studied the sniper, frozen like a snake in the grass, waiting for its prey to wander too close. The rifle seemed to disappear into the shadow that was the man. Brady blinked and refocused his eyes, and a new shape appeared, a hand. The rest came in a rush as he found a shoulder and hair, straight and black with a dull sheen, and then the kill zone. He set the binoculars aside and slid his own rifle onto the rucksack to his front.

Finding the crosshair in his scope, he snugged the forearm dee-per into the rucksack and steadied himself as he caressed the trigger ever so slightly. Seven hundred meters, he figured, maybe seven twenty-five, normally not a terribly tough shot, but there was the crosswind and the uphill angle to calculate. He studied the afternoon breeze, watching the swirl of the grasses on the hillside, then the drift of the rising heat vapors in the scope. Blowing left to right, five to ten miles per hour, the breeze was steadier up higher on the slope. Down on the valley floor, where the trees dissipated the wind, the heat vapors rose almost vertically.

The man's head moved. Brady hesitated as he watched the sniper align his eye to his scope. Cutting his eyes down the valley, the blood drained from his head as he found the source of the sniper's attention. A single soldier—it had to be Will—crept along the edge of the banyan thicket, then ducked back into the trees, disappearing. He was intentionally giving away his position, but playing chicken with this guy was suicide.

Patience was suddenly no longer an option. Brady turned to find the enemy sniper aiming his rifle across the valley toward Will. If he found him in his scope, it would be over in seconds. Brady steadied himself, taking a deep breath, then partially exhaling. There was no time for careful calculations. Quickly figuring, he took a swag—a bit of humor he had learned at sniper school that stood for "scientific wild-ass guess." Except this was no joke. Will's life depended on it.

The average wind drift was one inch at five miles per hour for each hundred meters. He estimated the uphill slope at thirty degrees. Pushing the selector switch with his thumb, he carefully squeezed the trigger. A single bead of sweat trickled into his left eye as the crosshair dissected a leafy patch high and to the left of his target.

The echo of his rifle returned to him as a distant pop from the far slope, then again from farther down the valley, then silence. Remaining perfectly still, Brady maintained his watch through the scope as the man on the far slope came up on his hands and knees. He could see him plainly now as he aligned the crosshairs for a second shot, but the man's head was hanging low between his arms. Brady hesitated. A moment later, the enemy sniper's back bowed convulsively as he vomited a crimson stream of blood. A second shot wasn't necessary.

As the light of day faded into nightfall, Brady noted a single locust tree in a small clearing a few meters below the sniper's body. He marked it as a reference, and when it was dark, he began working his way across the valley floor to the ridge. Climbing the slope, it took nearly an hour to reach the locust. It was pitch-dark, and moving one step at a time, he cautiously approached the sniper's hide. He dared not use a light because snipers seldom worked alone. Squatting, he touched the ground in front of him. There was nothing, but he detected the odor of nuoc mam. The body was close. He stood, took a step, and stumbled over the corpse.

Kneeling, Brady ran his hands over the sniper's body. It was still warm, and the sticky blood soaked the man's uniform. He emptied the sniper's pockets, placing the contents with those in the haversack. When he was done, he felt about in the darkness until he found the man's rifle. Throwing it across his shoulder with the haversack, he began making his way back down to the valley.

* * *

An air of anticipation gripped those gathered at the battalion HQ the next morning as Brady emptied the haversack onto the table. And when a grease-stained deck of playing cards fell out, a chorus of whoops burst from the officers and NCOs. It was the moral victory everyone needed. They'd sent out their best to meet Rắn hổ mang, and they'd won.

The battalion commander was quick to confirm his promise for another three-day pass. He also submitted recommendations for both Brady and Will to receive the Distinguished Service Cross. It was a hell of an honor, or should have been, except somewhere amid the celebration, Brady found himself suddenly having to force his smile. He glanced at the brass shell hanging from the chain around his neck, and he remembered his promise to Duff.

His eyes met Will's, and they traded tight-lipped smiles. Will knew what he was thinking, but it didn't matter. His graveside promise to Duff was something nothing could change.

Later, when the celebration ended, the company clerk brought him his mail. There was the usual letter from Mama Emma, but this time, there was a second, and it was postmarked Nashville,

Tennessee. Brady's heart raced as he tore open the envelope and unfolded the letter.

December 15, 1967

Dear Brady,

I hardly know how to begin this letter, except to say that I love you. I know you think I have been insensitive and selfish, and if I could change the things I've done, I would. I've come to realize that no matter what happens, I will never forget that day when we first made love down on the Hiwassee. I know now, as I did then, that I will always be yours. I am so sorry for the heartache I have caused you, and I still don't understand why you had to go to Vietnam. But I want you to know that I will be here for you when you return. Please write to me. I miss you very much. Mama is doing well, and she reads me all your letters over the phone. She also said Hubert Brister has been asking how you are doing. I didn't know you and him were such good friends. Anyway, please take care of yourself, and please write me.

Love,
Lacey

Brady finished the letter, then read it again, but there was something that stifled his elation. It was the realization that somewhere along the way he'd given up hope for life after Nam. Vietnam was his life, and his only purpose was to find and destroy Duff's killers. The chance someday for a normal life was something he'd surrendered long ago.

He was a killer. Everything he had done since arriving in Nam was focused on the hunt and the kill. He lived for that moment when he put all the variables together and his quarry ended up flat-footed in the center of his crosshairs. Life after Nam hadn't even been an option, until now.

Could he simply turn and walk away, or had he already passed into that realm from which men seldom return, that place where the insatiable thirst for fighting eventually kills them or they go insane and are locked away forever? He folded Lacey's letter and put it in his shirt pocket. First, he would find Duff's killers. Only then would he know the answer to the other questions.

CHAPTER SIX

The Country Music Business

L acey glanced into the mirror behind the sun visor as she
rode with Hugh Langston to the club that Friday evening.
Nashville glittered with Christmas lights, and she should
have enjoyed the ride, but Langston seemed agitated, fidgeting
and driving too fast. No longer surprised by much of what he did
or the Nashville music business, she wasn't particularly alarmed,
but something wasn't right.

Langston was growing weirder every day, not in a major way,
but there were those constant little red flags. Tonight, it was his
insistence on picking her up and driving her to the club, saying it
was because some club owners and record producers were coming
to see her perform. His offhanded comments about her clothes
were probably the most worrisome, except she did allow that he
had some say in the way she dressed at his club.

When they arrived at the club, the neon signs on the strip were glowing in the gathering twilight, but Langston's pupils were pinpointed, and he was jittery as he dropped his keys getting out of the car.

"Are you OK, Mr. Hugh?"

They walked up to the front entrance of the club, where he stopped, studying his reflection in the glass door. He adjusted his string tie.

"I'm fine, little lady. Just don't you go getting too big for your britches tonight. If those club owners make you any offers, just remember we have a contract. I have to agree to anything they offer you."

He was no doubt popping pills again. It always started with the pills and ended with him getting drunk.

"I know that, Mr. Hugh. Have I done something wrong?"

Langston opened the door and walked in ahead of her. She'd never met a man who so thoroughly lacked courtesy of any kind.

"You just need to remember that business contract we signed. We'll talk about it tonight after the show. And don't believe anything these people tell you. You hear?"

He didn't wait for a response as he disappeared through a door leading to the back office. Lacey walked over to where several of the band members were tuning their instruments. There was no use talking to them about Langston. Whenever his name was mentioned, they grew tight-lipped. That they had problems with him was evident, but they weren't certain of her loyalties.

The club filled, and Lacey was already onstage singing when three men arrived around nine. Instinctively, she knew it was the men Langston had mentioned. Two wore string ties and cowboy hats like Langston's, the other a white shirt, khaki pants, and a sports coat. Langston showed them to a table and ordered drinks. During the next break, he called out to Lacey, motioning her over to the table. She shook hands with the men, and they complimented her singing. The small talk went well until one asked about her future plans.

Langston stood, clearing his throat as he glanced around the room. "OK, honey, let's get ready for the next set. People are getting restless."

The men laughed, and one murmured something into another's ear as Lacey excused herself. There were still ten minutes remaining on her break. She walked to the bar and got a glass of water.

Despite the abbreviated introductions, it turned out to be another routine night, and the men were gone long before closing time. It was well after midnight as Lacey shivered and waited in the car for Langston to take her home. She was tired, and the neon light from the motel across the street flashed monotonously on the windshield as she watched her boss lock up and walk to the car. After cranking the engine, he reached into his coat pocket and produced a bottle of liquor.

"Try this, baby. It'll help warm you up. It's peach brandy."

Lacey, not wanting to seem unappreciative, sipped tentatively from the bottle.

"Pretty good, huh?"

She nodded as Langston lit a cigarette and seemed satisfied sitting in the parking lot with the engine running.

"Want one?"

She shook her head. "No."

"You need to learn to be more sophisticated," he said. "Have you ever been to New York or LA?"

He didn't wait for her response.

"Those are real cities. Nashville is just a big country town compared to them. Out in LA, there's Hollywood and the Sunset Strip. And in New York, you got Broadway, Times Square, Radio City Music Hall, and millions of people, all trying to get someplace at the same time, people who someday will fight to get your autograph on their ticket stub. That's why you've got to polish your image. You're good, baby—real good—but you've got to learn to project yourself, and that's what I aim to teach you."

His voice had the ring of a carnival huckster, making her dreams of a music career seem ever more distant. The compliments from the other club owners had at least seemed more genuine.

"Just remember who brought you to this dance, little girl," he said. His bloodshot eyes appeared yellow in the glow of the dashboard lights. "OK?"

"Why are you saying that, Mr. Hugh?"

"Don't go playing the innocent little country girl with me. You know exactly why I'm saying it. Those bastards wanted to buy out your contract, but I'm the one who brought you here, and I'm the one who's going to make you a star—nobody else."

"I've done everything you've asked," Lacey said.

Langston tapped his cigarette in the ashtray.

"OK then, but it's time we started putting a little more image into your act. You've got the body, you've got the looks, you even talk like a woman, but you still dress like a schoolgirl, wearing those Sunday dresses and highheels. You need to wear cowboy boots and a miniskirt, you know? Men like the look, and you've got the tools."

"Mr. Hugh, I'm willing to try the cowboy boots thing, but I'm not wearing a miniskirt, not for you or anybody else."

She glanced at Langston, who downed the remainder of the brandy and tossed the bottle into the backseat.

"You don't know enough about this business to argue with me, baby. If I tell you to wear a damned propeller beanie on your head, you need to trust me."

"Well, I'm not wearing a miniskirt, not now, not ever."

Langston pulled from the club parking lot.

"That's what I mean. You think like a schoolgirl. You need to strut your stuff, and I'm going to teach you how."

Lacey didn't respond as she thought of her mother's parting words, "People with real talent don't have to sell their morals. You're one of those people."

"Why don't we go somewhere quiet and talk?" he said. "Maybe we can work this out."

"Mr. Hugh, I'm tired. I worked at the restaurant all day, and it's nearly two a.m. All I want is to go home and get some sleep."

"OK, maybe I was too rough on you. How about we make some coffee and have a little talk back at your place?"

Lacey was exhausted, but whatever it took to get home and get out of her high heels...

"Whatever," she said.

Langston turned south on Broadway, then down Twenty-First Street, past Vanderbilt, and out the Hillsboro Pike. She liked living out from town. There was less noise and a beautiful view of the surrounding hills. After a few minutes, Langston turned into the apartment complex and parked his Mark IV beside her Malibu. They walked up the steps to the second floor.

"Mr. Hugh, can we talk another night?"

"I thought you said we could talk?"

Lacey, too tired to argue, left the front door open as she walked inside.

"Why don't you make the coffee while I change clothes?" she said. "These shoes are killing my feet. All the fixin's are there in the cabinet above the stove."

She went to the bedroom and pried the heels from her feet, slipped out of her dress, and peeled herself free of the panty hose. Pushing aside the clothes hanging in the closet, she searched for her jeans and favorite T-shirt. It was the one Duff had sent her, black and gold with parachute wings and the words "Airborne Ranger" on the front. The hinge on the bedroom door squeaked behind her, and she turned to find Hugh Langston standing in the doorway.

"Where do you keep the cups, darling?"

She stepped backward into the closet, clutching the T-shirt across her bare abdomen.

"Mr. Hugh! What are you doing? The cups…uh…yeah."

"You don't have to be afraid of me," Langston said.

He walked into the room, coming toward her with a wrinkled smile on his face.

"I'm the one who brought you to this dance. Remember?"

"But…"

He put his arm across her shoulders as she cringed and held her breath. Ever so gently, he squeezed her shoulder as his other hand came to rest on her bare waist. Lacey's embarrassment gave way to fear. Dumbfounded, she clutched the T-shirt against her breast and pushed him away with the other hand. She finally found her voice.

"Mr. Langston, please, let me put my shirt and pants on."

A hurt look fell across his face, and for a moment, she wondered if she had overreacted. Langston grasped her chin, bending forward as he spoke.

"Baby, you don't need to be afraid of me. Just remember, together we can go places. Remember what I told you about New York and LA. All you need is to learn how to be a real woman."

The stale odor of cigars and liquor on his breath always turned her stomach, but never as much as it did now. She began trembling as he pulled her chin closer to his face. He attempted to kiss her.

"No!" Her fear turned to panic, and she tried to push him away. "Get away."

Langston was nearly fifty, but he was a big man, and his strength was overpowering. Try as she might, she couldn't break away. Panic gave way to terror as he pulled the T-shirt from her grasp, exposing her torso. Bare but for her panties and bra, Lacey grabbed for the shirt, but he held it out of reach.

"Please, Mr. Langston, no!" she shouted.

He laughed, then clamped his hand across her mouth. "Not so loud, spitfire. You'll wake the neighbors."

His huge palm blocked her nose as well, and Lacey found she couldn't breathe. She fought and squirmed, but he held her fast.

"Relax, honey. Old Hugh is your daddy, and I'm going to teach you to be a real woman."

The words sent a chill through her body. Her father had been a good man. Langston was a pig. As his wet tongue groped along her neck, he lifted his hand from her mouth.

"No!" she screamed. "You're not my daddy. Get your hands off me."

He clamped her mouth shut again. "You're a regular wildcat, ain'tcha?"

A rush of fear overcame her as Langston clawed at her panties. With one desperate heave, she broke free, stumbling backward and falling across the bed. Langston lurched forward and fell on top of her. It was as if she was pinned beneath a fallen horse, and try as she might, she couldn't squirm free. Langston began rubbing himself against her hip.

There was nothing she could do. Outweighed by more than a hundred pounds, Lacey fought to breathe as stars danced before her eyes. It seemed she was about to lose consciousness, until Langston slowly lifted his hand from her mouth. Sucking air into her oxygen-starved lungs, Lacey trembled, but she fought the urge to scream. As her head cleared, she regained her wits.

Langston would hold her tight as long as she resisted. *Breathe*, she thought. *Don't scream. Just breathe and relax.* Her heart pounded, but she forced herself to take a deep breath. He continued slobbering on her neck as he pulled her bra away, and as he sensed her lack of resistance, he, too, began to relax. The weight of his body eased somewhat as he crawled farther onto the bed, still straddling her with his immense frame.

"See, baby," he said in a soothing voice, "this isn't so bad now, is it?"

He rose to his knees, then unbuckled his belt and dropped his pants. This was her last chance. She pulled her legs back as if to remove her panties, but with all the force she could muster, she thrust forward with the heels of both feet. She did it just like Brady had taught her to do to defend herself. She used the muscles in her hips and focused on a point beyond her target.

Her aim, though, was high, as her heels missed his groin, but the blow sent Langston tumbling backward with a lung-draining grunt. Wrenching free, Lacey scrambled off the bed and stumbled into the living room, where she grabbed a brass table lamp. She stood ready as Langston walked into the room, holding his lower abdomen. A scowl was etched into his face. Hot tears streamed down her cheeks as she brandished the lamp like a club.

"Don't come near me," she cried.

He stopped, staring at her in silence. After a few moments, he began buttoning his pants, then snatched his jacket from the couch. He started toward the door, but stopped and looked back at her.

"You shouldn't have invited me up here if you were just going to be a tease," he said.

Lacey had never been a violent person. Never in her life had she struck anyone in anger, but this pretense, this lie Langston was attempting...She attacked with a fury, swinging the lamp like a baseball bat. Langston threw his arms up to fend off the blows, but the heavy brass base of the lamp struck his head. He stumbled, bleeding from a cut above his ear. Lacey struck him again, this time in the ribs, leaving him gasping for a breath.

When he offered no further resistance, she opened the apartment door and shoved him out onto the front balcony, tossing the ruined lamp after him. The entire apartment house shook when she slammed the door. It was over. Everything was over. Any chance for a music career was gone. She collapsed on the couch, and cried until sleep relieved her agony.

CHAPTER SEVEN

Keep Your Enemies Closest

The Christmas and New Year holidays were nonevents for Brady and Will, except for the food. The resupply choppers flew a hot meal into the firebase: turkey and dressing with warm beer and a cinnamon-tasting lump they tried to pass off as pumpkin pie. But no one was complaining because anything was better than C rations. Brady encouraged Will to drink the beer first, savoring not the taste but the little golden buzz that for a moment made them forget this was Nam. They were grinning at one another before eating the first bite.

After he'd licked the last speck of turkey and dressing from his fingers, Will wrapped himself in his poncho liner and fell asleep, snoring like a fat cat. Brady sat beside him, gazing out at a flat gray rain falling straight down into the hundreds of muddy boot prints outside the hooch. He doodled with his pen on a sheet of paper, still trying to make his letter to Lacey work. It had been several weeks, and he'd been unable to respond. What could he say? He wadded the stationery and tossed it in the corner.

The undercurrents of the war grew into an ominously rising tide as the month passed, but Brady remained determine to write Lacey. He dated a fresh sheet of stationery, January 28, 1968, and stared at it for several minutes. What do you say to make someone truly understand your situation? "The weather sucks, the war sucks, life in Nam sucks…" Will snored contently while Brady tried to write something positive, but it was useless. He wadded yet another piece of stationery as sloshing footsteps came from outside the hooch. The rains had continued unabated, and the unit had been on standdown for the last couple days. One of the lieutenants from battalion stepped into the doorway. His steel pot and poncho were drenched.

"Battalion CO wants to see you ASAP, Nash."

The officer was gone before Brady could reply. After shoving the pen and remaining stationery into his rucksack, he left Will sleeping and made his way through the maze of bunkers toward the battalion CP. As he trudged up the muddy hill, he tried to figure what the colonel wanted. They'd already canceled his three-day pass. The CO said it was because of the upcoming Tet holiday. It seemed the whole of Nam was a powder keg, and no one wanted to give up a single man if it blew wide open.

The marine firebase up at Khe Sanh had been under siege for nearly a month, and the rumor was General Giap was looking for another Dien Bien Phu. Army intelligence reported increased enemy movements everywhere in the country. With the Vietnamese New Year only days away, the VC were thought to be traveling among the hordes of homeward-bound holiday travelers, probably getting into position for a strike, but Tet was supposed to be a time of peace. The data simply didn't make much sense.

When Brady opened the screened door at battalion HQ, the sergeant major didn't bother with formality. "Go on back, Nash. The old man is waiting."

Brady walked into the colonel's office and saluted. "Reporting as ordered, sir."

"At ease, Brady, sit down, and let's talk"

The colonel was a West Pointer and one of the officers all the men respected. Despite his familiarity, the mere tone of his voice indicated something wasn't right.

"I've got a telex here from General Buckingham at MACV in Saigon. You've been ordered to report to his office for redeployment to the OSA. Were you expecting this?"

He looked the colonel in the eye. "I was expecting redeployment to the 101st."

"Buckingham is a liaison for a number of groups, including the OSA, but he doesn't normally handle orders for the 101st. Do you know what the OSA is?"

"No, sir."

"The OSA is headquarters for the CIA. Have you spoken with anyone about joining special operations?"

It came at once, a mixture of fear and elation. This had to be the result of his visit to the embassy house in Da Nang. Someone there had listened.

"Never mind," the colonel said. "I just hope you know what you're getting into. If special operations is recruiting you, I can't think of but one reason they'd want a sniper. Just keep one thing in mind: much of what they do is beyond the auspices of army regulations, and for that matter, from some of the rumors I've heard, beyond the Geneva Conventions. You'd better think carefully before you commit yourself to anything."

"I will, sir."

He heard the hollow ring of his own words and was certain the colonel did as well, but he didn't care. He wasn't thinking about anything, except this marvelous stroke of luck. He was going into the lair with Duff's killers.

The colonel handed him several folded documents.

"Those are your orders. There's a resupply chopper coming in around fifteen hundred tomorrow. Have your gear at the LZ, and be ready to go. You'll catch a C-130 out of Dak To. Good luck."

* * *

"Keep your friends close, but your enemies closer." It was one of Maxon's favorite maxims, and one that had served him well. He was going to keep this Nash person close for a while, at least until he was certain of his intentions. That was how he'd discovered Coleridge's plan to talk. A little wide-eyed sympathy and some keen-eyed friends made him realize that Coleridge could blow things wide-open if he left the unit. Now he intended to find out what Nash was up to. Maybe he really was after adventure, but it was his inquiry about Lynn Dai Bouchet that didn't make sense. She and Coleridge had been in cahoots. Of that he was certain.

Maxon awaited Nash's arrival in the office of Buckingham's aide. He had planned it carefully, pulling the right strings to have the higher-ups order Nash to Saigon. This prevented him from knowing the exact location of the IOCC near Da Nang, at least until he was ready for him to know. It also made things look official, a job interview, so to speak. It would allow him to size up this guy.

He heard a voice outside the office. "Specialist Fourth Class Nash reporting as ordered, sir."

Maxon involuntarily rocked forward in his chair. The accent and the tone were identical to Coleridge's, so much so it momentarily spooked him.

The captain poked his head through the open door. "Nash is here. You ready for him?"

"Send him in."

Maxon wore his usual tiger-striped fatigues with his .45 strapped in a shoulder holster on the outside. The .45 and tiger stripes always impressed the young ones. He made a point to prop his boots on the desk and remain seated as Nash stepped into the office.

"Specialist Fourth Class Nash reporting as—"

"Can the army crap, Nash. I'm not military. Shut that door, and sit down."

He looked across the desk at a kid who couldn't have been more than twenty, a little over six feet tall and with a kind of pretty-boy blondish hair, what there was of it with his paratrooper crew cut. The kid's eyes, though, were steady and with a spooky hard-core look Maxon had seen in only a few men that age.

"I understand you've been in Da Nang, asking questions about joining special operations."

"Yes, sir, that's right."

"So how is it that you know about operations that are considered top secret?"

"I had a friend who was in special operations."

"Yeah, and who was that?"

"His name was Duff Coleridge. He got killed in action."

Maxon fixed Nash with a penetrating stare. This kid was incredibly naive, but unlikely as it seemed, he might be trying to pull some shit.

"What did Coleridge tell you?"

"He just said it was exciting work and that he loved it, but later, we were notified he'd been killed in action."

"Is that all he told you?"

"Yes, sir."

"And so now, even though he got killed, you still think you want to do the same thing?"

"I don't know. I've had second thoughts."

Maxon studied the young ranger. If he was blowing smoke, he was doing a masterful job. The kid didn't blink. He didn't stutter. He gave no indication whatsoever that he was nervous or might be lying.

"Why is that?" he asked.

"I figured your men didn't want me to join. I mean, that day when I went to Da Nang to find you, they acted like I was doing something wrong. All I did was tell them I was interested, but if you don't want me…"

Maxon found himself grinning. This guy was one dumb son of a bitch.

"Maybe you're right, Nash. You might not fit in with real warriors, but I reckon if you still want to join, we might consider you. First *y'all* need to answer another question or two."

Nash didn't seem to notice him mimicking his accent, more evidence that he wasn't all that bright.

"What about this Vietnamese national you were asking about?" Maxon paused, and although he knew her well, he glanced at his notepad as if to find her name. "Let's see, Bouchet—that's it, yeah, Lynn Dai Bouchet. How do you know her?"

"Oh, she was a friend of Duff's. He wrote me about her in the letter. Said I should look her up when I got over here."

"Letter? How many letters did you receive from Coleridge?"

"Quite a few, but there was only one where he told me about special operations. I know he wasn't supposed to write about it. He said so in his letter. Said he could get in trouble. He mailed it while he was on R&R in Hong Kong."

Maxon almost began feeling sorry for him. This stupid bastard was spilling his guts. Coleridge at least was half-assed bright. This guy was an idiot, but if he could shoot half as good as people were saying, he might be put to good use. Besides, another idea was taking shape in his mind. Maxon grinned. Sometimes, he even made himself proud when things came together in his head.

"If Coleridge was still alive, his ass would be in a sling right now for running his mouth. As for you, you're lucky. You've stumbled onto one of the best gigs there is in Nam. I can use a man with your shooting ability, but you'd have to be a whole lot smarter than your buddy Coleridge."

"What do you mean?" Nash asked.

"What I mean is, I know a good bit about how Coleridge died, and word was that he really wasn't killed in action."

The young soldier's eyes widened. It was like laying a trail of bread crumbs for a fat pigeon.

"We think he was killed by a Vietnamese double agent, but we can't prove it. We were never able to finger the one responsible, but your buddy's friend Miss Bouchet remains the prime suspect."

Maxon watched with satisfaction as Nash's face paled.

"Do you have a clue what this war is really about?"

Nash nodded. "Stopping the Communists from taking over South Vietnam."

"Damned right," Maxon said. "I've fought these bastards for almost three years, and they are the sneakiest fuckers on Earth. Try to make sense out of who's a Communist and who's not, and you'll go nuts. Your buddy's friend Bouchet is a perfect example. Me, I think he made a mistake messing with her. I can't prove it, but my gut tells me I'm right."

Nash's face had gone expressionless.

Maxon slapped the table. "So you say you're not sure you want to be a part of my group. Well, it's up to you, but I guarantee you, if we don't stop them here, we'll be fighting them in California before long. You can run back to your unit if you want, but I'm going to do my part to make sure we stop them here in Vietnam.

The young ranger remained blank faced.

"OK, I tell you what. I'll give you twenty-four hours to make up your mind. In the meantime, we're going out tonight to have a little fun. Have you ever been here in Saigon before?"

The kid wagged his head, and Maxon laughed. This kid probably hadn't seen a town with more than a dozen streets before joining the army.

"Well, sonny boy, you're going to see how real warriors spend their free time. You join up with us, and you'll get the best of everything—food, women, you name it. Let's go."

Maxon opened the office door.

"Where are we going?" Nash asked.

"I have a room at a villa down near the Cholon District, just down the road from the presidential palace. I'm taking you there to get some rest. You stay there until I come back. Understood?"

"Yes, sir. You gotta name?"

Maxon paused as he thought how to handle the question.

"You mean Coleridge didn't give you anyone's name?"

"Just one."

Maxon turned to face the kid. "Who was that?"

"He said someone named Spartan was in charge."

The more he heard, the more he wondered what Coleridge hadn't put in his letter.

"I don't remember anyone by that name, and I wouldn't be throwing names around like that. It could get you in trouble. My name is Maxon, but I don't want you to ever refer to me as anything other than Max, especially when we're around other people. Understood?"

Nash nodded.

"While you're taking it easy at the villa, look under the bed. There's a black case there with a sniper rifle in it. Take it out and get a look at it. If you decide to join us, it'll be yours. It's an M40 with a bull barrel and a Redfield scope like the marines use, accurate out to a thousand yards. They don't make them any better than that. And you can also thank me for keeping your ass out of the fire tonight."

"What fire?"

Maxon worked up his best patronizing half-assed grin and shook his head as he sighed. "They don't tell you grunts anything, do they?"

Nash shrugged.

"Our intelligence points to some heavy shit coming off real soon. We're not sure exactly when, but we figure it'd be pretty slick if the gooks timed it with the lunar New Year, Tet. That's tonight, but you'll be safe here in Saigon. It's the firebases that are going to catch hell, especially the ones up in I Corps."

CHAPTER EIGHT

Saigon, Tet 1968

After his meeting with Nash that morning, Maxon stopped by the OSA. It was almost laughable when he considered the name, the Office of the Special Assistant. It probably drove the gooks nuts trying to figure out who or what it represented. It was, of course, the people he worked for, the ones who really called the shots in Nam. He was at the top of the food chain, running with the big dogs. No one told him, or anyone at the OSA, how to fight their war. Even now, after the military had stolen it from them, it was still really their war because the CIA intelligence apparatus was what everyone depended upon most.

As soon as he walked through the door, Maxon realized something was up. People were poring over maps, and the telex machines were going nuts, chattering and spewing paper onto the floor. He grabbed one and read as the dispatches continued coming across. All hell was breaking loose in the provinces. New intelligence reports coming in from advisors all over the country said it wasn't the firebases that were being hit hardest. He cocked his head as he read. This was strange. The cities were being hit full force by both the VC and NVA regulars. Pleiku had been hit the previous night, as were Phu Bai, Qui Nhon, and several other cities.

This was a curveball. Charlie was taking on a new strategy, and the military was probably looking for answers, because obtaining intelligence and knowing how to use it were entirely different concepts. Of course, he already had it figured out. It was simple. Anyone with sense knew the enemy was hitting the cities because they were too weak to hit the firebases. These attacks were probably last-minute punches before the holiday cease-fire, nothing much to worry about. Whatever the enemy's strategy, the military and the grunts out in the bush could worry about it tonight. He was safe in the middle of Saigon. Besides, he had more pressing business.

Heading down to the Cholon district, Maxon worked his way through a crowded market and turned down a back alley. His black market connections would provide what he was after, something with absolutely no connection to him or the IOCC. Suspicious eyes followed his every move as he knocked on a door. Someone peeked from behind an adjacent window. After nearly a minute, an aged man, slight with gray hair and wrinkled eyes, opened the door and motioned him inside.

The odor of incense greeted him. In a corner of the room, atop a frail but lacquered altar, was the household shrine with smoldering joss sticks. Several children huddled on a mat, wide-eyed and silent, as he crossed the room and passed through a beaded curtain into the next room. The rank odor of nuoc mam clashed with that of the joss stick as the *papa-san* led him out into another alley. The odor there was even worse, rotting garbage and sewage. Walking with choppy steps, the old man hurriedly led him down the alley to another door.

Inside, it took only a few minutes for Maxon to get what he came for, an untraceable .45. The old gook was so happy with his fifty US dollars. He smiled with betel-browned teeth and gave him an extra clip loaded with ammo. Maxon shoved the .45 automatic under his belt and dropped the loaded magazine into his pocket. The warehouse in Da Nang was full of .45s, but this one had no traceable connection to him or the company. A few moments later, he slipped back onto the street and flagged a taxi.

The streets of Saigon were packed with the holiday crowds, and progress was slow, but Maxon felt good. He was in control. This was his game and his playing field. He was going to make sure Nash understood that by putting the fear of God in him. Catching a cab, he sat back and closed his eyes.

Never had he imagined studying law enforcement would land him in Nam. He was supposed to train the local Vietnamese police, but had ended up on contract as a special advisor. He kicked ass and took names; not a bad gig for a Detroit boy. But he didn't get the credit the ass-kissing ex-military types and the Ivy Leaguers got. He had slipped in the back door of their little club, and his spook bosses treated him like a step-child, but his PRU and special police unit were the most feared and respected in I Corps.

The only part of his job he didn't like was enforcing the code. Black ops meant no one man was more important than the overall mission. Everyone lived by it, and no one was allowed to put the mission at risk without paying the price. Coleridge had learned that the hard way, and Lynn Dai Bouchet as well. He hadn't shut her up entirely, but she wasn't asking questions since her name showed up on a list of reported VC sympathizers. As for Nash, he would be easy to handle. It was the look in his eyes when he heard Bouchet may have been involved in Coleridge's murder. Maxon smiled as he thought of his own genius. He had this dumbass right where he wanted him, eating out of his hand while he fed him continuous bits of misinformation.

* * *

The new sniper rifle was spotless, and after running the last patch down the bore, Brady held the barrel up to the bedside lamp. Squinting with one eye, he peered inside. The spiral of lands and grooves gleamed like a mirror under the light. Satisfied, he set the rifle back on the table and flexed his hands outward, cracking his knuckles. The rifle was a fine piece of equipment, and he'd meticulously cleaned every component. He glanced at his watch. Maxon was long overdue.

Impatience was something he could ill afford. It was incredibly quiet in the apartment, and he nearly jumped out of his skin when there finally came two subtle taps at the door. It was about time. Unlocking the door, he turned the knob. The door exploded inward, slamming him backward as Maxon stepped inside and pushed a .45 automatic into his face. Caught flat-footed, Brady felt a surge of cold fear as he held his hands up and backed into the room. Maxon followed, holding the gun against his nose and glaring with a sickening grin. The barrel of the .45 looked like the bore of a cannon. If he so much as flinched, he would die instantly.

Brady's head buzzed as Maxon's grin faded and his finger flexed against the trigger. The trigger snapped. A lump stuck in Brady's throat as an involuntary shudder ran through his body. Maxon stepped back, laughing loudly as he tossed the pistol into Brady's hands. It was a joke, a warped practical joke. Brady started forward, but Maxon quickly drew another pistol from his shoulder holster. He didn't point the gun, but held it menacingly as he gasped with laughter.

"Now don't ruin the fun by doing something stupid," he said, his voice cracking.

Brady stood trembling at the center of the room while Maxon fought to stifle his laughter.

"You should see the look on your face," Maxon said. "Anyway, that forty-five is yours." Even after reigning in his laughter, Maxon maintained a grim smirk on his face. "You can take that as your first lesson in special ops. You're playing in the big leagues now. Don't answer doors without knowing who's on the other side. Keep acting like a dumbass hillbilly, and someone will shove a loaded one of those under your nose someday."

Brady fought to pull himself together. Maxon was testing his nerve. That was the only explanation.

"Take this," Maxon said, tossing a clip of ammo. "Chamber a round, and put it on 'safe.' Keep it with you even when you're sleeping. It might save your life someday."

Maxon pushed his pistol back into the shoulder holster, then slapped his hands together as he turned toward the door.

"OK, whatta ya say, country boy? How about we get an early start? Tonight, I'm going to introduce you to some women who know more tricks than circus dogs." Pausing at the door, Maxon suddenly wheeled about and stared at Brady. "Damn, you look young. You ever had any pussy?"

Brady didn't answer.

"Oh well. You don't have to answer. I don't want to embarrass you. Let's hit a few of the bars before we get some chop-chop. What do you want, steak, shrimp? You name it."

Brady remained standing at the center of the room, still trying to quell his anger. Perhaps the pistol was a setup, the firing pin removed. Maxon was waiting to see if he would use it.

"Oh, come on, country boy, you're not still mad, are you?"

Maxon took a boxer's crouch and hopped toward him, taking a playful swipe at his chin. He missed his face entirely as Brady reflexively cocked his head to one side.

Maxon gave a nervous laugh. "Pretty good reflexes," he said.

Without a word, Brady turned and walked to the kitchenette in the corner of the room. Bending over the sink, he splashed cold water in his face. After several seconds, he took a deep breath. He had to stay cool.

"I reckon I need to put the rifle away before we go."

"Sure nuff, Brady-Bob," Maxon replied, his voice laced with sarcasm.

Brady turned to face him. He had to play his cards carefully, but he wasn't going to be run into the ground. "Are you always such a smart-ass, Mr. Maxon?"

Maxon's face turned crimson. "You just remember one thing, Nash. It's Mr. Maxon here who calls the shots, and if you can't take a little ribbing, you're in the wrong business."

Turning his back on Maxon, Brady took the rifle from the table, placed it in the case along with the bolt and ammunition, and slid it beneath the bed. Maxon grew suddenly calm as he threw his arm across Brady's back. Brady resisted the urge to pull away as cold shivers ran up his spine. This could be the very bastard who had killed Duff. Maxon's arm rested like a cobra across his shoulders.

"You listen to what I'm telling you," Maxon said. "War leaves behind two kinds of people: the smart ones and the dead ones. I like to think I'm one of the smart ones, and I have three rules for this business." He ticked them off on his fingers. "Number one: never underestimate your enemy. Number two: nothing and no one is more important than the endgame. Rule three: there are no rules; you play to win."

Maxon's second and third rules matched his psychotic behavior, and despite himself, Brady couldn't help cutting his eyes at him.

"Don't worry," Maxon said. "You'll understand someday when you step into the nest with them and you're the only round-eyed fucker in the whole 'ville. You won't know if you're going to catch it between the eyes from a VC sniper or in the back from one of your Kit Carsons."

They walked outside into a late afternoon haze, heavy with the stagnant odor of the Mekong. Maxon hailed a cab and said something to the driver that sounded like "Tu Do Street." A few minutes later, when they arrived, he said something else, this time in Vietnamese. He paid the driver and began strutting away down the sidewalk, stepping aside for no one as Brady hurried after him. Brady felt like a pet dog keeping up with his master as he tried to catch up, excusing himself, dodging people, and weaving his way through the crowd.

The stench of the nearby rivers clashed with the aroma of cooking food, along with the odors of perfumed whores and burning incense. A hodgepodge of people flowed around him, all seemingly bent on completing some urgent task, and even as he followed Maxon, Saigon cast its spell on him. Rickshaws, cyclos, and motor scooters wove their way through the mass of humanity. Old and new, Eastern and Western, civilian and military clashed and blended simultaneously in a strange mixture like nothing Brady had ever experienced.

Saigon was a place he hadn't imagined even in his dreams. "Enchanting" didn't seem quite appropriate, but neither did "surreal" because it was all very real, and he was here in the middle of it. Vendors hawked every kind of ware, from fresh flowers to steaming fish heads in rice, and in the back alleys, Wild Turkey bourbon, Pentax cameras, military hardware, and drugs were available for those with the money. The black market was open to all.

Their first stop was at a place called the Papillion, where the warm haze of the drinks quickly took effect. After that, the bars ran together in a collection of disjointed memories. Maxon wore his tiger-striped fatigues like a red badge of courage as he swaggered about and bragged to everyone how he was a jungle fighter. They made their way up Tran Hung Dao Street as the evening sun dropped behind the buildings, and sometime later that night, they ended up at a place called the Baccarat.

"I need to know if you want to join my group or not," Maxon said.

They sat around a table as the women there pretended not to understand, but Brady noticed when one cocked her head slightly and cut her eyes. She understood perfectly, and she'd caught him staring. She walked around to his chair and sat in his lap. Taking her hand, he tried to get her to stand again, but she wrapped her arm around his neck.

"I don't think it's smart talking about this in front of so many people," Brady said.

"Quit trying to be superspy. I know what I'm doing. These people are my friends, and they're just like you and me. They just want to survive the war, so relax and enjoy the party."

Brady pulled the girl's arm from around his neck.

"Let the girl sit in your lap," Maxon said. "She won't bite, unless you want her to."

Brady made another halfhearted attempt to push her away, but the alcohol and the music had his head floating. At Maxon's insistence, the girl remained seated, her buttocks hot and soft against Brady's already aroused body. There was no past here in Vietnam, no home, no future, only the present. The woman again wrapped her arm around his neck, caressing his ear with her tongue. The exotic smell of her perfume filled his head. This was a timeless world where tomorrow might never come.

"Yes or no? Give me your answer," Maxon said.

Brady faced him across the table. It had always been a dange-rous gamble, but it was the reason he'd come here. His fingers tightened around the woman's torso.

"I'm in," he said.

"Good," Maxon said. "I thought a little pussy would bring you to your senses." He killed his glass of scotch.

The girl sitting in his lap whispered into Brady's ear, "You friend of Mr. Max?"

He didn't answer as he eyed Maxon across the table.

She whispered again. "Mr. Max important man. He work for CIA, you know?"

His body went cold. If this woman knew, who else must? He glanced around the room. Grim-faced Vietnamese bounc-ers stood at the door and near the bar. Standing rigid with their arms folded, they seemed to look straight at the table where he sat. God only knew how many of them were VC agents.

"I say something wrong?" the young woman asked.

Brady nearly dumped her on the floor as he stood up and felt for the .45 under his belt.

"Wha's a matter?" Maxon muttered. For the first time that night, he was beginning to look drunk.

"It's late." Brady glanced at his watch. "It's after midnight. We need to go."

Maxon rose to his feet, holding precariously to the edge of the table, as he grinned and cocked his head sideways. "What, you turn into a fucking pumpkin after midnight?" He pointed a crooked finger at Brady. "Qu-Quit being such a go-goddamn dumbass," he stuttered. "Sit back down."

Brady didn't answer as he turned and headed for the exit. He wasn't sure if he was running because everyone knew Maxon was CIA or because of the possibility of having sex with the young woman. He had to get outside for a breath of fresh air. He hurried to the door and stepped outside onto the sidewalk, but something made him freeze in his tracks.

There was no fresh air. The heat and the stale stench of the night air were stifling, but that wasn't what stopped him. It was a sound. From somewhere, not far away, came the distinct rattle of automatic weapons fire, then the echoing explosion of a rocket or mortar round, and people shouting. Maxon stumbled out the door behind him.

"You hear that?" Brady asked.

"Hear what? Maxon said.

There was a lull, but the gunfire broke out again down to the southeast, near the river and over in the Cholon district. Then it came from the other direction, back to the north, toward Tan Son Nhut Airport. Soon the sky was alight with rockets and tracer rounds. They stood watching, and Brady fully expected the light show to end at any moment, but it didn't.

"I thought you said this kind of thing didn't happen here," Brady said.

Maxon seemed unnerved as he gazed skyward. "It doesn't. Let's catch a cab back to the villa."

There was no such luck. Suddenly, no one was stopping.

"We need to get off the main drag," Maxon said.

With rubbery legs, he stumbled, and Brady stopped to help him. Whatever was happening, Maxon was definitely worried because he'd gone from sloppy drunk to fully alert.

A white Renault skidded around the corner from a side street. Maxon pointed to a dark alley, and they sprinted into the shadows as the car squealed to a stop. Two men jumped from the car with AK-47s and opened fire. As bullets ricocheted down the alley around them, Brady and Maxon stumbled over piles of trash in the darkness until they turned into a second alley behind the first row of buildings. Brady stopped and listened while Maxon continued running. From somewhere back up the alley came the clip-clop of sandals. He stepped into a dark alcove and waited as the footsteps grew louder.

Maxon's silhouette was still visible down the alley as the guerrilla approached and rounded the corner. He stopped only a few feet away and threw up his rifle, taking aim at Maxon. With swift and lethal silence, Brady stepped from his hiding place and fired his .45 point-blank into the side of the man's head. Dead before he hit the ground, the man collapsed as his AK-47 clattered to the pavement. Brady grabbed the rifle and hurried to catch up with Maxon.

The closer they got to the Cholon district, the worse it became. Confusion reigned as sporadic gunfire crackled everywhere and buildings exploded into flames. Corpses were scattered along the street, and people darted about in the shadows, no way to know who was friendly and who wasn't. Brady's heart still pounded nearly an hour later as they crept within view of the villa entrance.

"We'll make a dash for the door from here," Maxon said. "When you get inside, grab your gear. We'll go out the back way and try to make it to the embassy."

They broke clear of the alley and sprinted down the sidewalk, and it seemed they were nearly home free when a burst of machine-gun fire splattered across the stucco facade of the building. Shards of concrete stung Brady's face as he emptied the AK-47 in the direction of the gunfire. He stumbled forward, crawled inside the doorway, and looked back at the street.

Maxon continued up the stairway toward his room. "Come on," he shouted. "Don't stay down there. They'll fire an RPG in a minute."

Brady bolted up the steps, barely making it to the second floor before the building shuddered from the impact of a grenade exploding in the downstairs hallway. He made his way down the hallway to his room, where he slammed and bolted the door. From somewhere on the floor below came shouts, screams, and more shooting. The VC were going room to room through the building.

With the AK-47 now empty, Brady hurried to the bed, removed the sniper rifle from its case, and inserted the bolt. From down the hall came the sound of a door smashing, more shouts, more shots, and more screams. He'd lost track of Maxon, but it was too late to go back and search. Next door, he heard shrill shouts, "*Lai day. Lai day.*" Again the voices were punctuated by gunshots. Brady switched off the lights, leaving the room black.

No panic, he thought as he set his .45 on the table and began loading the M40, one, two… "Keep the rhythm," he muttered as he pushed the last shell into the magazine and wound the scope back to 3X. The clip-clop of sandals came from outside the door, and someone shouted something in Vietnamese. He heard a thud as the door splintered and flew open.

The alcove where Brady stood in the kitchenette was to the right of the door, out of the direct line of sight. He froze there, watching the vague outline of a VC soldier pointing a rifle through the doorway. Carefully inching his hand toward the .45 on the table, Brady realized time was running out. The soldier stepped into full view. He snatched the pistol from the table and fired three rapid shots. The impact of the heavy .45 rounds knocked the intruder to the floor, killing him instantly.

Shoving the pistol inside his belt, Brady raised the sniper rifle and pressed his back to the wall. A deafening roar filled the room as the walls shattered from the impact of bullets fired by another Vietcong commando outside in the hallway. Only a few feet to one side, Brady, with his back against the same wall as the door, was out of the line of fire. As the soldier continued firing, he stepped through the doorway, into view. Brady fired a single shot into the man's head. The lifeless body hit the floor with a thud.

There was a sudden silence, but he didn't move as he listened to the sounds outside. Muffled thuds and explosions continued, along with the crackle of small-arms fire, but only a few moans came from inside the building, now filling with smoke. The VC had torched it, and it was only a matter of minutes before the flames would race up the stairway, engulfing everything.

Still, he hesitated as he knelt beside the bodies and peeked around the edge of the doorway. A widening pool of blood soaked the knees of his pants as he searched the darkened hallway. Maxon's voice came from somewhere down the hall.

"Down here, Nash. Get your gear, and let's go."

Maxon held his .45 at the ready while waving the smoke away from his face.

"Where were you?" Brady asked.

"Let me put it this way," Maxon said. "I didn't run in my room and hole up like a rat."

* * *

As the sun rose that morning, Brady and Maxon made their way through the smoky streets of Saigon toward the MACV compound. Smoke and flames billowed from buildings everywhere, and corpses were scattered along the sidewalks and in the streets. Finding security seemed impossible until a military convoy approached from the south. Maxon flagged them to a stop. The vehicles bristled with weapons as the American soldiers inside knelt behind the sideboards. An arm extended from the rear, pulling first Maxon, then Brady into the back of the truck.

"What the hell is going on?" Maxon asked.

"The situation is ugly," an MP explained. "The VC are everywhere. They even breached the walls of the embassy grounds. Our guys have it cordoned, and the 101st Airborne is inside trying to ferret out the gooks."

Brady eyed Maxon. He seemed dazed, but after nearly an hour of stop-and-go travel, the convoy dropped them near MACV headquarters. Officers and aides scrambled frantically about while Maxon grabbed a young PFC by the arm.

"I need to get this man's orders," he shouted.

A captain stopped and glanced back as the PFC wrenched his arm free from Maxon's grasp. It was General Buckingham's aide.

"Sorry, sir, but standing orders right now are for all men to rejoin their units ASAP."

"Look," Maxon said, "his orders are already approved. All I need—"

"The general said if you came back with Nash, I was to tell him to return to his unit. You can resubmit the paperwork as soon as this crisis is over."

"Bull fucking shit, Captain. Where's General Buckingham?"

"Mr. Maxon, the general is not available." He turned to Brady. "We'll get you on a convoy to Tan Son Nhut as soon as we can."

CHAPTER NINE

The Boss of Belle Enterprises

L acey left the restaurant early that afternoon to go to the club and collect her last paycheck. As she pulled into the empty parking lot, a lone beer bottle still stood upright near the center of the lot, and the wind swirled loose papers and chip bags into an eddy near the front of the building. The sun lay bare what the night hid so well, a stark and drab exterior of aging stucco, much like seeing a used car in the light of day after buying it at night under the sparkling lights of a car lot. The sunshine exposed the building's chipped and faded exterior, the trash, and perhaps the false premise upon which she had built her dreams.

The only thing that didn't appear worn and dingy was a gleaming white Cadillac parked near the side door. The sun glinted from its chrome and glass. It was one she'd seen there before.

The car's owner, a woman who looked to be in her forties, was always polite, but Langston had never introduced them, and she spent most of her time in the back office. Lacey assumed she was a business manager or some type of accountant.

After parking her Malibu beside the Cadillac, Lacey found the side door of the building unlocked and pushed it open. The interior was cool and dark, and she began feeling her way through the maze of tables and chairs. Without the music, the bright lights, and the applause, it seemed eerily silent. Shadowy rows of glasses and liquor bottles glinted along a mirrored wall behind the bar, and the red vinyl stools appeared almost black in the darkness. The stale odor of alcohol and tobacco hung in the air, but it was the silence that left her unsettled, as if something was telling her it was all an illusion. She made her way down the hallway to where a light shone from beneath an office door. Taking a deep breath, she tapped lightly with her knuckles.

From inside came a shuffling sound, and after a moment, a woman's voice called out, "Come in."

Lacey opened the door. The woman behind the desk had a worried look on her face, but it quickly turned to a smile as she pulled her hand from the desk drawer and pushed it closed.

"Well, hey, girl," the woman said. "You scared me. I didn't know I had left that outside door unlocked. Come on in. I guess you came by to get your check."

Lacey nodded, and the woman pulled a ledger from the drawer, wrote the check, and handed it across the desk.

Belle Enterprises was the header on all her paychecks, but Hugh Langston had always signed them. This signature, though, read Belle Langston, and it became suddenly apparent who the real brains was behind Belle Enterprises—this woman with the long paste-on eyelashes, piles of bleached blonde hair, and a million-dollar smile.

"So what do you think?" Belle asked.

Lacey looked up at her.

"About what?" she asked.

"The raise!"

Lacey glanced down at the check. "Oh. Oh my…"

The amount was nearly double what it should have been.

"Ain't nothing like a little money to raise your spirits, is it, honey? I told that tightwad Hugh I was going to increase your salary so you might reconsider and think about staying with us. He told me y'all had a pretty ugly falling-out over you wanting to sing for some of the other clubs, even got his old butt whipped by one of the other club owners, but he wouldn't tell me which one. Anyway, I sure wish you'd think about staying with us."

So this was how he'd explained it, another classic Hugh Langston lie. Lacey stared Belle Langston in the eyes, and the truth hung on the tip of her tongue, but telling Belle her husband was a sleazebag would fix nothing. Lacey dropped her head and remained silent.

"Look here, honey, let me tell you something. You've got real talent, and I ain't saying that just to preen your feathers. That so called 'contract' Hugh had you sign, well, I'm tearing it up and tossing it in the trash. If you stay with me, I'll do what I can to get you going in this business. All I ask is that you help us out here at the club when you can and give me a shot as your agent, no contract, just a handshake agreement. What do you say?"

Lacey felt her hatred for Hugh Langston clashing with the sudden euphoria that came with this new opportunity. His wife was obviously more honest and open and certainly not the kind of woman Langston deserved. But more than anything right now, it was a second chance. She needed someone she could trust, someone who might take her through the maze of the music business. She hesitated. Everything she'd worked for hung in the balance.

"If you promise me that you and you alone will handle my business dealings, then I'll work with you. I don't want anyone else at the club to pay me, give me rides, or talk to me on the telephone—nobody. And I don't want to make you mad, but that includes Mr. Hugh."

Belle Langston furrowed her brow. "That man can be a real asshole when he's had a drink or two, and I know he must have been real ugly to you. I'm sorry, honey." She stood and extended her hand across the desk. "You've got my word."

As she shook hands with Belle, Lacey heard footsteps in the hallway. Hugh Langston walked through the office door and froze midstride. His mouth fell open, and his face paled. She turned to face him. His head and jaw were still bruised and swollen, and a line of black stitches crossed his cheek, but Lacey felt no remorse. He deserved every lick she'd given him with the lamp and more. Wide-eyed fear filled his eyes as he stood speechless, staring first at Lacey, then Belle.

Belle stood up, lips set firmly, and pointed wordlessly past him to the door. Langston didn't hesitate. Turning, he walked out, and the sound of his footsteps quickly faded up the hall. When she turned back, Lacey found Belle's eyes still locked on the now-empty doorway, her upper lip still firmly set. After a few moments, she seemed to exhale, and their eyes met.

"You let me know if he so much as looks crossways at you again, honey. I'll whip his fat ass."

It was almost as if Belle saw in her husband's eyes that there was more than either of them was telling her, but she seemed willing to let it go. Lacey took a deep breath, and for the first time since they'd met, she smiled at her newfound mentor. Belle was her kind of woman, but she didn't need her to whip Langston's ass. If he so much as looked at her again, Lacey would need no one's help. Belle would have to stand in line behind her.

"Whatcha thinking about, honey?"

Lacey looked up, and it came to her that she had achieved something through her experiences the last few days. It may not have been wisdom, but it was, at least, a newfound perspective. And it wasn't necessarily a bad one, but a perspective no longer gilded with the innocence of naïveté. Hugh Langston was right about one thing. He had been successful giving her a more sophisticated view of the world. She was no longer the blindly trusting country girl who had come to Nashville.

CHAPTER TEN

The Battle for Hue, 1968

When the MPs had secured the route, Brady rode with another convoy to Tan Son Nhut Airport, but his orders were not to rejoin his old ranger unit with the 173rd. Buckingham's aide had returned with orders that said he was to report to the 101st Airborne up near Hue. Will and the other rangers were probably already there with the new unit, and given the reports of heavy enemy attacks in I Corps, they were no doubt in an ugly fight.

Maxon accompanied him that morning as they boarded a C-130 to Da Nang, but he stood by late that afternoon, watching as Brady loaded his gear onto a chopper bound for Hue. The last forty-eight hours had been a nightmare. Much of Saigon had been overrun by the enemy, and he was nearly killed in the room at the villa, but the worst of it was dealing with Maxon. The jerk seemed to have accepted his alibi for wanting to join special ops, but he still acted like a paranoid schizophrenic. If there was a bright side to going into a city occupied by the NVA, it was that Maxon was staying behind in Da Nang.

"Here," Maxon said as Brady boarded the chopper, "take this with you."

He handed him the new M40 sniper rifle.

"Just don't forget where you got it."

Brady took the rifle, but wondered why Maxon would give it to him when he might not return.

"What's the matter? You don't want it?"

"No, I do, but..."

Maxon gave him his usual griffin-like grin. "Don't worry. You'll earn it before we're done."

For once, Brady was inclined to agree. "I'll bring it back."

Maxon winked at him. "I know."

"Strap in," the door gunner shouted. "We're outta here."

Maxon ran clear of the main rotor, and the chopper lifted off and swung northward. Brady knew he was heading into an ugly fight, yet his blood pressure began dropping for the first time in days. It was only minutes before the chopper began climbing over the mountains to the north, and when it cleared the clouds in the Hai Van Pass, the door gunner pointed out the huge plume of gray smoke on the horizon, coming from the ruins of Hue. They skirted Phu Bai, then began their descent toward Hue under a gray and rainy sky.

"Better grab hold of your nuts," the door gunner shouted. "We've taken fire every time in."

Buckingham's aide had told Brady that his new unit was a recon platoon with the 101st. They were in a blocking position southwest of Hue, where the enemy still held tenaciously to positions in the center and northeastern parts of the city. The marines were slugging it out toe-to-toe with them in ugly street fighting. Word was the streets and buildings were filled with enemy snipers, leaving some of the marine units pinned down and taking heavy casualties.

The chopper came in low and fast as it approached an LZ west of the city, near the Perfume River. Green tracers crisscrossed the sky around them, and the pilot flared, dropping rapidly into a soggy field beside a road clogged with trucks and soldiers. After jumping from the skids, Brady shouted at the men pulling the supplies from the helicopter, asking them for directions to his new battalion.

"Over that way," an officer shouted. "The CP is about four hundred meters down that levee."

It was getting late when he finally spotted a familiar figure sitting against the muddy wheel of a deuce and a half. It was Will.

"Hey, Willie boy!"

Will seemed startled as he opened his eyes and looked up. His face quickly broke into a broad grin.

"Well, if it ain't the Lone Ranger. They told me you were on the way, so I decided to wait on you." He stood and wrapped his arm around Brady's neck.

"So what's the story, Tonto?" Brady asked, slapping his back.

Will shook his head. "It's ugly, man, I mean really bad. You won't believe what's happening inside the city. They've carried so many dead marines out of there, they ran out of body bags. No shit. And there's still several marine and ARVN units pinned down, waiting for reinforcements. They're just trying to hold on until more line companies can move up into the city. The higher-ups have ordered our recon snipers up to help out, but I asked if I could wait on you."

Brady laughed. "What, you think I'm Superman?"

Will frowned. "Look, man, if I had to go in there with only one person, I wanted it to be you, so I asked."

"Thanks." Brady wanted to say more, but words no longer meant much.

"So what's that fancy rig on your shoulder?" Will asked, pointing to the M40.

Brady pulled the rifle from his shoulder and handed it to Will. "Check it out," he said. "It's a Remington 700, .308 with a bull barrel and a three-by-twelve Redfield."

Will sighted through the scope as he talked. "So what about the deal in Saigon? Was it what you thought?"

"Yeah, but I'll tell you about it later. I've got to report in. Where's the battalion CP?"

* * *

As dusk closed in, an ARVN scout joined them, and they received their orders. Their objective was an old house near an industrial area. The house was a marine command post. After cros-sing the river in a small boat, Brady and Will followed the ARVN scout, working their way into the heart of the city where the figh-ting was heaviest. A hellish pall of smoke glowed orange against the night sky, and the air hung heavy with the stench of decaying bodies. Gunfire and artillery explosions crackled and thudded intermittently. Every wall that still stood was pockmarked with bullet holes, and most of the homes were reduced to smoking piles of rubble. Nothing remained unscathed.

Somewhere nearby, glass shattered, and the scout froze. A stark silhouette in the drifting smoke and haze, he stood motion-less as he tried to determine the source. The scout wasn't young, but neither was he old, and war was his forte. Brady sensed it. He'd probably fought since he was old enough to carry a weapon, except now, his accoutrements were Americanized, a shiny black M16, a boonie hat, and ripstop jungle fatigues. The scout turned his head as slowly as the hands on a clock until he faced Brady and Will. Nothing was said as they remained motionless, nerves hum-ming, senses raw and alert.

After a few minutes, there was only the continued rumble of artillery and the crackle of small-arms fire in other parts of the city. The smoke and fog still drifted among the men as they be-gan moving again, slowly and deliberately, toward their objective. Two hours later, after they had crossed so many streets and check-points that Brady was certain he would never find his way back, the scout signaled for them to stop. He pointed to a small stucco building surrounded by the remains of several artillery-blasted palm trees. It was the only building that remained standing on the street up ahead. The dark forms of two sentries lay huddled behind piles of rubble near the doorway.

Brady motioned for Will and the scout to remain behind as he crawled up the street. After drawing as close as he dared, he called out to the sentries and got their signal to come ahead. The scout and Will quickly followed.

"Where's your CO?" Brady whispered.

"Ain't no officers left," the soldier said. "The gunny's in charge. Besides, ain't much more than a platoon of us left out of the whole damned company."

"Where's the gunny?" Brady asked.

The marine motioned with his thumb over his shoulder. "He's inside."

The gunnery sergeant, lean and hollow eyed, sat on the floor just inside the door. He wasted no time as he awakened another marine sleeping in the corner.

"Hang your poncho over the door so we can look at the map."

Spreading a dirty map on the floor, he waited until the poncho was in place before switching on a dim flashlight.

"OK, this is where we are," he said, pointing to a spot on the map. "We tried to advance up through this area yesterday and got cut to pieces. I've still got two squads pinned down out there. I want you boys to make your way up here to this old factory building. It's the highest structure in the area—maybe three or four stories, I don't really know, but you'll have a commanding view of no-man's-land from there. We've mortared the hell out of it, so I don't expect the enemy is still using it, but be careful.

My men have taken heavy casualties, and they've been out there since yesterday morning. Artillery hasn't done much good, and we can't get another company up here until tomorrow evening at best.

"Your scout here knows this area, and he's going to take you into no-man's-land. Once you secure your position on the roof of the building, you should be OK. Try to spot those goddamned snipers and the machine-gun positions and take them out. Just make damned sure you know who you're shooting at. We don't want any of our own people hurt. You got it?"

"No sweat, Sarge," Brady answered.

The gunny's eyes narrowed as he looked Brady up and down in the dim light. "Semper fi, Marines," he said.

He looked at them expectantly as if they might say something else. Brady obliged him as he coughed and cleared his throat. "Sorry, sarge, but we're not marines."

The gunny turned his flashlight into Brady's face. "Well, shit. I figured as much. What are you guys, army?"

"Yeah. We're from the 101st Airborne. Can you get that light out of my eyes?"

Turning the light aside, he eyed Brady, then Will. "I've got enough problems without you guys going out there and getting pinned down or killed. Are you sure you're up to this?"

Brady stood and slapped the dust from his fatigues. "We can handle it. Besides, you don't have a choice. Your men need our help."

The sergeant continued eyeing Brady. "If you're with the 101st, how come you're wearing a 173rd patch?"

"Just transferred in," Brady said.

"Shit," the sergeant said. He shook his head as if disgusted. "How long have you been in-country?"

"Sarge, have you ever heard of Brady Nash?" Will asked.

"Can't say as I have."

"Well, I'm sure some of your men have. Ask them about him. He's only one of the best snipers in the country."

Brady slapped Will on the back. "OK, Willie, that's enough bullshit. Let's get started."

"There's no bullshit to it," Will said.

The old gunnery sergeant's face glowed yellow in the pale light of the flashlight as he studied Brady's face. "You're that sniper from down at Dak To, aren't you?"

Brady nodded. "Just keep your artillery and mortars off of us, and we'll take out those snipers and machine guns. Deal?"

"Deal," the gunnery sergeant said. He extinguished his light and removed the poncho from the door.

* * *

Brady watched as the ARVN scout slowly signaled for him to move ahead. It had been nearly three hours since they departed the marine CP, but they had advanced only a few hundred meters through the rubble of the streets. First, a firefight broke out, red and green tracers snapping all around, only to be followed in minutes by an artillery barrage that pounded the rubble into even smaller pieces. Everything was working against them reaching their objective. Footsteps, voices, and breaking glass echoed from every direction in the spooky veil of smoky darkness.

Up ahead, the factory building loomed black against the orange night sky. They had to reach it before daylight, but giving in to impatience was a fool's game. Brady followed the ARVN scout step-by-step, knowing all the while a single mistake could be their last. The clouds overhead began turning gray with the first hint of dawn as they reached the factory. Crouching at the base of the outer wall, the three men gazed through a huge shell hole into the blackness of the interior. An imposing brick-and-concrete structure, it towered several stories above them.

"OK," Brady said, "I'll take the lead from here. Let's stay at least ten feet apart."

They eased through the opening. Dank and musty inside, the old building didn't offer a hint of light. Brady felt his way along an interior wall. Slowly making his way in the pitch-black darkness, he used his hands and toes as his eyes. After a hundred feet or so, a slight draft crossed his cheek. He sensed he'd reached a large open area. By now, they were somewhere deep within the building. The skittering of rats echoed in the ghostly silence, but he could see nothing, only an opaque wall of impenetrable darkness.

"This isn't working," he whispered to Will. "Get your rifle ready. I'm turning my light on."

The light instantly brought a surge of adrenaline as Brady stood ready with his weapon raised. After a few seconds, a sense of relief washed over him. They were alone—for now. He scanned about with the flashlight as he oriented himself. The yellow beam threw spooky shadows across a huge room, obviously some type of production area littered with a jumble of broken machines, piles of debris, and fallen beams. The ceiling, several stories above them, was obscured by a tangle of wires and hanging girders.

Climbing through some of the fallen girders, Brady moved carefully ahead, searching for a way to reach the roof. After moving only a few feet, he spotted a steel ladder attached to a column near the center of the room. Following it upward with the beam of the flashlight, he found an open hatch. At least forty feet above the floor, it was open to the sky and showing the first dim gray light of dawn.

He turned to the others, putting a finger across his lips. "Not a sound," he whispered.

Quickly but quietly, they made their way to the base of the ladder and began climbing. First, Brady, then Will, followed by the RVN scout, they climbed toward the roof. High above the concrete floor, the three men were strung out on the ladder when a sudden burst of gunfire erupted somewhere outside the building. Brady extinguished the flashlight. He waited and listened. Again the gunfire erupted, but this time, there was another sound. It was barely noticeable, but following each burst of gunfire came the faint tinkle of spent brass hitting the ground—or was it the roof? The shooter was close.

Will hung just below him on the ladder, but Brady didn't risk making a sound. Will and the ARVN scout both carried M16s, and Brady had the M40 sniper rifle slung over his shoulder as well as the .45 Maxon had given him. He had to make a quick decision: move up or down.

There was no sense in retreating now. He continued climbing until he was just below the open hatch. Despite the cold morning air, sweat dripped in his eyes as he pulled the .45 from his shoulder holster, freed the safety, and cocked the hammer. Taking a deep breath, he reached for the top rung, but the gunfire erupted again. He cringed. This time, it was much louder, and the tinkling of the spent brass was plain as it hit the concrete roof above.

With .45 in hand, Brady slowly raised his head though the hatch. If he were spotted, it would be over in an instant. They'd come shoot them off the ladder like treed coons. He peeked over the top. A couple of hundred feet away, two NVA soldiers sat with their backs to him, manning a machine gun, and looking out over the city.

He turned to check the rest of the rooftop. As he did, his heart crawled up into his throat. Two more soldiers were on the other side. They, too, faced away from him, but he couldn't risk climbing out of the hatch with enemy soldiers on both sides. Ducking inside, he holstered the pistol and pulled the M40 from his shoulder.

He signaled to Will that there were a total of four NVA soldiers on the roof, two on one side and two on the other. After bracing himself on the top rung of the ladder, Brady took a deep breath. Popping up, he fired, bolted another round, and fired again, killing the first two soldiers, but as he spun toward the others, they opened fire. Shards of flying concrete cut his face and stung his eyes. Half blinded, he fired, and another soldier fell, but the last one darted for cover, firing his AK-47 as he sprinted across the rooftop toward a smokestack.

Lunging out onto the roof, Brady rolled onto his belly and fired blindly at the running soldier. He missed, but there came the rapid cracking of an M16 from behind him, and the NVA soldier's arms began windmilling as his dead body crashed into the smokestack. Blurry eyed, Brady turned to see Will at the top of the ladder with his M16. He exhaled and rolled onto his back. Will and the ARVN scout climbed through the hatch, onto the roof.

"You all right?" Will asked.

"Yeah. Just got some shit in my eyes."

Will poured water from his canteen into Brady's eyes, clearing away bits of blood and sand until, after a few moments, Brady waved him off.

"You good to go?" Will asked.

Brady blinked several times. "Yeah, let's have a look at what's going on."

They crawled to the edge of the roof and began surveying the destruction of the city. Spread before them as far as they could see were piles of embers glowing in the dim morning light, and the sole remains of homes that had lined a street for nearly a half mile. In one area, some buildings still stood, but the tiled roofs were shattered with gaping holes. To the north were the smoldering skeletons of larger buildings standing like huge wounded animals, stark against the skyline. Orange flames reflected with an eerie glow against the low gray clouds while plumes of smoke rose from the rubble. The devastation seemed total.

"You gonna be able to see?" Will asked.

"Yeah," Brady responded, "as soon as I get the rest of this grit out of my eyes."

Brady rested while Will searched the early morning shadows with his binoculars. Several minutes passed.

"You see anything yet?" Brady asked.

"Yeah," Will answered, "I caught some movement near a court-yard wall over there, about two hundred fifty meters away. It's one of the marine squads. They're where the gunny said they'd be."

Brady peeked over the wall and peered through his riflescope. Most of the marines were huddled together, mostly hidden against the concrete wall, but several were lying in the open, covered with ponchos. Only their boots protruded. He continued searching for enemy snipers.

A solitary rifle shot cracked through the air, and a plume of dust leapt from the top of the wall above the marines.

"Where did it come from?" Brady asked.

Will scanned the windows and rooftops of the nearby buildings with his binoculars. "I don't know," he murmured quietly. "Too damned much echoing."

They waited and watched for several more minutes until another shot reverberated through the buildings, but this time Brady thought he saw something. A building, smaller than the factory and five or six blocks away, had several rows of windows, most of which were broken.

"You see that building out there with all the windows?" he whispered to Will.

"Yeah."

"Well, count from the left on the second floor. It's the eighth one, the one that's not broken. See it?"

"Yeah."

"Watch it," Brady said.

The ARVN scout also watched with curiosity as another shot rang out. The gray light reflecting from the windowpane rippled slightly as it vibrated.

"Yeah, I see him," Will whispered. "He's behind that window, shooting through the broken one next to it."

Brady rolled his poncho and laid it atop the wall. As he steadied the M40, he counted imaginary football fields to his target.

"What do you think, Will, seven hundred fifty meters, maybe?"

"I'd say closer to eight hundred," Will replied.

Brady pressed his cheek against the stock and peered through the scope. The shadow of a silhouette was barely visible behind the solitary windowpane. Will watched through his ten-by-fifty binoculars. A second passed, then two, and three. After nearly a minute, there was another shadow of movement behind the window. Brady's shot echoed among the buildings as the distant windowpane shattered.

"I think you got him," Will whispered.

The ARVN scout stared wide-eyed. "You damn good shot. You damn best shot I ever see."

After several hours and at least seven kills, they succeeded in lifting the crossfire that had pinned down the marine squads. Taking his turn, Brady maintained surveillance while Will and the scout slept. He couldn't get Maxon off his mind as he realized his was a no-win situation. Rubbing his half-smoked cigarette out against the concrete wall, he picked up the binoculars. Will cracked open one eye.

"Hey, man," he muttered, "don't waste my cigarettes."

"Sorry, Willie," Brady replied.

Will closed his eyes. "So what happened in Saigon?"

Brady scanned the horizon with the binoculars. "I think I'm getting damned close. Actually, this guy Maxon recruited me to join special ops."

"Sounds like you got what you wanted. You gonna do it?"

"I've got to. Maxon says he knew of Duff. Only problem is, he says Duff was killed by an enemy double agent. He said it was probably Duff's girlfriend, Lynn Dai Bouchet."

Will sat up and opened his eyes. "No shit?"

Brady looked back at him. "No shit, and that leaves me trying to figure what's true and what's not. Maybe Duff was wrong. Maybe he just messed up and got himself killed."

Will shook his head. "You know, that just doesn't make sense. The woman is half French, right?"

"Yeah, I know. The Vietminh and the French were mortal enemies. It doesn't make sense that she would be working for the Vietcong. You know?"

"I agree," Will said.

"Right now, I just can't figure out who's telling the truth. My gut tells me Maxon is lying, but everything he says makes perfect sense."

"Trust your instincts," Will said.

"I need more than instinct."

"You still have to trust your instincts. Right now, you're too caught up in all of it. If Maxon is blowing smoke up your ass, he'll show his hand sooner or later. Just listen to the things he says. My granddaddy was a judge in Georgia, and he had this saying: 'Truth has a resonance to it that fills the cracks where falsehoods hide.' If Maxon is feeding you a line of shit, his story just won't ring true."

Will closed his eyes and dozed off as Brady lit another cigarette. Could he trust his instincts? If instincts were all it took, he'd kill Maxon with a clear conscience the next time he saw him. He needed proof. If Maxon was involved in Duff's murder, he wanted evidence that no one could deny. The woman, Lynn Dai Bouchet, was the key. He had to find her.

Duff was too smart to have been fooled by a woman who wasn't being genuine. He saw things Brady had often missed, and he was the one who always handled matters so well, like the night they got jumped by the Tull brothers in Bradley County. It was another one of their secretive trips to play music at a roadhouse and make some spending money. Lacey had just finished singing when a beer bottle sailed out of the crowd, barely missing her and glancing off Brady's head. As Brady carefully set aside his guitar, Duff saw what was coming and stepped in front of him.

"Let me handle it," Duff said.

As he turned back to face the crowd, two men the size of dump trucks swaggered up to the foot of the bandstand. Wearing dirty bib overalls with armpit-stained T-shirts, the two looked like twins. The bar owner rushed up as Duff stepped off the bandstand.

"You Tull brothers ain't startin' no shit in my place tonight," the man said.

One of the Tulls pushed the old man away.

"It's all right," Duff said to him.

Brady had walked to the edge of the bandstand to shield Lacey as he stared at the Tulls, but he noticed Duff was smiling.

"What are you grinning about?" one of the brothers asked.

"Just trying to bring a little calm to the situation," Duff said.

"Well, maybe we don't want no *calm*."

"Maybe not," Duff said, "but I'm just trying to help you boys out."

"We don't need your help. Besides, it looks like your friend up there ain't as happy as you."

"That's what I need to talk to you about," Duff said.

He stepped closer to the Tulls, appearing almost dwarfed by the two brothers, who stood red-faced with fists balled. Duff began talking in almost a whisper, throwing his thumb over his shoulder, then twirling his finger next to his ear. The Tulls' eyes rose as they looked past him at Brady. After a few more moments of Duff's whispering, their eyes grew a little wider and more inquisitive. Duff cocked his head to one side and began slowly shaking it side to side.

"Tell you boys what," Duff said, "why don't you let me get him out of here, and we'll call it a night, OK?"

One of the brothers gave a slight nod.

"Yeah, reckon so."

Duff stepped back and turned toward Brady and Lacey. "Lacey you get the amp, mic, and one speaker. Brady, you carry the instruments and the other speaker."

It was obvious Duff intended to keep his hands free as they made their way to the pickup. After placing the equipment under the tarp in back, the three of them got into the truck, and Duff started the engine.

"What did you say to those guys?" Brady asked.

Duff put the truck in gear and pulled from the parking lot. "I explained to them how you had just got out of prison over at Brushy Mountain on an insanity plea for killing two guys."

Lacey let out a whoop.

"You what?" Brady said.

"Yeah, I told them you killed two fellows with your bare hands and how you had inhuman strength and all."

"We could've taken them," Brady said.

"Maybe," Duff answered.

"If they'd laid a hand on Lacey, I'd have killed them both myself."

"I know," Duff said, "and that is exactly what I was afraid of. Then we might really have ended up in Brushy Mountain."

It was vintage Duff. He saw things more clearly and later admitted how he knew Brady and Lacey had become romantically involved. Even in the heat of the moment, Duff recognized and reacted to things that completely went past Brady. Duff wasn't naive back then, and he hadn't been that way in Vietnam either. There was no proof, but Brady's faith in his stepbrother's judgment left him with no doubt. Lynn Dai Bouchet was the key to finding the killers, but she wasn't the one who killed him.

* * *

For the next month, Brady and Will worked with the marines and the 101st around the city of Hue, rooting out the NVA. The fighting was almost continuous, until one day, the enemy simply disappeared. The ones who hadn't been captured or buried in mass graves simply faded into the countryside. By March, their new recon unit was ordered to pull back, putting Brady and Will on stand-down for a few days. Exhausted, they were sitting under a poncho, looking out at another dripping afternoon rain, when a lieutenant walked up the muddy road from the battalion CP.

"Pack your gear, Nash," the young officer said. "Report to the colonel at battalion. You've got orders to report to an Intelligence and Operations Coordination Center near Da Nang."

"Well, I guess this is it," Will said.

"Wish me luck," Brady said. After gathering his gear, he and Will stood together in the rain.

"Good luck," Will said.

Brady forced a smile. "Yeah, thanks."

"Try to stay in touch."

"Sure," Brady said. "If we survive this mess, I might show up at your door in Georgia someday."

Brady extended his hand. Will grasped it but pulled him close, wrapping his arm across his shoulders.

"Watch your step, little brother. I'll have a six-pack in the fridge when you show up."

CHAPTER ELEVEN

Special Ops Initiation

When she got home from work that afternoon, Lacey retrieved the mail from the box outside her door and tossed it on the table. She had given up hope of getting a letter from Brady. It had been weeks since she'd written to him, and every day, she searched through the bills and magazines, until finally accepting he wasn't going to respond. She kicked off her shoes and sat on the couch, then propped her feet on the coffee table as she thumbed through a magazine. It was one of those rare nights when she was off work and could catch up on her sleep, but first, she made up her mind to write him again.

Tossing the magazine aside, she closed her eyes and rested her head against the back of the couch. Despite the shambles she'd made of her personal life, her music career was showing signs of life. She was doing more shows during the week and had little free time, but it was better to stay busy. Without Brady, her music was all she had for now.

Belle Langston had proven to be everything Hugh wasn't, sensitive and caring, but more than anything, she was honest. Belle treated her almost as a daughter, guiding her toward the fulfillment of her dream. That day when Hugh Langston had walked into the office, Belle quickly dismissed him, no questions asked. For Lacey, that was good enough. She had Hugh where she wan-ted him, and there was nothing to gain by hurting Belle with the truth about her husband.

Opening her eyes, Lacey began shuffling through the rest of the mail as she thought about her new mentor, Billy Wyatt. Billy was a lot like Brady, except he was also a songwriter, a bartender, a carpenter, and a sometime singer/guitar player, but most importantly, he was willing to work with her to get his songs recorded. Billy became the supporter she needed, working with her hours at a time, picking out tunes and reworking lyrics. And as her confidence grew, her performances improved, and she began receiving more recognition around Nashville.

Lacey suddenly found herself staring at one of the envelopes in her lap, one with a military APO address. Dropping her feet to the floor, she ripped almost frantically at the envelope, tore it open, and unfolded the letter.

March 1968

Dear Lacey,

I got your letter a while back, and I've wanted to write, but things have been crazy over here. Just the same, getting your letter has left me feeling better than I have in a long time. I'm sorry it took me so long to write back, but I've been moving constantly, and I really didn't know what to tell you about all the bad things that have happened. I suppose, more than anything, I just want to say that if I get through this mess alive, I want to come home to you. I hope you will forgive me, and maybe someday, I can explain all this. Don't worry about the phone calls from Mr. Brister. I talked with him about what happened and why I came over here, and he's just worried. I hope you and Mama Emma are doing well, and I promise I will write sooner next time.

Love always,
Brady

The letter was frustratingly short, and its cryptic message caused her brief euphoria to give way to anxiety. What was it that Brady had told Hubert Brister? Why hadn't he shared it with her? She'd always assumed he'd gone to Vietnam for the usual macho reasons men go to war. Never before had she thought there might be something more, but there was, and Hubert Brister knew what it was.

She had to find out. Picking up the phone, she clutched the letter in one hand as she dialed home.

* * *

Maxon tried to focus on the post-op report he was typing, but he was distracted. The paddle fan above his head did little more than stir the dank air in his office, a windowless corner in the sandbagged Intelligence Operations and Coordination Center. The IOCC was a large cinder block building with various other out buildings on the outskirts of Da Nang, surrounded by a concrete wall, piles of sandbags, barbed wire, and a contingent of ARVN soldiers. He stared at the wall map of Vietnam and found himself thinking about Nash. The kid didn't seem bright enough to be a real threat, but it paid to be cautious in this business.

His eyes drifted to the black-and-white photo hanging in a frame beside the map. It was autographed by LBJ, and there he was, Jack Maxon, standing beside the president of the United States at the White House. It was taken when he went home to recover from his war wound, a nasty knife slash on the side of his face, courtesy of a VC prostitute. At least, she became VC after the incident, a dead VC. The bitch couldn't take a little rough sex, and slashing him with his own knife was a mistake.

She didn't seem to understand that special operations people were not to be trifled with, and no one, Vietnamese or American, fucked with Jack Maxon. She had learned the hard way that he owned this little piece of the Nam, and no one crossed him here, not even his own men.

He began typing again, but paused. If Nash was telling the truth, Coleridge had somehow gotten a letter past him.

"I personally censored every letter Coleridge wrote," he mumbled.

Realizing he was talking to himself, Maxon slapped the carriage return on the typewriter. Had Coleridge told Nash about the arms deal or the high-level snatch and snuffs? Killing gooks had always been a big hang-up for Coleridge. The idiot actually thought there were good gooks and bad gooks. Now Nash was here, and for what? What did he really know?

When his men first told him about the young army ranger asking questions about Lynn Dai Bouchet, he worried that he was being investigated by Army CID, but that didn't make sense. CID couldn't fuck with the company. It would be a breach of protocol, and they certainly wouldn't send someone so closely connected to Coleridge to do an investigation. Besides, Bouchet, not knowing anything for sure, had only stirred up a lot of shit. Nash had given a pretty good explanation, but there was still no sense taking chances. He would simply isolate him for a while by putting him out in the boonies.

There came a knock at the door.

"It's open," he shouted.

The door opened, and Nash was standing there as if he'd somehow been conjured by mere thought. Maxon feigned nonchalance, focusing on the typewriter.

"Come on in, Nash. Get yourself a beer from the refrigerator and pull up a chair. Get me one too."

He watched the young paratrooper from the corner of his eye as he opened a can of 33. It was time to try again, to try to catch him flat-footed. His plans had gone awry in Saigon. After he had rattled him with the .45 in the room that afternoon, then gotten him drunk, he planned to spring more questions on him, catch him off-balance. But a little thing called Tet had gotten in the way. Now he was starting over.

For the first twenty minutes, they talked casually while drinking several beers. Maxon finished typing his report while lulling Nash into complacency with casual conversation.

"You've made a hell of a reputation for yourself, Nash."

"Just doing my job."

Maxon looked up from the typewriter. "'Just doing my job,' that's cute. According to everything I've heard, you're one hell of a sniper."

Nash shrugged, and Maxon gazed at him for several seconds. Nash was either simpleminded or coolheaded, but which?

"There's been so much new intelligence received since Tet. We don't have time to follow up on all of it. We've got high-level VC fingered all over the country, and after the shit they just pulled, we're not wasting time asking them to *chieu hoi*. Are you ready?"

"I don't have much choice, do I?"

Nash was hard to figure. He seemed dumb as brick, but then he said things that made sense. He was right. He didn't have a choice. He was committed, and he either did as he was told or else. By the time Nash finished his third beer, he seemed totally relaxed as his eyes wandered around the office. Maxon noticed he was studying the photo of him with the president. He was primed.

Maxon pulled the report from the typewriter, set it aside, and casually picked up one of the empty beer cans. He glanced matter-of-factly at it, then at Nash. Without warning, he smashed the can down on the desk, crushing it. Scowling, he stared across at Nash, but the young paratrooper barely blinked as he sipped his beer.

"Upset about something?" Nash said.

Maxon studied him.

"We need to get a clear understanding of why you're here."

Nash said nothing.

"Well?"

"I'm not sure what you mean."

Maxon motioned toward the photo of LBJ. "You see that man there?"

Nash nodded.

"Well, he's my boss, the president of the United States. I just want to make it real clear to you who you're fucking with."

"I'm not sure what you mean when you say I'm 'fucking with' someone."

"Look, Nash, why don't we just get all our cards out on the table? OK, you said you were friends with Duff Coleridge. You know about Lynn Bouchet. You came all the way over here looking to work for my group. How did you get your information?"

"I thought we already went over this."

"Humor me. Tell me again."

"It's like I said the first time. Duff sent me a letter. Why are you so paranoid?"

"Because it's my business to be. Coleridge couldn't have sent you a letter. All his mail was censored."

"Well, I got one, and he seemed damned proud to be working for you."

"Do you still have the letter?"

"No. I mean, if I do, it's probably back home somewhere."

"What did you want with Lynn Bouchet?"

"Duff said she was his girlfriend, and I wanted to look her up when I got over here, but if she's a double agent like you said, I'd like to find her for other reasons."

"Better watch yourself, no freelancing. Besides, you can't be too careful around these Vietnamese whores."

Maxon sat up, suddenly realizing he was subconsciously running the tip of his finger along the scar on his jaw. It was always sensitive, and the razor nicked it damned near every time he shaved.

"Did Coleridge tell you what we do in our group?"

"He just said it was special operations, and that I would probably like it. Look, you say you want me, but you've been treating me like crap since we met. Do you want me or not?"

Maxon fixed him with a cold stare. Nash was a cocky bastard, bold and stupid, just like Coleridge.

"First let me say this: We don't run a 'special operations group.' It's called a studies and observation group. Most of what we do is reconnaissance for the Vietnamese special police, but you may be required to pull the trigger from time to time, and you can't balk. Someone's life may depend on it. This is dangerous work. We hunt down known NLF cadre members, and most of them already know who we are. That makes them extra dangerous. So don't expect to be coddled by anyone. We trust no one, not even one another.

"You'll be sworn to secrecy and receive a top secret security clearance, which means you keep your mouth shut. Had your buddy Coleridge lived, he'd be in deep shit right now for running his. So are you still up for it?"

Nash nodded as Maxon studied his face, nothing there but a blank stare.

"Good. I've already run your security clearance. We'll sign some paperwork and get you squared away. Then I'll take you across the compound to an air-conditioned Quonset hut where you'll be billeted with some of the special police. Any questions?"

"I thought you said most of your men stayed near the Embassy House in Da Nang."

Maxon looked across the desk at him. He was keeping Nash under his thumb.

"They do, but you'll be working closely with the special police," he said. "And this is where they're billeted. Don't worry. I'm pairing you with one of my best men for a while to observe some villages out in the district. We'll see how you do with that assignment before you're turned loose with the gooks. Someone will come by and pick you up later."

Maxon couldn't help himself as he grinned. Nash could chase bugbears around the more secure villages, while one of his men kept him under constant surveillance for a month or two.

"And one last thing, stay the hell away from the embassy house in Da Nang, and stay away from Lynn Dai Bouchet. Like I said, no freelancing. I don't need you getting killed like Coleridge. Understand?"

Nash nodded.

"And if anyone, including any of the special police, begins asking questions, I want to know immediately. You don't answer to anyone but me. Is that understood?"

"Yes, sir," Nash said.

* * *

Brady felt it almost immediately, but it wasn't something overt. It wasn't one person or a single circumstance or action, but an accumulation of nuance that left him certain that Maxon had warned his men that he was not to be trusted. They held him at arm's length with an invisible but ever-present barrier of aloofness. The Vietnamese special police officers were equally as detached, acknowledging him with little more than occasional nods.

The weeks turned into a month as Brady realized he was getting nowhere. Maxon had him pulling recon missions day after day. Every mission, he was paired with the same man, John "Dibbs" Dibrell, a trash-talking Navy SEAL with a skull-and-dagger tattoo on his right forearm. Dibbs, who was fighting an occasional relapse of malaria, liked to brag about the gooks he'd greased and the missions he'd pulled, but he seemed to have forgotten everything he'd learned about reconnaissance tactics. Sloppy and careless, he smoked constantly and seldom sat still, and when he had to urinate, he stood up and walked about like he was in a park.

While lying in mosquito-ridden hides, they watched people come and go from houses and villages or along certain roads and trails. Oftentimes, Dibbs would hang back and send Brady slipping within yards of suspects' homes, where in spite of ants, snakes, and on one occasion, a herd of foraging pigs, he would lie unmoving for hours. They moved at night and laid up in the day as they circled villages, watching for suspicious activity. With it raining almost every day, the two men fought jungle rot and ate cold C rations chased with iodine-flavored water.

At first, Dibbs's scrutiny had been relentless as he questioned Brady, often asking the same questions repeatedly, but after a week or so, he became totally relaxed. Fighting a slight fever, Dibbs lay on his poncho beside Brady, who was searching a valley hamlet with his binoculars. The thatched roofs of the huts below glowed in the afternoon sunlight. There had been little activity, and after several hours, Brady set the binoculars aside.

"You know, we've been doing this for over a month, and we haven't seen a damned thing."

Dibbs, who was still lying on the poncho, cracked open one eye, grunted, and laughed.

"Boy, Max is right about you. You are one dumb son of a bitch. Why do you think I've been acting like we're on a fucking picnic? You haven't seen anything because these are considered secure areas. There hasn't been any enemy activity around these villages in months, maybe years."

"Then why are we doing this?"

Dibbs propped himself up on his elbow and glared at Brady. "Why don't you tell me?"

"What do you mean?" Brady asked.

"Why don't you tell me why Maxon has me babysitting you? I'm getting tired of this shit myself. Why doesn't he trust you?"

Dibbs's face was sallow and sweaty, and he mopped it with the tail of his shirt.

"You OK?" Brady said.

"Just a touch of fever," Dibbs said. "Answer my question."

"I'm not exactly sure," Brady said. "I had a friend who worked for him, and that's how I found out about you guys. Ever since I came around asking about joining, he's been acting paranoid."

"Who did you know?"

"His name was Duff Coleridge."

Dibbs sat upright and lit a cigarette as he stared out over the village in the narrow valley below.

"You knew Coleridge, how?"

"We're from the same hometown."

"Well, that explains some things."

"Like what?"

"For starters, Max didn't like Coleridge. I don't really know why, personality conflict, I suppose, but that's probably why he doesn't like you. Coleridge was going to quit the group, but he got shot on his last mission. It was all pretty weird. Max thinks he could have been killed by a VC double agent, one of the gooks in our own operations group."

"You mean one of the special branch police?"

"Yeah, I suppose if Max ever loosens up, you'll meet some of them. We pull missions with them all the time, kind of like advisors, you know?"

"What kind of missions?"

"You know, like we're doing now, except for real, maybe a snatch and snuff now and then, just whatever's needed."

"You've done snatch and snuffs?"

Dibbs grinned. "Mostly just snuffs. We don't waste time with the snatches much since Tet, unless one of Max's bosses wants them for questioning. Why?"

"Just wondering. Sounds like risky work."

"Can be, but we do our thing, and Maxon covers our tracks."

"Have you ever had any problems with him?"

Dibbs laughed and blew a stream of smoke into the air. "Maxon's just a fucking nut, thinks he's a superspy or something. You'll get used to him. Just don't cross him. I mean, he can be a real asshole, but you learn to put up with his shit because this is such a fantastic gig."

"So is there a particular one of the Vietnamese you think might have killed Coleridge?"

"Hell, I don't know. They're all a bunch of shady assholes, but that Major Loc is the sneakiest-looking bastard in the bunch. Besides, I think him and Maxon got a sideline going, selling arms out of the CIA warehouse in Da Nang."

"Major Loc?"

"Yeah, Loc Van Thuc. Of course, there're about a dozen others like him, but he'd be my pick. Still, there's really no telling. It could have been someone else altogether."

"Like Lynn Dai Bouchet?"

"You know, that's what Max—"

A crack of lightning startled them both.

"Shit! I thought we had incoming," Dibbs said.

Behind them on the opposite side of the mountain, a nimbus billowed skyward. Brady glanced at his watch. It would be dusk soon. That's when they planned to begin working their way toward the pickup point, an LZ farther up the mountain. The hamlet below was located in a steep valley between two ridges. The far slope rose only four or five hundred meters away. They had a good view of the entire area, but they had observed only what appeared to be normal day-to-day activity. To the south, the storm-fractured sunlight glistened on a patchwork of rice paddies. A large stream, bordered with thick jungle, meandered its way southward through the mottled country-side.

Dibbs pulled his poncho over his head as the rain began, and the sounds of the surrounding jungle faded in the downpour. "We might as well head up the hill to the LZ," he said.

"I don't think that's a good idea," Brady said. "Too much light yet."

"Huh?" Dibbs wrinkled his face.

Brady looked through his riflescope to make certain the rain hadn't totally obliterated the view. "It's still broad daylight. I can see all the way across the valley."

Dibbs stood up and threw his pack over his shoulder. There was a metallic clack as an unwrapped buckle banged his rifle.

"Nash, how many times do I have to tell you, this is a secure area? All this crap we've been doing for the last month is a charade. Don't you get it?"

"Lower your voice, will you?"

There came the low rumble of thunder as the storm drifted down the valley and the rain slackened.

"You know, you need to save that shit for a real mission. Now grab your gear and let's—"

Sssshhhhrrrraaack. The back of Dibbs's head exploded as the round exited. Brady rolled onto all fours and clawed madly up the hill, into the underbrush. There was silence again, deathly silence, except for the patter of rain on the leaves. Dibbs's body quivered one last time, but Brady dared not move as he searched the opposite hillside. Misty rain and smoke rising from the hamlet below obscured the wall of trees and vegetation on the far slope.

With no more movement than it took to cut his eyes, Brady glanced at his watch. The sun was only now settling into the clouds in the west. In Vietnam, the term "secure area" was an oxymoron, and Dibbs had been talking too loud, banging his gear, and standing in the open before dusk. Now with his position compromised, Brady knew he was the sniper's next target. If he so much as breathed, he would be spotted, but there was another problem. There were probably more of the enemy flanking him at this very moment.

With the mist rising from the vegetation and the leaves fluttering under the falling rain, it would be impossible to spot the sniper. The slope from where the shot came was at least four hundred meters away. He needed to use his binoculars, but that too would draw the sniper's attention. His choices were to wait until dark and risk missing the chopper or crawl back down the hill to retrieve the radio while it was still daylight.

If he waited until dark, it would mean staying out another night, and with the enemy aware of his presence, it could make for an interesting game of all-night hide-and-seek. Crawling down the hill while it was still daylight was almost certain death. He decided to wait until dark, then try to relocate somewhere closer to the LZ. That would be the tricky part. Now that they knew he was here, the enemy would be watching the trails, waiting to ambush him.

As dusk faded into nightfall, the mosquitoes fed ravenously on the exposed parts of his body. It was time to move. Crawling rapidly down the hill, he retrieved the radio and Dibbs's body. No doubt the enemy was moving too, probably rushing toward him at this very moment. He shed everything except his bandolier and canteens, and after slinging the radio onto his back, he pulled the corpse over his shoulder. Dibbs wasn't a particularly big man, but his dead weight was staggering. Brady paused—which way to go?

The hamlet was at the base of the ridge. It was also in the opposite direction from the LZ, but it was the last direction the enemy would expect him to go. Later, he could work his way around the base of the hill and back up to the LZ from another direction. With the body draped over his shoulders, he made his way down the hill through the undergrowth. The rainfall deadened the sounds of his movement, and a half hour later, he reached a trail skirting the hamlet. The overcast night sky made the jungle an opaque wall of darkness. There was no choice. He had to use the trail to circle back to the LZ.

He was about to step from the brush when he heard voices murmuring near the hamlet. He paused, and after a minute, there came the sound of footsteps squishing in the mud. They were coming up the trail from the village. Within moments, a line of armed men began passing within a few feet from where Brady knelt, a VC patrol, probably searching for him. Dibbs's body reeked of cigarette smoke, and the sweat poured down Brady's face as he held his breath.

If the enemy soldiers smelled the tobacco odor, it would be over in an instant. There wasn't a hint of a breeze as they passed within arm's reach. One, two, three, he counted as the column passed. When the last soldier was gone, he stepped into the trail. There were fourteen VC in front of him. So much for Maxon's "secure area."

The silhouette of the last man faded away up the trail as Brady fell in behind the patrol. They continued on the trail around the base of the mountain until reaching a second trail that turned up the hill. Remaining far enough behind the column so as to escape detection, Brady silently followed until he realized their destination. The patrol was heading toward the LZ. He paused and listened. Up ahead, the enemy soldiers talked in low voices as they deployed around the edges of the jungle clearing. They were setting up for an ambush. How the hell did they know this remote clearing in the middle of nowhere was the pickup point? He thought of Loc. The special police were kept informed of every mission.

This meant the alternate pickup point could be compromised as well, but it was his only remaining option. The other LZ was one and a half klicks south of the main village. Under normal conditions, he could reach it within an hour, but with a twenty-five-pound radio and a 170-pound body on his back, he'd be lucky to get there by dawn.

Sometime after midnight, he left the trail south of the main village and pushed into the undergrowth. A series of rice paddies and a wall of jungle along the meandering stream lay between him and the rendezvous point.

With only his compass for reference, Brady tried to maintain the azimuth while wading across the paddies, struggling through elephant grass, and fighting rushing torrents of water in the stream. Leeches covered his arms and legs, and after moving most of the night, he was near exhaustion. The pickup point had to be close, but he wasn't certain. He'd become disoriented.

It was 0550 hours, nearly time for the chopper to arrive in the area, but a solid wall of jungle still surrounded him. He might be nowhere near the pickup point. He pulled his poncho over his head and hid beneath it while examining the map and compass with his flashlight. Not a single landmark was evident. He switched off the light and pulled the poncho from over his head. It would take a few minutes for his eyes to readjust to the darkness. He decided to try the radio. It broke squelch immediately.

"Lucky Tiger Three-Three, this is Sky Patriot One-One. Do you read me? Over."

It was the pickup chopper. Brady keyed the handset on the PRC-25.

"Roger, Sky Patriot One-One," he whispered. "This is Lucky Tiger Three-Three. I read you Lima Charlie."

"Hey, you guys OK, Lucky Tiger?"

"Negative, Sky Patriot. We've got problems," Brady whispered. "I'm trying to reach Blanket Two."

"Roger, Lucky Tiger. We're on standby for extraction. How far are you from Blanket Two?"

"I don't know," Brady muttered. "I'll call you back in one five. Over."

"Roger that, Lucky Tiger. Stay low, bud."

Dibbs's body had begun to stiffen as rigor mortis set in. Brady's arms trembled with exhaustion as he struggled to pull the corpse over his shoulder. It was still drizzling as he pushed his way through the wet undergrowth. His fatigues were muddy and soaked, with as much blood as rain. After taking a few steps, he slipped and fell facedown in the muck, the corpse atop him. He pushed it away and pulled his rifle from the mud.

Wiping away the debris, he checked the bore. The M40 was OK, but he no longer had the strength to carry the body on his back. Struggling to his feet, he hooked his hand behind the collar of Dibbs's fatigue shirt and began dragging him. Up ahead, there appeared to be a break in the jungle. Brady tried to move faster, but stumbled and fell forward. This time, though, he broke through a wall of elephant grass, into a clearing.

As the first hint of gray dawn appeared in the sky above, he heard the thumping rotors of the chopper coming in low through the mountains.

"Sky Patriot One-One, this is Lucky Tiger Three-Three, over."

It took only a second or two, but it seemed forever before the chopper pilot answered.

"Go ahead, Lucky Tiger."

The sound of the chopper drew closer, echoing from the nearby hills.

"I think I'm at Blanket Two. I'm firing a starburst, Sky Patriot."

Brady watched the fiery crimson flare burst overhead. The extraction had to work this time because every VC within miles now had his position. He waited for confirmation.

"I've got you, Lucky Tiger. We're inbound less than a klick out. Pop me some smoke."

Brady pulled the pin on a red smoke grenade, and within seconds, the chopper flared overhead. He confirmed his red smoke, and the chopper descended into the clearing. Struggling to keep his feet, he dragged the corpse toward the chopper. The door gunner slogged across the boggy ground to help. After pushing the body onto the deck, Brady crawled in and collapsed on the floor. The high-pitched whine of the Huey's turbines was an alleluia choir singing his salvation as the chopper lurched skyward.

CHAPTER TWELVE

Lacey's Dream

S ipping her morning coffee, Lacey gazed out the apartment window at the green hills beyond the parking lot. The morning mist was drawing up in magical wisps and fading with the rising sun. It was late May, and the misty hills left her homesick and lonely, but relief was on the way. Billy was coming by with one of his midweek projects. With her singing engagements becoming more frequent and her earnings improving, she had quit her job as a waitress. This gave her more time to practice and the freedom to do the things she enjoyed. One of those was doing things with her new music coach and partner, Billy Wyatt.

Billy had become the friend she needed, filling the empty hours with his silly jokes and sometimes even sillier ideas for fun and entertainment. He reminded her so much of Brady. His latest escapade was an offer to share profits from a painting job he'd contracted down at Brentwood, if she helped. Painting wasn't exactly her idea of fun, but his pleading eyes made it difficult to say no, and she agreed. Besides, it beat sitting around the apartment, thinking of home and worrying about Brady.

Billy was simply a nice person, and theirs was a brother-sister relationship. At least that was how she saw it. Occasionally, he acted like it could be more, but Lacey made it clear that Brady was her only love. Billy claimed to understand, but he never sounded truly convinced. Still, she found his friendship comforting as they worked together rehearsing and rewriting music and lyrics for her performances. And today, though the work would be less gratifying, it would at least be fun to get outside and enjoy the weather.

After pulling on her oldest jeans and a T-shirt cut off above the waist, she was pinning her hair beneath a red bandanna when a horn sounded in the parking lot. She peeked out the window. It was Billy in his old pickup. Grabbing the lunch she'd prepared, she patted Sampson on the head and turned out the lights. Sampson had been a kitten when Billy gave him to her a few months back, and the little tomcat had purred his way into Lacey's heart. He was draped over the top of the television, still sleeping, as she went out the door.

The sun was barely above the horizon as Billy drove his pickup through the back roads over to Highway 31. He eyed the lunch basket on the seat between them.

"Whatcha got in there?" he asked.

Lacey leaned her head closer to the open window, basking in the cool morning air. "You'll have to wait till lunchtime to see."

"What, no breakfast?"

She turned to him, frowning. "I thought you were getting breakfast."

Smiling, Billy reached behind his legs and retrieved a white bag from beneath the seat. "Coffee and doughnuts," he said. "Why don't you serve it up?"

Lacey wrapped a doughnut in a napkin and handed it to him, then pried the plastic lid from one of the cups of coffee. When they reached 31, they turned south, and the sun was shining brightly when they pulled into a drive near Brentwood. Lacey swiped at the last of the doughnut crumbs on her T-shirt as they drove between two huge wrought iron gates hanging from brick columns. When Billy stopped the truck, she raised her head and gazed up the drive.

Long and gracefully curved, the drive stretched up the hillside for nearly a quarter mile to a mansion at the crest of the hill. Huge white columns lined the front porch, but it was the multitude of wooden gables, porch railings, and windows all decorated with ornate trim that left her staring in disbelief. It would take an army of painters to do this job.

"Well, here we are," Billy said. He wore a smug grin, and Lacey realized she was gazing openmouthed at the mansion.

"Surely, we're not going to paint that...are we?"

Billy scratched his head as he looked back up at the house. "Why not?"

"Because," she said, "it's too big. We'll never finish."

"Well, if you don't want to paint the house…" He paused as he pointed to the fence that paralleled the highway. It stretched for over a hundred yards on either side of the drive. "How about we just paint that fence?"

The white three-railed wood fence went forever as it followed the gently rolling terrain. Lacey stretched to see where it ended, but the fence disappeared into a hollow somewhere in the distance. "We aren't going to paint the house, just the fence, right?

"That's right. So, what's the matter?"

"Nothing, except that's still a lot of painting for just two people."

"Don't worry," he said. "A couple of buddies of mine, Rick and Terry, are coming to help. You'll see. We'll be finished before dark."

By late afternoon, they were still painting, but Billy was right— the end was in sight. Sunburned and splattered with paint, Lacey had followed behind him all day as he rolled the flat surfaces and she cut in the corners with a brush. Across the drive, nearly three hundred yards away, his buddies were approaching the opposite end of the fence, most of which now gleamed with a new coat of white paint. She gazed out at the white-faced Herefords grazing in the pasture across the highway. The grasses on the hillside swayed in a feathery breeze.

"You know, it's really beautiful out here," she said.

She turned back toward Billy, who was squatting as he rolled the last bottom rail on the last section of fence. He grunted and nodded.

"Well, it was, till I saw that," she said.

Shirtless, he duckwalked along as he rolled the rail. "What's that?" he asked without looking up.

"The crack of your butt is showing," she said.

"So don't look," he replied.

"So why don't you cover it up?"

"'Cause I'm busy."

"OK," she said, "then I will." She dipped her paintbrush in the bucket, then swiped it across the top of his buttocks.

"Shit! I'm not believing—" He jumped to his feet and ran his hand behind his back.

Lacey dropped the brush back in the bucket and folded her arms. "That's what you get for indecent exposure," she said.

But without warning, Billy pulled his paint roller down the length of her torso. She screamed as they wrestled playfully, smearing paint on one another, but he suddenly stopped. His face was only inches from hers. Their eyes met, and Lacey suddenly found her heart pounding, but it wasn't from the wrestling. Billy was a handsome man, deeply tanned with blue eyes and sun-bleached hair the color of honey. And neither was it his looks that made her short of breath. It was how much he reminded her of Brady. He kissed her tenderly on the lips. She wanted to pull away, but she hesitated. He caressed a wisp of hair dangling from beneath her red bandanna, and she shivered.

"We need to finish the painting," she said, carefully pushing free of his arms.

"Fair enough," he said. "Just make sure it's the fence and not my butt."

"Don't moon me anymore, and I won't."

* * *

Lacey stared out the side window of the truck that evening as they drove back into Nashville. She had to make Billy understand. Whatever moment of weakness that had overcome her was just that, and there was no chance she'd forget her heart's one true love. The eastern sky was already a deep violet, and she wanted to turn toward the sunset, but that meant she'd have to turn to face Billy. She couldn't.

"What's wrong?" he said.

"Nothing."

"Yeah, right."

"I just miss Brady, and I worry about him."

She turned to look straight ahead and saw from the corner of her eye as Billy tightened his grip on the steering wheel. It was enough. She had told him what a thousand more words couldn't, and she felt his frustration in the silence.

"So are you guys going to get married?"

Lacey felt her eyes moisten, and she tried to laugh, but it didn't work, as she made a sound more like the bleat of a desperate lamb. Swallowing hard, she fought to regain her composure.

"There are a lot of things I want, but more than anything, I want Brady home alive. And yes, someday, if he will have me, I want to marry him."

Billy glanced over at her. "What do you mean, if he will have you?"

"I let him down one time."

They were on the outskirts of Nashville, and the traffic was beginning to increase.

"What do you mean?" Billy asked.

"I was so wrapped up in my own feelings that I didn't take the time to really listen when he tried to tell me something. Now I just want to do something that will make him proud of me. It's something that's been kind of a far-fetched dream of mine for a long time."

"What's that?" Billy asked, his eyes remaining fixed on the road.

"I want to sing at the Grand Ole Opry some Saturday night, and I want everyone back home to hear me sing on the radio."

Many times she had wandered down to Fifth Avenue, gazing dreamily at the Ryman Auditorium, the ancient red brick building with windows like a church.

"My daddy used to listen to his radio every Saturday night. Melody Hill is up on a mountain, and he'd play with the knob until he got WSM. Me and my brother, Duff, would sit in that big old chair with him while we listened to the Grand Ole Opry live in Nashville. I'd like to sing there just once. You know?"

"Well," Billy said, "just keep doing what you're doing, and you'll make it to the Opry someday. I guarantee it."

For the first time since they'd begun the ride home, Lacey sat up and turned toward him. Her anxiety suddenly faded.

"You really think so?"

He grinned. "You don't realize just how good you are, do you?"

Lacey felt her cheeks burning as she looked away.

"I think I sing pretty good, but—"

"Believe me, girl, you don't just sing pretty good. You've got talent. When you do a country song, you bring real meaning to it. It's only a matter of time before you sing at the Opry."

CHAPTER THIRTEEN

Phung Hoang

I t was late afternoon when Brady awoke the day after the mission. His last conversation with Dibbs still smoldered in his
mind. He knew now that there were others who might provide information about Duff's killer, but Maxon was intentionally
isolating him. This left him with no choice but to push for a more
active role with the special operations group. He would never
learn anything if he spent the rest of his tour chasing shadows.
He had to start putting faces with names, even if it meant taking
some chances.

It was nearly 1745 hours, and he was supposed to report to Maxon for a post-op debriefing at 1800, but it was raining again.
Thunder rumbled low in the distance, vibrating the thin walls of
the Quonset hut. After lacing his boots, he donned the shoulder

holster with the .45 Maxon had given him, then draped a poncho over his shoulders. Trotting across the compound, he dodged the water puddles as he made his way to the white cinder block building that housed Maxon's office. Maxon was at his desk when Brady knocked at the open door.

"Come in, Nash. Take a seat."

His first instinct was to confront Maxon, but with Maxon's overblown ego, pressure of any kind would be the wrong move. He had to pick his words carefully. He let Maxon speak first.

"Looks like you and Dibbs got into some bad shit out there."

Brady nodded.

"Well, the rest of the team is real proud of you, carrying his body out like that. I can't say that I'd have done it myself. Sometimes, you've got to put your mission first, you know?"

Brady shrugged. "Just doing what I thought was right."

Maxon walked to the refrigerator and returned with two beers. Opening them, he placed one in front of Brady.

"So tell me what's on your mind?"

"What do you mean?"

"You seem down. This is a tough business. People are going to die. Can you take it?"

Brady felt the impulse to unload on him, but he caught himself. He had to take it easy.

"Yeah, I can take it."

"That's good. We just had another man rotate back to the States, and with Dibbs KIA, we need someone to step up pretty quick. You ready?"

The offer caught him off guard. Maxon seemed relaxed for once, and he was talking without his usual sarcasm.

"Yeah, I'm ready."

"OK. First you need to understand exactly what our mission is, and what I expect from you. You've got to understand. The bastards we go after are known Vietcong cadre members. That means they're part of the leadership infrastructure that runs the National Liberation Front."

Brady nodded.

"There are different levels. First you have the VC that the military fights every day. They're a dime a dozen. It's the next level we hunt. They're the studs in charge. When we go after these high-level gooks, we don't mess around because they're dangerous. Some are village leaders, and some are spies in the Vietnamese government. You understand?"

"Exactly how do we go after them?"

"That's up to my bosses," Maxon said. "We do what's necessary. That's why you're here, and that's why we play our cards close to the vest. We are a counterterrorist group, and when we have strong enough evidence, we sometimes terminate them without any questions. You understand?"

Brady sipped his beer and nodded. This is what Duff had said was happening, but killing unarmed women and children was a long way from killing enemy agents.

"The important thing is that you discipline yourself to do exactly as I tell you, and you talk with no one about anything we do. We work closely with several different GVN groups, but mostly in conjunction with the National Police Force, Special Branch. You know that old gook in the camo fatigues, the one you saw when you first got here?"

Brady nodded. The graying Vietnamese officer had a distinct air of authority about him.

"That was Colonel Tranh. He reports directly to the province chief. Tranh's the big dog around here, and he's the one we work with most of the time. You'll get to know the pompous little bastard because he always reminds us that we're only advisors, but when the shit hits the fan, he does what I tell him."

Brady remained straight-faced. Duff was right. Spartan hated everyone, even the people he was sent here to help. Yes, Maxon and Spartan were no doubt one and the same.

"The most important thing you need to understand is what's at stake. You fuck up and you're dead meat. The VC are like the criminals back in the States. They understand one thing, and that's swift and certain justice."

Maxon turned up his beer. When he was done, he studied the can while rolling it in his fingers.

"Yeah, the liberal bastards think we can rehabilitate them with the Chieu Hoi program, but they don't understand the Vietcong perspective. You see, Charlie is a patient son of a bitch. He will wait for as long as it takes. He will tolerate anything for a while, even a rehab program like Chieu Hoi, but as soon as you let your guard down, he will kill you. He's an enemy that understands only one thing—a bullet between the eyes. Any more questions?"

Brady shook his head.

"We're starting a new program. Actually, we've been working on it since Tet, but we're finally getting buy-in from the South Vietnamese. In the past, things were hit or miss with gathering intelligence, but we've started using computers. You know how computers work?"

Brady nodded. "We read a little about them in school."

"Good, but remember, this is top secret stuff, so you need to keep your mouth shut. Anyway, once a gook gets his name in the computer, it stays there. We just add evidence as it comes in and make him a new punch card. The computer cross-references the information and ranks the suspect according to the evidence until we have enough to go after him. Bottom line, if the computer says his ass is ours, we don't need to worry about asking questions. We just take his ass out."

Brady nodded. This was what Duff had said: no questions, no arrests, no trials.

"Here's how we work. I normally have two or three of you military guys assigned TDY to me. You act as my middlemen of sorts, advisors with the special police and the Luc Luong Dac Biet. That's the South Vietnamese Special Forces. We also use indigenous forces like the PRU and sometimes the Montagnards. We work in teams anywhere from two to sometimes a hundred or more, depending on the mission.

"We also work missions in conjunction with other units, including the ARVN, the National Police Field Forces, and even some of our own units, but our part deals mostly with Vietnamese operations. We advise and assist them in performing very specific missions aimed at taking out the high-level VC in the districts around I Corps. So now you know what I know. Any questions?"

"You work for the CIA, right?"

"Officially, we'll have to call that need-to-know information, and you haven't heard it from me. Just get your head screwed on straight because this computerized intel is already giving us more business than we can handle. Now let's get this debriefing out of the way. The military is asking questions about Dibbs getting killed."

* * *

Several days later, Brady was awakened by a knock at his door. Forcing his eyes open, he looked at his watch. It was 0230 hours.

"Yeah," he said, still drugged with sleep.

"Be out at my jeep in thirty minutes," Maxon called through the door.

It was odd that there was no pre-mission briefing. Even routine patrols were planned and talked about in advance, but this time, Maxon remained silent while they loaded their gear into the jeep. The compound was stirring with activity, the special police loading their equipment and climbing into trucks. After several minutes, the smoky exhaust from the diesels hung in the thick morning air as the vehicles sat idling, the drivers waiting for the word to move out.

"We're going after some VC suspects carrying arms down the Cu De River."

Maxon got behind the wheel and cranked the jeep. That was the entire pre-mission briefing. The convoy followed as Maxon drove through the compound gate. A half hour later, they were boarding choppers at the air base in Da Nang. Things were moving fast, and it was still well before dawn when the choppers landed on a highway to rendezvous with a Provincial Reconnaissance Unit. According to Maxon, they were still several klicks from their objective, a village near the river. They moved out quickly on foot as the column moved up the highway in the pre-dawn darkness.

Just before first light, the PRUs had encircled the village. Maxon explained that their suspect, along with two other VC, had been seen in the village the previous evening before dark. He motioned Brady to follow as they split away from the main force, making their way in the darkness down a well-trodden trail. Silently, they slipped across an open field to a knoll, halfway between the village and the river. As dawn broke, the PRUs tightened the cordon and began their search operation.

"The special police force will check out the villagers while the PRUs do a house-to-house search," Maxon whispered. "We're going to wait out here and see if our boys make a break for the river."

As the full light of day fell across the countryside, Brady realized the position Maxon had chosen was ideal. They were hidden in some trees on a slight rise. To the east, three hundred meters away, was the tree-lined bank of the Cu De River. To the west, two hundred meters out, the heads of some of the PRUs bobbed just above the grass as they watched the village in the misty dawn. Thin columns of white smoke rose gently skyward from smoldering cook fires in the village. It was quiet for the moment.

The search proceeded for nearly an hour, but things remained peaceful. Waist-high grass with scattered scrub brush covered the area between them and the village. Unless someone was on hands and knees, they would be easy to spot. The minutes ticked away as the sun appeared across the river, a huge orange sphere burning through the morning mist. It could have been the most beautiful sunrise he'd ever seen, but Brady scarcely noticed as he unconsciously thumbed the safety on the M40.

Muted shouts and the sound of a baby crying came from the village. Suddenly, a pig squealed. Brady stiffened, but after a few moments, it was quiet again. He relaxed, but worried if he would do the right thing. Did he have the courage that Duff had, the courage to say no?

"So what if these guys aren't carrying weapons?" he whispered.

Maxon pursed his lips and cut his eyes at Brady. "It doesn't matter. We have the goods on them, and one's a really slippery son of a bitch. The marines did a search here before Christmas and couldn't catch him. We think he's a district chief. We're going to nail his ass this time. Understood?"

Brady nodded.

"If they're out here, we assume they're VC," Maxon said. "And we shoot them on sight."

This was it. Maxon was putting him to the test. If he failed, he might never find Duff's killers. His gut ached with tension, but as the sun climbed higher, the mission seemed destined for failure. Taking a deep breath, he glanced at his watch. Perhaps the suspects had slipped off in another direction, but the thought no sooner occurred than two pajama-clad figures sprang from the grass and sprinted toward the river. Both carried AK-47s and haversacks.

They were at least two hundred meters away, and the troops near the village failed to see them as the guerrillas ran for their lives. Brady raised his rifle and began following the man in the rear. Holding the crosshairs on his target, he tracked him as the two men raced wildly for cover.

"Shoot," Maxon hissed.

Brady continued following the man in the rear through his riflescope as they drew closer to the river. They were now over 250 meters away and less than fifty meters from the river.

"Shoot, goddamn it! You're letting them get away."

Then, for only the briefest moment, the man in the rear stopped to look back. The bullet ripped through his chest. The man in front stopped running as the rifle's report echoed against the distant tree line. He looked back at his dying comrade. It wasn't a long or contemplative look. He didn't even come to a complete stop as he backpedaled several steps, then spun to run the last few meters to safety, but it was too late. The second bullet exploded inside his heaving lungs, slamming him to the ground.

"Damn," Maxon muttered. He seemed in awe, but caught himself and quickly changed the tone of his voice. "Hell, Nash, I thought for sure you had let those two gooks get away. What the hell were you waiting on?"

Brady shrugged.

"Well, next time, don't wait. You understand?"

"Yeah, sure. Whatever you say."

"Be ready," Maxon said. "There may be another one. Those two must have come out of a tunnel."

The PRUs had formed a skirmish line and were working their way out into the grass when another man stood up. He, too, wore black pajamas, but he held his hands high in a sign of surrender. Apparently unarmed, he walked rapidly toward Brady and Maxon. Brady peered at him through the riflescope as the man drew closer.

"*Dung Lai*," the soldiers shouted, but the man continued walking with his hands in the air. The PRUs aimed their rifles at the man's back, but he ignored them.

When he was less than seventy-five meters away, he placed his hands behind his head and shouted, "*Chieu hoi. Chieu hoi.*" His voice was shrill and tentative. "No VC. No VC. *Chieu hoi.*"

"Now," Maxon hissed.

Brady looked over at him.

"Shoot, damn it!"

"But he's surrendering," Brady said.

"Shoot that son of a bitch now!" Maxon shouted.

The man continued calling "*Chieu hoi*" as he came forward, now within fifty meters.

Brady froze.

"I am giving you a direct order, Nash. Shoot that goddamned gook now."

Slowly, Brady raised his rifle and laid his cheek against the stock as he pulled the crosshairs below the man's chest. It was an easy shot, and the 7.62 mm round entered the man's chest at the top of his heart, knocking him backward into the tall grass. For several moments, Maxon peered through his binoculars, studying the spot where the man had fallen. Then he turned toward Brady.

"You listen to me. The next time I give you an order, don't ask questions. Is that clear?"

Brady continued staring straight ahead.

"I said, is that clear?"

"He was surrendering," Brady murmured.

Maxon's face went from red to purple.

"Goddammit, you said you wanted to do this. That son of a bitch is our man, and he's probably killed more GIs than you can count."

Brady said nothing.

"Look, Nash. You don't know enough about this business to question my judgment. For all we knew, that gook might have had a satchel charge or a grenade hidden in his clothes. You need to remember rule number one: never, ever underestimate your enemy."

Brady didn't answer as he stared across the field toward the village. Maxon grew suddenly calm again as the color in his face subsided. He stood and again searched the grass with his binoculars.

"You think he's down for good?" he asked.

"He's dead," Brady answered quietly.

"Good," Maxon replied. "Just remember, if I tell you to take 'em out, you do it. This is war. It's my business, and I know what I'm doing."

Brady remained silent as he stared straight ahead. After the PRU troops passed the bodies, Maxon stood and motioned him forward. "Let's go see what we have."

As they approached, Maxon drew his .45, but Brady knew when his shots were right. All three of these were on. He watched while Maxon searched the bodies and tossed aside their weapons. Afterward, he produced what appeared to be business cards. They were exactly like the one Duff had sent home in his letter, yellow with a green birdlike figure and the Vietnamese words "Phung Hoang" written in red. The hair tingled on the back of his neck as Maxon placed one on each body.

"What are those?" he asked.

Maxon smiled. "Just calling cards to let the rest of these bastards know we were here."

"Where do you get them?" Brady asked.

"I had them made in Saigon."

Maxon reached into his pocket and pulled out another. He handed it to Brady.

"The Special Branch gooks love it. Phung Hoang is the bird of a thousand eyes that sees everything. It's gook superstition, scares the hell out of the VC."

Brady looked at the card, then handed it back to Maxon.

"Does everyone use them?"

"Yeah, but I designed them myself. You want some?"

"Yellow, red, and green, that's a good play on the national colors," Brady said.

"Yeah, thought of that myself."

It wasn't proof, but it was the best evidence yet. If it wasn't Maxon who'd killed Duff, it was someone in his group—not Lynn Dai Bouchet.

* * *

By early afternoon, Brady returned with Maxon to the IOCC. Up since 0230, his eyelids drooped as they got out of the jeep and walked toward the door of the operations center. A young ARVN guard with an M16 and an oversize American helmet stepped into Maxon's path. Brady hadn't seen him before, probably a new replacement.

"I must see identifications, sirs."

Brady reached for his wallet, but he hesitated when he noticed Maxon put his hands on his hips. He was looking off to the side, licking his lips and smiling. Without warning, Maxon's arm shot out, pinning the guard by the neck against the wall. The young soldier's rifle clattered to the ground as Maxon kneed him violently in the groin, then grabbed him by the chin.

"Look at my face, you greasy fuck!" Maxon shouted, pointing his finger back at his own face.

The soldier's eyes bulged with fear as he held his hands up in surrender.

"You look at it good, and don't ever forget it. Because the next time you step in front of me at my own IOCC, I'm going to kill you. You understand?"

Maxon didn't wait for a response as he shoved the soldier aside, knocking him to the ground.

Glancing over his shoulder, he said, "You have to make these greasy bastards respect you."

Turning, he sauntered into the building, leaving Brady staring down at the frightened ARVN soldier. Bending, he retrieved the man's M16 and helmet, then extended his hand and pulled the soldier to his feet. The soldier trembled, and his face was still contorted with fear and anger as he rubbed the red marks on his neck.

"Sorry," Brady said as he handed the man his M16 and helmet.

He wanted to tell him that not all Americans were crazy like Maxon. He wanted to ask him not to hate Americans. He wanted to say anything that would make a difference, but it was useless. Words could never fix what men like Maxon and the Communists were doing to the Vietnamese and their country. Besides, he was now as much a part of it as Maxon. Brady turned away from the young soldier and walked inside the building.

CHAPTER FOURTHEEN

Xin Loi

S leep should have come easy that afternoon following the mission, but Brady was restless as he tipped up the fifth of Wild Turkey. He sat in his little room at the back of the Quonset hut, mulling the morning's events. Maxon's kill card was evidence that he was close to putting a name and a face on the killer. It should have been encouraging, but something bigger was eating at him. He'd crossed a line he had hoped to never cross. He'd shot an unarmed man.

"*Xin Loi*, fucker," Brady muttered as he again saw the man's face in his riflescope.

"He would have blown your ass to hell," Maxon's men had said. "Besides, what's one more dead gook?"

190 | RICK DESTEFANIS

As it turned out, Maxon was wrong. The man was unarmed, and he wasn't the district chief either. He was a young VC recruit, but it was all a matter of numbers to people like Maxon. What was one more death? And perhaps they were right, but Will's words kept coming back: "Truth has a resonance that fills the cracks where falsehoods hide." This bell had no resonance. Shooting the first two guerrillas was no problem, but the third man had his hands in the air. Despite Maxon's order to shoot, Brady had made his own decision to walk in that gray area between right and wrong.

There was only one solution. That was to put it out of his mind. He had to think about something else, and he thought about Lacey back in Nashville. He wondered what she might be doing at that very moment. He thought about home, the crisp mountain air of Melody Hill, and the crystal waters of the Hiwassee River, places and things that now seemed like distant memories.

Sitting on the side of his bunk, he gazed up at the ceiling fan swirling in the rafters above, and he soon realized that he was coming to understand schizophrenic personalities like Maxon's. Finding the truth in Vietnam was nearly impossible, perhaps because there was no truth. There were only instincts to go on. Corking the bottle, he fell back on the bunk.

If he made it through this mess with his sanity intact, it would be a miracle. Still, he refused to quit as long as Duff's murderers were free. The problem was what to do next. He had to have a plan. Brady finished nearly half the bottle, but still found no answers as he fell into a swirling cauldron of drunken sleep.

* * *

His room at the back of the Quonset hut was windowless, but Brady sat bolt upright when he realized it was morning. His watch said it was 0630, and his head throbbed like a boiler with a bad relief valve, but an idea had come to him in the night. He pulled on his fatigues, laced his boots, and eased out the door, trying not to disturb the Special Branch police officers in the adjoining rooms. The air outside was dank and warm, and the compound was quiet as he hurried across to the operations building.

Maxon was billeted at the air base in Da Nang, and after the previous day's mission, he would probably be late coming to the compound. This was the opportunity Brady needed. If there was anything at all in Maxon's office that linked him to Duff's murder, now was the time to find it. He approached the door to the operations center, pausing as the morning sun set the clouds ablaze.

The front of the building was a reinforced concrete block wall. What if he was the one who was crazy? What if there really was a double agent who had used one of Maxon's cards to set him up? Perhaps he should wait a little longer. Perhaps he could make excuses until hell froze over. He promised Duff that day at his grave that he would find the ones responsible, and now he was among them. There would be no more waiting.

Adjusting his cap, he approached the Vietnamese guard standing grim faced at the entrance, M16 in hand. It was the same one Maxon had attacked. Flipping his ID confidently, Brady strode past him without stopping. The young soldier opened his mouth slightly as if to say something, but Brady continued on. The bluff worked. Maxon had all the guards afraid to challenge any Americans. Brady quickly made his way down the darkened hallway to Maxon's office, where he tested the door. It was open.

There wasn't a moment to waste as he began pulling open cabinets and going through drawers and files. He read everything he found, searching every bin and cubbyhole in the room. File by file and document by document, he searched and read memos, telex messages, and handwritten notes, but he found nothing. After nearly an hour, he stood frustrated at the center of the room, turning slowly in a circle. He noticed a door. He walked over and pulled it open. It was a closet. Inside were boxes of file folders marked "burn."

The first folder he grabbed was unmarked, but as he searched, he found others with tabs. One was marked "Communications." It was also stamped with red block letters, "Top Secret." His blood pressure throbbed in his head, and his hands trembled as he laid the folder open on the floor and thumbed through it.

Flipping through more dispatches and telex messages, he came across one with the same two words he'd seen on the cards that Maxon had placed on the bodies near the Cu De River—Phung Hoang. The message was in code, but someone had penciled between the lines.

"Until Phoenix-Phung Hoang transfer is fully implemented take initiative to continue program objectives beyond auspices of DEPCORDS with local SPFD. We will coordinate additional staffing and resources as needed."

DEPCORDS was military, but who was telling him to go beyond their authority? He was sanctioned, but by whom? The note was unsigned.

He picked up another paper. It was an un-coded carbon, apparently a copy of a note sent by Maxon, claiming evidence suggesting Lynn Dai Bouchet was an NLF agent, but there was another note ordering him to cease his investigation of Bouchet. He couldn't put it all together. Someone was ordering Maxon to stop investigating Bouchet, but why?

Thumbing through several more notes, he spotted one with two familiar names. "Terminate Coleridge-Bouchet relationship ASAP," it said. This jibed with what Maxon had said about her being a possible National Liberation Front agent, but there were still too many pieces to the puzzle missing.

Bouchet was the key, but the more he read, the more confused he became. He went through several more folders and was about to quit when he saw one marked "Coleridge." A lump stuck in his throat.

Almost reverently, Brady opened the folder. Two cards slid out on the floor. One he recognized immediately. It was identical to the yellow cards Maxon had placed on the bodies up at the Cu De, and it was splotched with what appeared to be dried blood. The other appeared to be an ID card, completely covered with the dried blood. Brady scratched through the blood with his thumbnail. As the picture became visible, the lump in his throat grew until it nearly suffocated him. In the photograph staring back at him were the baleful eyes of Duff.

Overcome with emotion, Brady didn't hear the footsteps until someone was just outside the door. He grabbed the kill card, pushed it into his pocket along with the ID and several telex messages, and quickly closed the closet door. As he turned, the office door flew open.

"What are you doing here, Specialist Nash?" Colonel Tranh asked. The Vietnamese special police officer seemed as much surprised as he was angered.

"I came here to wait for Maxon," Brady said. "Is something wrong?"

Brady felt his head burning as Major Loc walked into the room behind Tranh. Loc said something in Vietnamese to the colonel, but Tranh shook his head. Loc was insistent, but Tranh barked at him in Vietnamese.

"My operations officer feels you should be arrested for being here without your boss, Specialist Nash, but I feel he is overreacting. Please leave, and do not come here in the future without your superior, Mr. Maxon. This area is restricted."

"Yes, sir," Brady replied.

"I will also tell Major Loc that he may call Mr. Maxon and inform him of your presence here this morning. I am certain he will discuss it with you when he arrives."

* * *

Maxon slammed down the telephone, but it popped from the cradle and fell to the floor. What was that goofy son of a bitch doing at the operations center? And why hadn't Colonel Tranh called before releasing him? Instead, it was Major Loc. Loc Van Thuc was the only gook he trusted. The Bouchet woman was again asking questions, and now just as he was beginning to trust him, Nash was snooping around in his office. Too much was at risk. He had to deal with them both.

Loc informed him that Nash had left the operations center only minutes earlier, but he didn't know where he was going. Maxon grabbed his shoulder holster and headed for the IOCC. His jeep careened through Da Nang city as he sped toward the compound. He was going to kick Nash's ass. He had to know what he was up to.

The jeep was still rolling to a stop as he jumped out and headed for the Quonset hut. As he charged through the doorway, he collided head-on with Nash. He went for his throat with his hand.

"What the hell were—"

Nash caught his wrist in midair, holding it with unexpected strength.

"You better think about what you're doing," Nash said.

Nash's calm demeanor was unexpected, and his eyes, although bloodshot, were blue and steady.

Maxon snatched his arm free. "What the hell were you doing in my office, Nash?"

"You and those Vietnamese police are the most paranoid people I've ever seen. What the hell is wrong with you?"

Maxon felt the veins throbbing in his neck. "I asked you a question. Answer me. What the fuck were you doing in my office?"

"I was waiting for you," Nash said. "What is the big damned deal?"

Maxon paused. Nash was either the shrewdest or the dumbest son of a bitch he'd ever dealt with. He looked him up and down. Nash was too calm to have been caught doing something wrong.

"Boy, you are one dumb son of a bitch. You know that? What the hell do you think we're paranoid about? That's my office, and no one is supposed to be in there but me. You understand?"

"You never told me that."

"Well, if you can't figure that much, then you're pretty goddamned stupid. Just stay the hell out of there when I'm not around."

Maxon turned and kicked open the screen door of the Quonset hut, but after stepping outside into the morning sun, he paused and looked back. Even if Nash wasn't up to something, there was no sense in going through any more of this. Nash stood staring stupidly back at him.

"By the way, we're gathering new intelligence on an old suspect, and we may have a mission this weekend." He paused as he worked out the plan in his head. "I want you to pack your field gear and stay here until I get back. Don't leave the compound. Is that understood?"

Nash continued staring blank faced at him, but he didn't answer. Maxon turned toward the operations building. He had to meet with Colonel Tranh, not something he looked forward to, but it had to be done. Tranh was always a willing participant until a mission got ugly. Then he always tried to say the Americans were at fault. Maxon walked into the Vietnamese colonel's office without knocking.

"I need you to send me a scout from the PRU, someone who knows Quang Nam Province," he told Tranh. "Make sure it's someone who will follow orders and won't talk to anyone. Also, tell Loc to come see me. I want him to watch Nash. I think Nash is contemplating taking some kind of personal action against the Bouchet woman."

"Why would Nash want to do that, Mr. Maxon?"

Maxon paused in the doorway and looked back. "He's been asking a lot of questions about Bouchet. He thinks she had something to do with Coleridge's death."

"Why don't you simply warn her?" Tranh asked.

"She wouldn't believe me," Maxon said. "She still thinks I had something to do with killing Coleridge."

Tranh raised his eyebrows. The colonel had apparently heard the rumors. Maxon started to turn away, but stopped to face his counterpart.

"Of course, only a *very* crazy man would kill one of his own people," he said.

Tranh was tight-lipped, but he smiled. "Of course, only a very crazy man."

Maxon didn't reply, but he understood the colonel's implication. He hated slick-headed gooks like Tranh. They displayed shitty little facades of politeness to hide the contempt they held for Americans. It was ridiculous, but in their own screwy way, they thought they were superior. If it weren't for the Americans,

Tranh and the rest of the slopes would be living in straw huts and eating maggot-infested rice.

The only one he cared to deal with was Major Loc. Loc followed orders with no questions asked, and he was a viciously efficient bastard. He got things done.

Maxon walked down to his office. He'd set his plan in motion, and now it was a matter of working out the details. The idea had first occurred to him when Loc told him how Bouchet was still interrogating villagers and asking men in the PRU detachment about Coleridge's death. Loc was the first to suggest that Bouchet might be an enemy agent, perhaps because he felt threatened by her questions, but he was wrong. She was definitely up to no good, but she wasn't an enemy spy. Of that, he was certain because he'd been given a "hands-off" from his bosses.

The bigger question about Bouchet was the same one he had about Nash. Was she acting on her own, or was she part of something bigger, like an official investigation? He hadn't sold any guns in months. Hopefully, that trail had grown cold, but she continued trying to make the connection between him and Coleridge's death. If she did, it could lead to an official inquiry. He had to stop her.

* * *

Brady sat on his bunk, his head still aching. His mouth tasted like a dusty road in a garbage dump, but some more bourbon would snuff all his problems. He reached for the bottle beneath his bunk and uncorked it. His transistor radio was tuned to the

AFVN, and Johnny Rivers was singing "Summer Rain." Outside, the clouds were growing pregnant again as they blotted out the sun and promised another afternoon of drenching downpours.

He'd just received another letter from Lacey. After taking a swig of the whiskey, he set the bottle aside and tore open the envelope.

Dear Brady,

I hope you are doing OK. I miss you very much, and I wish you would write more often. Mama shares her letters with me, but she said she's no longer getting them as often either. I have some good news. Belle Langston has introduced me to a music writer named Billy Wyatt. He sings and plays the guitar. We are recording some of his songs, and we've been working together on a possible recording deal. He thinks I'm really making progress and will eventually go somewhere. I hope he's right. I quit the job at the restaurant and began singing in some other clubs several times a month. Billy took a bunch of pictures of me performing the other night. I will send you some when we get them developed.

I got a call from Mama the other day. News from home isn't so good. It's about Mr. Brister. Jessica told Mama that her daddy is in the hospital in Knoxville. He had another heart attack, and he's not doing very well. She also told Mama something about a letter you sent her daddy and how he wanted us to get it, but he's in such bad shape, she couldn't understand much of what he said.

If she comes across it, she's going to send it to Mama. Do you know what letter she's talking about?

Please write more. I miss you. In the meantime, take care of yourself, and remember I love you very much.

Yours always,
Lacey

Brady picked up the whiskey bottle and paused, looking at the label. There was a turkey on it, and he thought of Phung Hoang, the mystical bird of a thousand eyes. His was a totally bizarre situation. All his mail was being read. If Lacey or Mama Emma got Duff's letter and wrote him about it, their lives, too, could be in danger, but how could he warn them?

Getting caught in Maxon's office was a foolish mistake. Maxon had acted as if he accepted the explanation, but his eyes told a different story. If only he'd done as Duff suggested and gone to the authorities. It was obvious Maxon thought he was stupid and inept, and for the first time, he was inclined to agree. He tipped up the bottle and finished it.

CHAPTER FIFTHEEN

The Double Cross and Lynn Dai Bouchet

I t could have been an artillery barrage. It sounded no diffe-rent from one of those nights when he first got to Nam. Brady held his eyes tightly shut as he remembered the fire-base on the Cambodian border when the NVA Fortieth Artillery Regiment pounded them every night, night after night. It was hell. Shrapnel-shredded sandbags leaked sand inside the bunkers, and everyone's ears rang from the thunderous explosions, explo-sions so powerful they vibrated in your chest and sucked the air from your lungs. But that wasn't what he was hearing now. It was simply another bad dream, or was it? He fought his way from a deep sleep.

To no avail, he had tried drinking the surrendering guerrilla out of his mind. It was useless, and he cracked one eye to look at his watch. The odor of whiskey hung, stale and nauseating, in the room. He had no idea how long he'd been sleeping, but his head was pounding as loud as the person at the door. Slowly he'd come to realize the source of the barrage, a barrage of fists. The door shook as if it would disintegrate at any moment. It had to be Maxon.

"Damn," Brady muttered, trying to wish him away, but the pounding grew, and Maxon began shouting.

"Wake up, Nash, or I'm going to kick this goddamn door in."

Brady's head throbbed.

"Wake up, you son of a bitch."

Maxon's boot thudded against the door. Moving intensified the pain, but Brady slowly rolled off the bunk and crawled across the floor.

"I'm going to kick your goddamn ass if you don't open this door. You hear me?"

He reached up and turned the latch, and Maxon shoved the door open. Brady fell backward on the floor. Lying on his back, he didn't open his eyes.

"Look at you," Maxon yelled. "I'll be damned if you aren't the sorriest sack of shit I ever laid eyes on."

Brady said nothing as he opened his eyes and stared up at the ceiling fan. The circular motion made him dizzy, and for a moment, he tasted bile in his throat.

"Get your sorry ass dressed, and come with me," Maxon said. "You need to get some food in your stomach, and we need to talk."

Brady grunted and shook his head. "No way."

"Oh yeah," Maxon answered, "you're not going to quit on me now. Get your goddamned clothes on, and let's get some coffee. You can finish your nap after the briefing."

They climbed into Maxon's jeep and drove to a place in Da Nang city. When Brady got his first glass of water, he poured the entire contents over his head. The relief was welcomed, but short-lived, and the young Vietnamese waitress brought him a second glass, which he drank to the bottom.

"Bring more water and two cups of coffee," Maxon said.

Brady sought more relief from his raging hangover, resting his head on the cool surface of the table. It felt almost like ice against his burning skin.

"We received some new intelligence on another enemy agent, and you need to get your shit together."

The room spun crazily as the water he'd just drank belched violently from his stomach, forming a scummy pool on the table. He moved to the side and again laid his cheek against the cool surface. It brought a slight relief to his burning skull.

"Damn, you're a nasty fucker, Nash."

The waitress wiped the table and set a steaming cup of coffee in front of him. After a minute or two, he sat up and, with trembling hands, raised the cup to his lips. Maxon continued talking, but he scarcely heard him as the misery of the hangover raged.

* * *

It seemed only minutes passed before he jerked awake. Disoriented, Brady barely remembered going back to bed after the briefing that morning, but he was suddenly aware that he'd been sleeping for a very long time. He actually felt better, or so he hoped. He hadn't yet sat upright. He glanced at his watch. Maxon said they would meet again at 1800. It was nearly 1730 hours. Slowly and carefully, he rolled over, and when it felt safe, he sat up on the edge of the bunk.

His stomach felt hollow, and the pounding in his head was reduced to a dull ache, but he was taking no chances. He reached for a bottle of aspirin on his footlocker. After shaking several into his hand, he threw the tablets into his mouth and ignored the bitter taste as he chewed and swallowed them. He pulled on his boots, dressed, and shoved the .45 into his shoulder holster. It was time to see what the bastard had up his sleeve this time. Was Maxon going to make a move?

As he walked across the compound yard to Maxon's office, the sun was setting in the hills to the west, its splintering orange and yellow shafts piercing the remnants of an afternoon thunderstorm. He would have taken pause to do as he'd done so many times back home, watching the sun drop into the hills, but there was no longer any sentiment left inside, only a growing lump of fear that had him drawing on survival instincts he never realized existed. He had to think. What to do next?

A wiry little Vietnamese man sat with Maxon in his office when Brady arrived. Sitting cross-legged in a stained easy chair, the man wore tiger-striped fatigues like Maxon's and smoked an unfiltered cigarette. He glanced up as Brady walked in. His eyes were confident, but exhibited little emotion. Perhaps it was his imagination, but Brady saw some of himself in this man. On the floor next to his chair was a Swedish K lying atop a small satchel and a poncho.

"Feeling better?" Maxon asked.

"Yeah," Brady said.

For once, Maxon didn't seem inclined to provoke him, another of those subconscious red flags.

"This is Captain Tri," Maxon said. "He's an interpreter with the PRU, and he's your guide for the mission tonight."

Brady nodded at the captain, but said nothing as Maxon opened a folder lying on his desk.

"This is a dossier on your target. I've suspected her for a long time, but I never figured she would be such a high-level party leader."

He began reading aloud. "Residence: Quang Nam Province." He looked up. "She lives here on the outskirts of Da Nang city." Looking back at the folder, he continued, "Known ties to the NLF and NLF sympathizers. Suspect is believed to have…" Maxon read the summary, and when he finished, he tossed the file aside and stared across the desk at the two men.

"Now this is where it gets tricky, so listen up. She's a double agent. Despite the evidence, there could be a lot of political fallout if we botch this thing. She has friends in high places. If we simply arrest her, she'll probably chieu-hoi and walk. Nash, this is what special ops is about, and you need to trust that we know what we're doing. Put any doubts out of your mind. You are our only hope to save a lot of soldiers' lives. Discuss this mission with no one, understood?"

Brady nodded, but alarms were going off in his head. He could hear the deceit in Maxon's words and in the tone of his voice.

"OK, you and Captain Tri will take one of the jeeps. He'll drive you to a location near the suspect's house. It's a pretty simple snuff. Do it and get back here before daylight. Any questions?"

"What's her name?" Brady asked.

Maxon hesitated as he glanced inside the dossier. "Not that it should make any difference, but according to this report, one of her aliases is Nguyen Cai Li. You never know their real names because these people change names more than I change shirts."

Brady glanced from the corner of his eye at the Vietnamese captain, but he remained expressionless while staring straight ahead.

"When you get the shot, take this woman out," Maxon said. "You understand? You can't hesitate. She's a murderous bitch responsible for giving away intelligence that's gotten a lot of GIs killed. Think you can handle it?"

Brady nodded, but this entire mission had the earmarks of a set-up. If it was so important, why wasn't Maxon going with him? Why was a low-level PRU officer his guide and not one of the special police? Was this how Duff's last mission had gone? Brady cut his eyes toward the man in the chair beside him. What did a killer look like?

"You need to get moving," Maxon said. "It'll be dark soon."

* * *

Captain Tri drove the jeep through the outskirts of Da Nang city at sunset. Chilled by the evening air, Brady felt goose bumps on his arms. He studied the road ahead. Shadows crept across the gravel and up the sides of the houses. The odor of wood smoke and steamed fish hung in the evening air. Nightfall came, and Tri turned on the headlights. The enemy could be anywhere, but it was Tri that Brady watched from the corner of his eye. The little man, squinting against the wind, seemed oblivious to the danger.

After driving a short distance, Tri swerved abruptly onto an unmarked side road. Brady nearly lost his balance as he grabbed the dash. He had barely regained it when Tri again snatched the steering wheel, this time tunneling the jeep directly into a road-side thicket. He burrowed the vehicle deep into the cover, stopping only when the jungle closed behind them and they were out of sight of the road. When he killed the engine and lights, it was pitch-black. A flashlight snapped on.

"Follow me," Tri whispered.

Things were happening quickly. Grabbing his rifle, Brady step-ped out of the jeep and hurried after him as they made their way up a ridge paralleling the road. When the trail reached the top of the ridge, Tri dropped to one knee and switched off his light. Brady did the same, but he held his rifle at the ready.

"We wait here till we can see good," Tri said. "Then we go down this trail to the house."

Mosquitoes buzzed incessantly, but the only other sounds came from the occasional rustling of a night breeze in the trees above. Brady gazed up at a nearly full moon coming and going among the broken clouds. His eyes adjusted to the darkness as the moonbeams filtered through the jungle canopy, casting spooky shadows all around. The minutes passed like hours as he thought about the target, a woman. She would probably have guards. The lunacy of a full moon sent his adrenaline flowing into overdrive.

Brady flinched at the sudden sound of Tri's voice. "We go now," he said.

He stood and signaled for Brady to follow as he moved down the trail. After several hundred meters, they stopped again. Standing on a steep hillside, it seemed they were in the middle of nowhere when the breeze suddenly parted the jungle. Almost as if it were a mirage, an old French mansion appeared at the foot of the ridge. Brady raised his binoculars. The exterior was dark, but dim lights inside cast a soft glow through several open balconies around the second floor. Ornately trimmed, the house was beautiful. Only spidering cracks on the interior plaster walls revealed its age.

Captain Tri moved down the steep slope toward the house, and Brady followed until they reached a small clearing. There the two men stopped, level with a balcony, now less than fifty meters away. It opened into a spacious second-floor bedroom. Tri turned and sat with his back against a tree before raising a pair of binoculars to his eyes.

"Mr. Maxon described this place well," he said as he studied the house through his binoculars.

Brady sat beside Tri and turned his rifle toward the house, scanning it with the scope. There was no one around, and after a few minutes, he lowered the rifle and settled in for the wait. It seemed now that this could be a legitimate mission, but he refused to lower his guard. Something still wasn't right. If this woman was an enemy agent, double or otherwise, how could she live on the outskirts of the main city with no security?

The sound of an approaching vehicle interrupted his thoughts. Back toward the main road, there came the drone of an engine, then headlights flitting among the trees. The vehicle slowed and turned up the narrow access road toward the mansion. A few moments later, a dark, perhaps black, Citroën rolled to a stop in front of the house. The driver switched off the engine and lights, and stepped out.

Brady quickly raised his rifle as the shadow of a person walked up the wide front steps toward the door. This had to be the target, but he couldn't find his crosshairs in the dim light. No more than a vague silhouette, the figure quickly disappeared inside. Brady looked over at his counterpart, but Tri gave no indication of what was to be done. Brady looked back at the house, studying the dim interior.

After a few moments, a light came on inside the bedroom. The soft vanilla glow flooded through the open doors of the balcony and out onto the adjacent hillside. Sudden and bright, it caused Brady to instinctively move behind a tree. When he peeked out again, she was there, the woman, but she was nothing like he expected. Tall and beautiful, she stood near a vanity table, shedding her clothes. He raised his rifle and peered through the scope as her skirt fell to the floor. The riflescope provided a depthless, but crystal-clear and close-up view.

Setting the rifle aside, Brady raised his binoculars. The powerful magnification put him in the room with the woman as every detail of her body came into sharp focus, her rounded but firm buttocks and the glow of her skin. She pulled a strap from each shoulder and shed her bra. Her breasts glowed in the soft light reflecting from the mirror. Completely naked now, she picked up a brush and pulled it through her flowing black hair. His eyes followed her legs upward, over her buttocks and across to the mirror where her full bosom bounced gently as she brushed her hair.

"*Cô ấy là đẹp,*" Tri whispered.

Brady lowered the binoculars and glanced at him. Tri's face was drenched with sweat, and his eyes glowed white in the dim moonlight, but his words seemed strange, almost a plea.

"She is very beautiful woman," Tri said.

"Yes, she is," Brady whispered, "but she doesn't look Vietnamese, at least not... Do you know her?"

There were alarms ringing somewhere in the back of his mind.

"I am not certain. I have never seen her without a scarf and sunglasses, but this woman could be the one who has come asking questions about the men in my unit and the special police officers in your operations group. Some believe she is a spy. I suppose that is why we were sent to assassinate her."

Brady again raised the binoculars and looked back into the woman's bedroom. The thought wouldn't leave him, but it was too far-fetched. This couldn't be Lynn Dai Bouchet. The woman was beautiful with mysterious dark eyes and flowing dark hair that surrounded her mostly Caucasian features. The serene beauty of her Vietnamese blood showed delicately around her eyes. She turned and walked toward the open double door of the balcony. Dropping the binoculars, Brady quickly raised the rifle and looked through the scope as Captain Tri sat wordlessly watching his every move.

The woman stopped at the doors, staring blindly into the darkness. With delicate feminine movements, she pulled one door shut, then stretched on the tips of her toes, reaching for the latch at the top of the other. Her ribs were outlined against the soft skin below her breasts, and as Brady carefully placed the crosshairs on her chest, he felt a throbbing deep within his body. Center mass, he thought to himself. But "mass" was this soft female body.

Her body filled the riflescope, but his eyes wandered down past her navel to the soft patch of dark hair on her groin. For a moment, the spell was broken. He was no longer the mindless killer. How could someone snuff out something, someone, with this kind of beauty? And what if it *was* Lynn Dai Bouchet?

He hesitated and looked up. A gentle breeze stirred in the trees, and the full moon turned the cirrus clouds silver. Far above the shadowy jungle, the sky was nearly bright as day. He had to kill this woman, just as he had killed the young VC recruit trying to surrender that day on the Cu De River. She couldn't be Bouchet, and killing this woman would buy him time. It would give Maxon the false confidence that would make him believe he still owned him. There was no real choice. He had to do it.

Brady again raised the rifle and centered the crosshairs on the woman's chest. As he gently tightened his finger around the trigger, a monkey howled from somewhere deep in the jungle, and an involuntary shudder ran through his body. For a moment, he thought that she, too, shuddered as she hesitated in the doorway.

The smell of the vegetation flooded his senses, and the naked woman seemed superimposed, in all her delicate vulnerability, on the harsh background of the jungle. The crosshairs were an obscenity worse than rape as they quartered and metered her body into increments of elevation and windage. She reached for the other door and began to pull it closed. Brady tightened his finger against the trigger. Slowly, almost reluctantly, it seemed, the door closed. A bead of sweat trickled into his eye as she disappeared from sight.

Lowering the M40, he bowed his head, holding his eyes shut while his heart pounded. Perhaps if he held them closed long enough, the nightmare would go away. Perhaps he would wake up in a greasy sweat in his hooch back at Ben Het and find it was just that—another nightmare. But nothing changed, and he turned to Captain Tri.

"If this woman is an enemy agent like Maxon says, she's not dying tonight. He'll have to find someone else to kill her. I'm not killing another unarmed person, especially one that looks like that."

Tri stared silently at him for several seconds before replying, "Mr. Maxon has made her seem an enemy agent, but I am unsure who is really the double agent."

"What do you mean?" Brady asked.

"I know nothing for certain, except that my unit's missions are often compromised, but this woman could not possibly have had the knowledge to do so. If she is a double agent, then there are two."

"Why didn't you tell Maxon what you know?"

"I tell Mr. Maxon nothing because I do not trust him. He lies, as he has lied about this woman."

"Why do you say that?"

"As I said, I do not believe this woman is Nguyen Cai Li. Although, I am still not certain, I believe she is the one who came asking the questions. That woman's name is Lynn Dai Bouchet."

Brady felt a cold knot in his gut, and began trembling as he realized he'd come within a breath of killing the only person who might help him find Duff's murderer. He sucked down a deep breath. He was stupid, and Maxon was playing him like a fiddle. He was so wrapped up in this mess, he could no longer think straight.

Brady turned to Tri. "This woman you think is Lynn Dai Bouchet, do you believe she is a double agent?"

"I have no way of knowing for certain, but your Mr. Maxon tried to make me believe she is the one responsible for the many failures of our missions. I am simply an officer with my Provincial Reconnaissance Unit, but I know his accusation does not seem true. This woman has little knowledge of our business, and her questions are usually about civilian deaths, not operations."

"So you believe she's innocent?"

"I did not say that. Although, I am confused like you, I follow orders. If they tell me to help you to kill her, then I must."

Brady no longer knew what to think. He wanted to believe that this woman, if she was Lynn Dai Bouchet, was deserving of Duff's trust. Every bit of logic said she was the key to finding his killer, but he was becoming like Maxon. He no longer trusted anyone, not even himself.

The only solution was to confront Lynn Dai Bouchet. Then it would be left to his instincts to find the truth, to listen for the resonance that Will had talked about.

"You must think I'm pretty weak, a coward, because I didn't kill her," Brady said.

"On the contrary, Mr. Nash, I find a man who stands up for what he believes to be a rarity, especially among Americans. You have my deepest respect. I only wish I had your courage."

Brady stood and turned to go. "I'm not sure if I'm standing up for what I believe or running from it. Let's get the hell out of here."

Brady racked his brain, trying to make sense of the situation as they made their way back to the jeep. Maxon had him set up to kill Lynn Dai Bouchet, but why did he lie about her identity? A person could draw any of a number of conclusions, but any one of them could be wrong. Bouchet obviously wasn't in Maxon's camp, but that didn't necessarily make her one of the bad guys. What did she know?

Tri led the way as they crept through a cane thicket the last few meters before reaching the jeep. When they arrived, Brady paused, and it came to him with sudden clarity—it *was* a setup. He caught a momentary glint in the moonlight, a metallic object on the far side of the highway. A keen surge of adrenaline coursed through his body as he grabbed Tri's arm. Signaling for Tri to follow, Brady turned and slipped silently back up the trail into the jungle.

"Hurry," he whispered.

They quickly made their way back up the ridge, putting as much distance as they could between themselves and the jeep. A moment later, an explosion of gunfire erupted from the woods near the roadway. The metallic clack of bullets striking the jeep came from below, and Brady looked back as red tracer rounds ricocheted through the trees around them. He had been right. After he had killed the Bouchet woman, someone was waiting to ambush him. He and Tri trotted over the ridge and circled back to the road leading into Da Nang.

The cards were all on the table, and there was no doubt that Maxon was bent on taking him out, but there were accomplices, faceless, but just as dangerous. Brady was chin deep in a swamp full of alligators. He could no longer wait for Maxon's next move. He had to dictate what happened next.

CHAPTER SIXTEEN

Cunning Tiger

"Someone knew we were to be here," Tri whispered.

Brady squatted with Captain Tri in the tall grass beside the road, watching for movement in the predawn darkness. Like hunted prey, their eyes searched the shadows. The attackers would not give up with the failed ambush. They were probably watching the road back into Da Nang city at this very moment. And now that Brady was certain of Maxon's involvement, returning to the operations center was almost out of the question, except that was where Duff's ID card along with the kill card and telex messages were hidden.

"Someone wants us both dead," Brady said.

The moon had yellowed and hung low and fat on the horizon.

"Who knew about this mission?"

Tri shrugged. "I am uncertain about anyone, except for Mr. Maxon."

"That's right," Brady said.

Their eyes, mere glints of light in the darkness, met, and Tri slowly nodded. "I do not know what is happening, except to say that what you have said is true. Your Mr. Maxon is the only one who knew we were here, and the weapons we heard were American M16s firing, and I saw only red tracers, no AK-47s. I would think it was the special police."

"Is there anything you can tell me about Maxon?" Brady asked.

"There is much, but now we must go. We must leave this place quickly. We will talk later."

Tri was right. Once daylight came, the ones who had ambushed them would search the area.

"We need to separate," Brady said.

Tri nodded, and without another word, he slipped away into the darkness. Brady crept along the edge of the road, stopping frequently as he listened and studied the shadow-splotched terrain. They were out there lying in wait. The compound was only a few kilometers straight-line distance, but taking the road back was out of the question. The only way was to loop north around the obvious ambush points.

Weaving his way along unfamiliar trails, through woodlots and behind rows of houses, Brady moved like a cat in the night through the outskirts of the city. The full moon eventually faded into dawn, and dawn into daylight, and by late morning, he arrived outside the compound gates. Muddy and exhausted, he stood watching the compound entrance. Maxon and the special branch officers weren't there, probably out scouring the countryside for him. He needed clean clothes, but most of all, he needed the evidence he'd taken from Maxon's office.

Boldness seemed the best tactic for getting past the guards. If they hadn't been forewarned, he could walk in with no problem. Throwing his rifle on his shoulder, he sauntered toward the compound gate. The gravel crunched almost too loudly beneath his boots as he walked, but the guard seemed relaxed and smiled, giving him a nod of recognition. Brady tried to appear confident as he saluted and walked past. It worked, and as he stepped inside the compound, he quickly scanned the buildings. The entire compound appeared vacant, for the moment. Trying to maintain his nonchalance, he walked across the yard toward the Quonset hut. There were no vehicles anywhere, and the only person visible was another guard posted at the operations center door.

Once he reached his room, Brady quickly toweled off and donned clean fatigues. He pulled the cards and telex messages from their hiding place behind a loose wall panel, and stuffed them into his pocket. He needed a weapon, but the rifle would only draw attention on the street. After stripping off the fatigue shirt again, he grabbed his shoulder holster with the .45, strapped it on, then pulled the fatigue shirt over it. After stuffing a poncho and change of clothes into a bag, he moved to the door, where he paused to look outside at the compound. It was still deserted, almost too quiet, but he couldn't stop. There was no time to freeze up now.

Casually, but wasting no time, he walked back through the main gate, giving the guards a friendly salute and this time a smile.

He hurried to reach a crowded street as he headed through the heart of Da Nang city. He'd been lucky so far, but he had to escape into the anonymity of the city and somewhere find a journalist or Army CID. Out of ideas and with desperation overtaking him, he studied every person and passing vehicle. A growing sense of paranoia left him raw-nerved as he flinched at a crack of thunder from a gathering thunderstorm. An upward glance revealed a looming thunderhead, but there was something else nagging him, a sixth sense. He cast a quick glance over his shoulder, and though he saw no one suspicious, he knew he was being followed.

He stopped at an intersection, turning to the side as he lit a cigarette and studied his back trail from the corner of his eye. There were scores of people walking the busy street, but no one stood out. None of them even remotely resembled a threat, except …He spotted a skinny kid, a black-haired boy wearing khaki shorts and Ho Chi Minh sandals.

The boy ambled along in the crowd, several hundred feet behind him, and though a child, he looked nervous, holding his head low while cutting his eyes up ahead. Taking his time, Brady turned and made his way through the center of an open-air market while keeping an eye on the boy. The youngster seemed unsure of himself, yet intent on following him.

When he reached the far end of the market, Brady found an isolated place in the shadows behind one of the wooden stalls. An old woman chewing betel nuts watched with squinted eyes as he ducked behind the stall and drew his pistol. A moment later, the boy rounded the corner and stopped abruptly, staring cross-eyed into the barrel of Brady's .45.

Brady stepped farther back into the shadows. "*Lai day,*" he said, motioning the boy closer.

The boy, wide-eyed with terror, stepped forward, extending in his hand a folded piece of paper. Brady snatched it away, but as he began unfolding it, the boy turned and fled.

"*Dung Lai!*" Brady shouted, but to no avail. The boy quickly disappeared. He glanced down at the paper. There was a note scrawled in black ink:

> M. Bouchet requests you meet with her in Saigon as soon as possible. She has information which may be of importance to you. Contact her through the man named Than at the Continental Palace Hotel.

It was not signed, but he read the name again, M. Bouchet. How? It had to be Captain Tri. He must have gone back to the house and told her what happened. Maxon wanted her dead for some reason, but why? Perhaps this was why Bouchet had gone all the way to Saigon. What was it that she knew about him? He thought of the chances Tri must have taken to warn her. People were risking their lives for what, certainly not so that he could fulfill his mission of finding Duff's killers. But maybe that was it. Maybe they hoped he could make a difference. Maxon was as much a threat to them as the enemy.

Stuffing the note into his pocket, he began walking as another tropical rain burst from the sky. The rain was a blessing. Brady donned his hooded poncho, knowing it made him difficult to recognize, but he remained cautious. If the boy had been able to find him, anyone could. Glancing over his shoulder, he hurried through the streets toward the Da Nang Air Base.

Despite his poncho, he was drenched by the time he hitched a ride into the air base. After looking over his SOG orders and military ID, the NCO at the operations desk seemed puzzled, but shrugged and informed him that the next flight to Saigon wouldn't depart until dawn. Wet and miserable, Brady found a large vinyl easy chair in the waiting area. It was stained and reeked with the odor of stale cigarettes, but it was better than sleeping on the floor.

Curled on his side between the huge foam-stuffed vinyl arms, he shifted his weight side to side, twisting and turning as he tried to get comfortable. But after a while, he gave up, lying catlike with one eye open. He noted every person who came and went. Maxon was no doubt searching for him, but was probably still focused on the countryside outside Da Nang. His only hope was to catch the flight before Maxon extended the search. He kept a nervous eye on the NCO behind the desk.

By the time the flight was ready to depart, another gray dawn had broken, and the sky was still dripping relentlessly. Brady glanced over his shoulder as he walked across the tarmac to the C-130. The crew in the cockpit above sat behind the wall of Plexiglas panes, going through their final flight checklist. There were only a few ARVN guards and some marines standing around the buil-ding. None of them looked particularly dangerous, but he was on borrowed time. Exhausted, Brady boarded the plane. Tossing his bag under the web seat, he sat and closed his eyes. The monotonous drone of the turboprop engines quickly drove him into a deep sleep.

* * *

Brady jerked awake as the C-130 hit the tarmac at Tan Son Nhut. It had been a sleep of death. He'd not even dreamed since leaving Da Nang, and he fought to gather his wits as he boarded the green army bus for downtown Saigon.

Stepping off the bus, Brady was immediately struck with déjà-vu. The city hadn't changed much since Tet. That night of terror down near the Cholon district seemed forever tattooed on his brain, and a familiar sense of foreboding reminded him that the war might explode anywhere at any moment. The scars remained everywhere in the city, bullet-riddled walls and boarded windows, stark reminders of the ferocity of the battle.

Entering the Continental Palace Hotel, he quickly found the man named in the note, Than. He was ancient. With brown leather skin and thinning gray hair, it seemed only his eyes glowed with life. He smiled and nodded, until Brady identified himself. After reading the note, the little man's face suddenly tightened, and a fine sheen of perspiration instantly appeared. His eyes no longer glowed. Only after casting furtive glances in several directions did he seem satisfied that no one was watching.

With his eyes continuing to dart nervously about, he whispered to Brady, "You come back later. You come at eight o'clock. I bring you word from lady."

"No!" Brady tried to whisper, but his voice cracked. "I've got to see her now."

"Phung Hoang see all," the little man hissed.

"Phung Hoang?" Brady whispered. "Tell me about Phung Hoang. I need to know more."

"*Xau Lem,*" the man said.

"What? What does that mean? You've got to tell me more."

The man wagged his head emphatically. "*Khong lau,*" he said and scurried away.

Brady stood staring as the little man disappeared. The fear and paranoia created by Phung Hoang apparently had its effect. Most likely spawned by the kill cards placed on the bodies, it had spread until even those working on the side of the government were terrorized. There was no use following Than. He was obviously scared out of his wits. Brady walked across the lobby and back out onto the street.

It was still early, and a hazy sunshine drenched the city. Ambling up the street, he found the restaurant where he and Maxon had eaten supper back in January. After ordering a Coke, he pulled Lacey's letter from his pocket. After all this time, it still remained unanswered, but now he had to warn her in case she somehow got Duff's letter from Mr. Brister.

Brady pulled an envelope and notepad from his overnight bag and began writing.

Dear Lacey,

I know I haven't written you enough during the last few months, but this letter is especially important. I want to tell you how much you mean to me. You have never understood why I came over here, but I hope you will believe me when I tell you again that I had no choice. Recently, I have found myself in the same situation as Duff. If you got the letter from Mr. Brister, you know what I'm talking about. I gave it to him before I left home. A soldier who knew Duff brought it to me in Melody Hill because Duff believed that all his mail was being read. Now my mail is being read too, except for this letter. I am mailing it in Saigon. Whatever you do, never write me about any of this, and above all, don't ever mention Duff's letter to anyone. It could be very dangerous for you if you do. I am not sure how all this will turn out, but I hope you will forgive me someday for everything I've put you through. Please know how much I truly love you. And if God is willing, we will spend the remainder of our lives together when I return.

Love always,
Brady

He slipped the letter into the envelope and glanced at his watch. Barely twenty minutes had elapsed. He looked at his watch a hundred more times before the hands finally crept close to 2000. By then, he was tense but ready as he stepped back onto the street. Taking a deep breath, he paused and looked about. The evening air in Saigon was stifling compared to the Northern Highlands. Two white-helmeted policemen with M16s stood at the nearby intersection, and the sidewalks were crowded, but nothing suspicious caught his eye. Wasting no time, he hurried back to the Continental.

Than was waiting for him when he walked inside. Motioning for Brady to follow, the little man ducked into a darkened alcove, where they met in the shadows. Than refused to make eye contact as he again cast furtive glances all about. When he seemed satisfied it was safe, he handed Brady a note. The paranoia was infectious, as Brady caught himself looking around before reading it.

Mr. Nash,
Please meet me in the L'Amiral restaurant at 8:30 p.m. I believe you know my face. I will be seated alone.
M. Bouchet

Than gazed steadily out at the hotel lobby. Perhaps a little incentive would get him to talk. Brady pulled a wad of piastres from his pocket and shoved them into the man's hand. Than quickly shoved the money into his pocket.

"You numba one, guy," he said. "Many thanks."

"It's not that simple," Brady said. "The Ps are for information. Tell me…"

Than turned and walked away, shaking his head. "You talk to lady. It too dangerous us talk here. Phung Hoang see all."

Whatever the little man feared was now exerting the same influence on Brady, as he found himself infected. Thirty minutes later, his paranoia peaked as he walked into the L'Amiral restaurant. There were people seated everywhere, but only one woman was seated alone at a table near the back wall. Despite a scarf and dark glasses, he recognized her immediately. It was Lynn Dai Bouchet.

As he made his way toward the table, Bouchet glanced his way and removed her glasses. Their eyes met, and Brady gave a clumsy grin. She acknowledged him with a slight nod. Never had he felt as inept as he did now standing at the table. He didn't know whether to treat her like a kitten or a cobra.

"*Chao co,*" he said.

"*Bonsoir,*" she said. "I am Lynn Dai Bouchet. I do speak Vietnamese, and also French, but I presume you would prefer English. You are Mr. Nash?"

Her complexion was firm and clean and her features delicate in the dim light of the restaurant. Her face was even more beautiful than her body—if that was possible. Brady found himself mesmerized, the same as he was two nights before on the hillside outside her bedroom.

"Oh, uh, yes. Yes, ma'am. Brady Nash."

She extended her hand. "You are so much younger than I imagined, Mr. Nash. Oh, but please forgive me. Would you be so kind as to join me?"

The pungent odor of peppers and rice wafted through the restaurant as Brady sat across from her.

"I appreciate that you have traveled this far to meet with me. I know that it was a very long distance to come, but I had no choice except to leave Da Nang. You see, I no longer feel safe, and I am leaving the country tomorrow to live with relatives in France. If you are willing, I wish to talk with you before I go."

"Well, I am here, Miss Bouchet. What would you like to talk about?"

She seemed to accept his terse reply as if he were the most gracious gentleman in all of Saigon.

"Please, call me Lynn Dai," she said. "As I was saying, I am leaving the country and wish only to talk briefly with you."

A waiter approached the table.

"Bring me a double bourbon over ice," Brady said. He noticed Bouchet had a glass of white wine. "You want another glass of wine?"

She shook her head. When the waiter left, he looked across the table at her.

"I suppose we can talk, but how much I say really depends on what you want to talk about."

"Mr. Nash, I do not know why you did not kill me the other night, and perhaps you do not wish to tell me, but I wish to express to you my deepest gratitude for sparing my life. Also, I want to give you information in return that may be of help to you."

"The reason I didn't kill you is simple, Mi...Lynn Dai. It's because I have a problem with killing unarmed people, especially women."

"But why were you sent to kill me?"

"Maybe I need to ask you the questions first," he said.

"What is it that you would like to know, Mr. Nash?"

"I suppose we could start with your explanation for asking me to come here," he said.

Brady glanced around the restaurant. There were several Americans and Europeans sitting at tables, but one other table was occupied by a lone Vietnamese man. He sat facing away from them, but Brady felt as if he was being watched, nothing concrete, just another of those strange premonitions that had become so frequent in recent months.

"There is no need to be alarmed, Mr. Nash. To the best of my knowledge, we are alone, and my intentions are in no way meant to bring you harm."

Brady realized he was telegraphing his every thought.

"I heard the gunfire near my home the other night, and it frightened me. Later, a man, Captain Tri, came to inform me of what had happened. He said it was your mission to kill me. I know of the man for whom you work, Mr. Maxon. I also know of his organization, and I also know of your own reputation among the Vietnamese. You are held in high esteem by those in both armies."

"Oh?"

"Let me come to the point, Mr. Nash. First of all, I am not a member of the National Liberation Front, the Vietcong you call them. The reason I am telling you this is because I was told that this was the reason you were sent to kill me, but this is truly irrelevant. My purpose here is to return your favor by informing you of the imminent danger to your own life."

Brady said nothing.

"Let me explain," she said. "I am sure you are aware of the price placed on your head by the National Liberation Front."

The waiter returned with his drink. Brady paused until the waiter was gone again.

"I don't know what you're talking about. Why is there a price on my head?"

"Do you mean that you have not heard what they call you in the enemy camps?"

Brady shook his head.

"They call you Xảo Quyệt Hổ. Let me think. I believe an appropriate translation would be 'Cunning Tiger.' You are as much revered by your enemy as you are feared."

Brady grunted while giving her the slightest hint of a humorless grin. Mr. Tiger had his ass in a bind at the moment.

"Do not take yourself so lightly, Mr. Nash. Your enemies in the NLF have not, and that is why they have placed this price on your life. I have heard from people as far away as Hue who know of you, but I must warn you. You are in far greater danger from the people with whom you are working."

Brady paused for a moment before he spoke. "Who are these people? Give me some names."

"I have no proof, but I believe one is Mr. Maxon. I believe he is seeking to have you killed."

Brady wanted to grab hold of this information and cling to it as final verification, but paranoia ruled his life. There was still a chance that this could be an elaborate scheme of manipulation. What if this woman was an NLF agent? Reason and logic made it seem impossible, but...

"If you aren't NLF, how come you know so much?"

"I am employed by my country's Military Security Service, and for many months, my primary duty has involved this one mission. You see, because their operations have been continually compromised, we are reasonably certain the An Ninh have an agent among the officer cadre of the special police unit that Mr. Maxon advises. Up until now, I have reported only to the MSS office here in Saigon. Therefore, no one in Da Nang is supposed to know that I am an agent. I have tried for a long time, without success, to expose the spy."

Brady said nothing as the pieces to the puzzle began falling into place.

"You see, the Military Security Service recruited me, because of my job at the Civic Action Center. I worked there as a liaison for the South Vietnamese government, representing Vietnamese civilians making claims against the United States military for the deaths of family members and relatives. I worked closely with many groups, including Mr. Maxon and the special police at the operations center to determine if claims for retribution are legitimate. At the same time, I have worked to determine who among them is the NLF agent, but because there is a great deal of politics involved, I have had to work slowly and unobtrusively."

"What politics are those?"

"I have been given strict orders that my investigation must not interfere with Phung Hoang."

"Phung Hoang?" Brady said.

"Yes, the Phoenix Program is the name used by your government. The activities of Mr. Maxon and the Special Branch are condoned at the highest levels of both governments; thus, Mr. Maxon is protected because even his own government fails to realize that he is murdering innocent people. He is cunning and deceitful and uses this protection to further his own agenda. Yet he fears his superiors will discover his treachery, and this is the reason he seeks to have those killed who may hold such information."

"People like yourself?"

"Yes, and people like you, Mr. Nash. I am unsure why he wants to kill you, but I believe I know why I am now a target. I suspect this is because the spy in Mr. Maxon's group knows of my MSS mission, but the only way he could have gotten this information was from someone here in Saigon. I believe this happened when Mr. Maxon sent false information to my superiors to make it seem as if I were an agent for the An Ninh. When he was told to take no further action against me, I believe he informed the Special Branch officers, and the actual An Ninh agent there deduced my role."

Brady sipped his bourbon as he contemplated the things Bouchet said. "Why would Maxon send false information about you?" he asked.

"I am afraid that this becomes even more of a complicated story, Mr. Nash. It began two years ago, when Mr. Maxon took a personal interest in me and asked me for dates on several occasions. I refused, but he persisted. I felt as I did for the obvious professional reasons and also because he and his special operations people were known in the northern part of the country for their arbitrary and ruthless acts of violence. Then in January of nineteen sixty-seven, I met a young American soldier much like yourself. His name was—"

"Duff Coleridge," Brady said.

Lynn Dai's face paled, and her eyes widened. Experiencing the acute awareness brought on by the adrenaline coursing through his veins, Brady heard the metallic ticking of his Seiko watch as clear as his own heartbeat. Suddenly vulnerable, Lynn Dai swallowed hard, obviously fighting to maintain her composure. A lump grew in his throat as he saw something in her eyes, something he hadn't noticed before. It was a deep melancholy. Lynn Dai cocked her head ever so slightly, her eyes moist.

"You knew Duff Coleridge?"

Taking a deep breath, Brady forced himself to remain calm. "Yes," he said. "Duff was murdered by someone in this country, and I came here to find that person."

"Mr. Nash, I believe you are working for that person. Although I have been unable to obtain conclusive proof that he murdered Duff, I can tell you that Mr. Maxon was at the center of the treachery that caused Duff's death."

Brady studied her face. He was certain now of Lynn Dai Bouchet's innocence, but he had to put her to one more test.

"Maxon told me that it was you that killed Duff."

Lynn Dai's facade crumbled as tears welled in her eyes. "No! No! I loved Duff with all my heart! He meant more to me than anything in this world. We hoped to be married someday."

He had become as cold and callous as Maxon, but every hint of doubt had disappeared. Her love for Duff was something she couldn't hide. Lynn Dai quickly regained her composure. Taking a deep but quavering breath, she paused, then spoke.

"Allow me to explain further," she said. "You see, I found Duff to be an honorable person, but I also discovered that he was working with Mr. Maxon. I went to Duff and explained to him my concern about his boss's activities. During this time, Mr. Maxon discovered our relationship and became jealous. He threatened Duff, but Duff confronted him about the murder of innocent people.

When Duff refused to unjustly kill civilians, Mr. Maxon became enraged. Duff told me of this.

"He also told me how Mr. Maxon was selling weapons on the black market that were meant for the Provincial Reconnaissance Units. Because of his knowledge of the killings and the stolen weapons, Duff said that he felt threatened. It was soon after this that he was killed.

"A few days after his death, I began questioning the PRU members who were on that mission. Later, a Captain Truc came to me at the embassy house in Da Nang. He had heard that I was asking questions about Duff's death. He seemed very frightened, but he told me that Duff's death was not an accident. He said Mr. Maxon was involved, but that it was one of the special police who actually murdered him. That moment, before Captain Truc could tell me the person's name, Mr. Maxon came into my office. He seemed not at all surprised to find Captain Truc there and told him to report immediately to Major Loc at the operations center for a pre-mission briefing.

"When Truc had gone, Mr. Maxon told me that I was asking too many questions. He became angry during our conversation and said that I was interfering with my own government's special police, and if I didn't stay away, he would have them come talk to me. He left my office, and the next day, I learned that Captain Truc had been killed. It was also soon after this incident that my name began appearing as an NLF sympathizer.

"When I spoke with Captain Tri last night, I questioned him extensively, and he also told me that he had heard rumor of Maxon attempting to recruit someone to kill an American shortly before Duff was murdered. Mr. Maxon obviously found someone, and I believe it was the NLF agent within his own operations group. I believe this agent is manipulating him, and he doesn't even realize it. I believe it is this agent who murdered Duff and will murder you also if you do not flee. I also believe Mr. Maxon is responsible for your attempt to kill me, because he knows that I suspect his involvement with Duff's murder as well as his other illegal activities."

Brady reached across the table and put his hand atop Lynn Dai's. "I'm sorry I hurt your feelings. I know now why Duff cared for you. You're a strong person."

A fat teardrop welled from her eye and trickled down her cheek. Lynn Dai wiped it away and nodded. "Please forgive me. My thoughts of Duff—"

"There is no reason to apologize, Lynn Dai, but I need to ask you another question."

She drew a faltering breath and put a sad smile on her face. "Please, continue with your questions."

"Who is he, the NLF agent?" Brady asked. "Do you know?"

"I have narrowed the possibilities to two men. The agent is either Colonel Tranh or Major Loc."

"I think it's Loc," Brady said.

"It could be, Mr. Nash, but Colonel Tranh is not yet beyond suspicion. Whoever this agent may be, he is very clever and very ruthless. Major Loc could be simply following orders."

"There is one thing I don't understand," Brady said. "Why was Captain Tri willing to let me kill you, yet afterward, he went to warn you?"

"Captain Tri did not know that I worked for the Military Security Service. He had also heard the fabricated rumors that I was an enemy agent, but he recognized the sounds of the weapons used in the ambush that night to be American M16s, not the SKS rifles and AK-47s used by the Vietcong. The only one who knew you and Captain Tri were there was Mr. Maxon. Captain Tri had also heard rumor of an MSS agent investigating Maxon's activities. He knew then that I must be that agent because of the inquiries I had made among the men in his unit. He also realized that he had become an unwitting pawn used to kill me. I have aided him in escaping as well."

"My God," Brady muttered. "This is total insanity. How do you ever hope to separate the people you trust from those you don't?"

Lynn Dai nodded and smiled, her soft brown eyes glowing in the dim light. "You are much like Duff. You make wise observations. Allow me to tell you some things about the politics of this country. You see, I have no certain knowledge of the allegiances of many of the people whom I must question. That is why I am very careful in the things I say and the questions I ask. It is this way with many people in Vietnam.

"Those who suspect their neighbors are members of the National Liberation Front often choose to ignore it for the well-being of their families. Yes, it is a false hope that has been violated many times by both sides, especially the Communists, but it is the only one remaining. Many people believe this complicit ignorance will protect them from whichever group next comes to power.

"Although Captain Tri is not an NLF agent, I assure you many of the people who give me information are. There are many agents and double agents in our government, even at the very highest levels. That is why I am careful with the information I obtain. You see, there is no simple right or wrong, good or bad. And this conflict is not simply one between the capitalists and the Communists.

"Many people have chosen the NLF, but not all of them are Communist. Diem ruled with an iron fist until he drove many people to the other side. They only want freedom for their country, but they cannot see the folly in their allegiance with the Communists. If they take control of this country, I believe the Communists will become even more oppressive than Diem's government.

"Your government has come to this country in ignorance, and they have ignored these things. This is truly a civil war, which can be solved only by the Vietnamese people. Yet your government tries to gain allegiance and solve problems with men like Diem and Mr. Maxon. The people of South Vietnam do not know whom to trust or with whom they should place their allegiance. And now, I have reached that point myself. That is why I am leaving."

She was silent, and for several seconds, Brady looked into her eyes. There was something mysteriously attractive about Lynn Dai Bouchet, something more than the physical attraction. He understood how Duff had been drawn to her. She was herself as complex as her country.

"How can I thank you?" he asked.

"There is no need," she said. "You have given me the opportunity I need, and I am leaving tomorrow. I am going to France to live with my father's family until a time comes when I can return safely to my home in Quang Nam Province."

"Miss Bouchet, I need your help."

"Certainly, if I can," she answered.

"First, will you please mail this letter when you get to France?"

He slid the envelope beneath a napkin and pushed it across the table to her.

"I also want to contact a journalist, a war correspondent perhaps."

"There are several residing at the Continental Palace Hotel, where you were earlier. I do not know their names, but the man, Than, whom you spoke with, he can help you."

Brady stood and extended his hand. "Good enough."

She gripped it lightly.

"Good luck to you, Mr. Nash. Perhaps someday we will have the opportunity to meet again when circumstances have changed. I believe it would have been a pleasure to have known you better."

"Thank you. My sentiments are the same, and you can rest assured the people who killed Duff will pay."

Their eyes locked for several moments before Lynn Dai nodded carefully. "Your title is well deserved, Mr. Nash. I have no doubt that Mr. Maxon will someday face his reckoning with *Xảo Quyệt Hổ*. I wish you well."

CHAPTER SEVENTEEN

The Bird of a Thousand Eyes

As he made his way up Tu Do Street, Brady again felt the paranoia. Somewhere in the back of his mind, he sensed the ticking clock, the one that said his time was running out. A sea of cyclos, pedicabs, and motorcycles clogged the street, and people crowded the sidewalks: men with black slacks and white shirts, white-helmeted policemen, soldiers in uniform, and women, some in *ao dais* and others wearing sundresses or pantsuits. The crowd flowed and intermingled, and Brady felt that sixth sense as he glanced about. He was being watched, but the nighttime lights and shadows camouflaged his stalker.

Than was still on duty at the Continental when he arrived, and the little Vietnamese man again glanced about in fear when asked about the correspondent. Backing away, he acted as if Brady was a leper.

"Three men, they stay room two oh seven. One there now, but you go away now. Do not come again."

A few minutes later, Brady tapped at the door to 207. There was no answer. He knocked again, this time louder. From inside came a faint shuffling, and someone coughed.

"Yeah, who is it?" came a groggy voice.

"My name is Nash, and I need to talk with a war correspondent."

An interminable wait ensued until the doorknob slowly turned, and a man wearing green boxers stood before him, rubbing his eyes. The man eyed Brady, then pushed his longish brown hair back on his head as he turned and walked back to the bed, leaving the door open. He looked to be in his midtwenties with a flak jacket tan. Brady stood in the doorway.

"Come in. Come in. Shut the door. What'd you say your name was?"

Overhead, a rusty ceiling fan slowly pulsed in monotonous circles.

"Nash, Brady Nash, and you?"

The man yawned, then bent over to an ashtray on the floor. He picked up a Zippo and a half-smoked joint. The lighter made a metallic ping as he flipped it open and lit the joint.

"I'm Richard Mathis, freelance correspondent on assignment for about a dozen different publications. What can I do for you, Mr. Nash?"

Brady held out his hand, and the man gingerly switched the joint from his right hand to his left, then shook hands.

"I need to talk with you and give you some information, information that's, well, let's say it's dangerous for the person who has it."

Mathis closed his eyes and sucked the smoke into his lungs. "Dangerous, huh?"

Brady nodded.

"Here," Mathis said as he stood and threw a dusty rucksack from a chair, "have a seat. You want a joint?"

Brady looked at him, and though the look was subtle, he was certain Mathis understood.

"Well, how about a drink? There are a couple of bottles over there beside the sink."

Brady walked over and picked up one of the bottles.

"The glasses are up there in the cabinet, and there's ice in the freezer. Just bust the tray over a bowl in the sink."

After filling a large glass with ice, Brady poured it full of Jack Daniel's.

"Damn. You don't mess around. Do you?"

"I guess we all have our ways of dealing with this crap," Brady said, eyeing the joint.

Mathis smiled and took another drag. "So tell me about this information you have."

Brady sat in the chair. It was covered with a fine red dust from the rucksack Mathis had just thrown on the floor. "I was originally assigned to a ranger recon platoon attached to the 173rd Airborne Brigade. My last regular assignment, though, was with the 101st up at Camp Eagle, but I've been with a special operations group the last few months, working out of Da Nang."

Mathis closed his eyes and sucked hard on the joint, then held his breath.

"If I give you this information, I want you to promise me you will do your best to get it printed in a newspaper, but you need to understand something. It's stuff that can get you killed."

Mathis stood and grabbed a pair of fatigue pants from the end of the bed and pulled them on. "I've got an incredible case of the munchies, man. Just got back from three days up around Tay Ninh. Nothing but Cs the whole time."

Brady shrugged. "You should eat Cs for months on end."

Mathis gave a dry laugh as he began buttoning his shirt. "Yeah, I suppose I shouldn't complain. Let's see…Nash, Nash…damn, that rings a bell. Do I know you?"

"I doubt it," Brady said. "I worked as a sniper up around Dak To for a while, then—"

Mathis stopped buttoning and looked up. "I know who you are. You're him, the one the gooks put a bounty on, right?"

"So I've heard," Brady said.

"Shit. I was heading up-country to interview you, but all of a sudden, no one knew where you were. They said it was temporary duty, but the orders were classified. Man, you're the stuff legends are made of. You know that?"

"Yeah, but legends are usually about dead people, and I'd like to avoid that for a while."

"Man, this is great," Mathis said. "Let's go find something to eat, and we'll talk. How about it?"

The late-night air on Tu Do Street was thick and heavy, but the crowds had thinned considerably. Brady glanced over his shoulder.

"You expecting company?" Mathis asked. Despite being stoned, he seemed to have the instincts of a vet.

"You ever hear of something called Phung Hoang, or the Phoenix Program?" Brady asked.

Mathis locked eyes with him for several seconds as he stopped walking. "Let's forget the food," he said.

They found a bar a few blocks away, and when they'd sat down and ordered their beer, Brady laid the wrinkled telex dispatches along with Duff's ID on the table. Mathis didn't bother with his beer as he lit a cigarette and began examining each paper. After a few minutes, he looked up.

"Where'd you get these?"

"From an advisor's office at an interrogation and operations coordination center office outside of Da Nang."

"CIA?" Mathis asked.

Brady nodded. "Yeah, I'm pretty sure he is. Officially, he advises the Vietnamese special police detachment there, but he also has an American SOG unit and a Provincial Reconnaissance Unit working for him."

Mathis glanced back at the dispatches, then at Brady. "We've investigated dozens of kidnappings and killings that we thought were related to covert programs, but we never got anywhere. You're right about one thing, this is some dangerous stuff. The CIA doesn't want it in the *New York Times*, that's for sure. How much do you know about this business you're involved in?"

Brady shrugged. "Enough to make them want to kill me. I got involved almost two years ago when I received a letter from a friend, Duff Coleridge. That's his military ID there. I was still living at home, and…"

After several minutes, Brady finished his story and sat back.

Mathis held up two fingers to the waitress as he ordered two more beers. He turned to Brady. "Let me fill in some of the blanks for you. You see, Phung Hoang is the Vietnamese legendary bird of a thousand eyes that sees all. It's also the name for the Vietnamese version of a top secret program the CIA has put together. It grew out of ICEX, another program developed to ferret out the VC, but we think there's been a lot of unofficial freelancing, if you know what I mean. Corpses have been turning up with Phung Hoang kill cards on them, and other people are simply disappea-ring altogether.

"The Americans call it the Phoenix Program, but most of what I've gathered up to now has been hearsay. I believe a new version of the program has been under development since Tet, but I heard the Vietnamese hadn't bought into it. But you're saying the special police were already involved a couple years ago. And this loose cannon, Maxon, an American killing another American, this is really crazy. Do you think he knows you're talking to the press?"

"I'm not sure," Brady answered. "I've had the feeling that I'm being followed ever since I got to Saigon, but it's probably just paranoia."

"Do you realize the possible ramifications of what you're doing?" Mathis asked.

Brady glanced down at Duff's bloody ID. "I reckon so."

"Same thing could happen to you, but they really don't have to kill you, you know?"

Brady shook his head. "What do you mean?"

"They might simply discredit you," Mathis said, "or they could bring charges against you, saying you acted independently when you tried to kill the Bouchet woman. They might do a number of things. These are some slick bastards you're running with. I just want you to know what you're facing. We can go after them, but there's no guarantee how things will turn out."

"Life has no guarantees," Brady replied. "Just do the best you can, and I'll fend for myself."

"I want to pick this apart," Mathis said. "The more facts I can get, the better our case will be. I can't go to a bureau chief with a bunch of unsubstantiated crap."

Mathis flipped the page of his notebook, and for several minutes, he asked questions and took notes. When he finally laid his pen aside, he looked across the table at Brady. Mathis wasn't a big man. He wore little wire-rimmed glasses while he was writing, but his eyes were hardened, and his face and arms had that raw Vietnamese suntan.

"This is the kind of stuff that wins Pulitzer Prizes."

Brady tried to restrain himself, but it was no use. He set his beer down hard on the table. "Mr. Mathis, I don't give a fuck about any damned prizes."

Red-faced, Mathis avoided eye contact as he carefully folded the papers and put them inside his notebook. He then tucked Duff's ID into his wallet and looked back across the table at Brady.

"Sorry," he said. "Really, I didn't mean that the way it sounded."

Brady didn't acknowledge him as he stared out the window at the street outside. A jeep passed slowly, red and violet neon reflecting from the windshield.

"I'll do my best with what you've given me," Mathis said, "but it may take a while to get it out in the open. They always want to verify the facts and sources before we send anything back to New York. Where are you going in the meantime?"

"I'm heading back to Da Nang."

Mathis paused as he lit a cigarette. "Why?"

"I'm going back up there and sleep with those bastards. I want them to try to do to me what they did to Duff."

"Man, are you crazy? Why don't you just stay cool? Lay low somewhere here in Saigon. As a matter of fact, you can stay with us at the Continental."

Brady shook his head. "Can't do it. Just get your ass in gear and bring CID up to Da Nang as soon as you can."

"Look," Mathis said, "I don't want to seem pessimistic, but let's say you go back up there and get your ass greased. What am I going to do without my star witness?"

"I've given you enough names and information to nail Maxon, but you're only my backup."

"What are you saying?"

"I'm saying, I'm going up there, and I'm going to finish this thing the way they finished Duff."

Mathis shook his head. "You're screwing up. If you don't get killed, you'll end up in Leavenworth for the rest of your life."

"You do your part, and I'll do mine," Brady said.

Mathis waved off the waitress and ground his cigarette in the ashtray. "OK, have it your way, but I still say you're fucking up. How can I get a copy of that letter Duff Coleridge wrote to you?"

"Contact Hubert Brister. He's a neighbor of mine back in Melody Hill, but he's in the hospital in Knoxville right now. He's got the letter."

Mathis stood and extended his hand across the table. "Good luck, but I really wish you'd reconsider going back to Da Nang until I can get back with you. I'll move quick as I can."

"Sorry," Brady said. As he shook hands with Mathis, he looked up and down the street. "You need to watch your back too."

"Don't worry about me," Mathis said. "I can take care of myself. Besides, I've already been to hell and back in this country. I'll catch up with you in a couple of days."

Brady instinctively touched the lump of the .45 beneath his shirt as he watched Mathis head up the street toward the Continental. Several women in *ao dais* passed by, but it was a skinny Vietnamese man wearing gold-rimmed sunglasses that caught Brady's attention. Why was the son of a bitch wearing sunglasses at night?

Nearly a block away and on the opposite side of the street, the man was too far away to be recognized. He wore the standard black trousers and white shirt, but when he stopped to light a cigarette, he somehow seemed familiar. The man exhaled a cloud of smoke into the night air, then glanced back in Brady's direction. After a moment or two, he turned and slowly sauntered up the street.

"Damn!" Brady muttered under his breath.

Everyone seemed suspicious, but Maxon couldn't possibly know he was in Saigon, could he? He turned slowly in a circle as he looked up and down the street. The paranoia crawled around inside his skull like a trapped insect. Phung Hoang was controlling his every thought. He shook his head. The longer he stayed in Nam, the more believable the legends became.

CHAPTER EIGHTEEN

Missing in Action

Brady checked his watch as the C-130 Hercules touched down at Da Nang Air Base. He'd been gone over twenty-four hours. Maxon and the special police had probably searched all of Da Nang city by now. As he hitched a ride to the embassy house, he debated how he would handle the situation. He had to play his cards carefully, see how Maxon reacted. To simply walk in and blow him away wouldn't work. He had to bide his time until the right moment, probably while they were on their next mission, to do him the way he did Duff. This was probably when Maxon would make his move. Brady stepped from the cab and trotted up the steps at the embassy house.

Maxon was sitting at a table, drinking beer with several men, but the raucous laughter in the room fell silent when Brady stepped into the doorway. Staring poker-faced, he waited as Maxon stood and walked around the table, the purple veins on his temples instantly bulging.

"Come here," Maxon said, reaching for Brady's shirt.

Brady caught his wrist in midair. "We need to talk in private," he said.

The men at the table cast wary glances at one another as Brady and Maxon stood toe-to-toe.

Maxon snatched his arm free. "Get over to my office at the operations center. We'll talk there."

Brady said nothing as he turned and walked out. He had hoped it would be anywhere other than the IOCC, too many witnesses there.

After riding out to the IOCC, he walked in to find Maxon waiting. Maxon slammed the office door, jarring a picture frame from the wall. The glass shattered as it hit the floor, leaving the black-and-white photo of him with LBJ crumpled among the shards. An inscription on the photo read: "To Max, A Hell of a Warrior, Lyndon B. Johnson."

Maxon had strapped on his pistol since leaving the embassy house.

"Where in hell have you been? And where is Captain Tri?"

"Maybe I'm the one who needs to ask the questions," Brady said.

"Look, Nash, I've had people out looking for you all night. I know you blew the mission, but I got word you came back in yesterday. Where have you been?"

"I didn't blow shit. It was a setup, and you know it. That wasn't the woman you said it was."

"What the fuck are you talking about? I go with the intel the gooks give me."

"Who tried to ambush us afterward?"

"What ambush? Are you saying I had something to do with it?"

"You tell me. As far as I know, you're the only one who knew we were going to be there."

Maxon shook his head and threw up his hands. "Nash, I've had it with you. I've trained you. I've taken care of you, and I told you right off that this was a risky business, but something goes wrong, and you act like I had something to do with it. What do you want? You want out? Hell, I'm sick of dealing with you. Just tell me what you want."

"I want the truth," Brady answered.

Maxon slammed his fist against a metal file cabinet, then spun and pointed his finger in Brady's face. "I'll tell you the truth. The truth is you're a crazy fuck, Nash. You aren't cut out for special operations. The shame is I don't have enough men right now, and we have a critical mission coming up in three days. You're going to participate. After that, you can do whatever the hell you want."

One more mission, that was the plan, except unlike Duff, he was ready. He knew what the murderous bastards were capable of doing.

"I'll send you back to your outfit as soon as it's over, but you need to be ready for this one. You understand? If you go AWOL again, I'll have you reported as a deserter. As a matter of fact, I may just put you under armed guard until Monday. What do you think about that?"

Brady refused to break eye contact with him. "Don't worry. I'll be here."

A brief uncertainty flashed in Maxon's eyes. "Well, OK, but I'm warning you. You make damned sure you're ready to go. And stay off the liquor, 'cause hungover or not, you're going. We move out at oh-four-hundred, Monday. You understand?"

Brady nodded.

"You need to carry a full combat load. We'll probably be out for several days. You got any questions?"

"Yeah," Brady responded, "where are we going?"

"Elements of the 101st Airborne, First Cav, the Marines, and the ARVNs are heading into the A Shau Valley to shake out some villages we think are providing sanctuary for the NVA. The hundred and first, the marines, and the cav will provide security against any main-force NVA units while the ARVNs sweep the villages. In the meantime, we'll do our usual with the special police, interrogating prisoners. We might catch some of the bastards that escaped from Hue back in February and March. Does that tell you what you want to know?"

"Yeah, I reckon," Brady said. "Except, I have one more question for you."

"What's that?"

"What's your role with Phung Hoang?"

Maxon's eyes widened. "Phung Hoang is nothing but Vietnamese superstition. We use it to keep them spooked."

"That's not what I was told."

"Trust me, Nash. The less you know about it, the better off you are, but since you think you know so much, I'll tell you this. You can book it, Phung Hoang is watching you. Just like the gooks say, Phung Hoang sees all. Keep that in mind when you go sticking your nose where it doesn't belong."

Brady nodded. "I'll see you Monday morning."

With that, he turned and walked from Maxon's office. It had begun raining again as he trotted across the compound toward his room. Soaked by the time he arrived, he stripped off his clothes and lay on the bed, staring up at the ceiling. The sky outside rumbled and thundered, and he thought back to that night when the firebase near Ben Het was overrun. It seemed as if it had been years ago. He thought about Lacey and how they'd grown so distant and how Melody Hill seemed like a faraway dream.

Drifting into a troubled sleep, he found himself in a nightmare, one he'd had before. He was in a never-ending struggle to get home, and just as he was about to board the freedom bird back to the States, Maxon came running up, shouting that there was one more mission. It always ended the same way, with a vicious battle where he found himself running toward home. He ran until Melody Hill was just beyond the next rise, but the enemy always caught up with him before he reached the crest of the hill, shooting at him with their AK-47s until the bullets shredded his flak jacket.

Jerking upright, Brady found himself panting for breath. He threw aside the blanket and put his feet on the floor. He was still trembling as he reached for the towel hanging on the end of the bunk. After mopping the sweat from his face, he glanced at his watch. It was barely after midnight.

* * *

The huge air base at Da Nang was never a quiet place, but it was awash with activity that morning when they arrived in the predawn darkness. Although he'd slept little, Brady was tense and alert as he watched humans and machines intermingled in a frenzy of organized confusion. Scores of Hueys, their rotors drooping, lined the ramp like a legion of giant insects disappearing into the shadows. Jeeps and trucks crisscrossed the tarmac in every direction while men shouted above the scratch and squawk of radios.

It was cool following the rains of the night before, and the headlights cut through the mist with spooky shafts of light. Landing lights popped from the mist only seconds before huge Chinooks and C-130s roared overhead. Maxon parked the jeep behind a large hangar.

"Bring your gear," he said. "We're going inside to the ops room where they're giving a final briefing. We'll go to the choppers from there."

Brady didn't bother to reply as he pulled his rucksack over his shoulder and unsheathed his rifle. He followed Maxon into the room, where the glaring lights made him squint. Thirty or forty officers were gathered inside, and the briefing was already in progress. The colonel at the front of the room paused with noticeable aggravation at their late arrival. After several seconds of silence, he turned and pointed to a large map to his rear.

"As I was saying, gentlemen, this is a relatively large operation. There will be units from several branches involved, so we need to make certain that we're all on the same page. All units should have their individual briefings by now, and you should have your operations orders, call signs, radio frequencies, and other necessary information. Our aim here is to give you a final overview and answer any last-minute questions. Then we'll get on with our business."

The colonel moved his finger across the map.

"OK. Listen up. These circles indicate our objectives. These landing zones are approximately sixty miles northwest of here in the A Shau Valley. As you are already aware, there are two large and well-trained NVA regiments known to be in the area. At first light, we'll begin prepping the LZs with heavy concentrations of both air and artillery, but be ready. Some of your units may come in on hot LZs. We'll have plenty of TAC air on standby if it's needed. The marines will hit this series of LZs along these hills on the northern edge of the valley above Highway 548."

He rapped the map forcefully with his middle finger.

"The 101st and the First Cav will come in here above this blue line on this side of the valley. Most of the 101 will be coming in from Evans, Eagle, and the firebases up here around Phu Bai. This circle here is where Colonel Dang's rangers and the rest of the ARVN troops will land, down here in the middle of the valley, closest to the villages and hamlets. Our primary mission is to provide a blocking force, but we need to be ready to move up to reinforce them if necessary. Colonel Tranh's special police will be divided among the various units sweeping the villages. They will handle the classification and interrogation of any non-uniformed prisoners. Any questions?"

Brady glanced around the room. Some of the Vietnamese officers were familiar, but he recognized none of the marines.

"All right, gentlemen, if there are no further questions, we'll board the choppers and depart at first light. Good luck to you all."

This was it. Except this time, unlike Duff, Brady knew exactly what was about to happen, and he had no intention of waiting for Maxon to make the first move. He wouldn't take his eyes off the murderous bastard. And as soon as there were no witnesses around, Maxon would die. The move would be swift and certain, with no hesitation.

As they walked down the ramp toward the choppers, Maxon caught Brady's arm. "Nash, you're going on the chopper with Major Loc. Stay with him no matter what. You understand? I'll be in the C&C chopper with Colonel Tranh. We'll rendezvous with you and Loc north of the villages."

Brady glanced around at Loc. It was Loc. Loc was the An Ninh agent. Of all the officers in the operations group, Loc was the most reclusive. Other than that day when Brady was caught in Maxon's office, he had never seen Loc at close quarters. Even now, he remained aloof as he walked up the tarmac apart from the group. He had to be the one, but there was still doubt. Where was Tranh?

* * *

A cold blast of morning air buffeted Brady as he sat in the open door, watching thundering swarms of helicopters lifting away from Da Nang Air Base. His own chopper climbed with them into the sky as a misty dawn broke over Tourane Bay. Within the hour, they would arrive at their objective in the A Shau. His mind raced into dead-end alleys of inconclusive doubts as he thought about killing Loc. Killing a man on a hunch, no matter how certain it seemed, wasn't something he could do.

The helicopters paralleled Highway 1, climbing over the Hai Van Pass before turning on a more westerly heading. Behind them, the coastal villages faded into the distance as the sun climbed above the horizon. Up ahead, the green hills were splotched with the shadows of clouds. The valleys, still protected from the morning sun, were pocketed with mist. It was all deceptively beautiful, deceptive because beneath this sparkling veneer was a fog-shrouded jungle inhabited by the NVA, a large and lethal force that called this jungle home.

Brady glanced upward at the vapor trails stretching across the sky, jets heading for targets in the A Shau. In the sky across from him, the Vietnamese soldiers lined the bench seats of the open-sided Hueys flying in formation. No doubt, some would be casualties before day's end, and he couldn't help but wonder about his own destiny. His was an especially dangerous situation because he had to wait for Loc to make the first move.

The first village was assigned to a detachment of ARVN rangers under a Major Dang. Located near the hills on the southwestern edge of the valley, the village was in a rugged area, where the landing zone was relatively close to higher ground. It could get ugly if the LZ was hot. They began their final approach as Brady watched the expressions of the American flight crew tal-king back and forth through the intercom system. They seemed noticeably nervous, more so than normal. The chopper descen-ded quickly, dropping into the valley and passing over the first villages. The approach into the LZ was low and fast.

The door gunner bent over and shouted into Brady's ear. "We've got a hot LZ. The scout ships are reporting heavy ground-to-air."

The gunner shook his head in resignation as he readied his M60. Brady glanced over at the stone-faced Major Loc. He was gazing steadily off into the distance. Several F-4 Phantoms roc-keted past, making a bombing run near the LZ. Major Dang gave a hand signal to his men, and the ARVN troops locked and loaded. Brady bolted a shell into his M40 and set the safety. Glancing over his equip-ment, he made his last-minute checks. Frags, smoke, flares, ammo pouches, he was ready.

A line of green tracers rose up from the jungle and zipped past the chopper. They missed, but he heard metallic clacks as more bullets struck the thin-skinned chopper from below. An involun-tary shudder ran through his body, and his mouth went dry. The door gunner swung about with his M60 and began firing. Sitting in the open doorway, Brady felt like a duck in a carnival shooting gal-lery. More tracers zipped past. The choppers were at treetop level as they approached the LZ.

The Huey on their right suddenly exploded into an orange fireball and plummeted into the trees. A moment later, another was hit. It smoked and spun crazily as the pilot fought to maintain control, but it, too, disappeared into the jungle. Swallowing hard, Brady prayed.

His chopper was streaking over the treetops when he heard the metallic clacks of more bullets striking its underside. One of the ARVN rangers slumped as the others held him. The chopper broke out over a clearing where red smoke canisters were bur-ning, and the rotors clacked loudly as the pilot pulled the nose up and set down hard. Another helicopter set down too hard only meters away and rolled, scattering its human cargo like hapless puppets.

Mortar rounds blew clods of grass and dirt everywhere as Brady leapt with his Vietnamese counterparts from the chopper and sprinted into a gauntlet of machine-gun fire. They raced for a tree line fifty meters away. Several men fell before reaching cover, but Brady made it, dropping quickly to the ground as he looked around for Loc. Loc, too, had reached the trees. He was crou-ching behind a large one a few meters away. Several feet to his left, Major Dang was sprawled on his back, yelling into the handset of a PRC-25 for more air support. Enemy bullets hissed and cracked everywhere, clipping the vegetation. They were pinned down.

Mortar rounds continued thudding into the ground, explo-ding with loud *karoomph*s. Every explosion sent shards of shrapnel whiz-zing in all directions. Finally, Brady spotted a pith helmet bobbing in the brush ahead. Centering the crosshairs, he fired a round. The helmet spun into the air, and Brady looked for his next target. The vegetation off to his right fluttered furiously from the muzzle blast of an enemy machine gun. He fired several rounds into the brush. The gun stopped firing.

It seemed to take forever, but within minutes, a flight of F-4 Phantoms brought relief as they dropped canisters of nape, scorching the surrounding jungle with towering flames. It brought an immediate cessation of the enemy fire, and the battered rangers slowly began moving forward.

Brady raised himself to a low crouch, looking around for Major Loc. He was no longer in sight. Panic gripped him. He'd made a critical mistake. He'd lost track of Loc. A sudden jolt racked him. It felt like a high-voltage shock, and Brady realized he had been knocked to the ground. His head spun, and stars floated before his eyes. The mortar rounds continued exploding, but the sounds receded as if they were far away. He'd been hit.

The numbing sensation of shock quickly gave way to excruciating pain as he fought to open his eyes. There was no one around, and with only the greatest effort, he sat up, propping his back against a tree. Carefully, he ran his fingers around the edges of the flak jacket, searching his torso for the wound—nothing. He looked down at his legs, expecting to find one or both mangled or gone, but that wasn't the case. Unzipping the flak jacket, he ran his hand inside, finding a wet spot below his .45. It was in his left side, near the bottom of the flak jacket, where the jagged hole of an exit wound oozed into his hand. He had been shot from behind.

He jerked his head upright. Still he saw no one, but using a morphine syrette was out of the question. He pulled the snap on his first-aid packet and tore open the paper wrapping. With sweat dripping into his eyes, he pushed the gauze inside his flak jacket and against his side. Blood formed a puddle in his lap as he shook uncontrollably. Shock, he thought. He was going into shock. Instinctively, he pulled his rifle closer to his side. The sounds of the fighting faded even more, and soon, all he heard was the pounding of his own heart.

Time disappeared. He didn't know how long he'd been there with his eyes shut, gasping for breath, but suddenly he became aware of a presence. Opening his eyes, he found Major Loc standing over him. He made a move for his rifle, but Loc quickly pinned it to the ground with his boot. It was hopeless, and at that moment, he knew he was looking into the eyes of the man who had killed Duff.

"You can kill me," Brady said, "but I've already got you."

Loc said nothing.

"I gave your name, along with all the information about both you and Maxon, to a correspondent in Saigon."

"Yes," Loc said, "I know, but Richard Mathis is now dead. I saw to that."

Loc glanced about as he pulled a bright yellow card from his pocket. He tossed it into Brady's lap, then opened a pack of cigarettes and shook one out. Cupping his hands, he lit the cigarette and inhaled deeply.

Clutching the bandage inside his flak jacket with his right hand, Brady picked up the card with his left. He trembled as he glanced at the green bird strutting in a symbol of death. The doorman at the Continental Palace had been right. Phung Hoang had been watching all along.

"Before I kill you, you should know," Loc said, "Mr. Maxon has been one of my most effective weapons. The People's Liberation

Army has been well supplied with CIA weapons, and he has been persuaded to assassinate many of our enemies in the Vietnamese puppet government. He is a very foolish man, and we have used him for many years."

Defiantly, Brady threw the kill card back in Loc's face. Loc simply smiled as he bent down to retrieve the card, but as he did, Brady released the bandage inside of his flak jacket and quickly slid his hand upward. Loc raised his eyes to find the pistol barrel resting at the tip of his nose. His smile faded only an instant before Brady pulled the trigger. The impact of the heavy .45 round knocked Loc backward, but Brady instinctively held the pistol on him. Even while blood spurted like a small oil well from a hole between Loc's eyes, Brady held the gun on the man he knew had killed Duff.

Picking up the yellow card, he stared at it for several seconds before shoving it into his pocket. His survival was questionable at best, but if he somehow made it back alive, he'd give the card to Maxon personally before killing him. Rolling to his knees, he clung to the tree as he struggled to his feet. The surrounding terrain spun crazily around him in a mad carousel of trees and smoke. As he swayed back and forth, Brady retrieved his rifle and an ammo pouch. When he was steady, he forced himself to limp toward the sounds of battle.

From beyond the hill to the northeast came the crackle of gunfire and the dull thuds of mortars and grenades. An occasional F-4 streaked overhead, followed by another black cloud of smoke rising above the trees, evidence of another napalm strike. Forcing each step, Brady moved toward the sounds of battle, but the blood seeped down his legs. He had failed both Duff and Lacey. He was going to die and leave Maxon still very much alive.

Following a trail up the hillside through thick cover, he struggled, as each step became an agonizing jolt. At the top of the hill, he spotted smoke rising from a nearby ridge where the rattle, crack, and thud of a firefight raged. To reach it, he had to cross a deep ravine and climb the opposite slope. Gritting his teeth, he started into the ravine.

His fear now was that he would die somewhere in the trackless jungle below, becoming just another MIA. No one would ever know what had happened. He thought of Maxon's reaction when they declared him missing in action. Not knowing for certain if he was dead or alive, the paranoid bastard would go insane. He almost smiled as he limped to a tree and rested for several seconds. The pain was molten lead burning in his guts, and he looked down at his hand gripping his side. The bleeding had stopped, but it was only a matter of time if he didn't find help.

CHAPTER NINETEEN

Maxon Covers His Tracks

When Lacey found Brady's letter in the mailbox, the first thing that caught her eye was the postmark from France. She ripped open the envelope while standing outside the apartment door, her purse still hanging on her shoulder. The letter was cryptic. There was something about another letter, the one Brady had given Mr. Brister, but she didn't understand. Something was terribly wrong. Leaving the front door standing open, she walked into the apartment and stood at the center of the room rereading the letter.

Apparently, the letter Brady had given Mr. Brister was the key. It was one Duff had written, and it would explain everything. This was it—the one thing that Brady had never told her, his real reason for going to Vietnam. She had to talk with Mr. Brister, but the last she'd heard, he was still in a Knoxville hospital. She glanced at the clock. It was already after five. After quickly thumbing through her address book, she grabbed the phone and dialed a number in Chattanooga.

Brister's daughter, Jessica Payne, answered. She and Lacey had been in the same Sunday school class through childhood. As they talked, Lacey explained how she hoped to talk with Jessica's father and perhaps even get Duff's letter from him. It all should have been simple enough, but when they finished talking, Lacey hung up the phone and stared blankly across the apartment. Jessica's father had died over a week ago. She promised to search for the letter, but for now, there was only hope.

Lacey switched on the TV. Walter Cronkite was on, and he was again saying the war was a lost cause, an unwinnable stalemate. She picked up Brady's letter again. As she read, tears blurred her eyes. She'd been so selfish. If only she had taken time to really listen.

* * *

Brady paused and gazed into the darkened depths of the huge ravine. Descending into the jungle below seemed almost hopeless, but if he was to reach the battle on the next ridge, it was his only choice. The eerie twilight swallowed him as his surroundings took on different dimensions. Small streams turned to waist-deep torrents, and the emerald treetops transformed into briar-filled morasses of dripping vegetation. And what from a distance appeared as a minor folds in the terrain became steep and almost impassable ravines.

Slowly, he traversed the slope, clinging to vines and saplings, pulling, scratching, and clawing. It was no wonder entire NVA regiments disappeared in the A Shau. This one ravine could hide a battalion. With his strength waning, he discarded more equipment. The flak jacket went next, leaving his belly exposed and distended from internal bleeding. He touched the tender and now-purple flesh, and winced with pain.

If only he could find a medic. If he didn't soon, he was finished. His skeletal remains would be scattered in the undergrowth, food for the rodents. Just over the hill, the rattling gunfire and thudding explosions of the firefight continued, but his nausea intensified. For only a moment, he had to find someplace to rest.

At the bottom of the ravine, a rocky stream meandered through the jungle. Carefully, Brady lowered himself into the cold water and lay on his back against the rocks. The water was numbing, and the pain abated as long as he remained perfectly still. After a while, he contemplated simply staying there and letting it all end. There was so much relief that it would be easy to stay here, easy to simply close his eyes and die.

Shaking the cobwebs from his head, Brady fought back and, with his last ounce of strength, pushed himself to his feet. He retrieved his rifle from a shallow pool and looked up the hill. A solid wall of jungle still separated him from the waning sounds of the battle, but if he could make it the two or three hundred meters to the top ridge, there was certain to be a medic there. With his first steps, the pain and dizziness returned, and as he began climbing, the crackling crescendo of small arms slowly subsided to an intermittent staccato of rifle shots.

The air reeked with the odor of napalm and burnt cordite, and a smoky haze dimmed the jungle. But up ahead, the skyline shone through the trees. He was nearly there. His hopes rose as the steep slope began giving way to gradually flattening terrain, and he pushed his way through the last of the undergrowth, stumbling into the open.

The shooting had stopped, and there was no one in sight. Below him on the ridge, the landscape was one of devastation and destruction. What little timber remained was denuded of vegetation, splintered and blackened by the napalm. The ground was burned down to bare earth, and greasy rivulets of muddy water seeped into smoking logs, hissing and sending puffs of steam into the air. The breeze stirred an occasional eddy of ashes, sending it skittering across the hillside. Brady's hope faded as he stared into the pits of hell.

Where had they gone? His eyes wandered down the hillside and across the desolate landscape to the opposite slope, where the jungle remained intact. Despite his blurred vision, he caught movement as several figures, lean and cautious, emerged from the jungle. There were at least a dozen of them, and he nearly shouted until he suddenly realized they were NVA. Spread in a skirmish line, they crossed a stream at the base of the hill and began making their way up the slope. It seemed as if they expected resistance.

Brady began backing into the jungle, but paused as a moan came from the hillside below. He stopped, and the enemy soldiers slowed their advance, becoming more cautious and spreading farther apart. With a closer look, he began noticing charred bodies sprawled among the broken and burnt timber, soldiers apparently caught in the blast of napalm that destroyed the hillside. It was difficult to tell, but the weapons among the bodies appeared to be AK-47s and SKS rifles—NVA armaments.

He decided the moan must have come from one of the wounded NVA and was again about to retreat when he spotted something else. Raising his rifle, he peered through the scope. But this time, he found a line of GIs. Unlike the dead NVA, the Americans weren't burnt by the napalm, but most were sprawled in contorted configurations of death. They must have been sweeping down the bombed hillside when the NVA ambushed them from the opposite slope. The enemy had all but wiped them out, and now they were about to finish them off.

As he moved his scope from man to man, Brady saw most had disfiguring wounds, but two appeared to be alive. Suddenly, one of the Americans rolled to his knees and threw a grenade toward the advancing line of soldiers. The enemy skirmishers disappeared into the folds of the terrain, and after the explosion, they unleashed a withering torrent of fire up the hill.

Two American soldiers returned fire. Fighting his blurred vision, Brady propped his rifle across a fallen tree. The skirmish line split as the enemy soldiers moved to gain position on the surviving Americans. A particularly energetic enemy soldier in a pith helmet scurried up a shallow ravine and positioned himself above the Americans. Brady blinked one last time, and his eyes momentarily cleared.

The scope's crosshairs dissected the soldier's torso, and the rifle's recoil sent jolts of pain shooting through Brady's body. He didn't hesitate. He bolted another shell and moved to the next target. Stars floated before his eyes as he squeezed off another round. The impact of the bullet flipped the second enemy soldier backward down the hill. His pain worsened, and Brady lowered his rifle. Pausing, he sucked in a shallow breath. After a second or two, he again forced the rifle to his shoulder.

Another enemy soldier, apparently an officer, jumped to his feet and was pointing in Brady's direction. He was shouting commands to the others. The 7.62 mm round from Brady's M40 caught him center mass, knocking him backward down the hill. Three of the enemy rushed the Americans as Brady quickly reloaded and methodically squeezed off more shots. He missed twice, but when he finished, all three were dead. As he reloaded, the stars continued floating before his eyes, and he thought he would pass out.

"No!"

His own voice surprised him, and he gulped another breath.

"Can't pass out," he muttered.

Another enemy soldier stepped into the open. Brady pulled the trigger. The lifeless body thumped to the ground, sending puffs of ashes floating into the air. Pure adrenaline and raw instinct were the only things that kept him going, but he was sinking fast. He waited for yet another shot, but with seven of their comrades dead or dying, the remainder of the enemy patrol scurried for cover. Brady sent several parting shots after them as the bitter taste of bile filled his mouth.

After waiting until he was certain the enemy was gone, Brady struggled to his feet. The napalm had destroyed a large enemy force, and the nauseating odor of burnt flesh filled his nostrils. Clinging to tree stumps, he made his way down the hill, past the smoking remains of NVA soldiers scattered about in the timber, bodies everywhere, swollen and charred, with the flesh split and oozing reddish translucent fluids.

When he reached the Americans, he recognized the horsehead-and-shield shoulder patch of the First Cav on their uniforms. The death gazes of men who stared at nothing surrounded him as he searched the hillside for survivors. After a minute or two, he found a man lying in a muddy hole, squirming in agony. He pulled the semiconscious soldier to a dry spot and bandaged his wound. Moving on, he passed several more lifeless bodies until he found another soldier still alive.

The man, probably the one who had thrown the grenade, sat perfectly still with his back against a burnt stump. His breathing came in shallow gasps, and his eyes were glazed with shock. Covered with mud and the blood of his comrades, he had several small shrapnel wounds, but nothing that appeared life threatening. A small clump of mud hung near the corner of his mouth. Brady gently rubbed it away, but the soldier remained oblivious to his presence.

Somewhere in the hills nearby, the sound of helicopters reverberated as Brady moved on, finding yet another body lying in a shallow ravine. The soldier's corpse might have been staring skyward except the entire front of his head was missing. For several long seconds, Brady gazed at the gruesome sight as an idea began taking shape in his mind. He eased down the hill to where the body lay.

272 | RICK DESTEFANIS

Shedding his fatigue shirt, Brady removed Loc's kill card from the pocket, then knelt beside the body. The sound of approaching choppers grew steadily as he began frantically exchanging dog tags, watches, wallets, and fatigue shirts with the corpse. When he was done, he laid his sniper rifle across the body and backed away.

A helicopter shot in low across the hillside, quickly disappearing over the ridge. But as Brady glanced skyward, it circled in the distance. He had to send a signal. Finding a smoke canister hanging from a discarded rucksack, he snatched the pin. Purple smoke spewed forth, and after struggling to the top of the ravine, he waved his arms frantically. The helicopter skimmed the hillside once again, the door gunner and copilot peering in his direction.

The purple smoke surrounded him, trailing away with the breeze across the ridge. At first, he thought they missed him, but the chopper slowed and circled again. He was sure now they had seen him. But as the helicopter flared overhead, a sudden sensation gripped his body, and he felt himself falling backward into a deep black hole.

* * *

After Maxon read the dispatch from Major Dang, he grabbed the young Vietnamese soldier who had delivered it. "What the fuck does this mean? Nash is missing in action? You tell Major Dang I want his body. You hear me? You tell—"

Maxon felt a hand on his shoulder and spun around. It was Colonel Tranh.

"Mr. Maxon, this soldier does not speak your language, and it would please me if you would remove your hands from him."

Maxon shoved the young soldier away and stuck his finger in Tranh's face. "Colonel, I suggest you get in touch with Major Dang and tell him to find my man. According to this dispatch, Major Loc has been killed, and they can't locate Nash. What the hell is going on?"

"Mr. Maxon, I have been in radio contact with Major Dang all morning, but he is in no condition to search for your man. He has been gravely wounded, and his unit has taken many casualties. There are elements of your First Cavalry Division and 101st Airborne Division moving into that area now. Perhaps they will find Nash."

"Shit," Maxon cursed.

He flashed back to the notes Loc had taken from the correspondent's body in Saigon, including the telex messages stolen from his office. He turned and walked away. He had to get up there ASAP and make sure Nash wasn't still alive.

* * *

After several hours, Maxon had walked over much of the battlefield searching, but he had found no sign of Nash. Never in his life had he seen such a lucky bastard. Nash might be the *Xảo Quyệt Hổ* the gooks called him, and he was one with nine lives too. He'd even somehow slipped away from Loc in Saigon. Now Loc was dead, and it may have been Nash who killed him, but that was unlikely. Loc was shrewd, and he knew his business. A cold rain began falling as Maxon gave up his search and made his way back to the CP.

When he arrived, Tranh was still helping evacuate the wounded, and he told Maxon of a chopper pilot from the First Cav who said he had recovered several KIAs, including a sniper's body almost a kilometer north of the LZ. He was short on details, but the body had been taken to the Graves Registration Unit in Phu Bai. Hurrying to the LZ, Maxon commandeered a ride on one of the medevacs taking out the wounded. He arrived in Phu Bai just before sunset.

Maxon wasted no time as he quickly made his way to the GRU, where a young lieutenant was sitting behind a desk. He walked up, leaned forward, and stared intently at the man until the young officer looked up. With a fixed scowl, Maxon said nothing. Fucking little butter bar probably hadn't been in-country three months.

"What can I do for you, partner?" the lieutenant asked.

Maxon didn't move. The lieutenant signed a form and set it aside, then glanced up again, studying Maxon's collar for the rank or insignia that wasn't there.

"My name is Colonel Maxon. I'm an advisor with ARVN special operations, and I'm here to check on one of my men, if it won't trouble your tired ass."

The lieutenant banged his knee under the desk and nearly fell backward as he leapt to his feet and saluted.

"Sorry, Colonel! I didn't, ugh…I didn't realize you were a colonel. I mean you're not wearing any—"

"Save your salute, Lieutenant. What I need is information. Are you going to help me, or do I need to go to your commanding officer?"

"Yes, sir! I mean, no, sir! I mean, whatever you need, sir."

"OK. What I need to know is if you have the body of a soldier here named Brady Nash."

The lieutenant quickly ran his finger down a list of names.

"Ugh, yes, sir, we do. His remains are back there in the refrigeration unit. He arrived a few hours ago, so we haven't done any processing yet."

Maxon breathed a sigh of relief. "Where are his personal effects?" he asked.

"Just a moment, Colonel."

The lieutenant left the room and returned a few moments later with a small bag. Inside, there was a set of bloody dog tags along with a Seiko wristwatch and a leather wallet. Maxon opened the wallet and dumped the contents out on the desk. It contained Nash's military identification card, a Tennessee driver's license, and several photos.

In one photo, two young men stood together in front of wooden bleachers, wearing football uniforms. One was Nash, and as he looked closer, he realized the other was Coleridge. After thumbing through the odd greenback, piastre, and military scrip, he picked up the dog tags. The coagulated blood on them smeared under his thumb. They were Nash's. He tossed them back into the box and wiped his fingers on some reports lying on the desk.

"Where's the body?" Maxon asked.

"Like I said, sir, it's back in the refrigeration unit, but I don't think you can identify him. We can do that from his personal effects with your approval."

"Why is that?" Maxon asked.

"Well, sir. It's his head. It's…well, sir, I don't want to upset you, but his head is kind of messed up. I mean it's…" The lieutenant's voice escalated until he nearly shouted, "Well, it's damned near gone, sir!"

The lieutenant was visibly shaken, and Maxon fought back his feelings of satisfaction.

"All right, Lieutenant. I don't want to upset you more than you already are."

He put the ID in his pocket and walked out.

"*Xin Loi*, Mr. Tiger," Maxon muttered. "You fuck with the Spartan, you pay the price."

CHAPTER TWENTY

A Never-Ending Nightmare

When they told her she had a telephone call back in the office that evening, Lacey wasn't particularly surprised. With her new friends and business relationships, she often received calls while at work, but when they said it was her mother, the blood drained from her head, and she felt dizzy. There was only one reason her mother would call her at work. Leaving the stage without excusing herself, Lacey all but ran to the back office, her heart pounding. She hurried down the hall, and when she burst through the door into the office, Belle was standing ashen faced behind her desk. She held the phone in her hand.

"It's your mama, baby," Belle said.

She offered Lacey the phone, but Lacey hesitated. Gazing at the receiver, she could hardly make herself take it, but slowly and reluctantly, she pressed it to her ear. Several seconds passed before she could muster a word.

"Mama?" she said softly.

"Honey," her mother answered.

There was silence on the other end, and Lacey strained against the void, listening and praying for anything other than what had to be the reason for her mother's call.

"Mama?"

"It's Brady, baby. He's gone."

Lacey felt the room drop away as her knees buckled and her eyes lost focus. Belle Langston caught her before she fell to the floor.

* * *

Trapped in total darkness, he was surrounded by a chorus of quiet moans, the kind heard from people resigned to interminable suffering. It was as if all the souls in hell were enduring the torment of eternal damnation, except there were other voices as well, happy voices, seemingly unaware of those crying in pain. They talked about cheeseburgers with real French fries, the Beatles, and going home. None of it made sense, except that he knew who he was. He was Brady Nash.

Gradually, another sensation penetrated his darkened hell. It was an odor, the septic stench of wounds. And there were others, chemical odors, ether and alcohol. His mind swam in and out of a hazy consciousness until one sensation dominated all the others, a burning pain in his abdomen. His face itched, and he tried to scratch, but nothing happened. It was as if he was in a straitjacket or paralyzed.

He tried to force his eyes open, but they didn't budge. He tried to call out, but gagged. Again, he tried to force his eyes open, and for a moment, he thought he had, but there remained only a fuzzy grayness before him. Something was terribly wrong. It wasn't a nightmare. He knew who he was, but where was he? What was he doing? He couldn't see. He couldn't move.

Slowly, it came to him. He was in the army, but all he recalled was that first day when they gave him the OD green uniforms, baggy shirts, and pants that smelled like mothballs and had labels with backward names like "Shirt/Fatigue." Everything was backward in the army. Nash/Brady, Specialist Fourth Class. That was the way they put it on your orders, your commendations, your medical records. Medical records—it came to him. He was wounded. But how?

A hint of familiarity came to him as a strange and beautiful place, a place with green hills, flowing rivers, and flaming sunsets. And the name came to him as well, Vietnam. Although familiar, it seemed more a name you heard when thinking of faraway imaginary lands. His mind toyed with the word as he saw holy men in golden gowns standing before a red pagoda. It was a land of ivory and jade, orange tigers and huge gray elephants dancing under a crimson sun. He smelled incense burning and felt a soft breeze drifting through green mountain jungles.

The beauty of it all was almost overwhelming, until there came a brief flash of something ugly. A huge black cloud billowed skyward, then burst from inside with an inferno of orange flame. More flashes, streaks of red and green, shot past him. His memory suddenly returned as nightmarish chunks of recollection, and he saw the napalm, the tracers, the war, the fearful eyes, soldiers dying. He had been wounded, but he still couldn't remember how or when.

His eyes detected something, a pattern, and he studied it until recognition suddenly leapt out at him. It was the geometric pattern of ceiling tiles. He was in a darkened room, staring at the ceiling. The sound of heels clicking on hard tile registered somewhere in his mind, and he tried to turn his head to see who was walking.

His eyes, it seemed, were the only part of him he was able to control. A figure in white, a mirage, it seemed, approached down a long corridor lined with beds. A hospital, that made sense. He lost sight of the approaching figure until something warm touched his forehead. Brady found the blurred vision of a woman's face, gazing down at him. Smiling, she held her hand against his forehead.

"Welcome back to the world, Private."

Her voice was as soft and warm as her hand.

"Nod if you understand what I'm saying," she said.

With the greatest effort, Brady managed a slight nod, and despite his blurred vision, he saw the woman's smile expand. She leaned across the bed, and he heard the static scratch of an intercom.

A male voice came from the speaker. "Yoa?"

"Guess who's awake, Wendell," she said.

"Weeellll, let me see," the voice answered. "By the looks of the light, it's...Hey, is that PFC Gordon?"

"Sure is," the nurse answered.

"Well, I'll be...Welcome back to the world, Ray baby."

The voice was that of a black man, but why did he call him Ray and Gordon? He had to tell them his name, but his throat burned, and he gagged.

"No, no. Don't try to talk," the nurse said.

She pushed a thermometer under his tongue, but he spit it out. He had to call Lacey and his mother. He had to tell them he was alive. He tried again to talk, but nothing happened.

"It's the tubes in your throat, Ray. You have to be patient. It won't be long before we take them out. Just try to get some sleep for now. OK?"

Brady shook his head, but managed only a gurgle in his throat.

"What is it, honey?"

He cut his eyes over at his wrist restraints. If he could get free, he could write a note and tell her who he really was.

"Oh, your arms. I'm sorry. The doctor ordered the straps because you were tossing and turning so much, and you kept pulling your IV out. We were afraid you were going to hurt yourself. Don't worry. He'll probably take them off in the morning. Just relax for now. OK?"

His thoughts returned to his wounds as he craned his neck to look down at his legs. That was the worst one. He'd seen it too many times. Booby traps and land mines had blown the legs off so many men, until it became an obsession with every grunt in the Nam. "Just let me die quickly," men prayed. "Please, don't leave me without my legs."

It was as if the nurse read his mind.

"Don't worry, fella. You've got everything except a few inches of your intestines. Your biggest problem right now is infection, but from the feel of your head, I'd say you've licked that too. I think you're going to be just fine."

She held a finger on his wrist and looked at her watch. After another minute, she pulled the thermometer from his mouth.

"One hundred point three," she said. "That's the lowest it's been in two weeks."

Brady's eyes flew open. Two weeks? Where was he?

The nurse marked his chart, then continued her telepathy as she responded as if he'd spoken aloud. "I'll bet you don't even know where you are, do you? You're on an intensive care ward at Camp Zama, Japan. You know, I didn't think to tell you…"

Her voice faded as he fell asleep.

* * *

When Brady awoke, the fluorescent lighting revealed a large hospital ward bustling with activity. A little man in a white lab coat stood at the end of his bed, making notes on a clipboard. He had prematurely thinning hair and stress creases around his eyes. His wire-rimmed glasses had slipped down on the bridge of his nose. Finally, the man arched his eyebrows and glanced up.

"Oh! Good morning, Private Gordon. I see you're doing better. I'm Dr. Bagley."

Brady said nothing as he stared up at the doctor.

"You know, you've kept us all on the edge of our seats. With the nature of your wound and the delay getting treatment, your prognosis was pretty bleak. There was also a problem with your blood type. Somehow, the incorrect type was entered on your records, but I believe you're out of the woods now. We have you on one of our favorite antibiotic cocktails, and from the looks of it, it's working well. How do you feel?"

Brady didn't answer as he suddenly recalled Maxon. And for the first time, he remembered killing Loc. He looked up at the doctor. Did he know?

"Oh, don't worry. I'm going to have the nurse remove those restraints and the tubes shortly. We'll need to do some more tests and take some more X-rays, but it won't be long before we'll have you on solid food again. What do you think about that?"

Brady wanted to answer, but he was suddenly remembering those last minutes of consciousness up in the A Shau when he swapped identities with the dead soldier.

"I believe we have some mail from your parents," the doctor said. "I'll get one of the nurses to bring it to you. As a matter of fact, you can probably call them as soon as you can get up and around."

At first, Brady nodded. Then he shook his head from side to side. His mind raced in confusion.

"You can tell them you'll be on a plane home within a couple of weeks. Of course, you'll have to stay in a Stateside hospital a little longer."

Brady knew he could carry this ruse only so far. What would happen when they discovered his true identity? He had to come clean and tell them everything. Sooner or later, they would find out, but what if Maxon got to him while he was still in the hospital? Who would question his death then? He had to wait.

* * *

With each passing day, he felt improvement, and the first afternoon when they moved him from intensive care, Brady sat up in bed. Later, he stood beside his bed, and the next day, he was walking around the ward. Rehabilitation was exhausting, but mobility equaled survival at this point.

It was after midnight when he crept to the nurse's station at the end of the hall. The duty nurse was on the ward, and there was no one around as he bent over a typewriter and pecked out a letter.

11 November, 1968

Mr. and Mrs. Charles Gordon
4895 Prairie Road
Strayhorn, Missouri

Dear Mr. and Mrs. Gordon,

It is with deepest regrets that we must inform you of an error in the reporting of your son's status. The status of Private Raymond Gordon has been changed from that of "wounded in action" to that of "missing in action." Due to the nature of the wounds of another soldier, he was misidentified as your son. We regret this unfortunate error, and you will be informed of any additional information concerning this matter as soon as it becomes available.

Respectfully,

John R. Hurdle, Colonel

United States Army, Commanding

"Whatcha typing, soldier?" the nurse asked.

She walked in and peered over Brady's shoulder, but he snatched the letter from the typewriter.

"Nothing. Nothing. Just a letter home."

"It's OK," the nurse said. "You can use the typewriter."

"Oh, uh, well, thanks," Brady stuttered. "I guess I'm finished anyway. Is there a PX around where I can buy some envelopes?"

"Sure, but it's not open at this hour. Besides, you don't have to buy them. We've got plenty right here."

The nurse pulled one from a drawer and gave it to him. The hospital's letterhead was printed on the front.

286 | RICK DESTEFANIS

"Here you go."

She handed him a blank envelope.

* * *

A week later, when they wheeled his gurney up the ramp into the C-141 medical transport, Brady no longer felt weak. He could have walked on board the plane, but they insisted he travel to the air base in the big square ambulance and ride a gurney into the back of the aircraft. He still felt dizzy on occasion, but his strength had returned. Bound for Seattle, and eventually, a VA hospital in Kansas City, he prayed that Raymond Gordon's parents hadn't questioned his bogus letter.

More wounded vets were boarded in the same manner, many missing arms or legs, but the ones who stared silently at nothing spooked him the most. They reminded him of his situation. He wanted to find a mirror and look into it to see if he, too, was hollow-eyed and looking back inside himself. Like them, he was lost, not because of his wound, but because he'd stolen a man's identity and failed to keep his promise to Duff. Not only had he failed, but he'd become like the ones who killed Duff. He tried to wipe away a tear as a nurse walked up.

"Can I get you something to help you sleep?" she asked.

"You don't have anything that strong."

"Maybe not," she replied, "but you lay back, and I'll bring you a couple of pills to help you feel drowsy. OK?"

It was only a minute before she returned with a cup of water and two red pills. Brady swallowed them and fell asleep before the jetliner left the ground. It seemed like only minutes passed, too little time to cross the Pacific. But when the aircraft landed, he was ready to get off and kiss the sweet ground of home.

The plane taxied to a stop as he grabbed his duffel bag and hurried down the aisle toward the door. The other soldiers talked excitedly as they, too, shuffled along, but when Brady stepped into the doorway, he froze. There was a huge sign prominently displayed on the building across the tarmac:

WELCOME TO BIEN HOA AIR FORCE BASE
REPUBLIC OF SOUTH VIETNAM

"No!" he shouted.

But the other soldiers pushed him down the stairway as they cajoled and called him chicken.

"No, it's a mistake. I'm not supposed to be here. I'm going back to the United States."

At the bottom of the steps, Maxon stood waiting.

"Come on down here, country boy," he shouted. "We've got another mission, and there's no time for screwing around."

Brady tried to force his eyes open, but nothing happened. He tried to rub them with his fists, but he realized his arms were restrained once again. Why? He kicked violently as he tried to free himself. Finally, with only the greatest effort, he forced his eyes open. Everything was blurry. No matter how hard he tried, he couldn't focus on anything. Then he felt something touch his forehead, and he heard a woman's voice.

"It's OK, Ray. It's OK. You're going home. Just take it easy."

It was the nurse who had given him the sleeping pills. For a moment, he felt relieved, but everything remained blurry.

"Please. Please. Just untie my arms," he begged. "Please untie me. I can't stand it."

"Just try to sleep. When the medication wears off, I'll loosen the restraints. OK?"

Brady spit his bloody tooth into the NVA officer's face. "Fuck you," he shouted.

Running, he found himself pursued by dozens of enemy soldiers as he neared the top of a hill. He fired his rifle as they swarmed about, the bodies falling until they were three and four deep, but the enemy kept coming. He saw the face of one of the dead men. It was the one he'd shot that day, trying to surrender outside the village. He looked at another. They all had the dead man's face.

He looked over his shoulder toward the crest of the hill. Hiwassee Knob was in the distance. Just beyond was Melody Hill. He turned and ran, but the enemy bullets tore at his flak jacket. He had to get home, but no matter how far he ran, the mountaintop remained in the distance. He fell as his knees buckled in the dusty jungle trail.

After a while, a squeaking sound rose from somewhere in the back of his mind, a constant nagging sound that seemed to vibrate throughout his body. Listening, he tried to determine the source, another nightmare? The bed shook beneath him, and he opened his eyes. It was nighttime, and flashing red lights were everywhere. There were also long lines of blue and white lights trailing away into the distance, and the sounds of aircraft. He was at an airport and being moved on a gurney. The wheels squeaked continuously as they pushed him toward a nearby ambulance.

"Where am I?" he muttered.

He heard the nurse's voice. "You're in Seattle, Washington, Ray."

A wave of relief washed over him. He was back in the United States.

"Where are you taking me?" he asked.

"You had a pretty rough trip over, so we're taking you to a VA hospital here in Seattle to rest a while," she answered.

"To rest a while," the words sounded strange. Perhaps it was the tone of her voice that set off the alarms in his head. No one ever let you rest in the army. Hurry up and wait, perhaps, but never for the sole purpose of getting rest. "Take five. Smoke 'em if you got 'em." That was the cue, but it was because they needed time to check their maps or plan their next move. Rest was something you got when they had nothing else left to do.

"Can you take the wrist straps off now?"

The male orderly pushing the gurney spoke before the nurse could answer.

"You've been a bad boy, Ray. Spitting in the nurse's face doesn't build you brownie points. I don't think we're going to untie you right now."

"I was drugged! I wouldn't spit in anyone's face on purpose."

"Yeah, and we got a call from the army. They want to ask you some questions."

"Shut up, Carter," the nurse shouted. "It's OK, Ray," she said in a soothing voice. "We're going to put you in a room tonight.

The doctor will check you out, and I'm sure you'll be on the way home by tomorrow."

The ambulance pulled away from the airport, and Brady found himself distracted as he gazed out the window. The sights and sounds were at once familiar and strange as the ambulance passed crowded sidewalks, lines of parked cars, and people, like silent mimes, laughing and moving about or standing in lines at movie theaters. They wore flowery shirts, leather jackets, jeans, and all had long hair. These were clean people, smiling, happy people, and people living carefree lives. The aroma of French fries and hamburgers filled the air, and as the ambulance passed through the crowded streets, an occasional fragment of music quickly rose and fell away.

They were much too much happy to be thinking about Vietnam. These people probably had jobs or went to school. The war was only a sideshow for them to watch on TV, something only the unfortunate few had to deal with.

The ambulance backed up to the glass doors at the emergency room entrance. Still strapped to the gurney, Brady found himself being pushed into a long corridor. The ceiling was filled with rows of fluorescent lights. Turning his head to one side, he avoided the lights and saw a group of men sitting along the corridor wall. They wore old army fatigue jackets, but looked like bums and hobos with long hair and scraggly beards.

The orderlies left his gurney against the wall opposite the row of bums and disappeared down the hallway. Why were these men allowed to hang around inside a veterans hospital? One man was bent double in a metal folding chair, shaking uncontrollably, while another sat beside him, scarcely seeming to notice as he read a newspaper. Most of them simply stared with haunted eyes, but after a minute or two, one of them stood and shuffled up beside Brady's gurney. The man stared down at him. Young with chubby cheeks, he almost looked like an overgrown fat kid, except his eyes were very old.

"Hey, man, you just get back from the Nam?" he asked.

"Yeah," Brady answered.

Strapped to the gurney, Brady felt helpless as the bum bent over him.

"Where were you stationed?"

"I Corps, Da Nang, Phu Bai—"

"You a marine?"

"No, army ranger."

"Airborne ranger, huh? Well, I'll bet you ain't near as gung ho now, are you?"

Brady didn't answer as he turned his head and looked the other way.

"Aw, man, I was just teasing you. Don't get pissed. I was in the Nam too, Twenty-Third Infantry Division down at Chu Lai. Saw some bad shit myself. You know?"

Brady turned his head back toward the man. Their eyes met, and they stared at one another for several seconds.

"Yeah," Brady responded, "I reckon you did."

The scruffy vet moved his eyes up and down the gurney as if searching for something. "Where'd you get hit, man?"

Brady tried to move his arms, but he was still restrained. "Hey, loosen these wrist straps, and I'll show you."

The man's fingers trembled as he gave a halfhearted tug at one of the buckles, but he made no real effort to set him free.

"How come they got you tied down, man? You ain't really whacked-out, are you?"

"Heck no," Brady replied. "I just came in on a hospital plane from Japan. They strapped everybody down because of the turbulence. Come on, man, these things are hurting my wrists. Untie me."

"That's not what that nurse told the doctor over there a minute ago. They said you're getting a psychological evaluation, and the army is sending people to ask you some questions."

Brady grinned. "Come on. Look at me, man. Do I look like a nutcase? Gimme a break, and loosen the straps."

"Well, I suppose you look OK to me. I mean, I don't guess it'll hurt anything. Besides, we're brothers, right?"

"That's right," Brady said. "It's just like back in the Nam. We've got to stick together."

The man glanced around the room as he began loosening the straps. It took forever before he released the last strap, and Brady sat up quickly on the gurney, rubbing his wrists.

"That's right, partner," he said. "We're brothers. Hey, have you got a car outside?"

"Yeah, but it ain't much, just an old Chevy Nova. It's got, like, over a hundred thousand miles on it. Why? You want to go somewhere?"

"Man, I just want to run down the street. I need some food, some real food. Can you take me somewhere to get a hamburger?"

"Yeah, sure, I guess so. You buying?"

"Sure, grab my duffel bag there at the end of the gurney." Brady stood up, but his head began spinning, and he braced himself against the gurney.

"You all right, man?"

"Yeah, yeah. Just a little dizzy. Stood up too fast." As his head cleared, he put his hand on the man's shoulder. "You ready?"

The vet glanced up and down the corridor. "Yeah, but we need to be cool."

"No problem," Brady replied. "Let's go."

With that, the two men walked casually down the corridor and out into the Seattle night.

295

CHAPTER TWENTY-ONE

The Salvation Army

The mountains of Tennessee were in their full autumn glory as the sun shone brilliantly on the gold, red, and yellow leaves trilling in the breeze. The afternoon warmth had spread across the hillsides, but for all their beauty, the hills back home were a place of sorrow for Lacey. A soft mist rose from the Hiwassee River Valley far below as she stood hand in hand with her mother at the cemetery behind the church. The grass had finally covered Duff's grave the previous summer, barely healing that ugly scar, but there was now a new one.

The army had brought Brady's casket home to Melody Hill, but this time there were no cracking rifles from a twenty-one-gun salute, nor were the plaintive notes of taps heard echoing through the hills. There was only the silence and the whispering of the wind in the treetops. Lacey had asked for a funeral without the military ceremony. Her mother agreed, and they watched with tear-blurred eyes as the casket was lowered into the ground beside Duff's grave. Like the time before, there were hymns and prayers, and a few days later, she drove back to Nashville.

Her heart was broken, and the mountain roads went on forever as she reflected on her years with Duff and Brady. She had never completely gotten past Duff dying, and now with Brady gone, she couldn't help but think if she hadn't moved to Nashville, he might still be alive. She tried to tune the car radio, but the music only irritated her, and she twisted the knob in frustration. Music no longer lightened her heart, and had there been something else to do, she would have given it up altogether. It had been a fool's gold. Emotionally spent, she now did only what was necessary to move ahead with her life.

Billy was waiting in the parking lot at her apartment that evening when she returned to Nashville. They greeted one another in silence as she unlocked the door and went inside. He followed with her overnight bag.

Billy had offered to drive her to Melody Hill for the funeral, but she refused. It was something she wanted to do alone. And it wasn't that Billy was a bad person, but that she needed this private time to grieve. Despite this, Lacey couldn't make herself send him away that night, and as always, he tried to cheer her with his gentle humor, something about being the faithful dog waiting on her doorstep. He went to the kitchen and mixed drinks.

* * *

As the days turned to weeks, Lacey's grief remained unabated. She knew she had to pick up with her life again, but Brady still owned her heart, her soul, her very being. Despite returning to work, life seemed flat and meaningless. Billy remained at her side, returning every day to spend time with her, at least until she sent him away as she had every time before. Sitting on the couch that evening, he tuned his guitar while she played with Sampson. The cat seemed to sense her sadness as he, too, tried humoring her by playing with the ribbon on her blouse. She pulled him close, burying her face in his soft fur. Tonight, for once, she was able to remain dry-eyed.

"So you're never going back to Melody Hill, huh?"

She rubbed Sampson's head as she turned toward Billy. "I reckon not," she answered. "There's nothing left there for me, except Mama." She swallowed hard as a surge of emotion welled inside. "I mean, I'll go back to visit, but I'm never going to live there again."

Billy laid his guitar on the carpet beside the couch and moved closer. As he massaged her shoulders, Lacey closed her eyes and began to relax. After a few minutes, he got up and went to the kitchen.

"I'll fix us a drink. Maybe it'll make you feel better."

The drinks helped, and it had become a nightly ritual of sorts. Sampson closed his eyes and began purring as she rubbed the little tomcat behind his ears. With Brady gone, nothing seemed important anymore. Life was a prison where she marked time and wondered what she could have done differently. Reason said she needed to pick up the pieces and move on. Reason said she needed to regain focus on her music career. Reason said a lot of things, but her heart wasn't listening.

From the kitchen came the tinkle of ice cubes, then the rattle and hum of the blender. Moments later, Billy walked back into the room with a glass in each hand and a smile on his face. With a halfhearted grin, she took her glass. The first few times he'd made them, the drinks seemed too strong, but lately, she'd grown accustomed to the sharp bite of the alcohol. The warm, fuzzy feeling always came on quickly, dulling the raw edge of pain.

"You said earlier that Brister's daughter in Chattanooga called," Billy said, "but you didn't finish."

"Yes. She said they searched everywhere, but still couldn't find the letter."

He kissed her cheek, and Lacey closed her eyes as she put her head on his shoulder. Billy began strumming a sad chord on his guitar. He was such a sweet guy, and he was always understanding and patient. He had helped her prepare for the funeral, and now he helped with her grief.

"I suppose we'll never know the real reason Brady went to Vietnam," Lacey said.

Sampson stood in her lap, stretched, and jumped to the floor. Billy set the guitar aside and finished his drink.

"You need to put it out of your mind," he said, "before it makes you crazy."

Pushing her blouse up her back, he began gently rubbing her shoulders. His callused fingertips were soothing, and she snuggled closer while he nuzzled her softly with his chin. Their lips met, and he held her tight as his hand dropped to her side, then moved gently across her abdomen. An increasing warmth filled her body as she fell back on the couch, and Billy fumbled with the button on her jeans.

She thought back to that day on the Hiwassee with Brady, when they'd made love. Everything had seemed so right then, but now a tear trickled down her cheek. She needed to move on. Billy's hand caressed her breast, and she wanted to draw away, but he held her close. Perhaps there really was no reason to draw away. All she wanted was to be close to someone, but something wouldn't allow it. A sob escaped, and she pushed him away.

"Damn," he gasped.

Lacey pulled her knees against her chest as she curled up on the couch. "I'm sorry," she said.

"It's OK. It's OK. I understand."

She wanted to die. The thought occurred to her. Dying was the only way she would see Brady again. The thought wasn't so terrible. If only she could be with him again, she would be whole again. She couldn't abandon the realization that everything she had done was in some way guided by her relationships with Duff and Brady.

After Duff died, there was only Brady, but even after she had pushed him away, she met every new day with the subconscious security that he was always there, a solid anchor holding her, unseen but secure, while she bounced on the waves. But the chain had broken, and now her heart drifted aimlessly in an ocean of loneliness. She cried until sleep brought her merciful relief.

* * *

Exhausted by the slightest exertion, Brady still felt the ache deep within his belly, but he was free. The dumbass medical attendant in Seattle had tipped him off. The army, probably because of the letter he'd sent to Gordon's parents, had sniffed him out. Or at least, someone knew something was amiss, and they were trying to sort it out. He only hoped it wasn't the CIA.

As he held up his thumb to hitch a ride, he looked about for police cars. A misty rain swirled in the backwash of the trucks speeding by on Interstate 5, and the sky hung low and gray. He had to maintain a low profile if he was to get back to Tennessee and find Lacey, but he had to tell her he was alive. More importantly, he had to warn her. If Maxon got wind that he was still alive, there was no telling how far the murderous bastard would go.

His first impulse was to call Mama Emma by phone to tell her to contact Lacey and tell her what was happening, but the phone lines could be tapped. If they were confronted, the less they knew, the better. Once he got to Nashville and found Lacey, he would go to Old Man Brister and get Duff's papers.

The warning from Richard Mathis kept coming back to him. He could give himself up, but the CIA might simply discredit him. They were experts at disinformation. He'd go to prison, or worse, a psychiatric ward, where they'd shoot him so full of drugs he wouldn't even know his own name. People would simply look at him as a paranoid fool.

Standing in the rain, Brady continued holding his thumb high, waiting, hoping, and praying that the cops didn't nail him before he caught a ride. His first thought was to head east, but that would take him through the sparsely populated areas of Montana and

Nebraska, places where he'd stand out like a tree on the prairie. Instead, he opted to head south, down through California.

Luck finally appeared in the form of a dilapidated '59 Chevy station wagon pulling to the side of the highway. Two suitcases and a plastic gas can were strapped to the roof, and the back of the car was filled with loose piles of clothes and household goods. Two men, two women, a crying baby, and a fuzzy brown cur were packed into the remainder of the car, but Brady wasn't complai-ning. They were going south toward San Francisco.

The old station wagon wove a smoky trail of exhaust along the freeway, but the group seemed oblivious as they passed around a joint. The man behind the wheel closed his eyes and sucked fu-riously for a moment while the car wandered across several lanes. In Nam, Brady had seen men smoke everything from simple "dew" to opium-laced "Thai sticks," but he'd never participated. His pro-mise to Duff always came first. But now that promise was broken, and when one of the girls offered him the joint, he didn't hesitate. Pinching it between his thumb and index finger, he pressed it to his lips and inhaled deeply.

The harsh smoke made him cough, but it did little else. There was no glorious high, nothing but the irritating laughter of those in the car. The woman in front turned up the radio. It blared with the sounds of an electric guitar—a racket almost unbearable at first, but after a while, it grew on him. The miles and minutes slipped by, and somewhere along the way, Brady found the beat and rhythm in the music. He was on a magic car-pet ride with Steppenwolf. He began tapping his fingers against the window.

By the time they dropped him off on the outskirts of Oakland, he was smiling for the first time in months. The pain had subsided in both his abdomen and his heart. Waving good-bye to his benefactors, Brady stuck out his thumb again as he finished the last of the joint. He smiled as he threw his head back, looking up at a beautifully cloudless sky. It was the best he'd felt in years.

As he made his way eastward, the weather worsened, and a few days later, he arrived in a snowy and wet Denver, Colorado. It was December 24, and the California sunshine had given way to a Rocky Mountain blizzard, one that was worsening by the hour. His thin fatigue jacket, better suited for the chill of the Central Highlands, did little to protect him as he sat shivering beside the snow-covered highway.

Too many sleepless nights had caught up with him as he hung his head in exhaustion. Cold, wet, and hungry, his shivering ceased. Hypothermia had set in. When a police car stopped beside him, Brady didn't move as the policeman rolled down his window and looked out through the drifting snowflakes. It was already nightfall, and Brady no longer cared what happened. He was ready for it all to end.

"Where you headed?" the policeman asked.

Brady felt his tongue thick and unresponsive as he tried to talk. "East, to Tennessee. I'm going home for Christmas."

"Well, you're not going to make it tonight, buddy. It's Christmas Eve. How about I give you a lift over to the Salvation Army house? You can get some hot food there and a warm place to sleep until this storm blows over."

As he tried to stand, Brady swayed on unsteady legs, and when he tried to open the squad car door, his hands were like stone. The policeman stepped out and walked around to where he stood. Brady tensed.

"Just relax," the policeman said. He patted his pockets and squeezed his bundle.

"You arresting me?"

"Nope, just being careful. There are a lot of crazy people around nowadays."

He threw the bundle on the front seat, then helped Brady into the back. With the deep snow muffling the highway sounds, only the occasional interruption of a female dispatcher's voice broke the silence as Brady felt drowsiness coming on. He nodded off to sleep.

"What are you doing out this way?" the policeman asked.

Brady jerked awake. He must have heard the question because the answer came to him immediately.

"I got out of the army a few months back, and I've been looking for work."

"I take it you haven't had much luck."

"Not much," Brady replied, "mostly just temporary labor."

"I hear there's a good bit of construction going on down in Texas," the policeman said. "Have you been down that way?"

"No, maybe I'll head down there after Christmas."

He sat quietly, hoping the policeman would stop asking questions. Just as he was about to nod off again, the car rolled to a stop in front of an old building.

"Here we are," the policeman said.

A large red-and-white sign above the doorway read: The Salvation Army. The policeman walked around and opened his door. By now, the snow was several inches deep on the sidewalk, and the cold night air cut through Brady's drowsiness as he stepped from the squad car.

"Merry Christmas," the policeman said, "and good luck."

* * *

Army CID officer Major Gil Gilardi stood beside FBI agent Huey Gates as they watched the backhoe operator carefully scooping the dirt from the grave behind the Melody Hill Methodist Church. On a small knoll a few yards away stood the two women, Emma Coleridge and her daughter, Lacey. They had insisted on being at the disinterment and clung to one another, teary eyed and shivering. Gilardi thought of his own wife and daughter, and it was difficult to simply stand and watch the two women suffer, but this was a professional investigation.

With the Christmas and New Year holidays, it had taken a while to get this far with the investigation. Raymond Gordon's parents had notified the army when they received an obviously forged letter saying their son's status had been changed from "wounded" to "missing in action." CID initiated an investigation, and Gilardi had planned on interviewing Gordon in Seattle, but he slipped away. At least they had thought it was Gordon, until evidence brought Brady Nash's name into the equation.

Two laborers attached cables to the gray metal coffin, and after raising it from the hole, they used brooms and rags to clear away the last of the mud. After the coffin was pushed into the back of a gray army hearse, Gilardi gazed out at the hills extending to the far horizon. If his hunch was right, the body in the casket was Raymond Gordon's, but it didn't make sense. Everything about Nash said he was a hero. He had a list of commendations a mile long, including a Purple Heart, Bronze and Silver Stars, and the nation's second-highest award, the Distinguished Service Cross. All of his former unit commanders said Nash was as straitlaced as they come.

"Well, I guess that's it for now," Gates said.

Gilardi awakened from his thoughts and glanced over at his FBI counterpart. Gates had given the response he'd hoped for. The military orders in Nash's file were marked "Top Secret," and all of the names and locations were blacked out, something he hadn't yet shared with his FBI counterpart. Gilardi had done his part by taking it up the chain of command, but he'd been ordered to keep his investigative findings in-house.

Someone higher up knew something, but they were staying tight-lipped, probably because of the questions Congress was beginning to ask about certain military and CIA activities in South Vietnam, some with which Nash had apparently been involved. His orders showed "Temporary Duty" with the Republic of Vietnam's National Police Force as an assist to the special advisor. The NPF was one of several groups with ties to the CIA, but inquiries with Langley had also come back negative. The CIA claimed no

306 | RICK DESTEFANIS

knowledge of him. Someone was stonewalling big-time, but who and why?

"Yeah," Gilardi answered. He shook Gates's hand. "I really appreciate the help your people have given us. I'll let you know what we find with the autopsy. Give me a call if you find anything new."

* * *

Jesse Harper had just picked up his mail at the store and was driving his old truck up the hill through town when he spotted Sheriff Harvey. The sheriff had parked his car at the Melody Hill Church entrance and was standing, gazing up the slope toward the cemetery. Jesse slowed and pulled up beside Sheriff Harvey. Several people were gathered at the edge of the cemetery behind the church.

Jesse rolled down his window. A yellow backhoe sputtered and clanked as it rolled across the rocky ground on the hill.

"Who passed?" Jesse asked.

"Nobody," Harvey said. "The army just dug up Brady Nash's grave. Said they might have buried the wrong body in it."

The weather was bitter, and the sheriff stood with his back hunched against the cold mountain air, his vaporized breath escaping in the breeze. Jesse pulled his truck to the side of the road and walked back to where the sheriff stood.

"Damned if that ain't something," Jesse said. "It's just like the military to screw up a burial." He pulled his cap back and scratched his head. "Bastards can't get nothing right anymore."

"You should know," Harvey said.

The sheriff cast a sideways glance at him, but Jesse remained focused on the activity up at the church. Harvey was right. He'd gotten a bellyful of military bureaucracy during his two tours of Nam back in '65 and '66.

"The worst of it is poor Miss Emma and little Lacey are up there now with those army people," the sheriff said. "Think how they must feel."

"They ain't gonna open it in front of them, are they?" Jesse asked.

"Hell, I don't reckon. Miss Emma said she just wanted to be up there. Know what I mean?"

Jesse nodded, and several minutes later, when the gray army hearse came around from behind the church, he pulled off his cap. The vehicle rolled slowly down the hill with the muddy casket inside. Sheriff Harvey removed his cap as well, and Jesse squinted as the sun reflected from the windshield of the hearse when it passed.

"You know," Jesse said, "there's something that just ain't quite right about that whole mess."

"How's that?" the sheriff asked.

Jesse replaced his cap and pulled the bill down low over his eyes.

"Well, first, Duff gets killed, and there were all kinds of rumors about how Brady went over yonder 'cause he thought Duff was murdered, and now this. It's all just a little bit too strange."

Sheriff Harvey remained tight-lipped as he shoved his hands into his pockets and watched the hearse disappear down the road.

Harper cut his eyes at the sheriff. Harvey knew something, but wasn't letting on.

"I reckon I'll be on my way," Jesse said.

"You take care," the Sheriff said.

Jesse walked back and got in his truck, but the sheriff called out to him.

"Hey, Jesse, wait a minute."

The people from up at the cemetery had begun walking back down beside the church. Lacey and her mother were holding hands. With the group still several hundred feet away, Jesse waited while the sheriff sauntered up to his truck.

"You were over there," Harvey said. "What do you think?"

"Think about what?" Jesse asked.

"The rumors, you know, about Brady and Duff."

"That's a damned crazy war, and I'm seeing a lot of smoke right now. I mean, with all the things I've heard about them boys getting killed, there's a fire somewhere."

The sheriff turned and gazed down across the rooftops of the little town below. Jesse followed his gaze, looking out toward the Hiwassee and the Little Tennessee River Valleys. The distant horizon was hazy in the afternoon sun.

"I'd be obliged if you'd give me a call if you notice anything strange hereabouts," the sheriff said.

"Strange like what—the ghost of Brady Nash?"

The two men faced one another, and Harvey's jaw tightened almost imperceptibly.

"I believe you're jumping to conclusions," the sheriff said.

"Am I, Sheriff?"

Harvey didn't answer, and Jesse smiled.

"You have a good day, Sheriff. I'll let you know if I see anything unusual."

Jesse cranked his truck. There was a lot more going on than anyone wanted to admit, but his tours in Nam had been enough drama for one lifetime. Unless someone came to him for help, he'd sit this one out.

* * *

As she walked down the hill from the cemetery, Lacey watched the hearse disappear down the road. The two investigators walked with her and her mother: one, an army criminal investigator; the other, an FBI agent. The FBI agent was tight-lipped, but the army man, Major Gilardi, seemed sympathetic and explained how he thought it was a good chance that the body in the grave was not Brady's.

"If that proves to be the case, your son's status will be changed to 'missing in action' until it can be verified otherwise."

Lacey refused to allow herself hope that might end in another disappointment. Unless something else happened, something that truly caused her to believe Brady was alive, hope was something she would not allow in her heart.

Gilardi held the car door as he helped her mother inside. A few days before Christmas, when the two government men first arrived, they began questioning her and her mother about Brady. Their questions had made it clear they were unsure as to the identity of the body in the grave. And when they called it a "possible clerical error," she had seen through their story. Gilardi was too honest of a man to tell a straight-faced lie. This also made her believe he was someone who could be trusted.

She had told him about Duff and the mysterious letter that Hubert Brister had gotten from him. She also told him about the cryptic letters from Brady. She sensed Gilardi already knew something was amiss, but he didn't offer any explanations. She pressed him for an explanation, but he only asked more questions. Gilardi acted as if he'd expected to hear some of the things she said, but he wasn't telling her anything.

As the car's engine gurgled to life, she rolled her window down and looked up at Gilardi. "We will appreciate it if you give us some answers when you can," she said.

The FBI man remained hard-eyed and stared out at something in the distance, but Gilardi nodded as he made eye contact with her. "I promise, I will tell you what I can when this is all sorted out."

Lacey let off the brake, and the car rolled from the church parking lot. She glanced at her mother, who sat stoically, lost in thought. Now more than ever, Lacey realized she had to give her mother something to live for.

CHAPTER TWENTY-TWO

The Grand Ole Opry

The army investigator promised to notify her as soon as the autopsy was complete, and Lacey found herself torn between the possibilities and the reality of the situation. She wanted to remain in Melody Hill to care for her mother, but her mother said she should go back to Nashville and meet her commitments. But it wasn't so much a commitment as it was a reward, because she had been invited to appear at the Grand Ole Opry.

Despite the emotional roller coaster, Lacey realized her mother was right. So many people had parts of their lives invested in Lacey's career, and she couldn't let them down. She had to make the most of this opportunity. Yes, it was the fulfillment of a dream, and it was the greatest opportunity of her musical career, something that could take her beyond her dreams. She would be seen and heard by people all over the country. And when the big night finally arrived, Billy Wyatt, Belle Langston, and all her friends from the restaurant and the club were in the audience.

It was a bitter cold January evening in Nashville, but the Ryman Auditorium was packed, and Lacey trembled as she peeked out at the huge audience. Her invitation here should have been one of the happiest moments of her life, but she could barely focus. Devastated by Brady's death only two months ago, she had been ready to quit when Belle came to her with word of the Opry invitation. And only days later, the investigators had come to Melody Hill with the court order to dig up Brady's grave. The assault of emotions had left her reeling.

Belle stood backstage, holding her hand and offering quiet words of encouragement, but the stage lights, the musicians, and the packed auditorium left her mesmerized. Even Loretta Lynn was there, along with several other well-known country music entertainers, speaking to her and Belle as if they were old friends. Nearly catatonic with fright, Lacey realized she had to find some relief, some pause, if only for a moment, to get her head right. This was her big opportunity, yet it seemed her mind was parting at the seams. She needed to put everything else out of her mind, step out on that stage, and do what she had worked so hard for.

After patting Belle's hand, Lacey excused herself and walked down a narrow hallway to a quiet corner backstage. She found an old chair, where she sat and closed her eyes. It was the quiet place she needed, if only for a moment. Drawing a deep breath, she relaxed and listened to the muted sounds of the voices and applause. The long months spent cleaning tables and sweeping floors were finally about to pay off. All the things that had led to this moment, all the people who had helped her—Duff and Brady, and the years they shared together—had culminated with her having this opportunity. This was it. Someone from Melody Hill had finally made it. And as she thought of these things, she felt for the first time a certain confidence. She would do this for Duff and Brady.

Standing, she drew another calming breath, smoothed her dress, and turned back toward the stage. Despite her resolve, she fussed with her clothes. The producer had wanted her to wear a low-cut black dress, split nearly to her hip, but it was too slinky. Hugh Langston made his bid again for the miniskirt and cowboy boots, but she would wait tables the rest of her life before she would give in to that old pervert. Then Billy came up with something that looked like a red-and-white checkered tablecloth. In the end, she'd gone shopping with Belle.

They'd gone through several stores before choosing a stylish, but conservative crushed-velvet dress. Belle said it was the perfect stage dress—a deep blue, cut to a mid-calf length, and sprinkled with a tiny mother-of-pearl sequined floral pattern that matched Lacey's pearl earrings. It clung beautifully to her figure, and Lacey was in love with it until she thumbed the price tag. It nearly took her breath. Paying $375 for a dress was out of the question, no matter how perfect it looked. Walking from the dressing room, she gave the dress back to Belle and showed her the price tag.

Belle laughed and said, "Don't sweat it, sweetheart. This one's on me."

Before she'd even walked onstage, Lacey was already a success with the people backstage as they gave her rave reviews on the dress. Loretta complimented her as well and offered words of encouragement. Everything, it seemed, was going her way. Even Billy had been supportive when she opted to sing a remake of an old Hank Williams song, "I'm So Lonesome."

She stood backstage as another performance ended, and Tennessee Ernie Ford did a commercial for Goody's headache powder. As always, the show was live on WSM radio, but it was also now being televised across the country, and Lacey thought of her mother back home in Melody Hill. With the mountain roads too icy for travel, she was sitting in her favorite chair in front of the TV along with several neighbors. Even though she wasn't actually in Nashville, her mother's presence was as real to her as if she was sitting in the front row. It all seemed like a dream until the deep voice of the announcer echoed her name throughout the auditorium.

"Ladies and gentlemen, let's welcome Miss Lacey Coleridge."

She felt the gentle nudge of Belle's hand against her back. The blood drained from her head, and she felt her feet moving, carrying her to center stage. Cameras flashed throughout the auditorium as the lights went down low. Bowing, she pulled the microphone close, and when the applause died away, it was quiet as a church at midnight. For several seconds, she stood in silence. One of the musicians behind her gently cleared his throat, and Lacey awoke from her trance. Looking back, she nodded, and with a voice that windowed her soul, she began singing a cappella.

Hear the lonesome whippoorwill
His song's too blue to fly
The midnight train is a-winding low
I'm so lonesome I could cry

By the time the band joined her for the second verse, not a person in the auditorium stirred. And perhaps because she was singing from her heart, the audience was spellbound as her voice filled every corner of the auditorium. The band was perfect. She was perfect.

The silence of a falling star
Lights up a purple haze
And as I wonder where you are
I'm so lonesome I could cry

When her song ended, Lacey bent one knee and nodded her head. An interminable void of silence hung over the auditorium. And it seemed it might go on forever, until the mesmerized crowd suddenly exploded. The applause roared in her ears as Lacey's eyes filled with tears.

Behind her, one of the band members shouted, "She nailed it!"

Tennessee Ernie Ford walked to her side as he acknowledged the applause, waving and smiling at the audience. There were whoops and yells coming from backstage, and before she realized it, not a single person in Ryman Auditorium remained seated as the applause thundered unabated.

Tennessee Ernie Ford put his mouth up to her ear and nearly shouted to make himself heard. "Baby, these folks want to hear you sing something else, but I don't see how you can top that. Do you have another song rehearsed?"

The applause faded as she nodded, then turned to the stage musicians behind her. They huddled briefly, and after a few seconds, she turned to the audience.

"Ladies and gentlemen, I recently lost the second of two…" She paused as the emotion welled up inside her. Swallowing hard, she continued, "These were two people who were very dear to me, and they both died in the Vietnam War. I would like to dedicate this next song to their memory. This is for my brother, Duff Coleridge, and my friend Brady Nash."

She cued the musicians, but the emotion overcame her as she shook her head and hesitated. The music stopped. Lacey again swallowed hard and took a deep breath. After several seconds, she turned and once again cued the band. The musicians were perfect, and with the same inspiration that had held the audience spellbound the first time, she sang "Amazing Grace."

Her voice resonated with passion, and as she reached the last verse, several of the entertainers walked from backstage, motioning for the audience to join in. Everyone came to their feet and sang with her until the last notes faded in silence. Another ovation thundered across the auditorium. Smiling radiantly, and with the tears still in her eyes, Lacey walked offstage, waving and blowing kisses as she went. She'd gotten her chance, and she'd stolen the show.

* * *

The temperature plummeted that night with the passing cold front, and Lacey shivered as she left the auditorium with Belle and Billy. Walking down the steps from the side entrance, she shielded her face as snowflakes darted beneath the streetlights. Despite the bitter northwest wind, everyone was smiling and talking enthusiastically of her success. The response of the audience and the other performers had been nothing short of phenomenal, and Lacey felt better than she had in months.

Pulling her collar tight around her neck, she hurried across the lot and opened the car door. But as she was about to climb inside, she noticed a commotion beneath a streetlight up on Fifth Avenue. A policeman was wrestling a vagrant to the ground, and for a moment, she thought she heard someone call her name. She paused as a strange feeling came over her. The policeman shoved the man into the back of the squad car, but the vagrant seemed to be trying to get her attention. She tossed her purse into the car and began walking across the parking lot toward the squad car.

"Where are you going?" Billy shouted.

Lacey could scarcely explain what she was doing. She ignored him and began trotting clumsily in her high heels. She ran down the side of the building as the radiant smile she wore so well moments before faded in the nighttime shadows. She hurried, but before she reached the street, the police car pulled from the curb and sped away.

"Wait," she shouted.

It was no use. The car continued up the hill and out of sight as Belle and Billy ran up to her.

"What are you doing?" Billy asked.

It was something too crazy to explain. "Nothing," she said. "I just thought...Never mind. Let's just go, OK?"

* * *

Lacey awoke with a start. The phone was ringing. Outside her apartment window, the sunlight shone brilliantly on the snow-covered hills. The call no doubt was her mother calling from home, or maybe Billy or Belle, ready for an early breakfast celebration. Picking up the phone, she propped herself up in bed.

"Hello?"

"Lacey, whatever you do, don't hang up. Just listen. This is Brady. I'm not dead. I'm alive, and I'm in the Davidson County jail here in Nashville."

She stared at the receiver.

"Lacey, you there? Listen to me, baby. That was me outside the Ryman last night, and I need your help."

"Brady?"

She couldn't think. This was a terrible joke, but no...

"You're..."

She couldn't speak, but the person on the phone finished her sentence. "In the Davidson County jail. I need you to come bail me out."

"But…"

The voice dropped to a barely audible whisper. "When you come down here, ask for Raymond Gordon. You understand?"

Raymond Gordon was the name the army officer had mentioned. Her head spun as she nodded her acknowledgment to the voice on the phone and hung up. What was happening? It was Brady. She would recognize his voice a hundred years from now. Lacey jumped from the bed, pulled on a pair of jeans, and ran to the front door.

A flood of brilliant sunlight reflected from the newly fallen snow, nearly blinding her as she clung to the icy railing, but she turned around and ran back inside. She'd forgotten her shoes. She quickly put them on, then ran back and made her way down the steps. Last night's storm was gone, and the fresh snow crunched beneath her feet as she hurried across the parking lot. The chilled breeze whipped her hair into her face, but she hardly noticed. Was it really Brady? Of course it was. It had to be. She couldn't face another disappointment.

Reaching the car, she fumbled in her purse for the key. Her teeth chattered, and the frozen vapor of her breath clouded the windshield as she turned the ignition switch. The starter only grunted.

"Come on," she pleaded.

Again, the starter grunted, then again, and when she thought the engine wouldn't start, it suddenly sparked and roared to life.

Yanking the transmission into reverse, she floored the accelerator. Wheels smoking on ice, she backed from the parking place.

* * *

"You're mistaken," she said. "I know he's here. I talked with him a few minutes ago. Don't you have some kind of arrest records somewhere?"

Lacey refused to believe the jailer. It had to be Brady. She was certain. But the jailer insisted that there was no one there by that name. He sent her back to the front desk, where she confronted the desk sergeant.

"How can you say he's not here? He is. He has to be. Check again. His name is Brady Nash, and he was arrested last night on Fifth Avenue in front of the Ryman Auditorium. I know it was him."

The tears dripped from under her sunglasses.

"No, ma'am, Miss Coleridge," the sergeant said. "But you wait a minute, and I'll double-check the shift log. You say he was arrested sometime before midnight over on Fifth Avenue, right?"

She nodded.

"Let's see. Well, here's one. His name is Raymond Gordon, but he fits that description."

"Raymond Gordon?" she said. She was an idiot. She'd blown it.

"Yes," the policeman replied, "he's back there in the drunk tank. Why don't we bring him up where you can get a look at him? Maybe he gave you a bogus name. You know how these characters can be. Are you wanting to press charges?"

"No! No, not at all. It's just that…well…I need to see him. I need to talk to him, and…" Lacey blushed as she fumbled for the right words. "Like I said, I know him—and he just kind of disappeared, and…"

The desk sergeant pushed his cheek outward with his tongue and glanced over at a clerk sitting nearby. Their eyes met, and the sergeant winked and smiled. Lacey knew what he was thinking, but it was better to endure the embarrassment. Nothing mattered except finding Brady.

"I think I understand now," the sergeant said. "So are you wanting to make bail for this guy?"

"Well, yes," she answered. "Can I?"

* * *

"Hey, Gordon," the jailer shouted. "Come on out here, boy. This is your lucky day. There's a good-looking woman up front making bail for you."

Brady was sitting in the back corner of the cell when he heard the keys jangling at the door. The wreckage he'd made of life was certainly more bearable drunk, but buying the bottle of liquor had been a mistake. Wasting no time, he picked his way through a jumble of comatose drunks as he made his way across to the cell door.

The jailer shook his head. "Women nowadays are crazy, making bail for you hippie bastards. Must be the dope."

Brady scarcely listened as the steel door clanked behind him, and he walked up the hallway to freedom.

* * *

Lacey finished signing the release papers.

"You better ask him for his ID," the old police sergeant said. "I believe that fella has pulled the wool over your eyes, little lady."

Lacey didn't reply as they showed her to an outside hallway to meet him. When the heavy steel door finally opened, Brady was there, bearded and dirty. But it was his eyes, the ones bluer than the mountain sky, except they now seemed cold, almost predatory. Lacey wanted to grab him, to hold him close, but it suddenly seemed she shouldn't. Wordlessly, she took his hand and led him to the car.

* * *

Police Sergeant Roy Barnes had a feeling there was something amiss, but he couldn't put his finger on it. The Coleridge girl made Gordon's bail, but she seemed confused about his name. He had apparently lied to her. After watching the two of them leave, Barnes walked back to the office and sat at his desk.

"Hey, Clyde, did you send that Gordon fella's prints to the Army Records Center in Saint Louis?" Barnes asked.

"Sent 'em first thing this morning," Clyde said.

The sergeant scratched his chin. "You know there's something fishy about this whole thing. Did you compare his fingerprints with the ones on the ID?"

"I sent them over to fingerprinting along with the ones on his ID a little while ago."

"I don't know," Barnes said. "Something just ain't right. We might should have held him a little longer, but of all people to make bail, Lacey Coleridge. Did you see her on the Grand Ole Opry last night?"

He looked down again at the papers she'd signed.

"Say, how long is it taking those verifications to get back from Saint Louis these days?"

"Depends," Clyde answered. "Sometimes, less than twenty-four hours, but sometimes it takes two or three days. Same as it's always been. You just never know."

"What about fingerprinting?"

"Tomorrow morning. They're off on Sunday, and nobody said it was urgent."

The sergeant propped his feet on the desk.

"Oh well. I guess we'll just have to wait and see. At least we know where to find him."

* * *

Brady sat in silence as Lacey drove, almost recklessly, toward her apartment. Tears streamed from her eyes as the car slipped along on the icy road. When they reached the apartment, they embraced beside the car, oblivious to the wind and snow. After a while, he gently held her chin and gazed into her eyes. There, he saw fear and confusion and, at the same time, hope.

"It's going to be OK," Brady said.

"Why didn't you call me and tell me you were alive?"

"I couldn't. I was afraid the phones might be tapped."

"Tapped?"

Brady hardly knew where to begin. "Yeah, bugged."

"By who?"

"Let's go inside."

As they walked up the apartment steps, Brady began, "It all started a few days before Duff got killed. Because his mail was being read, he had sent a letter home with a friend. This friend was a soldier Duff trusted, and the guy brought the letter to me down at the bus stop on 411, a few days after Duff's funeral…"

Brady suddenly found he couldn't stop talking. He told Lacey about the letter and the reason for his odyssey to Vietnam. He also told her about Maxon and the dangers that remained. They talked for nearly an hour as Lacey revealed Hubert Brister's death, the still-missing letter, and the exhumation by the army and FBI.

"I'm hungry," Brady said.

"What are we going to do?" Lacey asked.

"Let me think a minute. I'm going to take a bath."

Lacey arose from the table and opened the refrigerator. Brady went into the bathroom. It was his first bath in weeks, and he drew the water as hot as he could stand. When he finished, he wiped the steam from the mirror and began shaving. How could two such basic items as soap and hot water seem so luxurious? He rubbed his face. It felt good to be clean again, but it would be a short-lived pleasure. He had to get going again.

He saw Lacey in the bathroom mirror, standing behind him.

"I have breakfast ready," she said.

"They fingerprinted me in jail," Brady said. "They'll do a background check with the army, and I expect the police will come here looking for me."

"Why can't you just give yourself up and tell them everything that's happened?"

"It's like what that correspondent in Saigon said, they might just discredit me, make me look like a wacko, and throw me in prison, or worse, an insane asylum. I need to find Duff's letter and the other papers that are with it."

"But it's lost," Lacey said.

"Maybe not," Brady answered. "If his kinfolk don't have it, it has to be in the old house. You said no one is living there now, right?"

Lacey nodded.

"It's got to be hidden there. I'm going to Melody Hill and try to find it."

"And if you don't find it?"

"We'll see."

CHAPTER TWENTY-THREE

Return to Melody Hill

L acey was frustrated. It hadn't taken long, but they were already at odds again. Brady was being his old stubborn self. Sitting beside him on the living room couch, she tried to come up with a plan. It was only a matter of time before the police would come looking for him, but Brady was insisting that she stay behind.

"No way, buster," she said.

She'd cried that day when he left for Vietnam without saying good-bye. She was so certain he would call, and only now had she learned of the call that Hugh Langston never told her about.

"You're not leaving here without me. By some miracle you've come back, and I'm never letting you out of my sight again."

He tried to pull her closer, but Lacey stiff-armed him away. She had to make him understand.

"You're not leaving me again. I mean it."

"But you have no idea what you're saying," he whispered. "These people are ruthless. We could both be killed."

"I don't care. I'd rather die with you than live without you. Just don't leave me, please, not again."

Brady pulled her down on the couch to talk. He was a self-described assassin and an army deserter, and she was hiding him in her apartment, but she knew his heart. He was a good man, and she wanted only to cling to him and to never let him go. He gently grasped her shoulders and held her at arm's length. His eyes remained dry, but for the first time, she saw a hint of emotion somewhere deep within. He gazed steadily at her, and she at him.

"I am not leaving you behind, but we have to do this my way," Brady said. "I need you to stay here for just a little while, while I go ahead to Melody Hill. The police will come looking for me, and I need you to be here to send them in the wrong direction. You have to buy me some time."

She pulled his hand from her shoulder and held it tightly against her breast as a new tear trickled down her cheek. She didn't want to stay behind, but she'd made the mistake of not listening to him once before. Brady seemed to know what had to be done. He pulled her close, kissing the tears from her cheeks. Afterward, she put her head against his chest, hugging him tightly.

"What will I tell them?" she said. "They know I bailed you out of jail."

"That's OK. Tell them everything you know except where I'm really going. Tell them about Duff and Maxon. Tell them all of it, but make them think I'm going to New York to meet with a newspaper editor."

"Then what?"

"Once I've found Duff's letter, I'm writing a statement with enough names and dates that no one will be able to say I'm crazy. I'll send it to the newspaper, and then I'll give myself up."

"How will I find you?"

"You won't have to. I'll find you. Now stop worrying and help me figure this thing out. I've got to find a way to get to Melody Hill."

"I know someone who will give you a ride there, or maybe you can borrow his truck," Lacey said.

She told him of Billy, and they talked through their plans. When they were done, Brady kissed her forehead and stood up.

"The clock's running," he said. "I've got to get going."

"No," Lacey said, "not right now." She pulled him back down on the couch. "Not until you make love to me the way you did that day by the river."

* * *

Brady had driven through the night, arriving in Melody Hill just before dawn. He parked Billy Wyatt's truck up the road from the Coleridge house. In the first gray light of day, he eased up a wooded slope where he could see the surrounding area. Having spent several hours with Lacey before bidding her good-bye, he

330 | RICK DESTEFANIS

was tired. It had been something special, but the stark reality of his situation had returned. He was still in a fight that could end in death.

The house below was quiet, as was the rest of the town, dark except for the first kitchen lights now glowing orange as people began brewing their morning coffee. The streets were empty, and only the telltale streams of smoke from rooftop chimneys gave any hint of activity in the town below. Satisfied that he was still ahead of the authorities, Brady returned to the truck, drove up the road, and turned into the drive at the house.

As he walked to the front door, he glanced at the windows of the neighbor's houses, the outbuildings, and the yards, searching for signs of danger. The very thought was repulsive. The war had followed him home, and he was sneaking about as if he were near some enemy-held village.

Stepping up on the porch, he tried the doorknob. As always, it was open. Glancing around, he checked one last time, still no sign of danger. After slipping inside, he quietly closed the door and knocked on the doorframe with his knuckles. He called out.

"Mama Emma, you awake?"

He quickly searched the room, then went to the front window, where he glanced out at the street. It was still quiet. He heard the sound of footsteps coming from the back bedroom, and within moments, Mama Emma appeared. She looked so much older now than when he left a year ago. Her eyes were flooded with tears, but she was smiling.

"Lacey called me last night. Oh, baby, I just can't believe this. What are you going to do?"

Brady held her close, stroking her gray hair as she trembled in his arms. "Look, I've got a plan, but I'm going to need some help."

"Why don't you just give yourself up to Sheriff Harvey, baby? He'll take care of you. Please? It's the best thing."

"Because the government people won't let me stay in his custody. They'll take me, and the next thing you'll hear is that I'm being sedated in an insane asylum somewhere, or else shot, trying to escape."

Her face paled, but Brady held her hand as he led her into the kitchen. "I need to search Hubert Brister's place, find the envelope, and send it to the newspapers. I need some food and water and my hunting gear. Once I get the letter mailed, I'll have to lay low for few days before I give myself up."

"Oh, Brady, it seems so complicated."

"I know, but I have to buy time. Now listen. They'll probably come here looking for me sometime in the next day or so. I want you to tell them that I came here for food and that I just wanted to tell you that I was alive. I also want you to tell them I said I was going down to 411 to catch a bus to New York."

Brady opened a cupboard.

"Can I take some of this food?"

"Of course."

Mama Emma quickly brewed coffee and began heating a skillet. Within the hour, Brady had packed his hunting gear and some canned goods, stacking all of it at the back door. He set his hunting rifle atop the pile. Mama Emma stared wide-eyed at the rifle.

"Why are you taking your rifle?"

"Trust me. It's because I have to."

"You can't take all that stuff with you on the bus," she said.

"I know. I'm going to leave the truck I'm driving at the bus stop on 411. I called Jesse Harper last night, and he's going to pick me up and take me to Brister's place to look for the letter."

"Oh, Brady, what if I say something wrong?"

"You won't. Just be smart and don't say anything on the phone or even around this house that you don't want the government to know because they'll probably have all the phones and the house bugged before long."

As her eyes widened, Brady kissed her forehead. "I've got to go."

* * *

A stained percolator hissed and gurgled in the corner of the dispatcher's office that Monday morning, filling the Davidson County jail with the aroma of fresh-brewed coffee. Sergeant Roy Barnes was sitting at his desk, looking over the night log, when Officer Clyde Blevins burst into the room. With a look of grim excitement on his face, Blevins charged toward Barnes and slapped a piece of paper down on the desk.

"There! Read that, Sarge," Blevins said.

Barnes looked over the top of his glasses at the patrolman. Clyde was a good cop, but the word "understatement" didn't register anywhere in his vocabulary. He stood in front of him, lips pressed firmly together and nodding his head with satisfaction. The old desk sergeant forced himself not to roll his eyes as he picked up the telex message.

"You'd make a great movie actor, Clyde."

With that, he tilted his head back as he read through his bifocals.

Department of the Army
US Army Record Processing Center
Saint Louis, Missouri

NAME INQUIRY: File Flagged: Notify Federal Bureau of Investigation and Army Criminal Investigation Department with all inquiries.

Gordon, Raymond C 410 88 4357 PFC USAR
Wounded in Action, Republic of Vietnam, 23 Sep 1968
Status: AWOL, Seattle, Washington, VA Hospital, 20 Dec 1968

FINGERPRINT ANALYSIS:
Nash, Brady 411 02 3334 SP4 USAR
Killed in Action, Republic of Vietnam, 23 Sep 1968

"Well, I'll be damned," Barnes said. "I believe you do have something to get excited about. I knew there was something funny about that guy. Says here he was killed in action."

Blevins nodded. "You want me to find out where that Coleridge girl lives and dispatch some cars?"

The young patrolman was already backing toward the dispatcher's office. Barnes stared at the paper for several seconds before shaking his head.

"No. Hold on a minute. I don't reckon we better," he said. "We need to bring the federal boys in on this one. Get Huey Gates on the phone. We'll turn it over to the FBI. If he wants our help, he'll let us know."

* * *

Lacey had just finished touching up her lipstick in the bathroom mirror when she heard the knocking at the door. She glanced at her watch. It was 9:50 a.m. Brady had left before midnight, and she'd been expecting the police ever since, but it had taken nearly twelve hours. Stepping back, she looked at herself again in the mirror and picked a thread from her sweater. As she turned to walk to the living room, the knocking began again, this time louder.

"Who is it?" she called through the door.

"FBI," a man's voice shouted.

She opened the door. A big man in a suit held a badge and ID in her face.

"FBI, ma'am. Can we come in?"

Lacey nodded. "Sure."

She didn't recognize the man who shoved the badge in her face, but the other was Huey Gates, the stone-faced FBI man she'd met at the cemetery in Melody Hill. The two men glanced around as they entered the apartment. The younger one edged his way cautiously toward the hallway.

"He's not here," she said. "He's gone."

Both men stopped moving and looked at her.

"Who's not here, Miss Coleridge?"

"Brady Nash."

The men cast glances at one another.

"Where is he?" Gates asked.

Lacey hesitated. Brady was probably well into his plan by now, most likely on his way to the old Brister place.

"He told me he was going to New York to meet with a newspaper and give them his story."

"You mean he's going to tell them why he's deserted from the army and using another soldier's identity?"

"Yes, but that's only a small part of what's happened," Lacey said.

"How long has it been since he left here?" Gates asked.

"He left yesterday."

"How did he leave?"

"What do you mean?"

"I mean did he walk away, or did someone give him a ride?"

"He borrowed a friend's truck."

"What kind of truck is it?"

Lacey turned and walked toward the couch. She had to delay them. The more she stalled, the more time Brady would have to complete his search.

"Don't you even want to know why he's doing all of this?"

"My job isn't to find out why he's broken the law. It's to apprehend him."

"Well, I'm not telling you anything more until you let me tell you what made him do this."

"Miss Coleridge, if you don't cooperate, I'll have you arrested for obstruction of justice. Now tell me what kind of truck he's driving."

"I fully intend to, but first, I'm going to give you some more important information, information that could save some people's lives."

Lacey picked up several sheets of paper from the coffee table. Although she'd cleaned and polished it, the old table was scratched and worn. Her entire apartment seemed suddenly inadequate, the old brown couch with Sampson curled up on one end and the television sitting atop an old whiskey barrel from Lynchburg. These men probably saw her as some kind of seedy criminal.

"These are notes I took while Brady and I were talking yesterday morning. The only things missing are the names of the witnesses. He doesn't want the government to get to them before the news-paper has a chance to interview them."

A tight-lipped Gates took the papers and began looking over them. The younger agent glanced over his shoulder.

"OK, what does all this mean?" Gates asked. "Who is Duff?"

Lacey took a deep breath before she spoke. "I thought you knew all of this. Isn't that why you dug up the grave?"

"Answer my question, Miss Coleridge. Who is Duff?"

"Duff was my brother, and he was murdered by the people he was working for in Vietnam. That's why Brady went to Vietnam, to find them."

Gates turned to the younger agent. "Call Major Gilardi and tell him he better get back here as fast he can. Tell him we're starting to get some answers about Nash."

Gates glanced down at the notes again.

"Wait a minute," he called to the other agent, "I also want you to send an inquiry to the CIA. Says here Nash was on a temporary duty assignment with them in Vietnam." He glanced up at Lacey. "Is that right?"

"Yes."

"Miss Coleridge, since your friend Mr. Nash is still a member of the armed forces, I'm notifying the Army Criminal Investigation Department. I'm sure they'll want to interview you in the next twenty-four hours. I'm also going to contact the CIA to see if they can provide us with any information. In the meantime, I want you to stay put. Understood?"

"Yes, but you need to understand that Brady is a good man. He's done nothing wrong."

"Miss Coleridge…" Gates paused as he looked at the floor and shook his head. "I hope you're right, but right now, I don't know what to think."

* * *

As Brady rode with Jesse in his pickup back up the mountain to Melody Hill, his eyelids felt like lead. They'd left Billy Wyatt's truck at the bus stop on 411, hopefully buying them more time. Brady had been awake nearly forty-eight hours. Jesse was asking questions, rightly so, but they were nonetheless aggravating.

"So how come you called me?" he asked.

The heater fan in Harper's old pickup roared, doing battle with the icy air leaking in around the doors.

"'Cause you're a vet, and I can trust you. Besides, Lacey said Hubert Brister told his kinfolk you know where Duff's letter is hidden."

Harper scratched at his beard. "I hate to disappoint you, bubba, but Old Man Brister never told me nothing about no letter. The only thing he ever said to me was just before he died. I went to see him at the hospital in Knoxville. He said if you ever came around asking, to tell you your stuff was safe as long as nobody stole his tools and the cows didn't eat him out of house and home."

"What the hell did he mean by that?" Brady asked.

"Damned if I know. Maybe he hid it in a toolbox, but I think he was all doped up on pain medicine and talking out of his head."

Brady thought about the toolbox for a moment. Closing his eyes, he lay back. When he opened his eyes, he was momentarily disoriented. Jesse stood beside him with the truck door open. Only his boots crunching in the snow broke the eerie silence of the snow-covered hills.

"Where are we?"

"We're home, bubba, Polk County. Come on, let's go inside so you can get some sleep."

Harper's vaporized breath whipped away in the breeze. His cabin sat on a bluff beside the Hiwassee. The icy waters of the river tumbled over the rocks below.

"I can't. I've got to go to Brister's place first."

"You're a walking zombie, bubba. If you don't get some sleep, you're gonna pass out."

"I don't care. We've got to go now."

"OK, bubba, I didn't want to tell you this, but I saw several strange vehicles on the way in, ones I haven't seen around here before. And they all had tinted windows. The whole area is under surveillance. That's why I detoured and came here to my place."

"You think any of them followed us?"

"Nah, they weren't looking for a couple of hillbillies."

Harper's cabin was headquarters for his canoe and tube rental business, and the front porch was lined with an assortment of paddles and fishing tackle. Brady stepped out of the truck. Across the road, a small airplane sat in a field, its wings laden with snow.

"You ain't wrecked it, yet?"

Jesse gave a grunt and a laugh. "Hell, I've tried a few times."

Despite the cold, Brady paused as he glanced at the airstrip. It couldn't have been much over a hundred yards long.

"How the hell do you take off?"

"I took off and landed on strips just like it in Nam."

"Yeah," Brady said, "but that was because you had to."

Jesse wiped his nose with his sleeve and laughed. "You ground pounders are all the same, scared of anything that gets more'n a foot off the ground."

"I was airborne," Brady said.

"Oh yeah," Jesse said, "I forgot. Never did understand men who jump out of perfectly good airplanes."

The men walked up the steps to the cabin. The warmth of a wood-burning stove quickly broke his chill as Brady removed his coat.

"Feels good in here," he said.

"Come to the back. I'm gonna put you up in the den. I got a couch in there that makes out like a bed. We'll sort through the rest of this business after you finish your nap."

A smallmouth bass hung on the wall along with an eight-point buck, but it was a framed photo that caught Brady's attention. It was Jesse standing beside an OV-1 reconnaissance plane. In the background were several Hueys, parked with drooping rotors. Another photo showed him standing beside the wreckage of a second aircraft, poking his fingers in what appeared to be bullet holes.

Brady had eventually heard the entire story about Jesse's tours of duty. He'd been shot down twice, and the last time, he'd been given up for dead until he walked out of the jungle three weeks later. Jesse had seen his share of hell. This was why Brady had gone to him for help.

Jesse pulled a blanket from a nearby closet and tossed it to him. "Make yourself at home, bubba. I'll wake you up in a little while, and we'll head back around the mountain to the Brister place."

Brady didn't bother taking his boots off as he lay back on the couch and passed out again.

CHAPTER TWENTY-FOUR

Rise of the Phoenix

Maxon wasn't exactly surprised when he got the telex from the Office of the Special Assistant a few days after Christmas. He was being recalled—no explanation, just ordered to report to Langley, Virginia. His bosses at the embassy house were tight-lipped about it, but he hoped it meant his contract was being converted to a full time staff position. That was the way the company worked. It was time. He'd been hard at it for three years in Nam, three contract extensions, and with the numbers he'd turned, there was probably a promotion in the works.

After packing his gear, he warned his men. Things were going bad in Vietnam. The new Vietnamization program was a joke, because without America, the South Vietnamese Army didn't have a chance against the NVA. And with the army now running the Phoenix Program, it, too, was a joke, no teeth. Those silly army fucks thought they could play by the rules, but they found killing VC was like killing roaches one at a time. Of course, the lily-livered politicians didn't have the stomach for real solutions. They were caving in to the liberals and longhairs at every turn. They were quitting, giving up because someone was afraid they were killing the wrong gooks.

He didn't know why he even worried about it. None of it really mattered anymore. Vietnam was a lost cause, and he was home free. He hoped. There was that subconscious apprehension that gnawed at him, niggling phantoms of thought that came and went, leaving behind an indefinable anxiety. He'd covered his tracks well, but there was one person still alive who could cause him trouble, Lynn Dai Bouchet. She'd gone into hiding, but if she resurfaced... He was being too paranoid.

From Da Nang, it was on to Japan, then Anchorage, arriving at Dulles International by midafternoon the next day. He was supposed to report in upon arrival, but with his internal clock screwed up, Maxon opted to get some sleep first. After catching a cab over to the Hilton in Crystal City, he checked in to a fifth-floor room. He opened the curtains wide, fell back on the bed, and looked over at the bedside clock. It was nearly 4:00 p.m. local time.

Just twenty-four hours ago, he had been listening to the echoing booms of rockets impacting near the outskirts of Da Nang city. Now he was back in the world, lying on a soft mattress and looking out over Northern Virginia. He'd made it, and he'd made enough money on the black market to be on easy street the rest of his life. His years in Vietnam had been a hell of a gamble, but when the cards were shown, he pulled the pot.

He reached for the phone and dialed the number down at Langley.

"Greener," the man answered on the other end.

"This is Maxon, sir."

"You've arrived?"

"I'm at the Hilton in Crystal City. I figured on coming down first thing in the morning."

"Best come now," Greener said.

His new boss came across like an OK guy, but he wasn't wasting any time.

"I'm pretty much exhausted from the flight, sir. Can I report in the morning?"

"We have to meet now. How long will it take you to get here?"

The prick had probably never been someplace like Nam. Probably one of the McNamara types, another Ivy League bean counter.

"No problem, sir. I'll be down in about an hour."

"I'll be waiting."

As he hurried to catch the cab to Langley, Maxon felt the veins in his temples throbbing. His new boss was in too much of a hurry to see him. Something wasn't right. Someone had stirred up trouble, probably Lynn Dai Bouchet, wherever in hell she was. He should have greased her when he first had the chance.

After passing the security checkpoints, Maxon got directions to Greener's office. And when he arrived outside the door, he paused, wiping his palms on his trousers. Whatever the issue, he needed to remain cool. Taking a deep breath, he put a smile on his face, gave a cursory knock, and walked into Greener's office.

"Good afternoon, sir," he said.

Too goddamn cheery, he thought as Greener raised his eyebrows. He'd caught it too. Benjamin Greener was said to be a tough, no-nonsense boss who spoke plainly and to the point. He stood, reaching across his desk as he offered his hand to Maxon.

"Jack Maxon, I presume?"

"Yes, sir. Just call me Max."

"Good. Have a seat, Max, and tell me what you know about Brady Nash."

The jolt of apprehension left Maxon unable to respond. "Uh…well…"

"You recognize the name, I take it?"

"Yeah. Yeah. I recognize it. Why?"

Greener had caught him off guard and was no doubt about to ask some hard questions.

"Issues, Max. Issues. You know?"

Maxon felt the sweat beading on his forehead. "What kind of issues?"

Greener rocked back in his chair and smiled. "Why don't we take this one step at a time? Start at the beginning, Max. Tell me what you know about Brady Nash."

Maxon took a deep breath. Greener was fishing. He had to fi-gure out what he knew. After all, this might be a simple deb-rie-fing. "Well," he began, "there's really not much to tell. Let's see…"

Greener stared intently at him.

"He came to the attention of some of the Vietnamese officers with the NPF special operations group I advised up in I Corps. Let's see…" Maxon held his forehead with his thumb and index finger pressing against his temples. "It must have been around January of last year. Yes, that's right. It was right before the Tet Offensive. Anyway, it started when he came to my SOG unit and asked if he could get assigned. We checked him out. He had a pretty good reputation, so we let him join."

"Why did you want him?"

Maxon shifted his weight in his chair and gave a little laugh. "Well, Nash had a reputation for being a hell of a sniper. He was with a ranger outfit at the time, attached to the 173rd Airborne. They said he had this phenomenal number of kills. I don't remember how many, but Colonel Tranh agreed with me, and we decided he'd be a good fit for our operations."

"Go on," Greener said.

"So he worked pretty close with Tranh and his people until both he and one of Tranh's best men, a Major Loc, were killed during an operation up in the A Shau back in late October."

"Were there ever any problems with Nash, anything out of the ordinary that you were aware of?" Greener asked.

Greener knew something. It had to be Bouchet. She was the only one who was still alive, but after Loc missed her in Saigon, she'd completely disappeared.

"No, not really. Except…" Maxon rubbed his chin as if he were in deep thought.

"Except what?" Greener said.

"Well, there seemed to be some personal animosity between Nash and Tranh. Nash always wanted to argue with Tranh and the other Vietnamese officers. He also had some kind of interest in a Vietnamese local named Lynn Dai Bouchet. I'm not exactly sure what that was about, but I told him to stay away from her because we suspected she was a VC sympathizer."

"Is that all?"

The mention of Bouchet didn't seem to make a difference. It had to be something else. He had to keep fishing.

"I think so. Nash was a misfit in my opinion," Maxon said.

"Why do you say that?"

Maxon sat up on the edge of his chair as he clasped his hands together in a fist. "Because he began bitching and trying to say we were killing innocent people. I set him straight real quick and went to Tranh. We planned to send him back to his unit, but he got killed before that happened."

Greener sat poker-faced, saying nothing.

"What's all this about anyway?" Maxon asked.

Leaning forward, Greener rested his elbows on the desk while carefully rolling a black-and-gold pen between his fingers. He stared down at the desk for several seconds before raising his eyes to meet Maxon's.

"What would you say if I told you Nash is still alive?"

Maxon felt his facade dissolve under the white-hot light of reality.

"As the American advisor for a Vietnamese special operations group, I would think you'd have confirmed any Americans killed in action while they were attached to your unit."

"But...but I did," Maxon stuttered. "I went to the Graves Registration Unit where they had his body. I picked up his personal effects myself."

"Did you actually see his body?"

"Ugh, yeah. Yeah, I did, but his head was blown off. You couldn't tell anything. I mean...damn! Are you sure he's alive?"

"We're certain," Greener answered. "Army CID matched his fingerprints to a person in Seattle. And they're certain enough about the match that they've exhumed the body from what was supposed to be Nash's grave. We haven't heard back on that yet, but I can guarantee you it's not Nash."

Maxon looked up at Greener. How much did his boss really know?

"But how did he...Why..." he stuttered.

"That's something I was hoping you could explain," Greener said.

"I don't know."

"Well, here's what we think happened," Greener began. "Apparently, he was wounded during that last operation and exchanged IDs and dog tags with a dead soldier from the First Cav. No one knew anything about it until he sent a bogus letter to the other soldier's parents. Army CID was going to intercept him in Seattle and question him, but he went AWOL. The FBI and the army have begun an investigation. There was an inquiry made with us, but we've denied any knowledge of him for now."

"So where do we go from here?" Maxon asked.

"The FBI contacted us again a few hours ago, asking more questions. From what we could get out of them, Nash's girlfriend told them about a mysterious letter her brother sent Nash from Vietnam. It supposedly contained some pretty serious allegations along with handwriting samples, names, and some telex messages. Nash actually went over there, and they think now he's probably got more of the same type of information, and he's going to the *New York Times* with his story. So here we are."

Maxon remained dumbfounded. Greener raised his eyebrows and pursed his lips.

"The way I see it, Nash must be planning on making some pretty serious allegations if he's going to the newspapers. Now I want some answers before this thing gets really ugly."

Maxon rubbed his temples with his fingertips. The top of his head felt as if it would explode. Should he simply tell Greener everything?

"Why do you think he went to the trouble of doing what he did?" Greener asked.

"I don't know," Maxon answered. "This guy was really strange from the very beginning. He had all kinds of delusions and paranoia—a real nutcase. That's why we were sending him back to his unit."

"What do you mean? What was he paranoid about?"

"Oh, he had some warped idea that someone in the special operations group killed his girlfriend's brother and that we were out to get him too," Maxon said. "He also believed we were indiscriminately shooting innocent civilians. I tried to work with him by explaining our system and how we classified all our suspects, but he was just too dense to comprehend much."

"The FBI is working with Army CID," Greener said, "and they think he's headed back to his hometown, a place called Melody Hill, Tennessee. What do you think he's up to?"

"Hell, Mr. Greener, I don't know. My guess is he's laying low and waiting for the heat to pass, but I really don't know for sure."

"Why do you think he went there first and not directly to a newspaper?" Greener asked.

"I don't know. Maybe he's going back for that letter."

Greener continued almost rapid-fire with his questions. "What exactly do you think is in that letter?"

"Hell, I don't know, probably a bunch of bogeyman conspiracy crap about the Phoenix Program. That would be my guess. Is that what you're driving at?"

"I need a complete debriefing of every operation in which Nash and the man who sent that letter participated. Right now, I need for you to tell me what Nash really knows. Was he an active participant in the Phoenix Program?"

"Yes, sir. I mean, no doubt Tranh and his people pushed the envelope a few times, but there's nothing that can reflect directly on us."

"Goddamn it, Maxon, anything this man says will reflect on us. You know and I know he has information that is almost certainly detrimental to our interests and the interests of the nation. I don't have time to sit here and play games. What does this guy know? Answer my damned question!"

"He had a top secret clearance."

"Don't you think I know that by now? Did he have access to any of your documents?"

"Not directly...I mean, we caught him in my IOCC office last summer, but we figured he was just a dumbass and didn't know any better."

"My God! Did you report it to anyone?"

"Uh..."

"Never mind. Did he witness or participate in any covert operations that involved snatch and snuff?"

"Uh, yes, yes, sir."

Greener's face grew dark red. He turned in his chair and stared at the wall.

"OK. We have several choices on how to handle this, but we have to move quickly and be discreet about it. I want this guy isolated. I want to talk with him myself. He must be intercepted before he goes public. With all that's happening, our people are pretty damn nervous about this situation. This has the potential to blow up into a really ugly affair, and we don't need any more of that right now."

Greener rubbed his chin. "You know this man better than anyone else. I want you in Melody Hill tonight. I've already got four of our best men down there. I'll have them all meet with you so you can coordinate the mission."

He paused. "As of now, you are in charge of this mission, but let me make one thing perfectly clear. There will be no freelancing. This situation already reflects badly on you and our organization. I want this guy brought in for debriefing."

"Do they know where he is?" Maxon asked.

"The FBI shared some pretty good leads with us before they clammed up. I don't think he's going to New York, at least not right away. The FBI thinks they can catch up with him in a few days, but we need to find him first."

Greener stood and walked around the desk.

"The men I have in Melody Hill are all top-notch weapons specialists. All you have to do is work with them. This Nash might be a sniper, but these guys are some of the best we have. You need to help them isolate him and push him into a corner. When he sees there is no way out, he'll surrender. Do you think you can make that happen?"

Maxon nodded.

"The FBI probably has people in the area as well, but they can't know we are there. Your cover is you're all on a deer-hunting trip and hoping to get permission to hunt on these people's property. We need to contact Nash's girlfriend and try to find that letter. If we can do that and get Nash back here, we just might work through this mess. Just remember one thing. We have to keep this low profile. Understood?"

"Understood," Maxon said.

He stood and shook Greener's hand.

"Make me a list of what you need, including personal items. I'll have everything for you inside of three hours, along with your travel arrangements. You'll probably fly out of Andrews. I'll call down and have a car out front to take you to get your things at the hotel in Crystal City. Call me when you get to Tennessee. I want updates twice daily until this thing is resolved. You must bring this guy in."

Maxon's blood pressure pounded in his head as he stood to leave. Greener wanted Nash brought in, but that option had to fail. It might cost him his permanent position with the company, but one way or another, he would take Nash out this time. If Greener found out about the missing weapons or that an American had been terminated, he would make Maxon the sacrificial lamb. That wasn't going to happen.

Maxon's mind raced as he rode in the company car back to the Hilton in Crystal City. It was amazing how this stupid hillbilly stumbled out of every trap he had set for him. First, Loc's ambush had failed at Lynn Dai Bouchet's place. Then Loc was supposed to kill him, but Loc ended up dead instead. And at the GRU in Phu Bai that day, there was no doubt in his mind that Nash was finally dead, but the bastard was a cat with nine lives. He would make damned certain he ran out of lives this time, even if he had to personally pull the trigger.

CHAPTER TWENTY-FIVE

Home Turf

I t was near dusk when Brady awoke with a start. The cabin's metal roof rattled with rain, a hard rain, and there was a phone ringing in the other room. He heard footsteps on the wood floor of the cabin, and Jesse Harper's voice as he answered the phone.

"Yes, ma'am, Miss Lacey. Just a minute, I'll see if he's awake. No, it's OK. We need to get going anyway."

A large window framed the river behind the cabin, where fog was rising from the dimpled gray waters. A warm rain was rapidly melting the snow. It was near dusk, and Brady realized he had slept too long.

"It's Lacey. You can pick up that phone there." Jesse pointed to one beside the couch. He noticed Brady looking out the window. "Warm front," he said.

Brady picked up the phone.

"Mama called," Lacey said. "A telephone man came by the house this afternoon to fix the phone. He said something about static in the line, but she told him there wasn't any." Lacey's voice was tight, and she spoke rapidly. "He told her he was putting a filter on the line, just in case. She said he also asked some questions about me and if she was my mother. Then he acted like he knew me, and she told him about my singing at the Opry, but when he kept asking questions, she figured something wasn't right. She called me as soon as he left. I'm coming home. I'll be there in a few hours."

"He bugged the phone," Brady said. "Tell her to be careful what she says, and please take your time driving in this rain. There's no need to hurry."

After hanging up, Brady sat on the edge of the couch, trying to gather his thoughts. The phone began ringing again.

"I'll get it," Jesse called from the kitchen. "You come on in here and get some supper."

Brady no sooner sat down when Jesse stuck his head through the kitchen door.

"It's your stepmother."

"Hang up," Brady hissed.

Harper furrowed his brow.

"Just hang up. Don't say anything. Just hang up."

After Jesse carefully set the receiver back into its cradle, Brady walked over and picked it up again. He listened for a dial tone. When he heard it, he set the receiver aside.

"Leave it off the hook. That first call was from Lacey. Some creep masquerading as a telephone repairman bugged Mama Emma's phone."

"No shit?" Jesse said.

"Yeah, he came by her house this morning. Mama Emma called Lacey, and she's on her way from Nashville."

"Well, she just asked for you by name, and I told her to hang on."

Brady nodded. "That's OK. I already figured as much. We're busted, and whoever planted that bug will probably show up here before long. I need to get moving."

"Where?" Jesse asked. "We can't go out on the roads now. They'll nail us for sure."

Brady forked the fried steak from his plate, chewing it as he talked. "I'm going on foot, up into the hills and work my way over to Hubert Brister's place."

"Man, are you crazy? Let me hide you in the back of the truck and drive you around there. We can be there in thirty minutes."

Brady shook his head. "No, it's too risky. Where's my gear?"

"It's in there behind the couch. What do you want me to do?"

"I want you to stay here. If they traced that call from Mama Emma, they'll come here, and I want you to tell them I'm up there in those hills."

"Now I know you're crazy, bubba. Why do you want them to know where you are?"

Brady pulled the backpack and rifle from behind the couch. He took a box of shells from a side pouch, opened the bolt, and began loading the rifle.

"It'll keep them occupied, searching for me, while I get across and search Brister's place for the letter. I'm crossing Hiwassee Knob tonight and heading straight to his place."

"This is insane," Jesse said. "It'll take you all night and most the day tomorrow to cross that ground on foot. Besides, you don't need that letter."

"Yes, I do. The evidence in that envelope ties Maxon directly to all of this. Without the kill cards, the telex messages, and that list of names that's in Maxon's handwriting, we only have circumstantial evidence."

"So what are you going to do if you find it? They aren't going to simply let you walk out of here with it."

Brady sighted through the riflescope as he pointed toward the back window, but with the darkness outside, he saw nothing.

"If I find the letter, I'll let you take it to the newspaper. Just watch after Lacey and Mama Emma for me till this is over, will you?"

Jesse was right. The overland trek to the old Brister place would be treacherous, but the Overhill was Brady's backyard. He knew every ridge, hollow, and trail out there, and the straight-line distance was only a few miles. The jumble of gorges would take time to negotiate, but taking the circuitous twenty-three miles of highway and county roads was too risky. Whoever bugged Mama Emma's phone would now be watching the roads even closer.

* * *

Maxon sat in a van parked on a road outside Melody Hill. Night had fallen, and he was planning his next move. He removed the headphones monitoring the Coleridge woman's phone and switched it to the speaker. The bug had paid off.

"That woman knows where Nash is hiding, and when we get that telephone number run down, we will too, but I'm not sure we can afford to wait."

The man sitting beside him was one of Greener's handpicked snipers, Nick Werkman. He was second-in-command now that Maxon had taken over, probably a good thing since he was a little green. According to his file summary, he hadn't been to Nam. Other than some time spent in the Middle East, his only real operational experience had come from a stint in the Congo.

"You may be right. The guy on the line acted like he was going to bring Nash to the phone, then hung up," Werkman said. "I think they suspect we're onto them."

"I say we grab the old woman and squeeze it out of her," Maxon said.

"Bad move," Werkman answered.

"Why?"

"Greener said to keep the op low profile. If we grab the woman, the FBI and the local law will know something's up. I say we wait. We'll have a location for that phone in a few hours. Then we'll nail him."

"If he doesn't slip away tonight," Maxon said.

Werkman lit a cigarette and exhaled as he spoke slowly. "I don't think he's going anywhere without that letter. Call Sager and tell him to move over and watch the old woman's house. If Nash is somewhere close, she might lead us to him."

Maxon turned his head slowly to make eye contact with Werkman. Punk had his nerve, ordering him around.

Werkman pulled the cigarette from his lips and rolled his eyes. "OK, what I meant was I think that's what we should do, if you agree."

Werkman was a smart-ass, and for a moment, Maxon considered sending him out into the pouring rain to do surveillance, but he needed him. He was the electronics expert and handled the eavesdropping equipment.

"OK," Maxon said, "I think you're right. Go ahead and call Sager. Tell him to let us know every move that woman makes."

* * *

The rain poured from the roof above the front porch that night as Gil Gilardi and his FBI counterpart waited at the door of a small wood-frame house in Macon, Georgia. A barefooted man wearing a T-shirt and jeans opened the door. Scratching his head sleepily, he stared out at them through the screen door.

"William Cantrell?"

"Yes, sir, that'd be me," the man answered.

"I'm Major Gilardi, with the United States Army Criminal Investigation Department, and this is Agent Treller, with the Federal

Bureau of Investigation. Do you mind if we come in and ask you some questions?"

There was a pause before Cantrell laughed and pushed the screen door open. "You know, I thought I might hear from you guys someday. Come on in."

The two men stepped inside as they shook the rain from their clothes and removed their hats. "Why do you say that, Mr. Cantrell?"

"Does this have to do with Brady Nash?" Will asked.

Gilardi turned and raised his eyebrows at his FBI counterpart. It appeared another piece to the puzzle was falling in place. After nearly an hour with Cantrell, the picture in the puzzle was becoming much more recognizable. Cantrell's statements matched the notes that Lacey Coleridge had taken from Nash.

More and more witness statements were coinciding, and it was becoming clear that Nash probably wasn't the paranoid wacko everyone assumed him to be. There was also a growing urgency developing in the back of Gilardi's mind, because if Nash's fears were real, the people hunting him were probably closing in.

Everything pointed toward Maxon, but on whose authority was he acting? He had violated every form of law that existed, including military, civil, Vietnamese, and the Geneva Convention. How much did his superiors in the CIA know? They could already be acting on the information they'd received during the FBI inquiry, but how? Were they going after Maxon or Nash or both?

"We'll get back with you in the next week or two," Gilardi told Cantrell.

"So are you about to catch up with the people that killed Brady and his stepbrother?" Cantrell asked.

The two agents stood and began pulling on their coats.

"I guess I forgot to tell you," Gilardi said. "Brady Nash is still alive."

Cantrell's eyes widened, and his face paled slightly before he slowly nodded and gave a knowing grin. Apparently catching himself, he suddenly looked up at Gilardi.

"Brady is the good guy in all this. You really do believe that, don't you?"

Giving out too much information was ill-advised, but Gilardi recognized the bond between the two vets. "We're coming to believe that, Mr. Cantrell. That's why we're trying to confirm this information and bring him in before anything else happens."

"Are we going back to Melody Hill?" Treller asked.

Gilardi nodded. "I think that's where we'll find him."

* * *

Jesse Harper peeked through a gap in the front curtains as he looked out toward the road. Just before first light, the rain finally stopped, and Brady had slipped away. Jesse now waited for his expected visitors, but a hazy fog obscured the nearby hills. It wouldn't be long before the ones who'd bugged the Coleridge phone arrived. Of that, he was certain.

As he watched the road in the first gray light of day, something caught his eye. It was barely a glimpse of a figure in the mist near the base of the mountain. A man, stooped low, was running along the edge of the woods. He was dressed in camouflage and carrying something, probably a rifle. They were here. Jesse maintained his vigil at the window.

Back up the road, the fog thinned for a moment, and a white van became visible. It was sitting without any lights, but the engine was idling, evidenced by the smoky white exhaust gently trailing away in the still morning air. It was time to call Sheriff Harvey to get him up here. The sheriff might be good insurance against disappearing and never being heard from again. Jesse picked up the phone. It was eerily silent, no dial tone. He should have expected as much. These were the big boys, and they were playing for keeps.

Walking into the back room, he studied the river from the picture window. A mist, thicker than the surrounding fog, rose from the rippling gray waters, obscuring the riverbanks. But after several minutes, Jesse spotted what he already suspected was there, another man with a rifle, barely a shadow, working his way along the riverbank.

Jesse went to the bedroom, where he retrieved his .45 from a dresser drawer. If he was forced to use it, he'd probably die, but he wasn't going to let them walk in unchallenged. He snatched the slide back and chambered a round, then tucked the gun inside his belt. He grabbed his cap from a peg and pulled on a nylon windbreaker, then opened the door and stepped out onto the porch.

These bastards had already proven themselves capable by killing Duff Coleridge, a boy who was more of a patriot than any of them. He'd met their type before, highfalutin bastards who thought they could do whatever they wanted in the name of patriotism. He'd talked with them in the bars in Saigon, cocky bastards who were convinced no single person's life was as important as their mission. Now they were outside his cabin, and if they decided to kill him, he would probably die, but not before he took at least one or two with him.

Crows began squawking out near the corner of the grass airstrip where his airplane was parked. These super spooks couldn't sneak up on a dead cow. Jesse watched the crows diving and fla-ring at whatever it was disturbing them, probably yet another sniper.

Shoving his hands into his pockets, he eased to the edge of the porch and waited. The lights on the van suddenly lit up as it sped his way. He'd been spotted. A few seconds later, the van crunched to a stop on the gravel in front of the cabin. Jesse walked down the steps. Two men got out, but one remained on the far side of the van, while the other walked toward him.

"You must be looking for Brady Nash," Jesse said.

The man approached him, stopping only when he was face-to-face. Jesse smiled. Intimidation didn't work with him. Once you've flown a burning airplane into the jungle and spent three weeks playing hide-and-seek with the NVA, you find very few things intimidating.

"That's right. Where is he?" the man said.

He had a deep scar running down the side of his face. The man was trying his best to fix Jesse with a hard stare, but Jesse conti-nued grinning as he looked him in the eyes. This guy was dange-rous, but so was he, and Jesse would not be bullied.

"He said he needed my help, so I put him up yesterday, but he bailed out of here sometime last night, said he was going back up yonder in the hills till the heat is off."

"Did he have a letter with him or mention anything about one?"

"Yeah…yeah, as a matter of fact, he did mention something about a letter. He said it was from his old buddy Duff Coleridge, and it named some people who were trying to kill him."

The man's eyes widened slightly at the mention of Duff's name.

"Where is it?" the man asked.

"Where is what?" Jesse asked.

"Quit fucking around. The letter, where is it?"

"Mister, I'm not 'fucking around.' I don't know where the letter is, but I do know you're about to get yourself into a kind of trouble you really don't want."

"Oh, and what kind of trouble is that?" the man asked.

"You're in the Tennessee Overhill. This is Brady's home. Keep pushing him, and somebody's gonna get hurt."

The man smiled. "Does he have a weapon?"

"Just an old hunting rifle, but that's all he needs with this bunch of yo-yos you have following you around."

The man threw a glance back at his partner standing on the other side of the van.

"Not him," Jesse said. He threw his chin toward the corner of the airstrip where the crows were still squawking. "I'm talking about your boy over there, disturbing the wildlife."

The man's eyes hardened. "How do I know he's not hiding inside your cabin?" he asked.

"Because if he was inside, he'd already have shot that clown over there by the airstrip or that one sneaking up the bank of the river"—Jesse settled his eyes on the man in front of him—"or maybe you."

The man knew he'd been one-upped.

"If Nash comes back, tell him we only want to talk. Tell him we'll guarantee him amnesty if he comes in on his own."

Jesse nodded, and after a few moments, the man turned and walked back to the van. The van turned and headed back up the road, then stopped near where he'd first seen it. For several minutes, it sat idling, until a man appeared and climbed inside. Jesse continued watching as the van sped away. Apparently, there was one staying behind to watch the cabin.

* * *

Lacey reached home sometime after midnight and was still sleeping that morning when someone began knocking at her mother's door. Wrapping herself in her housecoat, she peeked out the front window. Two men were standing on the porch. It was the FBI agent and the army major who had interviewed her prior to the exhumation. She pushed her hair back and pulled the door open.

"How are you, Miss Coleridge?"

"Who is it, honey?" her mother called from the back of the house.

"It's the army people, Mama. Put your housecoat on."

She turned to the men standing at the door. "I'm fine, Major."

"May we come in?" the man asked.

Lacey pushed the screen door open and showed the two men to the couch in the front room.

"I'm sure you remember Agent Gates from the FBI, Miss Coleridge."

Lacey nodded. "How can I help you, gentlemen?"

The FBI agent remained silent while Gilardi spoke. "We are here to help your friend, Brady Nash. You do realize that our goal is simply to find him, don't you?"

"I'm not sure what you mean, Major."

"What I mean is we are not going to hurt him. So far, the preponderance of evidence indicates that he may not be guilty of any serious crimes, but his life is in danger. If you know where he is, you need to tell us now."

Lacey's mother came into the room, but she stood just inside the doorway as the men nodded respectfully in her direction.

"We were just telling your daughter that Brady Nash—"

"I heard what you said, Major. What makes you think we know where he is?"

"We don't, but it's logical that he might have contacted you. You must listen to what I'm saying. I'm telling you the truth. We've talked with several witnesses, including men who were in Vietnam with your foster son. I can't make you any guarantees, but I can tell you, he will be a lot safer in our custody than somewhere out there on his own."

"Is that why you bugged my mother's phone?" Lacey asked.

The two men turned and traded questioning glances.

"Bugged her phone?" Gilardi said. "What makes you think we did that?"

"The bogus telephone company man that came by here the other day, that's what."

"I'm not sure what you're talking about. Do you mind if we take a look?" Gilardi asked.

"It's in the hallway," her mother said.

"Do you have a screwdriver I can borrow?" Gilardi asked.

A few moments later, Lacey and her mother watched as Gilardi removed the plastic casing from the phone and set it aside. He tapped a small cylindrical device inside and glanced up at the FBI agent.

"Yours?"

"You know better than that, Gil," Gates answered.

Gilardi carefully removed the bug from the phone and wrapped it in his handkerchief.

"You say the man that did this said he was with the telephone company?" Gates asked.

Lacey's mother nodded.

"He's with a company, all right," Gilardi said, "one out of Langley, Virginia."

Gates nodded.

"What does that mean?" Lacey asked.

"According to the notes you turned over to us in Nashville," Gilardi said, "Mr. Nash believes the people he was involved with are from the CIA. The Company is a name they often use for themselves."

Lacey felt her heart thumping beneath her flannel gown as she glanced at her mother.

"Look, ladies," Gilardi said, "the people that bugged this phone do not have Brady's best interest in mind. I'm not sure what they intend to do, but it can't be good. If you know anything, you need to tell me now. Time is running out."

Lacey felt a cold lump of panic rising from within. Brady could be killed while she stood by and did nothing. Gilardi seemed honest, and at some point, she had to trust someone.

"Do you know something, Miss Coleridge?" Gilardi asked.

It was something that Brady had written in one of his letters. His best buddy in Vietnam, Will Cantrell, had told him that truth had a resonance to it that filled the cracks where falsehoods hide. She looked into Gilardi's eyes. He was a man to be trusted.

"I believe I know where he is," she said, "but I have to take you there, and I want the sheriff to go with us, Sheriff Harvey."

"Where is Nash hiding?" Gates asked.

Lacey wagged her head. "Not till we get the sheriff. Then I'll take you there myself. We can all go together."

CHAPTER TWENTY-SIX

From Skeptic to Believer

Brady had watched that morning from high on the ridge above Jesse Harper's cabin as a white van came down the road. They had arrived quicker than he expected, and rather than continue toward the Brister place, he decided to wait and see what happened. When the fog began breaking, he spotted a man with a rifle near the base of the ridge, then one stumbling along the riverbank behind the cabin. Within minutes, he had spotted three men altogether with rifles in various places around the cabin. Given the distance, there was little he could do to protect Jesse, but if they harmed him, there'd be hell to pay right then.

Two other men had gotten out of the van, and Jesse met them in the front yard. The confrontation lasted several minutes, and despite Brady's fears, everything seemed to have gone well. They picked up two of their snipers as they drove away, but one stayed behind, the one at the base of the ridge below.

The sound of the vehicle's engine echoed in the distance as it labored up the steep grade beyond the ridge and out of sight. It seemed the van was leaving, until it stopped. Brady listened, and they tried to shut the doors without making a sound, but the still mountain air gave them away. Two doors opened and closed. No doubt, the other two snipers had gotten out and were entering the forest above him. He'd screwed up, letting them get between him and the Brister place, but there was something more, something even worse.

It was Maxon. Brady was certain, if for no reason other than a predator's sixth sense. He was here. But this time the bastard had made two unforgivable mistakes. He'd come to Melody Hill, Brady's home, and he was now a direct threat to Lacey and Mama Emma. This time, there would be no hesitation, no defensive stance. He was going after Maxon and his cronies. He would do whatever it took to protect his family. Maxon had no idea of the nightmare he was about to experience. Hell was coming.

Brady contemplated his next move. He had to keep them from harming Lacey or Mama Emma, but with two snipers on the mountain above and one down below, he had let them put him in bad position. He studied his old hunting rifle. The Remington 700 didn't have the newest scope, or the bull barrel like the ones Maxon's men were carrying, but it would work. These people were sloppy. Had they been snipers in Nam, the VC would have nailed them to a tree within a matter of days. Just the same, he didn't have much choice except to sit tight and let them show their cards first.

A bird called high and clear from somewhere up the mountain, while in the pasture far below, Brady spotted a deer feeding near Jesse's airplane. At times, it was this same way in Nam, deceptively quiet and peaceful. Yet there was an ever-present undertow hidden below the serene and peaceful surface, one that, without warning, could suck you instantly into its torrents. Brady rested, and things remained quiet until midmorning, when two vehicles came down the road toward the cabin. They moved slowly, almost cautiously, it seemed.

From his perch on the rock outcropping, he was better than twelve hundred meters from the cabin, but he recognized the first vehicle as a Polk County sheriff's squad car. The second also appeared to be some type of police or government vehicle, a gray Ford LTD. He sat upright as he studied the little convoy.

The cars stopped several hundred feet from the cabin, and Brady cranked his scope up to 9X. The occupants seemed cautious as they got out and gazed at the cabin. The two uniformed officers had their hands in their pockets, but the men who got out of the Ford had weapons drawn. Brady watched with little more than curiosity until he saw Lacey emerge from the back of the squad car.

* * *

When the squad car stopped just in sight of Jesse's cabin, Lacey started to get out, but Sheriff Harvey told her to stay put. He and his deputy stepped out and gazed up at the cabin. Gilardi and Gates came up from behind with their weapons drawn. Lacey pushed the door open and jumped out. This wasn't what they had agreed to do. The men stood with the sheriff and his deputy as Lacey rushed to them.

"Why do you have your guns out?" she asked.

Neither Gilardi nor Gates answered as they looked at the cabin, then Sheriff Harvey. Lacey pushed in among the men. Harvey patted her gently on the back and turned to the others. Neither he nor his deputy had drawn their weapons.

"She kept her part of the bargain," Harvey said. "Why don't you give me a couple of minutes to talk him out? If that doesn't work, then we can do this your way."

After a few moments, the two men holstered their weapons, and the front door to the cabin opened. Jesse Harper stepped out onto the porch.

"Jesse," Harvey called out, "is Brady up there with you?"

Harper walked down the steps, shaking his head. "Nope, he's up yonder." He pointed to the mountain rising steeply beyond the little grass landing strip. "I reckon he's somewhere between here and Melody Hill."

"How come he went up there?"

"A bunch of men with sniper rifles and automatic pistols showed up here a few hours ago. They looked like a pretty rough bunch, and they seemed to want him and that letter real bad."

"What happened?" Gates asked.

"Nothing. I mean, we knew they were coming, so Brady had already gone. I told them he went to hide up in the hills, and they took off. I think they went to find him."

"Why did you tell them where he went?" Lacey blurted.

The old sheriff put his hand on her shoulder again, as if to calm her. Jesse looked at her and tugged gently at his bushy beard.

"I reckon because that's what he wanted me to do, Miss Lacey."

"But why?"

Jesse shrugged. "Maybe he's getting tired of being chased. Maybe they shouldn't have come here and gone into your home. Mostly, though, I think he did it because he wants to protect you and Miss Emma from those sorry bastards."

Gilardi turned to Sheriff Harvey. "We need to get some people up there to search for them. How many deputies do you have?"

"Not enough to search those hills," Harvey answered. "Besides, if there's a bunch of fools with sniper rifles up there, I'm not sure I want my boys out looking for them."

"Where's the nearest National Guard or Army Reserve unit?" Gilardi asked.

"I reckon that'd be down yonder in Cleveland. That's the biggest town between here and Chattanooga."

"Sheriff, I want to set up a command post here. I'm going to make some calls and get a platoon of guardsmen up here before dark."

"You won't catch Brady up there, Major. There ain't nothing but miles of straight-up and straight-down hills and gorges between here and Melody Hill."

"We don't have to catch Brady, but we need to stop the ones that are after him."

For the first time that morning, Lacey felt good about something that was said. As the sheriff and the other three men talked, Jesse Harper motioned her aside. They walked across the road and gazed at the little Cessna 182 sitting in the grass. Jesse had christened her *Miss Whippoorwill*, inscribing the name with yellow paint on the plane's red cowling.

"Brady is headed to the old Brister place to look for Duff's letter." Jesse spoke in a low voice as he glanced over his shoulder. "If he finds it, he's going to get one of us to take it to the newspaper."

"But the family moved everything out of the house over a year ago. What makes him think it's still there?"

"Hubert Brister said some things to me just before he died. I'm not sure if he was just talking out of his head or giving me a clue. He told me to tell Brady that if nobody steals his tools and the cows don't eat his last bale of hay, the letter will be safe."

"Makes perfect sense," Lacey said.

Jesse glanced over his shoulder again, then back at Lacey. "Huh?"

"Did anyone look for a toolbox in the hayloft of his barn?"

* * *

Earlier that morning, Maxon received a call from Sager, saying two men were at the Coleridge house. He said they looked like FBI, and it was only a few minutes after their arrival that the listening device on the phone went dead. Later, his man across from Harper's cabin called in on the radio, saying the same two men were there with some local cops and the Coleridge girl. Matters were getting sticky fast. He had to find Nash, snuff him, and get the hell out of the area.

After removing the surveillance equipment, they wiped the van clean, and Werkman ditched it in a gorge a few miles down the road. They switched vehicles, this time using an old pickup truck, something that blended better with the local surroundings. Werkman sat beside Maxon, studying a map.

"He's got to be heading back to Melody Hill," Werkman said, pointing to the town on the map.

"There's no telling what that dumbass is up to," Maxon said.

"I don't think he's as dumb as you think," Werkman said.

"Trust me on this one," Maxon replied. "I worked with this guy for several months in Nam. He's about as country dumb as they come."

Werkman gave him a sideways glance. "If he's dumb as you say, then he must be awfully lucky."

Maxon ignored him. Werkman was another know-it-all Ivy Leaguer, and half-assed jealous because Greener had made him a subordinate on his own mission.

"Call Brewton and Carney and ask them if they've seen anything of Nash. And call Sager too. Tell him we're coming to get him. We'll drop him up there with the others. Then we'll go back to set up surveillance in the town."

* * *

By late afternoon, Jesse Harper's yard looked like a military staging area. Lacey stood with Jesse on the front porch, watching while an army captain and Major Gilardi briefed the soldiers. Having arrived only minutes before, the soldiers, wearing new green fatigues and field jackets, had leapt from two canvas-covered deuce and a halfs. Each man wore web gear and carried an M16. They were gathered in a loose formation while Gilardi explained their mission.

They were to detain anyone found carrying a weapon or who appeared otherwise suspicious, but no one was to fire a weapon unless fired upon. When Gilardi finished the briefing, a young lieutenant ordered the squad leaders to spread their men on line. The plan was for them to sweep up the slope until dark, bivouac, and continue the search at first light.

Lacey stood watching with Jesse as the men spread in a line across the grass landing strip and walked into the woods. She had wanted to leave earlier in the day to drive around to Melody Hill to search Brister's barn, but Gilardi insisted that she and Jesse remain at the cabin. Despite her plea about her mother being alone, Gilardi remained steadfast.

"Why not just tell him what we need to do?" Jesse suggested.

"Because he might go find the envelope himself, and it might not ever get to the newspapers."

Gilardi and Gates came back through the front door of the cabin.

"I suppose all we can do now is wait," Gilardi said. "It'll be dark soon."

"So I have to spend the night here?" Lacey asked.

Gilardi nodded. "I'm sorry, Miss Coleridge, but I think it best you stay for now. If we don't find Brady tonight, I'll let Mr. Harper take you back to your mother's house first thing in the morning."

She turned to find Jesse looking her way. They were both thinking the same thing. That could be their opportunity to go to the old Brister place and find the letter.

* * *

Army Reserve Lieutenant Frank Baker was exhausted. He'd been called at the office of his accounting firm that morning and told to report to the armory for immediate activation. Now as dusk gathered across the mountainside, he called quietly on the radio for his squad leaders to begin moving into a night defensive position, not that an NDP was necessary, but it was the way he'd been trained.

"Let's make a tight perimeter," he told the platoon sergeant. "No reason to dig in, but I want every third man on watch tonight. Tell them to break out their Cs and they can smoke if they want. Just tell them to be careful. The leaves are starting to get dry again."

Baker had been briefed that afternoon by the CID officer Gilardi, but the briefing was all too vague, and he was still unsure exactly who he was after. The rumors were rampant, and he'd heard about a war hero supposedly returned from the dead, but that seemed far-fetched. He only wished he had more information. His orders, though, were simple: detain anyone he found and call down to the command post for instructions.

An hour or so after dark, it had grown quiet as the men finished their C rations and rolled out sleeping gear, ponchos with liners. The platoon sergeant had built a fire, and Baker stood around it with several of the NCOs speculating on what was happening. They had their poncho liners wrapped around their shoulders as they huddled close to the flames, the orange glow reflecting on their faces.

"This Nash is apparently from around here somewhere, and there are some people up here after him," Baker said. "It has something to do with the military."

"I don't get it," one of the squad leaders said. "This CID major, what's his name, seems to want us to catch him, but he doesn't want him hurt."

"Yeah, it's kind of strange."

"Well, if you think this is all strange, you really ain't gonna believe this," the platoon sergeant said. "I heard a guy telling a story about this Nash a few weeks ago. It was at the VFW in Cleveland. The guy was a Nam vet, but the story sounded so crazy, hell, I thought it was all bullshit—until now. He was telling about how Nash had all kinds of medals and how he was a sniper in Nam, but he got mixed up with a government death squad and disappeared."

"No shit?" Baker said.

"No shit. And to hear him tell it, this Nash is a real straitlaced kind of guy. He just crossed the wrong people."

One of the men shuffled up behind the ring of NCOs gathered around the fire. He was wrapped in a poncho liner and still eating from a C ration can. The others ignored him while they continued talking.

"You know, I read something similar in the paper a while back how Nash was killed in action and that he was a hell of a sniper and a pretty big hero."

"Yeah, I saw that article too," one of the others said. "Is this the same guy we're looking for now?"

"Yeah, he's supposedly alive again," Baker said, "but I can't fi-gure it, because he was such a big hero and all."

The man standing behind the NCOs grunted and gave a quiet laugh. "You can't believe everything you read in the newspapers," he said.

Baker and the others looked around as the man stepped up to the fire and tossed the empty C ration can into the flames. Baker didn't recognize him.

"Whose squad are you in?" he asked.

The man pulled the poncho liner from his head. He wasn't one of them.

"I'm Brady Nash, Lieutenant."

Baker looked out toward the perimeter.

"How'd you get past...Surely, those guys aren't already asleep."

"No, sir," Brady said, "but I've gotten past men with a hell of a lot more experience than yours."

The men around the fire stared at him as if he were a ghost.

"Is it true?" one of the squad leaders asked.

"Is what true?" Brady said.

"All the stuff in the newspaper article, all those confirmed kills and the medals."

Brady nodded as he stared into their eyes. "Yeah, I suppose it is, but it doesn't amount to much if they decide they want you dead."

"Who wants you dead?" Baker asked.

"Someone in the government," Brady said.

He bummed a cigarette and drew closer to the fire as he began telling the men his story. After nearly an hour, the fire had died down, and they stopped asking questions as they stared into the glowing embers.

"What are you going to do?" Baker asked.

"I'm going to find Maxon and kill him. Then I'm going to take that letter to the newspapers."

Baker knew there was no way he would hold Nash unless he went voluntarily, but he was compelled to at least tell him what his orders were.

"You know my orders are to detain you."

Brady looked over at him with raised eyebrows. "Yes, and?"

The other men laughed.

"Just wanted to let you know," Baker said.

"Don't worry, Lieutenant. I won't tell them I saw you."

"That's OK," Baker answered. "I'll tell them myself, and I'll be damned proud of it."

"Thanks, Lieutenant," Brady said. "And I need you to give them a message from me. Do you mind?"

Somewhere on a distant ridge, a coyote let out a series of yips and a long howl.

"Not at all, Mr. Nash."

"Tell them I've been watching their men up here with the sniper rifles all day, and this is their last chance. They need to leave. I will surrender to the FBI in forty-eight hours."

"According to that CID major, what's his name, Gilardi, he thinks you're pretty much innocent. Why don't you just go with us back down the mountain and surrender to him?"

"There are a couple of reasons. First of all, the ones up here with the sniper rifles won't let that happen. Their sole purpose is to see that I don't get off this mountain alive. And if any of you get in their way, they'll probably kill you as well. But what's more important is I still have to find Duff's letter. Along with that letter, there's enough evidence in that envelope to stop all their cover-ups or attempts to make me look like the bad guy in this thing."

After a while, the embers died to a dull orange glow. Baker watched a few minutes later as Brady turned and walked quietly away, melting into the darkness. He heard one of the men on the perimeter challenge him.

"Hey, where are you going?"

"To pee," came a voice barely above a whisper.

There was only silence afterward, and Baker found himself nodding. Nash was everything the newspaper had said he was and more.

* * *

Shortly after Lacey awoke that morning, she went to the front of the cabin to find Major Gilardi sipping coffee. Jesse was sitting there with him, as was the FBI agent Gates. The men told her how at first light that morning, the soldiers on the mountain above had called in, reporting no contact. This was her chance, and she made her bid. Reluctantly, Gilardi agreed to allow her to return home to Melody Hill, but he wouldn't let Jesse go with her. Lacey glanced at him. They made eye contact, and he nodded. It was all up to her.

"You can use my old truck," Jesse said. "I'll come get it later."

She nodded as he handed her the keys. Without another word, she turned and walked out, but Jesse followed her out to the truck. She climbed in and cranked the engine, but Jesse stood inside the open door. After glancing back at the cabin, he reached behind his back and pulled a large pistol from his belt.

"Take this with you," he said.

Lacey looked up at the cabin windows and at the various vehicles parked out front. No one seemed to be watching.

"Put it in your coat pocket," Jesse said.

When they were teenagers, Lacey had gone with Brady and Duff a time or two to shoot guns, but this pistol seemed heavy, very heavy.

"It's a forty-five automatic," Jesse said. "Be careful. The safety's off. All you have to do is pull the hammer back before you pull the trigger."

She shoved the gun into her coat pocket. Moments later, she circled onto the road and sped away.

The only things more difficult to negotiate than the rivers and rapids in the Unicoi Mountains were the hairpin curves and switchbacks of the gravel roads, but Lacey wasted little time as she pushed the old pickup to its limit. Gravel popped and pinged beneath the floorboard, and she gripped the steering wheel with both hands as she drove the circuitous route to Melody Hill.

It was up to her now to search the Brister place for the letter, but what she really wanted was to leap from the truck and run up into the hills to find Brady. She wanted to be with him, to protect him. Instinctively, she touched the hard lump of the pistol in her coat pocket. Her anger was growing. Brady had done nothing to deserve being treated like a criminal.

* * *

A foggy mist blanketed the mountainside as Baker rousted his men at first light. After putting the squads on line, he again ordered them to sweep the mountain, this time to the west and then back south toward the cabin. If he could simply disrupt the snipers and buy time for Nash, he would.

As the sun climbed higher, he called in a sitrep on the radio. Nash had told him these people were probably monitoring his frequency, so Baker was cautious. As he had done at first light, he told the RTO to call in no contact. By midmorning, it was time to swing south and head back down the mountain. He was about to call in the squad leaders when the radio broke squelch. It was the squad leader for Fourth Squad on the far right.

"We've got something, LT."

Baker called everyone to a halt and ordered First Squad to swing back up the mountain in a flanking move. Motioning his RTO to follow, he made his way up the ridge toward Fourth

Squad. As he approached, he saw several of his men standing and gazing up at a rock outcropping. A lone man stood above them with his back against a rock wall.

"He says he's a hunter, LT, but look at the goddamn rifle he's carrying."

The man had a bored look on his face as he stared down at the reservists. Despite the winter air, Baker found himself sweating as he removed his helmet and looked up at the man standing on the outcropping twenty feet above.

"Whatcha hunting, partner?"

The man turned and spit before he spoke. "Wild hogs," he said.

"Don't usually find them up this high," Baker said. "Besides, that's a mighty fancy rifle for hog hunting."

The man glanced down at his rifle, then gazed out across the wooded hillside. "Lieutenant, if I were you, I'd leave this one alone. I'm on official government business."

Baker turned to his RTO and whispered, "Walk over there out of earshot and call the CP. Tell the captain we've got a man up here with a sniper rifle and he's claiming he's on official government business."

"I don't know what government you work for, but I have orders from a US Army major and an FBI agent to detain anyone I find up here."

The man turned and walked to where the rocks stairstepped from the outcropping, but as Baker went to meet him, the man raised his rifle to waist level. Baker froze, but several of his men raised their rifles.

"Hold up, men," he said, raising his hand into the air.

The man seemed totally at ease. Baker felt the sweat running in rivulets down his face.

"Sir, I have several men with loaded M16s trained on you. Now I expect you need to just hand me that rifle."

"Lieutenant, they might be able to kill me, but I'm going to kill you and maybe one or two of them first. Like I said, you might want to leave this one alone."

A bird whistled crisp and clear from somewhere in the trees higher up the mountain. No one moved as their vaporized breath floated like a shroud above them. The frosted gray tree trunks shone silver in the morning sun.

"What's it going to be, Lieutenant?" the man said.

Baker wasn't ready to see any of his men hurt. "Lower your weapons, men."

The man held his rifle pointed at Baker as he began backing away.

"Wait," Baker said, "before you leave, I have something to tell you."

The man paused.

"I don't know who you are," Baker said, "but if your business is with Brady Nash, you might want to reconsider what you're doing. You're out of your element up here, and he's playing for keeps."

The man grinned. "I think I can take care of myself, Lieutenant. You fellows are the ones that make the easy targets."

"Yes, sir, except he's not after us. He said to tell you that he watched you and your partners up here all day yesterday."

Baker saw it in the man's eyes as his confidence wilted like lettuce under hot bacon grease.

"I take it you've talked with Nash."

"Yes, sir, I did. He showed up around our fire last night. Hell, he was standing there beside me eating from a can of Cs before I knew he was anywhere in the world."

"What did he have to say?"

"Said he doesn't want to kill any of you fellows. Said if you back off, he won't hurt anybody, and he'll give himself up in a couple days. I wouldn't push him."

"He's a cocky son of a bitch," the man said.

"No, sir, he wasn't cocky at all. He was just trying to tell you he didn't want to hurt you."

"You fellows can believe all that bogeyman crap about the great sniper if you want, but it's only military hype." The man backed away as he circled the outcropping. "I'll bring you Nash's nuts by dark. Now, Lieutenant, don't you or any of your men do anything stupid while I'm leaving, OK?"

Baker watched the man zigzag up the slope, out of sight. The men around him gave a collective sigh while Baker took the handset to the PRC-25.

"What'd they say down at the CP?" he asked the RTO.

"I told them what was happening, and they said just to let him go."

"Looks like they got their wish—"

There came a sound like cold water hitting hot grease, *sssssh-hhhraccccckkksss*, followed by a muted and distant boom. A single round had cracked and hissed from several hundred meters away across the mountainside above them. The report of the rifle came from somewhere back to the east. Baker and his men had already buried their heads in the leaves as they listened for another shot. There was none, but from somewhere above came a steady rustling of the leaves, and they raised their heads just high enough to see what it was. The sound drew closer, and Baker spotted movement.

"What the fuck is that?" one of the men asked.

As they watched, a rifle came sliding down the mountainside, skittering through the leaves like a lost ski. It struck a tree, skidded sideways, and finally came to rest on the flat ground beside the rock outcropping. It was the sniper's rifle.

"I'll bet he's a believer now," the RTO muttered.

CHAPTER TWENTY-SEVEN

The Snipers' Duel

When he dropped the crosshairs on Maxon's assassin that morning, Brady faced a new and sudden realization. It was difficult to pull the trigger. It was no longer the almost robotic response he'd learned in Nam. As he watched the gunman sneaking toward the shirt he'd hung on a tree, he felt hesitation and doubt. Killing was no longer easy, but as the sniper raised his rifle to shoot the decoy, Brady realized there was no choice. These people would kill anyone to avoid being exposed. This meant Lacey would likely be their next target. The shot was slightly over five hundred meters, and he did what he had to do.

As he slipped over the crest of the mountain toward Melody Hill, the adrenaline pulsed in his veins. He'd taken out the first sniper, and he'd do it again if they got in his way. There were at least two, maybe three more in the hills between him and the old Brister place, and he was running out of time. He had to move fast, and that meant exposing himself even more. If he ended up in their crosshairs, Duff would have died for nothing, and Lacey would likely die too. He had to stay alive, but he had to cross Reliance Creek Gorge.

A wet mist rose from the white-water rapids roaring several hundred feet below, but it wasn't the creek or the sheer rock walls that made him hesitate. It was the knowledge that even a mediocre sniper had to figure he was going to cross the gorge to get to Melody Hill. Somewhere along the gorge, they were probably perched and watching. Exposed going down and coming up, he'd be a sitting duck, except for one advantage he possessed. He knew the only place to get down into the gorge from this side and the only two places to climb out on the other, but he had to move fast. As soon as he was spotted, they would move in position for a shot.

Pulling his rifle sling over his head, he began the descent. For the moment, he wasn't particularly worried. Having already studied the surrounding terrain for a long while, he knew none of Maxon's hired guns were close. Carefully, he slid down a rock crevice, working his way almost straight down toward the bottom of the gorge. The slick gray rock challenged his every step, and every handhold was tenuous as he moved faster than he wanted, slipping, catching, and always cognizant that the slightest misjudgment could send him plummeting into the gorge, hundreds of feet below.

Twenty minutes later, he reached the bottom. Stopping to catch his breath, he rested with his back against the rock wall, facing the boiling roar of the rapids in Reliance Creek. Deafened by their roar, Brady was left with only his eyes to detect danger, but a wet mist blew into his face as he looked up at the sheer rock wall on the opposite side of the creek. The descent had been the easy part. Climbing up the other side would be much more dangerous. If he was spotted, he'd be shot off the side of the gorge with little effort, and the deafening roar of the rapids might keep him from even hearing a shot if he was lucky enough to survive the first one.

There was only one crossing on the creek, and it was dead in the middle of the worst rapids, a place where he'd seen huge trees sucked beneath the swirling waters for minutes at a time. The crossing was a string of rocks, stepping-stones, forty yards across. When he was younger, he could run and leap, and if he didn't slip on a wet one, his momentum carried him rock to rock across the entire creek. If he slipped, though, he'd bust his ass and get a wild ride down through the rapids, maybe a fatal one.

He remembered the time Duff slipped. Brady had watched, scared shitless, as Duff was sucked beneath the icy torrent. Standing in shock, he was certain Duff had drowned until his head suddenly bobbed to the surface, two hundred feet downstream. He was laughing and waving. It was dumb luck that he survived with only bruises and scrapes.

Brady studied the rocks, gray and soaked with the mist from the rapids. He hesitated only a moment before sprinting from beneath the rock wall, making a running leap for the first boulder.

Instinct was 90 percent of it, like shooting a rifle. You either had it or you didn't. His toe touched down on the first rock, but it was momentum that counted at this point. Despite his flat-out leaping run, Brady saw each step, each toehold, and each leap as if watching a slow-motion film. It was both studied and instinctive, yet blindingly fast as he crossed the creek, rock to rock, until finally crunching safely into the gravel on the far side.

It was tempting to slow down and catch his breath. It was tempting to look back up at the rim of the gorge to see if someone was watching, but his instinct told him that Maxon's men were up there somewhere, and they had seen him. He had to keep moving. Don't give them a stationary target. The next closest place to climb out of the gorge was a hundred meters downstream. He wasted no time as he sprinted in that direction.

When he reached the crevice, he ducked inside. For the moment, he was safe. For anyone to see him now, they would have to be directly across the creek. He allowed himself to pause and look up to the top of the rock wall on the opposite side of the gorge. No sign of movement yet. Still, it didn't matter. He had to figure they had been watching from somewhere along the gorge when he crossed the creek. They were probably hurrying his way along the rim at this very moment.

Turning, he began the ascent. At first, it was a matter of wedging his arms and legs between the rock walls as he climbed, but as he drew near the top, the crevice widened into a series of rock shelves. His every muscle ached, and his chest heaved for air as every step and every handhold provided opportunity for disaster.

There was still nearly a hundred feet to go to the top of the gorge as he felt the sand running from the hourglass.

The sweat poured down his face, and he gasped for breath while clawing rock to rock, refusing to slow down. He maintained a steady pace until it happened. Beside his head, a flat rock suddenly shattered into a spray of flying splinters. It was a rookie mistake. The shooter had gone for a head shot. Sniper's rule number one: always aim center mass. Brady reacted instantly.

A slight overhang up and to his right offered some cover, but he instinctively rolled left first, then lunged the other way toward the overhang. The move worked, as the rocks to his left exploded from the impact of another round. He'd thrown the sniper off, but his only hope for cover was the narrow overhang. Unslinging his rifle, he turned on his back and tried to squeeze beneath the rock ledge. At the same moment, he searched the opposite side of the gorge.

He spotted it, the blue-black reflection of a riflescope above, on the far side of the gorge, staring him in the face. He snatched his rifle to his shoulder and snapped off a shot. At the same moment, the rock ledge, inches from his belly, cracked and splintered from yet another round. Forced by the spray of rock shards to close his eyes, Brady quickly chambered another shell, but when he opened them again, he saw something falling. It was a rifle tumbling end over end down the rock wall as it plummeted into the gorge below.

* * *

When Maxon got the call from Sager, telling him both Brewton and Carney were down, he looked over at Werkman sitting in the truck beside him. Werkman had the looks of a Nazi, square jawed with blond hair, and he was a cocky bastard. He wasn't stupid like Nash.

"I thought you said your men were the best of the best," Maxon said.

"I thought you said Nash was country dumb," Werkman replied.

Werkman was a smart-ass, but he was right. Nash seemed to have something more than luck going for him. The son of a bitch had managed to knock off Loc, a pretty slick bastard in his own right, and now two supposedly crack snipers.

"Tell Sager to stay behind him," Maxon said. "Tell him not to get too close, but try to see which way he's going."

"I'll tell you where he's going," Werkman said. "He's headed this way, and all we have to do is wait for him."

"What makes you so sure?" Maxon asked.

"I don't think he has that letter yet. I think it's somewhere in this town, and he's coming to get it."

Maxon found himself subconsciously running his finger down the scar on his face, but stopped when Werkman noticed. Werkman was slick, like Loc and several other ruthless bastards he'd known, but dealing with these murderous bastards was his trade, and he was good at it. He smiled. There was always one son of a bitch who was meaner than the most ruthless bastard. That was his handler. He decided to humor Werkman.

"So you think you have him figured, huh?"

Werkman nodded. "I'm pretty sure Nash knew we were coming to that cabin this morning, and if he had wanted, he'd have taken every one of us out."

"What makes you think that?"

"Just a gut feeling. I don't know for certain, but if I had to bet, I'd say he's watched every move we've made up to now. And so far, we've played into his hand. We need to stop reacting and start anticipating."

Maxon laughed. "You're giving Nash too much credit. If it quacks like a duck, it's a fucking duck, and he's like all the other hillbillies around here."

"Being a hillbilly doesn't make him stupid."

Werkman was one of those new-breed bastards who didn't have any common sense, and there wasn't time to argue.

"OK," he said, "maybe he isn't a total doofus, but I think the two of us can outsmart him, don't you?"

Werkman nodded, and it seemed he was about to say something, when a pickup truck sped past on the road below. It was the one that had been parked in front of the cabin that morning. A young woman was driving. He glanced back at Werkman. His eyes had narrowed.

"You recognize her?" Maxon asked.

"Yeah, it's the Coleridge girl," he said.

"The Coleridge girl?"

"Yeah, I think she's got some kind of romantic connection with—"

"With Nash?" Maxon said.

Werkman cranked the engine. "She's our ticket, and I'll bet she knows where that letter is hidden."

Maxon smiled. Werkman was a Doberman straining at his leash as they sped up the road into Melody Hill behind the pick-up.

"Don't get too close," Maxon said. "Let's see where she's going."

They watched as she drove past a store with rusted gas pumps. According to the sign in the window, it was also the local post office. The Stars and Stripes rippled casually at the top of a rusted flagpole. Just past the store, she turned onto a narrow road that dropped down a steep hill as it led out of town. This was not the main road back to the highway, but a gravel branch that wound down a ridge, and it seemed to be going farther back into the hills.

"Where's she going?" Maxon asked.

"I don't know," Werkman said, "but I've got a hunch we'll find Nash there."

Maxon nodded. "Call Sager. Tell him we're following Nash's girl. Tell him to keep coming this way but keep his eyes open."

Werkman nodded as he called his partner on the radio. The signal was weak and full of static, but Sager acknowledged the message. Maxon knew he was now in control of the situation. The truck bounced along the gravel road as they stayed close to the vehicle ahead. She was his bait. They had only to follow her, and once they had her, Nash would show himself.

* * *

Brady watched as a third sniper made his way down into the Reliance Creek Gorge. He raised his rifle and centered the crosshairs on the man's torso. Like the others, this one had a new sniper rifle slung across his back. It was an easy shot, no more than 150 yards, except now Brady saw the man as he'd seen the surrendering VC that day back in Nam. It was easy to pull the trigger, too, as the cold-blooded expression suggested, "Kill them all, and let God sort them out." Yet at some point, he had to stop. He had to think about life after this was over.

The poor bastard climbing down that rock wall, like him, had probably made some bad choices. Apparently, he wasn't too bright either. With two of his partners dead, he was needlessly exposing himself. Brady decided to give him one last opportunity to make the right decision. After the sniper disappeared into the gorge below, he moved to the edge of the crevice. There he hid in the shadow of an oak tree and waited for the man to climb out.

After a while, despite the roaring rapids below, he heard the sound of falling rocks and the man grunting. Brady masked the condensation of his breath by wrapping a bandanna across his mouth and sat motionless, moving nothing but his eyes. He waited as he had so many times back in Nam, still and silent for the right moment, the moment when his quarry ended up flat-footed in his crosshairs.

The minutes ticked by, but he was patient as the man came into view. He was panting as he reached the top of the gorge and paused. Breathlessly dropping to one knee, he stared up the mountain, his eyes filled with fear and uncertainty. He may have thought of himself as a killer, but this time, he knew he was in way over his head. Brady decided to give him every opportunity to make the right choice.

After several minutes, the man stood, and despite his exhaustion, he crept slowly within a few feet from the tree behind which Brady stood. He remained oblivious as Brady studied him. Armed with an AR-15 with a starlight scope, the sniper scanned the mountainside above. He seemed to study every distant detail, but like so many of his kind who *thought* they had mastered the skills of the trade, he failed to see the obvious. Brady was less than five feet away. As the man stared up the mountain, Brady stepped silently from behind the tree and pressed the muzzle of his rifle against his head. When the cold metal of the gun barrel touched the man's temple, his face paled.

"If you so much as flinch, I'll blow your brains all over this hillside," Brady said. "If you want to live, very slowly, hold your rifle at arm's length and drop it. Don't say anything. Don't even blink. If you do, I'll kill you graveyard dead."

The man dropped the rifle.

"Where's Maxon?" Brady asked.

The man started to turn his head, but Brady stopped it with the muzzle of his rifle.

"Look, Nash, he probably has your girlfriend in custody by now. He was following her when I talked with him a little while ago. If you know what's best for her, you'll give yourself up."

A cold surge of fear welled inside, but Brady remained outwardly calm.

"How did you talk with him?" he asked.

The man lowered his right hand as if to reach for his pocket, but Brady nudged him with the rifle.

"Real slow," he said.

The man carefully pulled a gray walkie-talkie from his pocket. Brady snatched it from his hand.

"Sit with your back against that tree, and remove your boot-laces."

Using one of the laces, he tied the man's hands behind his back and around the tree. With the other lace, he tied the man's feet together.

"What if you don't come back?" the man asked. "I could die up here."

Brady cracked a hard smile as he flung the man's rifle into the gorge. "I suppose you better pray I do."

* * *

Lacey found the gate to Brister's place padlocked with a rusty chain. She climbed through the fence and trotted up the road to the barn. One of the doors to the hayloft swung idly in the wind as she approached, but the main door to the barn was only slightly ajar. Pausing, she looked inside, her eyes searching the inky darkness. Only a few dusty shafts of light penetrated from the loft above. The musty odor of moldy hay filled her nostrils, and she listened, but it was quiet as a graveyard inside.

Gathering her courage, she took the first tentative steps through the door, but a sudden commotion exploded above her. Wheeling about, she started to run, but caught herself and stopped. It was a flock of pigeons bursting from their roost in the rafters above. Pressing her hand against her chest, she hoped to keep her heart from leaping out of her body. A tear ran from her eye as she fought to catch her breath. There was no reason to be so frightened, but she could hardly swallow as she again started toward the ladder to the loft.

When she reached it, she forced herself to climb. A cobweb stuck to her face, and she clung to the ladder with one hand while clawing at her face with the other. From above came more sounds, the skittering of rats across the floor.

"Just keep moving," she mumbled. "This is nothing compared to what Brady has been through."

Reaching the top of the ladder, she found the loft flooded with blessed sunlight from the open door. Lacey rested on her knees as she breathed in the fresher air and glanced about. The loft was empty, except for a small pile of loose hay wedged in one corner. Finding the letter had been a long shot from the very beginning, and it now seemed that she'd guessed wrong. Brister's words came back to her as she glanced at the last little bit of hay. The cows hadn't quite finished the last bale, but they'd come close. She walked over and idly kicked at the little pile in the corner.

It didn't hurt her toe quite so much as it startled her when her foot struck something solid. Dropping to her knees, she pulled a small metal toolbox from its hiding place beneath the hay. She quickly pried it open. It was there, the brown envelope wrapped in waxed paper. Tearing away the wrapping, she recognized the handwriting on the envelope. It was Duff's, along with a penciled note, "James R. Noble, 410-43." This was Brady's handwriting. Noble was the soldier who had delivered the letter to Brady.

It was tempting to stop and open it, to sit down and remove the contents, read the letter and try to be with her brother again, but she had to hurry. Turning, she started for the ladder, but there came a sound from somewhere outside, a voice perhaps. She froze as she listened for several seconds, but she heard nothing more. It had to be her imagination.

Carefully, she turned and tiptoed back to the open loft door, where she could see the barnyard. Fluttering pigeons, spiders, and skittering rats hadn't made her heart beat as it did now. There was a man on the front porch of Brister's house, looking through the front window. She was about to step back into the shadows when she heard a sound directly below.

Craning her neck, she looked down. Another man was standing just below her, in front of the barn door. He wore camouflage and carried a rifle. She stepped back and hurried to the ladder. Her only hope was to reach Jesse's truck down near the gate, but as she reached the bottom of the ladder, the barn door swung open.

The man with the rifle stood silhouetted in the doorway as she ducked into the shadow of a stall. He stood unmoving, and after a few moments, he seemed to lose interest. Turning, the man walked around to the back of the barn. Lacey stood and crept to the door. This was her chance. She sprinted down the hill to the pickup, clutching the envelope as she ran. When she reached the truck, there was still no one in sight. She snatched open the truck door, slid inside, and reached for the ignition. The keys were gone.

She heard a jingling sound and looked up. Although she had never seen him before, she recognized Maxon immediately. Brady had said his face was shaped like a griffin's, a jutting jaw, a wide mouth, and heavy brows. He also had a scar. It ran from near his left temple, down his jaw, and across to his chin. Purple in some places and white in others, it cut a fine line down his acne-scarred face.

"Looking for these?" he asked.

The keys dangled from his fingers while he pointed a pistol at her head.

CHAPTER TWENTY-EIGHT

Duff's Revenge

The Vietnam War was something Jesse Harper had always tried to put behind him, but it seemed now to have followed him home to the mountains of Tennessee. It was only minutes after Lacey left that morning that the call came in from the army national guardsmen on the mountainside above the cabin. They were in a standoff with a sniper, no doubt one of those who had been sneaking around the cabin the day before. A few minutes later, a rifle shot echoed from the mountain above. Then late morning came, and there were several more shots. Jesse had one cigarette left in his pack by the time the platoon leader and his men returned.

Pale and breathing heavily, the lieutenant held a broken sniper rifle as he told of his meeting with Nash the night before and how

404 | RICK DESTEFANIS

Nash had said he was going to look for the letter at an old farm-house near Melody Hill. Gilardi turned to face Jesse, but Jesse turned his back as he cupped his hands and struck a match to light his last cigarette.

"Do you know where this farmhouse is?" Gilardi asked.

Jesse didn't respond as he inhaled deeply and protected his cigarette from the wind. The one thing that may have brought him back alive from Nam was his ability to think through even the worst situations. And the more he thought about this one, the more he realized it was time to open up. Brady was verging on legend, but even he had his limits. Lacey and other innocent people who lived in the area were involved, and there was only so much Brady could do. He needed help. Exhaling the cigarette smoke into the chilled morning air, he turned to face Gilardi.

"Yes, sir, I reckon I do."

Gates looked up from the notes he was taking. "Is that where the Coleridge girl is headed?"

Jesse nodded. "Yeah, she thinks the letter is hidden somewhere in the barn at the old Brister place."

"Damn!" Gilardi said. "Doesn't she know there are probably more of these people around?" He turned to the lieutenant. "I need for you to get your men into the trucks and get them around to that farm ASAP."

He turned to Jesse. "Harper, you show us the way."

"I can do you one better, Major. To get there by road, you have to go all the way back down to the main highway and come back through Melody Hill. Other than the highway, it's almost all gravel from here. With all the curves, it'll take at least forty-five minutes, maybe longer. Let Sheriff Harvey take the lieutenant and his men. I can take you and Gates in my plane. We can get there in ten minutes."

Gilardi cast a sideways glance at the old Cessna sitting in the field across the road. The plane was covered with rain-streaked dust. A wide-eyed look of doubt filled his eyes.

"Just me," Gilardi said. "Agent Gates can ride with the sheriff."

Gates nodded and gazed back at his army counterpart as if to say thanks, and as the convoy pulled away, Gilardi ran with Jesse to the airplane across the road. The two men climbed aboard, but after nearly a minute, Jesse pulled at his beard in frustration. The plane refused to start. He choked the engine again.

"Must have some moisture in the carburetor," he said.

But no sooner had he spoken, the engine sputtered to life. Coughing and backfiring, it filled the air with a smoky blue-white haze. Jesse adjusted the throttle. The prop scattered the smoke across the field as the little aircraft lurched forward.

"I usually warm her up for a few minutes," Jesse said, "but considering the circumstances—"

He didn't finish as he spun the plane into the wind at the end of the field and held the brake. Pulling the throttle, he increased the engine's RPMs until every rivet sounded as if it would pop from the skin of the aircraft. The vibrations became teeth rattling as he released the brake and the plane lurched forward.

The large sycamore trees at the far end of the strip seemed distant, but the little aircraft was almost lethargic, slowly bouncing along on the wet grass. Fighting to hold the nose gear off the ground, Jesse felt the plane slowly gain speed. The white trunks of the sycamores grew thicker and taller. Beside him, Gilardi gripped the instrument panel with both hands. Finally, the little plane staggered into the air.

"Damned trees," Jesse muttered. "They get taller every year. I've gotta come down here someday and cut me a hole through there with my chain saw."

The plane rushed to meet the sycamores, their splotched brown-and-white bark pattern now clearly visible. He had to take it to the limit, not an inch to spare. Squeezing every RPM he could from the engine, he held his breath.

"Steady," he murmured.

The sweat burned in his eyes. It was time.

"Hang on, bubba," he shouted.

The trees towered above. Jesse snatched the yoke against his belly. The engine screamed, and the little Cessna labored upward at a steep angle. From the corner of his eye, Jesse saw Gilardi lifting his feet from the floor as the plane shot over the trees with only inches to spare.

The tach was redlined, and just before stalling, he pushed the nose of the aircraft over and dove to the left, toward the river, skimming the boulder-filled waters. The trees along the riverbank blurred as he gained speed and pulled the plane into a slow climbing curve. The gray rocky rapids grew more distant. Gilardi looked back and exhaled.

"Now then," Jesse said, "that was the easy part."

"What do you mean?" Gilardi asked.

"We've still got to get this thing over that mountain before we reach the gorge at the far end of the valley."

"Shit!"

Jesse scratched his beard and laughed. "Aw, Major, this ain't nothin'. It really gets interesting when the North Vietnamese are shooting at you."

Gilardi looked out the side window, and Jesse followed his stare. The wingtip barely skirted the trees on the mountainside, and when they climbed clear of the river valley, he noticed the major breathe another sigh of relief. A vast expanse of rolling hills extended to the horizon.

Jesse pointed over the instrument panel to the hills below. "Can you see that white church steeple sticking up over there? That's Melody Hill."

Gilardi nodded. "Yeah, but there aren't any fields or roads down there," he said. "Where are we going to land?"

"Just behind that hill on the other side of town is the old Brister's place," Harper said. "We can land in his pasture."

It was only a couple of minutes before they cleared the bald west of town. Harper pointed to a barn and a house with two pickup trucks parked nearby.

"That's the Brister place," he said. "And it looks like Lacey has company."

"Where are we going to land?" Gilardi asked.

Jesse pointed to a tiny patch of cleared pasture adjacent to the barn. "Down there, if we can get through those trees."

Several large trees were scattered in yellow broom sedge growing in a tiny clearing.

"You're kidding, right?" Gilardi asked. "I mean, we didn't put choppers down on an LZ that small back in Nam."

Jesse gave his counterpart a tight grin as he dropped the nose and turned the plane into the wind. Gilardi was right. It was going to be a squeeze, but someone had followed Lacey, and he needed to get down there. It was just another gamble like many he'd taken in Nam. He'd do it again to bring back the men he'd lost during the war, especially the ones on that last day when he'd crashed into the jungle.

A five man LRRP team was being pressed by a large enemy force, and they were depending upon him to bring in air support, but that was before he'd lost them in the smoke and fog of the jungle. Instead, he crashed into a mountainside, and they became MIAs. But that was the past. Today, he had another chance, a chance to save Lacey.

* * *

Brady was high on the mountain when he spotted the Brister place. It was still well over twelve-hundred yards away, but he could see well enough to realize something was happening. A figure, probably a woman, was running from the barn toward a pickup parked near the gate. It was Jesse Harper's pickup, and it struck him. It had to be Lacey. Adjusting his riflescope to 9X, he knelt and braced against a tree.

Another figure appeared. It was a man, and as Brady watched him, he felt a tingling on the back of his neck. Even from this distance, he recognized the cocky strut of Maxon. A moment later, Lacey leapt from the opposite side of the truck and ran toward the house. Too far away to even think about an accurate shot, Brady watched as Maxon pointed what looked like a pistol at Lacey's back. The pistol bucked upward in his hand.

Accurate or not, he had to fire a shot in Maxon's direction. Without hesitation, he held the crosshairs well above Maxon's head and squeezed the trigger. Luck was with him. It was a miss, but close enough to send Maxon diving for cover behind the truck. Brady hesitated as he watched Lacey disappear into the woods behind the house. She seemed to be limping, but from such a distance, it was difficult to be certain. Maxon slowly raised his head from behind the truck.

Brady lowered his point of aim only a hundredth of a degree as he squeezed off another round. This time he thought he saw dirt leap into the air beside the truck. He had the elevation, but it was the wind drift that took him off target this time. Maxon ducked again, and Brady began running down the mountainside.

* * *

Just as she reached the corner of the house, Lacey felt a stinging jolt in her thigh, and she'd nearly fallen to the ground, but she kept running. The man had shot her in the leg, but she refused to give up. The impact of the round momentarily numbed her leg, and she fought to maintain her balance as she made her way up the hill, into the woods.

Now as she slowly hobbled up the hillside and into the shadows of the pine forest, she pushed her hand against the wound, but it was to no avail. The right leg of her jeans was soaked, and her tennis shoe was streaked with blood. The man who shot her had, for whatever reason, not continued the chase. She glanced back down the mountainside. Beyond the shadow of the forest, the sun still shone brightly in the open, but there was no one in sight.

Stopping, she removed her jacket, then tore away the bottom half of her cotton blouse and wrapped her thigh. It helped, but she was shivering as she put her jacket back on and picked up the envelope. She had to keep moving, but as she stood, the effects of the blood loss hit her. The forest spun in a dizzying swirl, and she fell to the ground. Slowly, Lacey sat upright and glanced at the envelope. She removed the contents and began reading Duff's letter. She wasn't sure why she read, except she had to know what it was that had sent Brady to Vietnam. When she was done, she laid the other papers out on the ground.

One was the handwritten list of names. They were Vietnamese names, and at least half had lines drawn through them. These were the dead ones. There were also several telex messages, but the words were strange and difficult to understand. Some were signed by the man using the name Spartan. She glanced inside the envelope to see if there was more. A small yellow card, somewhat like a business card, was wedged in one corner.

She fished it out with her fingers. The stylistic figure of a green-and-red bird brandishing arrows and sticks of dynamite was printed on the front. It was bracketed by Oriental script on each side, but it was the dried blood that brought tears to her eyes. Could it be Duff's? She clutched the card in her hand as she heard the crack of a stick from down the hill. Looking up, she saw him, but it was too late. It was the man who had shot her. He was walking up the hill, smiling and brandishing a pistol.

* * *

"Hold on to your jock, Major," Jesse said. "Me and *Miss Whippoorwill* are fixin' to take us down to Earth."

He pushed the left pedal and rolled the yoke to the side as he extended the flaps a full forty degrees. The plane dropped like a rock. The pasture was less than three hundred feet long, and the huge trees made the landing seem nearly impossible. Jesse held his breath and wiped the sweat from his face as he slipped the aircraft down at an incredibly steep angle. Clipping the treetops on the mountainside, the plane nearly stalled as it dropped toward the narrow slot of pasture below.

At the last moment, Jesse straightened the aircraft and pulled back hard on the yoke, attempting to flare for the landing. The plane hit hard, bounced, and hit again as several huge trees flashed past. The end of the pasture was there in an instant as they burst through a barbed wire fence and skidded into the barnyard. After spinning backward, the plane crunched to a jarring stop.

They'd made it. Jesse, realizing he hadn't breathed in nearly a minute, took a deep breath and looked over at Gilardi, who was still gripping the instrument panel.

"You OK?"

Gilardi nodded rapidly.

"Well, it wasn't pretty," he said, "but here we are."

Jesse kicked the door open under the wing, reached back, and pulled Gilardi from the wreckage. The two men stepped out and stood in the barnyard, surveying their surroundings.

"Isn't that your truck?" Gilardi asked, pointing to a pickup down by the gate.

"Yeah," Jesse said, "but whose truck is that?"

He pointed to another one parked under the trees farther up the road.

"Let's take a look around," Gilardi said. "Stay with me."

That worked for Jesse, especially since, having given his .45 to Lacey, he was now unarmed.

* * *

"I see you have the papers I've been looking for," Maxon said.

Lacey stared defiantly up at the man standing over her, but she remained silent. He took a small radio from his pocket and talked into it.

"I have the girl. We're about two hundred yards up the hill from the house. She's got the papers. Stay put. I'll be back down there in a minute."

The man thumbed the safety on the pistol and shoved the muzzle against the bridge of her nose. Despite her wooziness from the blood loss, Lacey's eyes and nose stung as the barrel pressed hard against her face. This was it, but she refused to give Maxon the satisfaction of showing her fear. She winced at the pain, but gazed steadily up at him.

"Sorry, chickie, but you shouldn't have gotten yourself involved in this mess."

"Maxon," a voice called from the radio.

He looked at the radio as if it were a rattlesnake.

"You hear me, Maxon?"

It was Brady's voice. The man's eyes darted up, then from side to side as he scanned the mountainside.

"Yeah, it's me, Maxon."

Maxon slowly raised the radio to his mouth as he feigned a smile, but he was noticeably shaken.

"Nash, is that you?"

"You know it is, Maxon. Now don't do anything stupid. I'm giving you this last chance."

Lacey studied the man standing over her. Brady had said Maxon was the one responsible for Duff's death.

"You're not giving me shit, Nash. I'm the one calling the shots because I've got your girlfriend and the papers."

"Maxon, you know yourself, Phung Hoang sees all. You can't get away with this. I can kill you, but I'm giving you a chance to live. Turn around and walk away from her, and I won't shoot."

Maxon let out a laugh and looked down at her as he keyed the mic on the radio. "Nash, there's just no hope for you. You're still a dumb fuck. Phung Hoang was just a bunch of gook superstition."

Lacey was certain that Brady was up there somewhere on the mountainside, but Maxon seemed suddenly at ease as he continued pointing the pistol at her head. He was either crazy or totally misunderstood the situation. Brady was in a position to kill him,

414 | RICK DESTEFANIS

but Maxon didn't seem to care. That was when she saw movement on a nearby ridge. It was the other sniper, the one she'd seen near the barn. He was kneeling beside a tree several hundred yards away, but he wasn't watching them. He was gazing up the mountain, searching for Brady.

"Your boyfriend is one of the dumbest sons of bitches I've ever known. He'd give his left nut to kill me, but when he said he didn't want to, he tipped his hand. Hell, that stupid bastard isn't close enough. He's bluffing."

Lacey thought about pulling Jesse's pistol from her coat pocket, but the man still had his gun jammed in her face.

"You're wrong, mister. Brady isn't stupid, and he really doesn't want to kill you. He told me he wants to stop killing, but he's not bluffing. He will kill you if you make him."

There was a barely perceptible blink of his eyes, but Lacey saw it clearly. Maxon knew he was treading on the edge of a precipice. He raised the radio to his mouth as he studied the trees and the mountainside above.

"Nash, you've made it on dumb luck up to now, but this time, you're in way over your head. You seem to forget who taught you everything you know about this game."

The radio popped with static.

"Maxon, do you remember your rules of war? You said rule number one was to never underestimate your enemy. Well, you did, and you're the one in over your head. Major Loc was a double agent for the National Liberation Front. You did just what he wanted when you assassinated those people in the South Vietnamese government. Don't make it any worse. Give yourself up."

"That bastard doesn't know what he's talking about," Maxon mumbled. "Besides, he's bluffing."

He continued looking up the mountainside, but cast a quick glance at Lacey. Despite her fear, she smiled.

"Brady knows exactly what he's talking about. You killed my brother, Duff Coleridge. That's why he went to Vietnam to find you. You see this?"

She held up the yellow kill card Duff had sent home. Maxon's eyes grew round as his face lost all color. He snatched the card from her hand.

"Where'd you get this?"

"It's the one your assassins left the first time they tried to kill my brother. You don't seem to understand that Brady isn't like you. He isn't bluffing."

* * *

Maxon threw the card back at her and turned to look up the mountain. He saw no one and turned back to the girl. She looked up at him with wide brown eyes, but there wasn't a hint of fear. Despite her bloodied jeans and impossible situation, she seemed totally relaxed, but it was her eyes that spooked him the most.

He'd seen the same thing in Lynn Dai Bouchet's, something he never understood before now. It was confidence even when everything seemed lost, except there was something more in this woman's eyes. He only wished he knew what it was, because only now was he beginning to understand that this magnificent edifice, this idea of himself as a patriotic hero, was crumbling.

Loc had been an An Ninh agent, and he never had a clue. The arms he'd sold had gone straight to the VC. The people who were assassinated were all made suspect by Loc. Coleridge, Bouchet, Nash and no telling how many others had figured it out, but he hadn't. He had used people as pawns and, when necessary, sacrificed them for the cause, but he was the one that had been stupid all along. The Company had trusted him to do the right thing, but he had become a pawn himself.

Maxon caressed his pistol nervously with both hands as he gazed up the mountainside. Maybe Nash wasn't stupid after all. He was certain he wasn't bluffing. His only hope was to use the girl as a bargaining chip. He quickly turned back toward her, and only at that moment, did he fully realize how badly he'd underestimated his enemies.

The girl had a .45 automatic aimed at his head. Yes, she was just a girl, or so it seemed, but her eyes said otherwise. And it suddenly came to him what he had not understood about her eyes. She had the same eyes as Duff Coleridge, and it was he, more than this girl, who now held the .45 leveled on his chin.

* * *

"Just run, mister," Lacey said. "It's your only chance."

And he did, with reckless abandon. Lacey lowered the heavy .45 back into her lap, resting her head against the tree, but the man, who had already run several yards down the mountain, suddenly stopped. Wheeling about, he quickly searched the mountainside above, then raised his pistol, pointing it directly at her. Despite her fear, she found herself too weak to move.

There came a dull thud, much like a hammer striking a melon, followed by a shrieking crack as Maxon's arms convulsed into the air, sending his gun and radio sailing outward. With the look of total surprise in his bulging eyes, he pitched forward, striking the ground. Brady's bullet had found its mark. The horror of the scene would have affected her more, but stars drifted in front of her eyes as she clutched the pistol to her abdomen. She was simply too tired to do anything else. Time lost all relevance until she heard his voice. She opened her eyes. It was Brady.

Laying his rifle aside, he held her head against his chest. The fear in his eyes confirmed what she already knew as he ran his hand over her thigh.

"You're going to be OK, baby. All we have to do is get you to a doctor."

"Don't leave the papers," she said.

Brady quickly gathered the papers and laid them atop the pistol in her lap. Running his arms under her legs, he was about to lift her when Lacey saw the man standing behind them. She gasped, and her eyes met Brady's. He carefully let her lie back on the ground, then lunged for his rifle, but the man gave it a kick, sending it sliding away. He held his own rifle, aiming it steadily at Brady.

"Looks like you finally got him," the man said, motioning toward Maxon's body.

"I tried to give him a chance," Brady said.

"Yeah, I was listening. Too bad you don't understand this isn't about chances, or being a good guy or a bad guy. It's just business. Move over there. Get on your knees and put your hands behind your head."

He motioned Brady aside.

"You should have had more sense than to involve your girlfriend in this mess, but it looks like she's pretty much done for anyway."

Brady's eyes said it all. He was out of ideas.

"You," the man said, pointing at Lacey, "give me those papers."

Lacey picked up the yellow kill card and extended it toward the assassin.

"All the papers," he said.

"This is the only one you'll need," she said.

The man snatched the card from her fingers and glanced at it. He grinned.

"What's this?"

Lacey cast her eyes toward Brady. "He can tell you," she said.

The man looked toward Brady.

"It's a kill card that belonged to one of Maxon's men in Nam," Brady said. "He left it the first time he tried to kill her brother."

"Interesting," the man said with unmasked sarcasm. He turned back to Lacey. "So do you want me to leave this one for you?"

"No, I'm leaving it for you," she said.

The man laughed and bent forward.

"Give me those damned papers."

He snatched the papers from her left hand, and Lacey extended the .45 she had hidden behind them, holding it under the man's neck.

"If you move, I'll pull the trigger."

Brady scrambled to his feet, took the man's rifle, and retrieved his own.

"Slowly and carefully now," Brady said, "back away from her."

As the last of her adrenaline rush subsided, Lacey lowered the pistol and closed her eyes.

* * *

Brady tucked the envelope inside his jacket and shouldered the rifles. Holding the pistol on the assassin, he directed him to carry Lacey down the mountain. As they reached the edge of the woods above the farmhouse, he heard a shout. Jesse Harper and another man came trotting up the hill toward them. In the distance, sirens echoed through the hills as more vehicles approached down the narrow road from Melody Hill.

Brady handed Jesse the .45. "Here," he said, "watch this bastard while I carry Lacey. We've got to get her to a hospital."

The man with Jesse stepped forward. He was obviously some type of lawman.

"I've got an army helicopter on the way," he said. "It should be here anytime now."

"This is Major Gilardi," Jesse said. "He's with Army CID."

Brady paused as he held the semiconscious Lacey in his arms "Please," he said, "just let me get her to a hospital. That's all I ask."

Gilardi didn't answer at first as he talked over a radio. "Roger. As soon as you arrive, we need a stretcher up here behind the house. You need to hurry. Also, tell the sheriff and Agent Gates we need them up here as well."

The group continued making their way down the hill as a distant *thump*, *thump*, *thump* heralded the approach of the helicopter.

"I'm going with you on the chopper," Gilardi said. "Once we get her safely to a hospital, I'm taking you into protective custody until we get this mess sorted out."

Brady nodded. "That's fine with me as long as she's safe."

Gilardi drew his sidearm and held it on the gunman.

"Help Nash," Gilardi told Jesse. "I'll take care of this guy."

"There's another one of these clowns tied to a tree over at one of the crossings on Reliance Gorge," Brady said. "Jesse can take one of your people up there later to find him."

The front yard of the Brister place was a scene of confusion as vehicles were quickly cleared for a makeshift LZ. Within minutes, the chopper landed, and the crew helped Brady and Jesse put Lacey's stretcher on board. Before he climbed inside, Brady glanced over his shoulder. Gilardi and Gates were standing clear of the chopper, talking.

Slapping Jesse on the shoulder, Brady shouted above the noise of the helicopter. "I'll call you from the hospital when we get there, but I need you to take care of something for me." With that, he pulled the envelope from beneath his jacket and quickly shoved it inside Jesse's coat.

"You know what to do with it," Brady said.

Jesse nodded and backed away from the chopper as Gilardi turned and trotted their way. The helicopter crew chief pulled him on board, and within seconds, they were airborne. Brady cradled

Lacey's head in his arms while an army medic inserted an IV attached to a plasma bottle. Afterward, he put a new bandage on the wound and took her blood pressure. When he was done, he looked up and nodded.

"Her vital signs are stable," he said. "She's going to be OK."

Epilogue

The summer sun was settling into the hills west of Melody Hill as Brady and Lacey walked along a bluff overlooking the Hiwassee River. Here, the river was relatively quiet, wide and straight, and the rippling waters below reflected the orange and purple hues from the sky above. Other than the occasional breeze stirring the leaves, the hills were quiet.

Brady glanced over at her as they walked hand in hand. Lacey's brown eyes reflected the soft evening sunlight, and she smiled. The gunshot wound to her leg had healed entirely, with no lasting effects, but it had been a hectic six months since January. Besides their wedding, they had spent considerable time in Washington DC, where the Phoenix Program had become the subject of a congressional investigation. The hearings continued, but for now, their part was done.

Brady found a large, flat boulder near the edge of the bluff and held Lacey's hand as she sat down. It wasn't that she necessarily needed his assistance, but she had begun showing more and more of the baby she'd conceived that night in Nashville nearly six months ago.

As the last of the sun disappeared in the west, the breeze died, and the soft echo of church chimes filtered from the hills above. Brady found himself thinking of Duff, buried there in the cemetery behind the church. Every time he heard the chimes, they brought back the memories. He had been unable to reconcile entirely with life since the war, but with Lacey's help, it was becoming easier with each passing day. He looked down at the brass M14 shell that he'd picked up at Duff's grave. It still hung from a chain around his neck, as it had for two years. Fingering it, he gazed out across the hills.

"Don't you think it's time we let him rest?" Lacey asked.

Brady smiled. Lacey was reading his mind, something she had always been able to do. She glanced at the brass shell around his neck, then back at her own softly rounded abdomen.

"We've got to look ahead and start planning for this one's future."

She smiled, and Brady smiled back at her. Standing, he stepped to the very edge of the precipice. Right or wrong, he'd kept his promise to Duff, and all that was left was to pick up the pieces and move on. He grasped the shell in his fist and gave it a firm yank, snapping the chain from around his neck.

"I'll see you again someday, buddy."

With that, he threw the shell and chain high into the air and out over the gorge, watching as it disappeared into the shadows below. After several minutes, he turned to Lacey. Tears pooled in her eyes, but she smiled. Somewhere back in the hills, the chimes from Melody Hill continued, but this time, it was a familiar melody. Brady walked over and sat on the rock beside Lacey. Embracing one another, they kissed as the gentle notes of "Amazing Grace" floated softly through the haze-covered hills.

The End

Glossary

3X–9X   Essentially a zoom lens scope adjustable from three- to nine-power magnification

30.06   "Thirty aught six," original high-powered rifle caliber used by US military

.45   Forty-five-caliber semiautomatic pistol (standard military-issue sidearm during the Vietnam conflict)

Airborne   The United States Army's designation for its paratroops

An Ninh   Vietcong counterintelligence and propaganda group

AK-47   Russian-made assault rifle

ARVN   Army of the Republic of Vietnam (the South Vietnamese Army)

AWOL   Absent without leave

C-130   US military four-engine turboprop cargo and troop transport aircraft

Chieu Hoi   Amnesty program set up for VC defectors

CIA   Central Intelligence Agency

CID   Criminal Investigation Department (US Army)

CP   Command post (usually for field operations)

C rations   Combat field rations for individual use (US military)

Cô ấy là đẹp   Vietnamese for "She is beautiful"

IOCC	Intelligence and Operations Coordination Center
Di du mau	Vietnamese for "move quickly" (literally, "travel quickly")
Dừng Lại	Vietnamese for "halt"
GRU	Graves Registration Unit, the group that handles the bodies of soldiers killed in action
GVN	Government of Vietnam
HQ	Headquarters
I Corps	"Eye" Corps, the northernmost operations sector during the Vietnam War
Klick	Military slang for a kilometer, or one thousand meters
Khong lau	Vietnamese for "never happen"
Lại đây	Vietnamese for "Come here"
LOCH	Light observation helicopter
LRRP	Long-range reconnaissance patrol
LZ	Landing zone
MACV	Military Assistance Command, Vietnam
MOS	Military Occupational Specialty (B112P is an airborne infantryman)
MSS	Military Security Service, counterintelligence group for the Vietnamese armed forces
M14	US military assault rifle (308/7.62 mm caliber), predecessor to the M16
M40	Military designation for a Remington 700 bolt-action sniper rifle

NCO	Noncommissioned officer (the sergeants)
NLF	**National Liberation Front (the Vietcong)**
NPFF	National Police Field Force (South Vietnamese)
NVA	North Vietnamese Army
OSA	Office of the Special Assistant (CIA headquarters, Republic of Vietnam)
Phung Hoang	Vietnamese mythological bird of love, name given to the Vietnamese version of the Phoenix Program
PRC-25	The standard US military portable field radio carried by ground troops in Vietnam
PRU	Provincial Reconnaissance Unit, local mercenary forces controlled by the CIA
PX	Post exchange, military department store
REMF	Rear-echelon motherf——r (term used by combat troops to describe their noncombat counterparts)
R&R	Leave granted for rest and recuperation
RTO	Radio telephone operator (the man who carried the radio)
Section 8	A military provision for discharge for reasons of mental instability
SOG	Strategic Operations Group (covert military units)
TAC	Tactical Air Cover
TDY	Temporary duty
VA	Veterans Administration
VC	Vietcong

Xau Lem   Vietnamese for "very bad"

Xin Loi   Vietnamese version of "tough shit"

XO   Executive officer (second-in-command)

Made in the USA
Charleston, SC
12 February 2016